'Brilliantly disturbing'
Ben Aaronovitch

'One extremely smart spe
William Gibso

'I absolutely seco
(and third, and fourth) Charlie Stross'
Paul Krugman

'A master of the imaginative thrill-ride'
Karl Schroeder

'Picks up pace with some startling plot twists
and ends with a clever cliffhanger'
Guardian

'For sheer inventiveness and energy,
this cliffhanger-riddled serial remains difficult to top'
Publishers Weekly

'One of the defining phenomena of
twenty-first-century SF is Charles Stross'
Time Out

'Fantasies with this much invention,
wit and gusto don't come along every day'
SFX

'Fast-paced and engrossing, and will leave
readers ravenous for the next instalment'
SciFi.com

Charles Stross was born in Leeds, England, in 1964. He has worked as a pharmacist, software engineer and freelance journalist, but now writes full-time. To date, Stross has won two Hugo Awards and been nominated twelve times. He has also won the Locus Award for Best Novel and the Locus Award for Best Novella, and has been shortlisted for the Arthur C. Clarke and Nebula Awards. In addition, his fiction has been translated into around a dozen languages. Stross lives in Edinburgh, Scotland, with his wife Feorag, a couple of cats, several thousand books, and an ever-changing herd of obsolescent computers.

antipope.org

 @cstross

EMPIRE GAMES

CHARLES STROSS

TOR

First published 2016 by Tom Doherty Associates, LLC

This edition published by Tor
an imprint of Pan Macmillan
20 New Wharf Road, London N1 9RR
Associated companies throughout the world
www.panmacmillan.com

ISBN 978-1-4472-4539-1

A CIP catalogue record for this book is available from the British Library.

Printed and bound by CPI Group (UK) Ltd, Croydon, CR0 4YY

Visit www.panmacmillan.com to read more about all our books
and to buy them. You will also find features, author interviews and
news of any author events, and you can sign up for e-newsletters
so that you're always first to hear about our new releases.

For Iain M. Banks,
who painted a picture of a better way

MAIN TIME LINES

TIME LINE ONE:

History diverged from our own around 200–250 BCE in time line one. Judaism, Christianity, and Islam are all absent and the collapse of the Roman Empire into dark ages was complete rather than just partial. Since then, civilization in Europe re-emerged and quasi-medieval colony kingdoms sprang up on the eastern seaboard of North America. (The western seaboard was settled by Chinese traders.)

The Gruinmarkt, one such kingdom, was home to the Clan—rich merchant-traders with the ability to cross between time lines. As world-walkers, they made a good living as the only people who could send a message coast-to-coast in a day in time line one. They could also guarantee a heroin shipment would arrive without fear of interception in time line two. But all good things come to an end, and the vicious civil war that broke out in 2003 (by time line two reckoning) led to the Clan's discovery by the US Government. Their escalating cycle of retaliation ended in a nuclear inferno.

TIME LINE TWO:

This is a world almost identical to your time line, as the reader of this book—right up to a key date in 2003. Here world-walkers from the Clan's conservative faction detonated a stolen nuclear weapon in the White

House. They assassinated the President and forced the government to reveal the existence of parallel universes and the technology for reaching them. Our story starts in time line two.

TIME LINE THREE:

This time line was discovered by Miriam Beckstein. In this alternate world, England was invaded by France in 1760 and the British Crown in Exile was established in the New England colonies. There was no American War of Independence and no French or Russian Revolutions. Therefore the Ancien Regime—despotism by absolute monarchy—shaped the world order until the Revolution of 2003. Here, the New British Empire's Radical Party overthrew the government and declared a democratic Commonwealth. The country is now known as the New American Commonwealth.

The French invasion of England stifled the Industrial Revolution in its crib, so industrialization began a century later than in time line two. But economics and science have their own imperatives. And even before Miriam led the survivors of the Clan into exile in the Commonwealth, the pace of technological innovation was beginning to pick up.

TIME LINE FOUR:

Currently uninhabited, this time line is in the grip of an ice age—with an ice sheet covering much of Europe, Canada, and the northern states of the US. But it hasn't been uninhabited forever. The enigmatic Forerunner ruins pose both a threat and a promise . . .

MAIN CHARACTER PROFILES

ERIC SMITH

Born in 1964 in time line two, Colonel Smith, USAF (retired) has been a government man all his life. He worked for the United States' National Security Agency, then inside a top secret unit within Homeland Security. It was tasked with defending the States against threats from other time lines; these included world-walkers, those who could cross between these alternative worlds and his own time line. Many might consider this easy—after all, most known time lines are uninhabited, or populated by stone age tribes at best. However, the exceptions are the problem. The notorious Clan and their world-walkers came from time line one. And contact with this secretive organization resulted in a national trauma—dwarfing both 9/11 and the war on terror.

Smith knows that there are other inhabited time lines out there. At least one civilization is far ahead of the United States' technology levels, fighting—and losing—a para-time war against parties unknown. And then there's the BLACK RAIN time line, where reconnaissance drones and human spies go missing.

Defending the nation is easier said than done, when you can't even be sure what you're defending it from. But you can make a good guess . . .

KURT DOUGLAS

Born in 1941 in time line two, Kurt Douglas grew up in the German Democratic Republic—East Germany—during the Cold War. Drafted at 18, he ended up in the Border Guards. Then in late 1968 he escaped over the Berlin Wall to the West, and emigrated to the United States. Marrying Greta, another East German defector, he made a new life for himself. Kurt raised a family, and lived quietly with his son, daughter-in-law, and their adopted children—Rita and River.

However, the East German foreign intelligence service didn't send Kurt to the West to spy on the United States—they had longer-term objectives in mind. However, that was before the end of the Cold War and the collapse of East Germany. Old skills don't fade easily, and Kurt has given Rita the best training he could for living in a police state. And she knows, if she ever gets in over her head, that she can count on grandpa Kurt—and his friends—for help.

MIRIAM BURGESON

Born in 1968 in time line two, Miriam grew up in Boston, Massachusetts. She worked as a tech sector journalist before discovering, in her early thirties, that her mother had been lying to her for most of her life. Mother and daughter were fugitives from the Gruinmarkt—a small kingdom in time line one, which had reached medieval levels of technology. They were women of noble birth, whose designated role was to produce more world-walkers and to serve the Clan. Miriam world-walks "home" by accident and is expected to conform. But that had never been Miriam's style. So in short order, she discovered a route to a new inhabited time line and built a business start-up—using it to import high-tech innovations into this new territory. This triggered a crisis within the Clan, reviving a dormant blood feud and causing civil war.

Now seventeen years have passed since the Clan and the Gruinmarkt were both destroyed. Clan reactionaries made a disastrous miscalculation that led to a very brief war with the United States—ending when the US nuked the Gruinmarkt. Miriam saw the writing on the wall and led anti-Clan survivors into exile in the new world she'd discovered. But here she found a revolution in progress—and a new vocation.

Miriam is now older and wiser, and a minister in government. She works for the New American Commonwealth, the ascendant democratic superpower of time line three. She'd taken part in the revolution that overthrew the absolute monarchy of the New British Empire, now defunct. And ever since, she's been warning the new government, "the USA is coming". For seventeen years, she's been working feverishly to ensure that when the US drones arrive overhead, the Commonwealth will be ready to meet them on equal terms. But she wasn't expecting them to be expecting *her*—and to have made plans accordingly.

RITA DOUGLAS

Born in 1995 in time line two, and adopted at birth by Franz and Emily Douglas, Rita was eight when Clan renegades from time line one nuked the White House. Growing up in President Rumsfeld's America, she has learned to keep her head down and her nose clean. But there's only so much she can do to avoid attention. The paranoid high-surveillance state has her under constant surveillance in case the woman who gave her up for adoption (and enemy of the state) takes a renewed interest in her.

Rita has a history and drama studies degree, a pile of student loans, and no great employment prospects. At twenty-five years of age she doesn't really know where she's going. But that's okay. Because the government has big plans for Rita.

See the end of the novel for a principal cast list and a glossary of key terms and vocabulary.

PART ONE

DOG AND PONY SHOW

The future is already here—it's just not very evenly distributed.

—William Gibson

Prologue

A grandfather and his granddaughter walked under the leaf-bare trees of late autumn:

"Tell me again about Grandma Greta, Grandpa?"

Her gloved hand was fragile and small in his. The clouds were gray overhead, and the chilly Boston air, not quite ready for snow, nevertheless bore the crisp smell of incoming rain. The grass to either side of the metaled path had been mown for the last time this year. Kurt swallowed, rewinding the tapes of memory to a more innocent time. He tried to decide how much more he could tell his adoptive granddaughter about the extraordinary woman who'd died when she was three.

She was ten now, in these chilly dog days of 2004, old enough for another eyedropper-full of truth. Kurt glanced round, checking for eavesdroppers: but Kurt and Rita had come to pay their respects to Grandma late on a weekday, right before Thanksgiving. The only other residents of this park lay silent and unhearing, marked for eternity beneath gravestones and sculpted memorials.

They came to a fork in the path. Here, a narrower trail led off between a grove of trees toward a cluster of grave markers now falling into evening's shadow. Kurt gently steered his granddaughter onto this path, proceeding on instinct. The cold air numbed his cheeks, matching his mood. Soon he saw the plot, and finally spoke: not looking at the girl, trying to order his thoughts.

"Look at the headstone and tell me what it reads."

Rita trotted across the grass with the unstudied spontaneity of a child who'd never lost anyone close. She bent to read: "Greta Douglas, wife and mother, born February sixteenth, 1942, Dresden, died August nineteenth, 1998, Boston." A puzzled frown shadowed her eyebrows at the next phrase: "'Finally among friends'?"

Kurt nodded. For a moment he choked on his memories. "Everything except the places and the date of her death was a lie."

"Lies on a gravestone?" The indignation of an outraged youngster had bite.

"Oh yes." A ghost of a smile tugged at his cheeks: or perhaps it was the proximity of tears. "She was very insistent toward the end. I was to maintain appearances at all costs. Her illness . . . She was very tired, Rita, but she didn't want her death to affect the rest of us."

"But. If it's all lies . . . is 'finally among friends' untrue too?"

"No." Kurt took in the rest of the graveyard with a jerk of his chin. "She was buried under a false name, in a country foreign to her, among people who would have been her enemies if they'd known what she was." Now he too stepped off the path onto the grass, shifting his grip on the bunch of flowers. "So lonely."

"But . . ." Monosyllabic awkwardness struck. "Wife and mother?"

"Um." Kurt squatted, going down on knees that creaked more with every year. He began to unwrap the paper from around the bouquet. "I suppose that bit was true, if you like." His hands worked busily, without his conscious intervention. Dead flower stems, cold under his fingertips. He remembered Greta's hands, the warmth of her shared laughter. Her voice a little throaty from the cigarettes, a warning of the emphysema to come. "As true as you want it to be. She was a wife and mother. And as misdirection, it's perfect: nobody looks twice at a hausfrau, no? Exactly what she wanted on her headstone."

"She wanted her headstone to misdirect people? Why?"

Kurt arranged the flowers in the empty niche before the headstone, his neck bent. He did this every season, and would continue to do so as long as he was able to. Greta, his one true love, had died while he was still in his fifties. He didn't expect to ever remarry: for a man in his position it was too risky. But he still had their son, Franz, and Franz's wife, Emily, and their adopted offspring. He thought of his adoptive grandson, River, and this curious gawky girl with the perpetually stunned-looking dark eyes and restless mind, her talent for deadpan impersonation. "She was a"—he stumbled—"a sort of actress." Fingers fumbled with a flower stem. "It was all an act for Greta. A role she played. Wife and mother, for example. Just as, before she came to the United States, she was a sergeant in the, the special police, assigned to the Dresden administration. That's where we met: Dresden, Germany, in '66."

"Grandma was a secret policewoman?"

"Ssh! Not so loud." He'd popped the batteries from their cell phones as they entered the graveyard, and there were no visible cameras here, nothing but the thin whine of an Air Force drone circling high overhead. But you could never be sure you were unobserved. "That's what she was when I met her, before we crossed the wall to the west. Now"—he placed the last flower in the grave holder, covering his hand as he palmed the coin-sized geocache hidden there—"it's best if we don't remember this. At least, not in public." He straightened up, head still bowed, a hollowness behind his breastbone as he stared at his wife's gravestone. "I think you are old enough to know the truth. But it's a family thing. Not for outsiders. You can talk to me or your father about it, but nobody else: it's not safe."

"I got that." Rita nodded vigorously, then fell quiet, caught up in his silence. He took a deep breath, trying to clear his mind. Here was where he ended, emotionally. To the left of Greta's plot there was another strip of ground, turf undisturbed. He'd join her there eventually, he was sure. He'd sleep the final sleep on an alien shore, unable to go home to a nation that no longer existed.

But there was a cold breeze tugging at his coat, and after a minute the girl began to stamp her feet, clutching her hands under her armpits, and he realized it was unfair of him to expect a coltish tween to indulge his chilly grief. So Kurt straightened and walked back toward the path. He checked his watch with a start. "We'd better go straight home," he told his granddaughter: "it's past five."

"Mom will want help with dinner. Will she be mad with us for being out so late?"

"Not this time, I think." Kurt checked himself. "But we should still go, before the curfew." Police and Department of Homeland Security operatives would be on high alert tonight, as on all seasonal holidays. A revenge strike for the previous year's nuclear attack seemed long overdue, so tensions would be high. And for Kurt, a curfew violation and subsequent investigation would invite risky attention. "Just remember the truth about Grandma. And remember to keep it to yourself, or there could be bad consequences."

"Grandma was an illegal," Rita whispered under her breath, so quietly that Kurt failed to hear her as they headed back toward the graveyard gate. And again, with her lips barely moving as she tested the fit of the idea: "Grandma was a *spy* . . ."

Hurrying to keep up with Kurt's lengthening stride, Rita smiled in delight.

Trade Show

Rita awakened to the eerie warble of her phone's alarm, followed by NPR cutting in with the morning newscast. (Oil hitting a thirty-year low, $25 a barrel: a Republican senator calling for a tax on imports from other time lines, to prevent global warming.) She rolled over on the sofa bed and grabbed for it, suppressing a moan. It was five o'clock in the morning, pitch black but for the faint glow of parking lot floodlights leaking into the motel room. Today was Friday: last day of the trade show. Tomorrow they were due to pack everything up and head home. But today—

Today was their last day on stage demoing HaptoTech's hardware while their boss, Clive, worked the audience for contacts and (eventually) sales. Last day of mandatory stage makeup and smiles, last day of booth-bunny manners, last day performing their canned routines under the spotlights. Last fucking day. Hoo-rah. The end couldn't come soon enough for her. HaptoTech sold motion capture gear for the animation industry: kits for digitizing body movements so they could be replayed in cartoons and computer games. Unlike most MoCap rigs, which were suits you wore or pods you strapped on, HaptoTech's consisted of tiny implants, injected under the performer's skin. Supposedly this gave more precision and better inputs on musculature. What the brochure didn't say was that the implants *itched*.

Rita sat up and stretched, trying not to scratch. Her muscles ached from yesterday's workout. She'd taken the folding bed in the motel suite's day room, happy not to arm-wrestle with Deborah and Julie over the twin beds next door. Deborah snored when she slept (and complained when she was awake), and Julie talked too much, oversharing her religion enthusiastically. Rita had agreed to double up with them only because it was that or no contract for the trade show gig, which paid just well enough to make it worthwhile. Clive was a cheapskate, but even a cheapskate paying her by the hour was better than no contract (and no money). But by day 4 of a week of twelve-hour shifts, she was well past second thoughts and into thirds, if not fourths.

She wove her way past the wreckage of last night's rushed takeout and padded into the bathroom. She'd been too tired to scrub off every last bit of greasepaint the night before: now she made good. By the time she finished fixing the oversight, someone else was banging on the bathroom door with steadily increasing desperation.

Rita opened the door and found herself nose to nose with Julie. "Hey," Julie squeaked angrily: "gangway!"

Rita sidestepped and the bathroom door slammed behind her. Sharing three to a suite was one thing, but three to a bathroom was something else.

"Sleep well?" Rita asked, trying to keep her tone light. Deb paused her brushing long enough to glare and shake her head, then went back to untangling. Rita turned to the coffeepot: she'd refilled the water jug last night before hitting the sack, a preparation that stood her in good stead this morning.

While the coffeemaker was burbling, she laid out her costume for inspection. There were no catastrophic stains: good. The nanotech fabric treatment might keep it smelling fresh for weeks, but couldn't work miracles. All it would take was one drunk conference delegate with a glass of red wine to ruin her costume and put her out of a job. "One more day," she muttered to herself. "Just one more day." The implants in her right arm itched momentarily, making a muscle twitch.

"Looking forward to getting home?" Julie asked behind her.

Rita tensed. "Yeah," she admitted. "And to getting these fucking things out."

"They itch like scabies," Julie said thoughtlessly, and a moment later: "A kid brought that to the summer camp I was at one year. Didn't go *there* again."

Rita gave in to the impulse to rub furiously at the inside of her left arm, then made herself stop. If she'd known what this gig would come with she wouldn't have bothered. Clive had worked them like dogs all week; she hadn't even had time to check Facebook, much less go for a walk and log some geocaches—her hobby. It was wake, eat, work, sleep all the time.

"I think Clive said he closed a five-implant deal with a German games company yesterday. That's a five-grand commission between us, right? If he gets the export licenses."

You needed an export license to send any kind of high-tech kit out of Fortress USA these days: it was optimistic to expect to be allowed to sell the implants to Germany. Julie invariably looked on the bright side of things. It probably explained why she'd tried to become an archaeologist, before the bottom fell out of the profession. Not that Rita was in any position to throw stones. She nodded, not wanting to burst Julie's bubble. Just over twelve hundred bucks would vanish into her student loan account like a bucket of water into a polluted reservoir. She made herself smile: "Let's go break a leg. Maybe Clive can sell another bunch?"

Through the bathroom door, the sound of a toilet flushing.

"Like, yeah. Whatevs. Wire me up."

They drank coffee in the predawn gloom, three mid-twenties acting temps sharing a cheap motel suite just off I-5. Then they helped each other into their demo outfits, first strapping on the battery packs and inductive chargers, then testing their implants before pulling on their costumes and taking turns applying their makeup. Finally they were ready to head to the Waterfront trade center. Rita drove, an Indian princess in sari and coronet, her passengers a sixties schoolmarm in beehive and butterfly glasses and a time-traveling Martian debutante in silver boots and shoulder pads.

She didn't know it yet, but it would be the last normal workday of her career.

———

When they hit the queue to the exhibitor entrance, the Indian princess ran into an unexpected obstacle: Homeland Security had decided to come calling.

When they arrived they found a crowd of casual-Friday techies, salesmen, and suited women with conservative hairdos backed up in front of a security checkpoint that hadn't been there the day before. Rita found herself corralled between crowd control barriers patrolled by local cops and DHS heavies in dull black body armor. A couple of small missile-carrying quadrotor drones buzzed overhead like angry hornets, scattering the seagulls.

"ID checkpoint!" called one of the officers, pacing along the side of the queue, watching through mirrored goggles with professional disinterest: "ID checkpoint! Everybody have your ID card and conference badge ready for inspection."

"Oh shit," whispered Deborah, clutching her handbag. She began to rummage through it. "Coulda sworn it was in here—"

Failure to present a federal identity card if challenged by a DHS officer was a misdemeanor at best. If it got Deborah barred from the convention center it was going to have consequences for all three of them: Rita knew that she and Julie couldn't shoulder the workload on their own, and Clive would be pissed if his showgirls didn't show on the last day. "Chill," Rita whispered, touching Deborah's arm reassuringly. *Please don't get us noticed,* she prayed. Debs and Julie were white but Rita's skin, although pale for her costume, was sufficiently Indian-looking to draw more than her fair share of attention from the cops. And she'd heard enough horror stories that the last thing she wanted was to come to the attention of DHS and CBP.

Deborah was shaking as she rummaged through her handbag again. Touch-up kit, emergency tampon, fatphone, data glasses, purse . . . a sudden gasp. "I found it."

"Good." Rita faked another smile as Deborah caught her breath. Panic averted.

"You. Step this way, please."

For a moment Rita couldn't believe her ears. She'd been so focused on Deborah that she hadn't noticed the DHS guy pause on the other side of the barrier. Now he was looking at her. "Me?" she squeaked.

"Yes, you. Step this way." He didn't say "please" twice. The DHS might have hired Disney to train their staff in better people-handling skills but he was still a fed, with or without the smiling mask.

The cop directed her to a desk beside the checkpoint, at the front of the queue where a couple more DHS officers were hanging out. Some of them were armed with electric-blue pump-action shotguns: crowd control tasers. Her stomach lurched when she saw them.

"ID card goes here," said the guy at the desk. He sounded so bored he could have been stoned. She handed the credit card–sized rectangle over and he ran it through the reader. "Okaaay, this is a cheek swab. You've done this before, right?" Blue-gloved hands extended a plastic test stick toward her. "Open wide. This won't take long."

Rita opened her mouth, let the cop collect a saliva sample and lock it into the tablet on the desk in front of him. "Please sit here." He pointed at a plastic chair. "This will take a couple of minutes to develop." Rita gathered the skirts of her sari and sat carefully. *No zip-ties*, she realized: *That's a good sign. Means it's just a random check.* Nevertheless, they were running a full genome sequence from the sample they'd just taken, comparing it against her record in the national database. Even with the newest nanopore scanners, it would take ten minutes. They couldn't do it to everyone: they'd be here all day. *Why me?* she wondered. *Well yeah, the usual*: skin color. Mom and Dad might be of Eurasian descent, but one of Rita's birth parents had apparently been Indian.

It had been bad in second grade, right after 9/11, but when the White House was nuked, the post-7/16 paranoia had taken things to the next level. The government had announced that the attack came from a terrifying new direction, hostile forces that inhabited another parallel version of our Earth. So that made any stranger a suspect, as anyone could be a secret "world-walker," able to slip between universes and visit from a time line whose history had diverged long ago. Then, as if that wasn't bad enough, there'd been the India/Pakistan nuclear war. From which point on, the US had become increasingly difficult for people who looked like her.

The machine on the desk beeped for attention and the DHS officer peered at it. For a moment she thought he was doing a double take; then he smirked. "Okay, you're good to go. You have a nice day now, Miss Douglas. You can go right in."

"Thank you," she managed, heartbeat fluttering for a light-headed moment. The National Identity Database would have reported back, *No criminal history.* Because Rita was a good girl, and keeping her head down was an ingrained habit. And good girls tried not to get the post-7/16 national security apparatus mad at them, didn't they? She faked a smile for the cop, then scurried hastily in the direction indicated, into the bowels of the bustling conference center, enormously relieved to be out from under the microscope. Behind her, Debs was staring daggers from the middle of the slowly shuffling line. As if *she* had anything to worry about . . .

HaptoTech was a Cambridge-based biomechanics start-up. Rita was a Boston native in her mid-twenties with a major in history, a minor in acting, an aptitude for interpretative dance, and no union card. This made her a decent fit for demoing HaptoTech's newest motion capture implants at trade shows targeting the film, TV, and games production industries, although she drew the line at their more adult-themed customers. She needed the money, but not *that* badly: at least not yet.

It wasn't a new field—MoCap had been around since the '90s—but HaptoTech had a new angle: accurate to fractional millimeters, its subdermal implants could capture actors' pulse, respiration, and sweat. All stuff that fed into that difficult skin texture model, making for a more realistic simulation. Rita, Deborah, and Julie spent the day being filmed as they acted out twenty-minute vignettes, with the results animated in real time and projected live onto a big screen. A brace of servers turned their motion capture streams into mythological monsters, animals, and famous dead film stars. Rita's angle was her arms: she had two of them in real life, but six of them—realistically rendered—in her role on screen as the goddess Parvati, played by the immortal (and long-dead) Bollywood star Madhubala.

By the end of day 1 her script had become almost second nature; now she barely noticed the spectators. They weren't looking at her, anyway: they were watching the dead goddess on the screen. When they did look at her she made a point of avoiding eye contact. It was hot, boring work, and the implants itched abominably. Food was on the company, a pile of breakfast rolls served beside Folgers coffee. By five o'clock on Friday Rita was burned out. Deborah and Julie were phoning it in too, their smiles fixed, limbs shaky with tiredness. The hourly rate was great, and working for an East Coast start-up as a bluescreen babe was far better than any acting job she could aspire to—not that anyone except an already established star could make money in acting anymore. But it was a career dead end, working on stage for six hours a day was draining, and the prospects for HaptoTech keeping her on did not seem good: so she was already worrying about what she'd do next.

Stepping off stage after her 5 p.m. act—trying not to trip on her hem or lose track of the end of her sari—Rita nearly ran into Clive. Hapto-Tech's VP of marketing was conventionally handsome in a rugged country-club way, with a five-thousand-dollar smile and an open-collared shirt under his linen suit. He smiled at her affably: "Rita, if you've got a moment, please? We need to talk in private."

"Sure, Clive! Anytime!" *Oh shit*, she thought. It was the end of the show: the perfect time for layoffs, especially if he was planning on screwing people over. Her heart sinking, she followed him off the stage. Behind their show area there was a small, airless space backing onto a couple of other stands. There were no chairs, but a man and a woman were waiting there. At first she almost thought they were sales leads, but the black suits, cheap haircuts, and government-issue surveillance eyewear was all wrong. They smelled of—

"Rita Douglas?" asked the woman. She held up a badge, unsmiling: "DHS, Officer Gomez. Come with us, please."

Rita froze. "A-am I under arrest?" she asked.

"No." Gomez glanced at her companion. "Your turn."

He made eye contact with Clive. "You can go now," he said. "You never saw us and this never happened."

Clive turned and left without a backward glance. *Bastard*, Rita thought tiredly. *Fair-weather boss. Snitch. Informer.* "What is this?" she asked, trying to put on a calm expression. Her stomach lurched.

"We want to ask you some questions," Gomez said bluntly. Her posture was tense. "Please look at this card and tell me what you see." She held out a badge wallet toward Rita, then flipped it open.

Rita stared. The cops watched her expectantly: "It's some kind of knot. Celtic knotwork?" Her brow furrowed. "Why? What's it meant to be?"

The two DHS agents shared a look. "Told you so," murmured the man. They both relaxed infinitesimally. He looked at Rita: "As Sonia said, we'd like to ask you some questions. It's about something you might have witnessed without realizing what was going on." He smiled, but Rita could tell a fake when she saw one. "You are not under arrest. You are not a suspect in any investigation, although I should warn you that anything you say will be recorded." He shrugged. "But we'd prefer you to come with us voluntarily. That way we can eliminate you as a material witness from an ongoing investigation and let you go." Rita, filling in the blanks, caught the implied *or else*.

"Uh, my rental car's—" Rita's head was spinning. "We're checking out tomorrow morning. Due to fly home." Flying with HaptoTech implants still embedded was a nightmare at every security checkpoint, and it would take outpatient surgery to get them removed. HaptoTech would pay for it, but in the meantime she'd be stuck with the itching, not to mention Clive's whining because the damned things were expensive. "I was supposed to give Julie and Deborah a ride—what about them?"

"We're the government: we can take care of *everything*." The male agent grinned at her humorlessly. "You're in suite 119 at the Motel Six on I-5, right?" Rita nodded. "Give me your rental's key fob. We'll sort everything out for you."

"How long is this going to take?" she asked dubiously, handing over the keys.

"Not long; we'll probably be through with you by Sunday."

Rita forced herself to conceal her dismay. Gomez added: "If you cooperate fully, we'll book you a replacement flight home."

What was that ancient Chinese curse? *May you live in interesting times, and may you come to the attention of people in authority.* "Okay," said Rita, trying hard to sound calm. "Whatever you want." *I am a cooperative citizen, sir. Nothing to see here.* She paused. "But can I grab something to eat, and some makeup remover pads?"

The female agent nodded. "We can do that," she said, and Rita felt the words with the force of imaginary handcuffs closing around her wrists. "I promise you won't regret this, Ms. Douglas."

She was lying, of course.

BALTIMORE, NOVEMBER 2019

FEDERAL EMPLOYEE 004910023 CLASSIFIED VOICE TRANSCRIPT

COL. SMITH: Okay, so today we're evaluating the prototype candidate identified by our data trawl. Name's Douglas, Rita Douglas. Age 25. Which is to say, at least 5 years too old to be part of the DRAGON'S TEETH world-walker breeding program we uncovered back in the day.

DR. SCRANTON: (throat-clearing noise) Messy.

AGENT O'NEILL: If she isn't one of the DRAGON'S TEETH children, where did she come from?

COL. SMITH: Douglas may not be part of the world-walkers' project but she's listed in the database we captured back in '03. So we ran her DNA profile with forensics against the, the FBI's Alternate World Terror Suspects Index. And it turns out there's a three-sigma maternity match with a world-walking terror suspect. We ID'd her mother back in the day but she's been missing for years, presumably returned to the hostiles' time line.

AGENT O'NEILL: How did Douglas slip beneath our radar? The kid, I mean, not the mother—

DR. SCRANTON: She didn't.

COL. SMITH: Correct. She was adopted by a childless couple in Massachusetts, eleven days after birth. Very fast. Very well-organized—her maternal grandmother took care of it. We dug the original hospital records up and it turns out her birth mother and father were medical students. She was an, uh, accident.

AGENT O'NEILL: Medical students? World-walking medical students? What is this, I don't—

DR. SCRANTON: Listen to him.

AGENT O'NEILL: Okay.

COL. SMITH: Douglas carries the recessive trait for moving between time lines—like all of the DRAGON'S TEETH children. The world-walkers used a fertility clinic in Boston to run a rigged artificial insemination program, to breed more children who were also recessives. We figure they were going to approach some of them, as adults, to become host mothers or sperm donors . . . The point is, the first-generation carriers aren't able to world-walk themselves. And that goes for Douglas. When the terrorists set up the DRAGON'S TEETH program they already knew about her, hence her name appearing on the database. But she was born years before they set that wagon rolling. Anyway, her birth mother is most definitely one of Them—Miriam Beckstein. In fact, she was one of their ringleaders. There's an outstanding warrant for her arrest. Charges include mass murder, terrorism, crimes against humanity, violations of the Espionage Act, theft, possession of weapons of mass destruction, and treason. Oh, and narcotics trafficking.

AGENT O'NEILL: Any outstanding parking tickets? Tax evasion?

DR. SCRANTON: I didn't see any reason to complicate things needlessly.

COL. SMITH: So we have this baby, born and adopted out long before her mother showed up on our radar. Back in the nineties, so long before 7/16. This terrorist baby is just a baby, and not her mother's responsibility anymore. We tracked down the father and it turns out he's on his third marriage. He's a successful clinical oncologist in a teaching hospital in the Research Triangle. Naturalized citizen, born in Pakistan, came over with his parents when he was three. He was investigated by DHS in the wake of the Indo-Pak war, but came up clean. More recently we screened him for that same JAUNT BLUE recessive gene trait the world-walkers share, and he's negative. Whereas the Beckstein woman was most definitely positive, an active world-walker.

AGENT O'NEILL: So you're saying she's an adult recessive carrier. Older than the DRAGON'S TEETH cohort, but still Generation Z? And she's not some kind of ringer?

COL. SMITH: Yup. She's clean. No criminal record. Two loving middle-class parents, three surviving grandparents, mixed-race adopted kid. She had a really good childhood. Not silver-spoon privileged, but she never went short of evening courses or hobbies or summer camps during vacation. Lots of Girl Scout stuff: I mean, you couldn't make this up—she's your all-American straight arrow. They put her through college, then got out of her way when she struck out to make a life for herself, but they've always been there when she needs them. She'd be totally normal if she wasn't a carrier for the JAUNT BLUE capability.

DR. SCRANTON: And she has no background with the world-walkers.

AGENT O'NEILL: Don't tell me this is new information.

DR. SCRANTON: Of course not. We've been tracking Rita Douglas since the bad old days. She was just a kid when they nuked the White House. She was on a watch list for eight years—one of my predecessors thought maybe Beckstein would come for her eventually, but it seems they're not that kind of family. Or maybe she's forgotten all about her college accident by now. Or thought she could protect the kid by burying her. Anyway, as a civilian and a recessive carrier, Ms. Douglas was of no use to us. Until now.

AGENT O'NEILL: What changed?

DR. SCRANTON: This is classified: the brainiacs in the lab under the Lawrence Livermore National Laboratory finally figured out how to switch on the JAUNT BLUE world-walking trait in carriers. Carriers such as the DRAGON'S TEETH teenagers and our current person of interest. You're now authenticated and listed for that particular code word. We're going to recruit, motivate, train, and run her as an intelligence asset. A para-time spy. And that's going to be your job.

AGENT O'NEILL: Holy crap.

DR. SCRANTON: The DRAGON'S TEETH kids are still mostly in their teens. They're too young for the job we have in mind. It demands a certain maturity. But Rita Douglas is in her mid-twenties and fits the profile like a glove. I mean, she's so clean it's eerie—almost as if her family were aiming her at the political track, or a job in national security. Maybe they knew something, or guessed enough to train her to keep her head down instinctively. Either way, she's almost the perfect candidate for this operation. Almost.

AGENT O'NEILL: You're talking about turning her into a world-walking agent. Actually taking the war to the enemy's time line?

DR. SCRANTON: Eventually, yes.

AGENT O'NEILL: They're still out there? We have confirmation? You've got a fix on them?

COL. SMITH: You bet your ass they're out there. As for their location . . . that's a need-to-know matter. Let's just say, we can't just barge in and trash the joint this time. Which is why you're being pulled into this sandbox as of now. We think Ms. Douglas is the right tool for the job. We want you to run Rita. Are you up to the challenge?

AGENT O'NEILL: That's a big responsibility you're putting on me, sir.

DR. SCRANTON: Don't blame me, blame Project Oversight. But yes. They've got a high opinion of you after Stockholm. Question is, are you on the team?

AGENT O'NEILL: I'll do my best, sir.

COL. SMITH: Well, now we need to get your authorizations upgraded. Lifelogger, disable code [REDACTED].

SECURITY LEVEL EXCEEDED

LOG REDACTED

Motivating Rita

Being questioned by the men (and women) in black from the DHS was a lot like being under arrest, minus the handcuffs, and with "please," "thank you," and makeup remover pads in return for cooperation. Rita was grudgingly grateful. *But,* as she kept reminding herself whenever they let her alone, *it could be a lot worse. Might soon* get *a lot worse, if . . .* She shied away from that thought. You didn't need to be guilty of anything to get into trouble with the feds: you just needed them to think that you *might* have something to feel guilty about.

They left the conference center in a Tesla with blacked-out windows, then drove her for half an hour through the trackless, office-zoned industrial yards of Seattle. Their destination was an anonymous warehouse with a loading dock and a windowless door. There was nothing to distinguish it from hundreds of others except for a couple of unobtrusive bird-drones soaring overhead like legless, featherless seagulls with telephoto eyes. Inside, it was furnished with office cubicles and, disturbingly, a shipping container tricked out as a motel room—if motel rooms came without windows and had doors that locked from the outside. Gomez and her sidekick—Rita gathered he was called Jack, but his surname remained elusive—ushered Rita into a room like a compact Holiday Inn, then locked the door. Half an hour later it opened again and a uniformed cop shoved her suitcase inside.

It had been searched and clumsily repacked, but everything was present.

She was gloomily going through her toilet bag when the door opened again. It was Gomez.

"Here's what you asked for," she said, holding out a bag at arm's reach. "Cotton pads, baby oil, the lot. We're calling out for food in half an hour: do you have any dietary restrictions?"

Rita took the bag and Gomez let go as if stung when their fingers made momentary contact. "I'm easy," she said quietly, trying to give no sign of discomfort that might put the other woman on the alert. *Am I a prisoner? A guest? A witness? What is this, anyway?*

"Get yourself cleaned up and make yourself comfortable. We'll interview you after you've eaten, then you can get a night's sleep and if necessary we'll continue tomorrow morning."

Gomez turned to go. "Wait," said Rita. "Am I free to leave if I want to?" She looked at Gomez imploringly. The fed wasn't wearing her government-mandated lifelogging specs. If their interactions weren't being recorded, what did that mean?

Gomez paused. "In theory," she said slowly, then stopped.

"But . . . ?"

"I wouldn't recommend leaving before we've had our chat. Be ready in half an hour, Ms. Douglas."

The door closed with a too-solid click behind her.

This is so fucking weird. Rita shuddered and pulled out her phone. They hadn't even bothered to take it off her. Instead of her regular carrier it was displaying the red FEDERAL OVERRIDE network ID. So the only phone signal in the building was supplied by a government agency pico-cell, and if she used it she was waiving her Fourth Amendment rights and explicitly consenting to her communications being searched. (Not that withholding consent meant anything these days: the Fifth Amendment— the right not to incriminate oneself—was a dead letter, too.) Her sense of unreality was almost overpowering as she turned the phone off. This was popularly supposed to prevent its bugging her—unless the feds had gone to the trouble of asking for a warrant to override the power switch. She collected a change of clothes from her bag of supplies, then retreated to the bathroom to remove her makeup and costume and seek comfort in simple routine.

Maybe it was her subcontinental outfit that had triggered Gomez, or maybe she was just a bitch. But off came the sari, choli, and lehenga and on went jeans, bra, and blouse. By the time her half hour was up, Rita was back to resembling her normal all-American self: hair in a ponytail, face scrubbed clean of greasepaint, costume ready to go back in Hapto-Tech's trade show wardrobe. But ten minutes later she was beginning to go stir-crazy: the lack of social feeds was almost as irritating an itch as her implants. So she turned the phone on again and was sitting cross-legged on the bed, poking frustratedly at a puzzle game, when the agent who had identified himself as Jack pushed the door open. "Ms. Douglas? Please step this way."

"Sure." She followed him down the indicated corridor. *I'll pretend I'm happy to be here and you can pretend I'm not under arrest*, she imagined herself saying. *Let's get this over with. Whatever it is.* The sense of dread rasped away at her shell of false bravado.

They want something. That much was obvious. *But they've got nothing on me.* Her parents and grandfather had raised Rita to be cautious, law-abiding, and risk-averse. She didn't have a criminal record: not even a parking ticket. If they had anything on her they'd have arrested her right from the get-go—once they had you in the system, they could get a warrant, go on a fishing expedition, and unravel your entire life if you didn't cooperate. But they clearly didn't have anything, otherwise why do the low-key approach? Either they were hoping she'd trip up and hand them something or they were going to try to co-opt her some other way, using threats, promises, and lies.

Grandpa Kurt was East German—he had escaped across the Wall during the cold war. His stories about the way the secret police worked you over when they wanted something had scared her half to death when she was a kid. She might have discounted them as she was growing up, the way kids always discounted their elders' cautionary tales, but some of it had stayed with her. Particularly the way he'd sat, staring at the rolling

TV news coverage of the mushroom cloud over D.C. back in 2003, muttering "Reichstag fire" until Mom shushed him, glancing in fright at the landline telephone. She'd been nine at the time, and already old enough to realize everything was wrong that day.

Her fugue state deepened when Jack ushered her into a boringly ordinary meeting room. Gomez was waiting with a plastic carry-out bag full of foil-wrapped burritos: "Qdoba," she said, pointing. "Help yourself." There were office chairs clustered around a bleached pine board table. A big bottle of Caffeine-Free Dr Pepper completed the still life. *So they're going to try seduction first,* she realized. Of course—the shortest way to an informer's brain was through her stomach.

Rita sat down, deliberately (and cautiously) mirroring the cops' body language. She accepted the offered burrito with unfeigned gratitude, then watched while Jack poured three cups of soda and slid one across the table toward her. This didn't match any of Grandpa's horror yarns—but these weren't ordinary secret police, were they? The DHS had a big concrete office block downtown. The DHS went after terror suspects with drones, GPS tracking, network taps, and Hellfire missiles. The DHS did *not* invite them round for burritos and soda and a fireside chat. *If these cops are regular DHS then I'm the tooth fairy,* Rita told herself. But they could call on the DHS for backup in the field. That, if anything, made them even more frightening. Whatever they wanted, they wanted it badly enough to be using kid gloves: that was the scariest realization of all.

"I expect you're wondering what's going on," Gomez said neutrally, raising her cup but not drinking from it.

Rita unpeeled the foil from her dinner. "I'm confused," she said noncommittally, remembering more of Gramps's advice: *The cops don't have to tell you the truth, they can lie to get you to incriminate yourself. And they can lie by being friendly.* "I'm not under arrest, right? Am I under investigation? Should I have a lawyer present?" Not that she could afford an attorney. Or that there was any guarantee they'd let her have one.

"You're not—" began Gomez, just as Jack interrupted: "Yes."

Gomez glared at him, but Jack cleared his throat, then looked back at

Rita. "You are not under suspicion of any crime, but you are neverthe-less under investigation." He paused. "Clear?"

Rita shook her head, then took a bite from her burrito to buy time and mask her confusion. She was starving: there was nothing like a day of one-woman performances to work up an appetite.

Gomez shot a look to her colleague and snorted. "Let me explain, Ms. Douglas. Rita. Have you ever met your birth parents?"

"Have I—" Rita closed her mouth and tried to chew without biting her suddenly dry tongue. "What?" She shivered, suddenly feeling cold and shaky. *What?* Gathering resentment began to boil over into indig-nation. "No!"

"Hey, take it easy," said Jack. He turned to Gomez. "I told you we should let her chill first before breaking it to her." He looked back at Rita, crow's-feet wrinkling the corners of his eyes. "Quickly, before we go into the details: your birth parents—"

"Donors," said Rita.

"What?"

"DNA donors." She laid down the partially eaten burrito. Her hands trembled with tension but her movements were slow and deliberate. "They put me up for adoption while I was still in the maternity ward. I have no idea who they are; they never called, and I never saw fit to ask. My *real* parents are Emily and Franz Douglas, and they raised me and my kid brother. They changed my diapers, nursed me when I was sick, loved me, and put me through school and college. So I'll thank you not to call those other people my parents, if you don't mind."

"Whoa." Jack leaned away from Rita's outburst. Gomez focused intently on a point just off to one side of her face. "Okay, I'm sorry. No offense intended. But, uh, we need to talk to you about them. Your, uh."

"Genetic donors," Gomez said drily.

"I don't know anything about them," said Rita, crossing her arms de-fensively. "And I don't want to." She abruptly realized that her heart was hammering and her palms were moist. Anger or fear or some less name-able emotion made her hunch her shoulders.

"Well, you see, we've got a problem right there." Jack was implacable.

"That's got to change. Because we got word that *they* want to know about *you.*"

BALTIMORE, NOVEMBER 2019

FEDERAL EMPLOYEE 004930391 CLASSIFIED VOICE TRANSCRIPT

COL. SMITH: Okay, motivational crack. Greg, what do you think? Can she do it? How do we put fire in her belly?

DR. SCRANTON: You scanned the backgrounder. She's just not interested in her birth mother. She's bedded in with her, her—

COL. SMITH: Adoptives.

DR. SCRANTON: Right. She doesn't give a rat's ass about Miriam Beckstein. Or if she does, she resents her.

AGENT O'NEILL: I don't think that's all there is to it. It's her, um, the adoptives. They were pretty damn good for her, apart from the whole moving to Phoenix thing when she was nicely settled in. It's a close family. She's an independent adult but she still likes them. Goes home for Thanksgiving and birthdays. Phones mom and dad every week.

AGENT GOMEZ: You could fridge them, pin it on the world-walkers to motivate her—

COL. SMITH: (emphasis) No, we *couldn't.* We don't do that shit anymore. We don't discuss that shit. We prosecute that shit, *'pour encourager les autres.'* It is illegal and off-limits. This isn't the fucking CIA.

AGENT GOMEZ: Hey! I wasn't suggesting—

COL. SMITH: Damn right you weren't.

DR. SCRANTON: Well, how about you come up with something legal that will motivate her instead? As it is she's got nothing you can sink your claws into . . . nothing. I mean, I read her file and I will concede it is eerily clean. In thirty years of intelligence operation oversight work, I've never seen anything like it. None of the three-felonies-a-day stuff. No sexting, no unusual Facebook drama, no underage drink or drugs. Even her hobbies are boring: painting, landscape photography, going for long walks with a bit of geocaching to liven them up. It's like she anticipated coming to our attention from the age of eight! Or as if she was trained by a professional paranoid—the grandfather perhaps. I can tell you right off that blackmail's not going to work. It's okay if an informant hates their handler, but a field agent in a foreign state— an illegal—has to love you. If you threaten her adoptive parents she'll hate you, so that's out too.

AGENT GOMEZ: You said she doesn't give a damn about her original parents. How about we make her give a damn, then give her a hand up? So she has to go through us to get them.

AGENT O'NEILL: Hmm. Like, if we can't fridge her encumbrances, how about we run a false flag op? Make her think Beckstein wants her dead?

DR. SCRANTON: She doesn't even know who the fuck Miriam Beckstein is. What are you going to do, reel her in and give her a background briefing first?

AGENT GOMEZ: Why don't we do just that? Crazier shit has worked.

DR. SCRANTON: Colonel, how about it? What do *you* think?

END TRANSCRIPT

SEATTLE, MARCH 2020

Jack looked sympathetic but continued implacably: "Back in 1992, two medical students met at Harvard and did what happens when two bright, not terribly worldly students strike sparks. He was a high-flying scholarship boy, the son of first-generation immigrants from Pakistan. She was adopted, like you: her parents were a lapsed Jewish political bookstore owner with a discreet trust fund and his left-wing activist wife. Anyway, our two students moved in together, and one thing led to another and they had a little accident with a burst condom which blew out the third year of her degree. He continued in medicine: she took six months out and transferred sideways, picking up credits in journalism after the adoption. They got hitched six months before he graduated, but separated eight months later and then divorced. It was a patch-it-up marriage, and it didn't work out."

Jack stopped reading from his tablet. *Why are you telling me this?* Rita wanted to scream. *I don't know these people! I don't want to know them!* But her lips felt numb, her tongue frozen. Gomez drained her cup of Dr Pepper and took up the thread.

"The father went on to a career in clinical oncology and moved to North Carolina. He remarried: you have a half-brother and two sisters. The mother—"

"I don't want to know this!" The pressure valve had blown: Rita's voice broke as she raised it, ragged and angry.

"Yes you do." Gomez stared coldly at Rita. "The woman I'm telling you about pursued a career in investigative journalism in Boston for some years before dropping off the radar in 2002. Subsequently she became a person of interest in the ongoing investigation into world-walkers. And yes, they are real. She and her adoptive mother—the father died in 1993—disappeared for good shortly before 7/16, but not before we confirmed that they were both world-walkers."

"What? The fuck?" The half-eaten burrito in Rita's stomach seemed suddenly to have turned to lead. "You're telling me I'm related to time travelers? The ones who nuked the White House?"

Gomez glanced at Jack, who took over: "They're not time travelers, exactly. And you are not under suspicion of having nuked the White House," he added, deadpan. "For one thing, you were eight years old. You also have a rock-solid alibi provided by your third-grade teacher, Mrs. Chu." Rita stared at his hands. It seemed like a safe thing to do. He wore a signet ring, embossed with the initials CTR. She noticed him glance at Gomez. *They're tag-teaming me,* she realized sickly. She'd seen enough TV shows and movies to recognize the good cop / bad cop dynamic. *Keep the subject off-balance.*

Gomez took over after a brief delay: "This is where it gets sticky. Please hand over your phone."

"What? Why?"

"Because I say so!" Gomez snapped. For a moment Rita saw something unnerving and hateful in the other woman's eyes, something that gave her unpleasant schoolyard flashbacks. She fumbled to comply.

"We're going to reflash the firmware," Jack explained. "You won't notice anything different, but if you dial 911, we'll hear you. If you're calling for fire or ambulance there won't be any delay. But if you need, uh, *help*, we'll be in the loop along with the local police. Again, if it's routine, we'll stand back. But if you need *us*, our department, we'll be there."

Rita released her phone with nerveless fingers. *They're going to root it,* she realized. No federal override icon: they were turning her phone into a full-time informer. Was there anything incriminating in there? Questionable photos? Sexts? Oddly phrased e-mails or text messages? It probably didn't matter: they could already grab anything they wanted off the net without her permission. The old-time secret police relied on informers; the modern ones just conscripted your phone. She felt sick to her stomach. "Why are you doing this?" she asked again.

Gomez gave her a tight-lipped stare. "You're not cleared. So we can't tell you," she explained. "It might be a false alarm. So, there might be no reason at all why we're having this meeting. Or it might be the most important meeting in your life, the one that saves you."

"What?" Rita's head spun. "You think—your bosses think—my genetic relatives might suddenly take an interest in me after a quarter of a century of neglect? Why is that?"

"They're world-walkers," Jack said as dismissively as he might have written off any other group of terrorists. "Who knows why world-walkers do what they do?"

"But I'm not a world-walker!" Rita quavered. She watched as Gomez pulled the back off her phone, plugged some kind of chip into it, and Vulcan nerve-pinched it into a reboot chime. The half-eaten burrito lay on the table in front of her, cooling. She didn't feel hungry anymore. She felt nauseous, bloated by a decades-long festering sense of emptiness and injustice. "I'm not a world-walker."

Jack shrugged again, an I-feel-as-uncomfortable-as-you-do gesture that fell flat. "We're not saying you are."

"But your relatives might disagree," cautioned Gomez. "So remember: 911 is your friend."

The not-exactly-cops invited Rita to stay the night. They positively insisted—with a formal politeness that said *don't even* think *about refusing*. They thoroughly creeped her out with their solemn last-meal formality, the inadvertent intimidation of power. She was getting a no-caffeine headache by the time Gomez finished with her phone. They made her bag up her burrito and escorted her back to her room, or cell, or whatever the hell you called it: the motel-grade accommodation with the handle on the outside and no window.

I'm not a world-walker, she repeated to herself as she lay sleeplessly on the narrow bed. *I don't come from another world, I can't wish myself between universes, and they're not my family.* But sleep came reluctantly, and she was troubled by incoherent dreams tainted by a nameless sense of urgency.

She woke early the next morning. Gomez knocked on the door at six thirty. Her black suit was spotless, as severe as a uniform. Her only sign of individuality was a brooch in the shape of an infinity symbol worn on the lapel. Rita was already showered and dressed. "Your ticket is on your phone," said the cop. "Jack will run you out to the airport. You're booked via Minneapolis on Delta." She looked as if she hadn't slept—didn't need sleep, like she was some kind of government terminator robot running on bile, paranoia, and electricity.

"Uh, right. Let me just zip up my bag."

"Take your time." Gomez's tone inverted the meaning of her words.

The agent stood at parade rest, waiting patiently by the door while Rita slung the last of her things into the suitcase. As Rita straightened up, she asked, "Who are you people? Really?"

"If you call the DHS and ask, they'll tell you we work for them."

"But—" Rita caught Gomez's quelling look. "If you say so."

Gomez relented slightly. "There are lots of operational directorates within DHS. We're part of a unit that not many people have heard of. You don't need to know more than that."

You have to be most afraid of secret police when they take you into their confidence and tell you things, she remembered Grandpa Kurt explaining: *it means they want you to believe.* But why would they even need that? They had the guns, the dogs, and the secret jails. If they wanted you to do something, they could force you to do it. *So they only try to make you believe something if they want you to convince someone else whom they can't touch. Your future self, or some future acquaintance. They do it and they make a liar of you.*

Rita smiled vaguely and nodded. Her forehead throbbed. "Great. I'm ready to go now. Wherever you want me to go?"

Jack drove her out to the airport: "We dropped your rental car off last night. And I processed your ticket myself: you're good for a checked bag, and you've got an hour until boarding."

"But I—" Rita stared at the e-ticket on her phone. "Hey, this is first class!" A stab of gratitude gave way instantly to suspicion. *They're trying to make me grateful. Why?*

"Least we could do," Jack said. "Have a good flight now." He seemed less inhuman and unbending, less inclined to hate her on sight, than Gomez. She found herself instinctively mistrusting him, resenting him for stimulating her pathetic sense of gratitude. *Good cop / bad cop,* she reminded herself. At least Gomez was honest.

Jack dropped Rita beside the baggage drop-off outside the terminal building. Dazed, she handed her suitcase over, then shifted her handbag up her shoulder and walked into the check-in area. Her head was spinning. *I need to talk to someone,* she realized. She instinctively reached for her phone, then stopped. *Wait.* More of Gramps's stories came back to her. *Not here, not on my phone.*

Security was the usual heaving human zoo, with people being called out for random DNA checks on either side of her and explosive sniffers buzzing around overhead. Miraculously, Rita didn't attract any unusual attention, despite the itching implants that had triggered the body scanners on the way out. She paid no attention to the cameras that tracked her across the concourse, the Segway-riding robocops, the whole panoply of national security displayed around her. With increasing confidence she walked toward her departure gate, knees weakening with relief at the realization that in another ten hours she'd be home.

The day passed in a blur of airplane seats and security checkpoints.

There was incoming e-mail on her traitor phone: she didn't dare reply to any of it. There was a *Call me when you get in* from Clive-the-bastard, the boss who'd sell her out as soon as look at her. An *Are you okay?* from her roomie Alice, to her surprise. A note about furnace repairs from her landlord. Nothing from her most recent ex. Irrelevant yatter and babble on the social side, pleas for support from her theatrical group's manager, marketing junk from bands she'd followed years ago. Normally the knowledge that the feds could snoop on all network traffic didn't bother her: but having seen her phone rooted right in front of her, she felt frozen, gagged by the knowledge of an intrusive presence. And all because they thought she might be carrying the virus of the paranormal around in her genes.

They think I've got world-walker connections? A hysterical laugh tried to bubble up. She took hasty shallow breaths to drive it back down again before someone noticed. World-walkers were shadowy nightmare figures, twenty-first-century reds under the bed. Terrorists who could flicker in and out of reality from other worlds where history had taken a different path, bearing stolen nukes or suitcases full of heroin. *The ultimate enemy,* the last president but two had declared them. She just about remembered her parents and grandparents gathered around the TV, red-eyed, trying to follow the news on their PCs as well. They killed the president in 2003, back before the government had built working paratime machines to go after them. Not to mention strip-mining fossil fuels from the neighboring uninhabited parallels. Back before they canceled the War on Drugs and replaced it with the Crisis on Infinite Earths.

Before the gig with HaptoTech, Rita had been too busy working to notice how her social life was shrinking and her days were sharpening to a bright workplace focus surrounded by a penumbra of exhaustion. But now, sitting on a plane with nothing else to do, all she could think about was how much of a mess her life was. She didn't have a job anymore, let alone a career. The outside world had decided to take an unfriendly interest in her, and she felt isolated and fragile, her existence liminal. So—the DHS having bought her a first-class ticket—she drank all the wine the cabin crew would bring her, and did her best to lose herself in the stack of tired romcoms that passed for in-flight entertainment.

At least the old and shabby planes had seatback video: she didn't know what she'd have done on a modern airliner, with nothing but a power outlet for her phone. She couldn't have forced herself to watch movies on it knowing its front-facing camera might be watching her right back, analyzing her face for micro-expressions indicative of terrorist sympathies.

Rita passed through the Minneapolis–Saint Paul airport like a ghost and made it to her connecting flight with time to spare. It was late evening by the time she spotted her suitcase on the baggage belt at Logan, dragged it off the line with a grunt of effort, and trundled it out to the exit and thence to the Silver Line, then the Red Line all the way south.

By the time she arrived at the parking lot where she'd warehoused her auto for the past week, she was exhausted. Cumulative sleep deprivation was catching up with her as she fumbled for the key fob. Her car was a '14 Acura hybrid her father had given her after running it for years, its battery pack halfway dead of old age and beyond her means to replace with a refurb. Hybrids were a dead-end technology anyway, killed when gas dropped below a dollar a gallon: but she loved it for its quiet start and creature comforts. Dragging her suitcase behind her, she hit the unlock button, saw the flash of her headlights reflecting off a concrete pillar, and hit the tailgate latch button.

As she did so she saw a bright blue flash—and felt a sudden breathtaking pain in her belly that doubled her over, retching. She collapsed to the parking lot floor. The pain was savage, as if she'd been clubbed, with additional cramps in her right knee and shoulder. A moment of panic. Footsteps coming toward her, then another stunning burst of pain in her stomach.

"Is she down?" someone asked.

Another voice, from a shadow bending over her: "Yup." Hands grabbed her and lifted: two strong men frog-marched her to her car as she retched. They pushed her headfirst into the open, emptied-out trunk and she began to struggle, terrified. *Kidnappers!* There were two of them, both bigger and stronger than she was, and the pain from the taser was dizzying. Resistance was difficult: it was all she could do to get breath into her lungs.

A click. Darkness and pressure. She gasped for air, tried to stretch, and found herself up against the ends of the trunk. It was cold and none too clean, and still smelled faintly of dog. Something dug into her midriff. She brought up her left hand, felt a wire and something sharp sticking into her. She pulled it free, shuddering and hyperventilating in fear.

The car bounced on its suspension twice, then the doors thudded shut. Rita felt the pressure change in her ears. Her abductors seemed to be having a muffled, distant conversation, but she couldn't make out any distinct words. She tried to roll on her back, banged her sore knee against the trunk lid with a flash of pain, and tried to remember which side the emergency tailgate release toggle was on. It was pitch black inside the trunk. Where was her handbag? They'd taken it: it contained her phone, her purse, and her ID card. Whimpering with fear, she twisted around, trying to untangle herself. The car shuddered and rocked, then began to move backward.

This is what Gomez and Jack were talking about, she realized, dizzy with pain. The implants in her left arm stung at the unaccustomed pressure of lying on metal. *Shit.* The car jolted, then stopped backing up and began to move forward, turning toward the parking lot exit. How did the DHS know? Words came back to her: *They don't tell us everything: we might unintentionally give something away when we talk.*

She fumbled around the interior of the trunk. She could feel the hole in the side of the trunk lid where the emergency release handle normally hung down: they'd cut it away while she was on the ground. Her eyes watered with frustration as the car angled down the exit ramp, then slowed, bounced over a speed bump, and came to a halt. Noises from outside were muffled, but she heard the whine of a barrier rising. The car began to move again, then turned into the street and accelerated, rolling her toward the rear of the trunk.

"Don't panic," she muttered aloud, scared out of her wits. Whoever her kidnappers were, they wanted her alive. *If I had my phone I could call the cops,* she thought. Then, *No, wait. The DHS or whoever they are want me to call them. But they're not my friends. This is a setup. I'm bait. They're probably tracking my phone.* If her kidnappers were world-walkers, then the feds would be much more interested in catching them than in rescuing her. But if her kidnappers were world-walkers, they'd probably ditched her phone before they left the parking lot.

Icy sweat drenched her, gumming her shirt to the small of her back. *What am I supposed to do in this kind of situation?* She'd once earned a Girl Scout merit badge for a course that covered surviving kidnapping attempts and hostage taking, among other unusual topics. *Observe, orient, act.* Her thoughts spun. *What if it's a different kind of setup? World-walkers could just grab me, couldn't they? I'd wake up in another world. But why would they take my car? What if they're ordinary carjackers? (But who? And why me?) Got to get out and run away.*

She had to change the parameters on them. Just like they taught in the (How Not to) Die Hard adventure course she'd taken all those years ago.

They'd moved all her normal crap out of the trunk to make room for an unwilling passenger, but did they know about her emergency kit? Gramps had insisted she stash it in the spare wheel well, under the carpet. Inchworming her way back into the trunk, she freed up enough space to grab the plastic handle in the floor. Predictably, she was lying across the hinge. By raising herself on her shoulder and bracing her feet against the opposite side of the trunk, she managed to lift herself off the panel. It rose, and she fumbled inside. Her fingers barked painfully on metal: the case of a socket set. Seconds passed as she frantically felt around it for the catch, popped it, and groped inside for the milled metal handle of the wheel nut wrench.

Fumbling around in the dark, knife-edged recesses of the swaying car, Rita wedged the end of the wrench between the trunk lid's catch and the back of the trunk itself, then yanked at the handle as hard as she could, bracing her feet. Metal gave, very slightly: but the lock was made of stern stuff, built to withstand casual thieves. Swearing quietly, she closed her eyes and thought for a moment. *What else?*

There were other items in the emergency kit, and she thanked Gramps silently for making her add it. Fumbling seconds passed as she navigated the contents of the small padded bag by touch. Finally her fingers closed around her target: the dumb emergency phone. It didn't do Internet or record video, but it had a standby life measured in months, a built-in flashlight, and GPS. She fired it up and waited for it to get a location fix through the aluminum trunk lid, and saw that open countryside was still a few miles away.

She flipped on the flashlight and shone it around the interior of the trunk. There was a compartment in the carpet-covered side, near her head, and big flat-headed screws held it closed. She vaguely remembered it holding electrical stuff: fuses, maybe. A minute's fumbling and she retrieved a flat-head screwdriver from the emergency kit. Behind the panel, the light from her phone shone on fuses and a couple of switches. The labels were hard to read in the dim light, but she puzzled them out eventually. BATTERY ISOLATION BREAKER.

The plan came together in a moment. *Here goes nothing,* she thought, and pulled up the phone's GPS again. It finally had a fix. The car was heading out of town, making almost thirty miles per hour. But she could see the blue line of a freeway up ahead on the screen, maybe a mile or two down the road. *I can't let them get there,* she thought, and shook the phone to call up the keypad. Thumbs on a fat screen dialed 911.

"Help," she said as soon as she heard a human voice pick up: "I'm being kidnapped. Two perps tased me and shoved me in the trunk of my own car. It's a silver '14 Acura hybrid, plates read, uh," and she rattled off her number. "They're driving me south through Dorchester toward Route 1."

"Please hold," the dispatcher crackled in her ear.

"Can't," she said quietly. "I'm bailing." She hung up, shoved the phone into her jeans pocket—it would have to take its chances—and reached for the battery isolation breaker by touch.

The car, her car, coughed and died. She brought her legs up as the car began to slow, then took the knurled grip of the socket wrench in both hands and waited.

BALTIMORE, DECEMBER 2019

FEDERAL EMPLOYEE 004910023 CLASSIFIED VOICE TRANSCRIPT

COL. SMITH: I'm just playing devil's advocate here, but what if she doesn't respond the way you expect?

AGENT GOMEZ: What? What do you mean?

COL. SMITH: You're playing her like she's a nice polite young Indian-American woman, deferential to authority, painfully clean and law-abiding. But what if—

AGENT GOMEZ: I'm not wrong—

COL. SMITH: —she takes after her mother?

AGENT O'NEILL: What?

DR. SCRANTON: Her birth mother, I assume you mean.

COL. SMITH: Yes.

DR. SCRANTON: Well, that would be . . . interesting.

AGENT O'NEILL: In what way?

COL. SMITH: Her mother looked like a nice middle-class tech beat reporter. Right up until she killed a lot of people.

AGENT GOMEZ: But she was a terrorist! Rita has no connection to her. She doesn't have any training—

DR. SCRANTON: How would we know? Deep-cover agents don't tell their children what they are. Any training is carefully disguised as childhood games. And what about her adoptives? Do you think her birth mother saddled her with a paranoid East German granddad who had run-ins with the Stasi by accident? What about all the Girl Scout wilderness adventure camp stuff they put her through? The self-defense courses?

COL. SMITH: It's almost like Miriam and Iris Beckstein chose her adoptive family to give her that type of upbringing. Perfect for a covert ops agent—or someone who'd keep a low profile because there's a seven-digit reward for her birth mother's head, dead or alive.

DR. SCRANTON: Until you crank up the pressure there's no way of knowing what Rita will do: whether she'll break down in tears or turn into a rabid grizzly bear with a hangover.

AGENT O'NEILL: Who were the Stasi? What do they have to do with this?

DR. SCRANTON: (groans quietly) Youngsters. Forget it.

COL. SMITH: Well, back to my point. We're running this motivation and evaluation scenario on her and we kind of expect her to do the reasonable thing—use the tool we handed her, take the hint we put in her head. And she looks like a nice polite lady who'll do the right thing.

But she's descended from pirates and monsters, even though they baby-farmed her out to a family who are so squeaky clean it's like they sleep in a laundromat. I've got a funny feeling about this. Better keep your ammo handy.

AGENT GOMEZ: Nothing bad's going to happen. Trust me, it's all going to go like clockwork.

DR. SCRANTON: Oh, really?

END TRANSCRIPT

Evasions

The ride roughened as the car rolled to a stop by the side of the road. Rita heard voices, muffled through the carpet. A door opened, then slammed. Footsteps on gravel coming round the trunk. *Okay, they figured it out.* She tensed.

Click.

The trunk unlocked and the lid began to rise. Rita bounced upright, uncoiling like a jack-in-the-box, and slammed the wrench right to left along the length of the gap, two-handed. The impact nearly yanked it from her grip. Someone gasped, trying to inhale; she shouldered the tailgate open and lunged from the trunk, landed sprawling on top of a man who was trying to lever himself upright. She heard the warble and scream of sirens in the distance. Dry-mouthed terror lent her strength as she whacked the wrench into the side of his head, rolled off him, and came up in a crouch.

Some subtle cue made her duck and spin; the fist that had been aiming for her face missed. She continued her turn and jabbed with the wrench. Her second assailant was a shadowy silhouette, backlit by the dim blue LED glow of the streetlights: he was taller and heavier than she was, and fast enough to dodge her inexpert attempt at punching him in the gut. She took a long stride backward, keeping the wrench extended, then another step, trying to open a gap. Long-ago classes in karate and Krav Maga and less-long-ago women's self-defense courses had stressed the importance of not letting a big aggressor get within arm's reach. The one she'd put down wasn't moving, but his friend was following her warily, reaching for—*oh shit*—

Rita spun and ran, jinking sideways. The taser dart whipped past her on its crackling tether. There was no traffic and no lit windows on this stretch of all-but-deserted highway, just shuttered exhaust shops and landscaping services. She made for the slope at the side of the road, looking for a gap between bushes and fences. Her phone buzzed in her pocket like a box of angry bees, but she ignored it. Then there were footsteps behind her. She was fast and he'd paused to ditch the taser, but if he caught up with her, this could only end badly. And if he didn't chase her, but had a real gun, he'd eventually get hyped up enough to use it. The sirens, still distant, were fading now. She found a gap, a driveway leading into a row of closed shop units, and dashed through it.

There was a whining noise overhead, and a pool of blindingly white light appeared around her. She threw up one arm to shield her eyes as an alarm began to beep frenetically. She heard a flat crack of gunshots— two, three—as she dove for the side of the nearest shop, trying to get out of view. The whine rose to a metallic screech above her, then cut off, followed half a second later by a tearing crash as something refrigerator-sized fell in the parking lot behind her. There was another volley of gunshots, then a roar of engine noise and a stentorian amplified voice commanding her to freeze.

Rita lay facedown, shaking with fear. Her kidnapper had a gun. She could see him silhouetted in the light from the second drone, this one keeping a healthy distance overhead. He raised it, fired twice more, then swept round toward a target she couldn't see. Two more shots rang out: not his. He dropped where he stood, like a marionette with cut strings. The amplified voice kept bellowing at him to lie still long after it was obvious he was beyond hearing. And her phone was still buzzing when the first cop—a for-real Highway Patrol officer, advancing in swivel-eyed starts with pistol drawn—reached her and put the cuffs on.

Frying pan, meet fire.

———

Shock can affect short-term memory. Rita retained only fragments of the next half hour, sitting in the back of a parked police cruiser with her hands zip-tied behind her back. She saw more cruisers with light bars flaring against the night converging on the parking lot. There were a few terse questions—name, what was she doing here—repeated in tones of angry disbelief when she explained she'd been carjacked and had escaped. Someone took her emergency phone. Kidnappees were not supposed to escape, she gathered. Someone else asked her to identify her handbag, her phone. More questions: what was she doing, where had she been, had she seen her assailants, why are you lying to us? While they were asking, her fatphone vibrated for attention. One of the officers answered it, asking a couple of brusque questions. Then his manner changed completely.

"Aw shit," he said. "Okay, we'll wait here." He ended the call. "Did you get the ID to match?" he asked his partner.

"Yup." The partner in question eyeballed Rita in the rearview. "Name check is—"

"Hey, listen up." The cop cranked his head round to look at Rita. "Your friends want you out of here. They'll be here in ten minutes."

"What friends?" she asked, but they had no answer for her.

A gathering dust storm and the thunder of full-sized rotor blades brought Rita back from the dark place. She looked up dully, squinting puffy, red-rimmed eyes against the wind blast through the open front windows of the car. She'd been scared sick before, wondering how she was going to make bail—they'd find something to charge her with, just for inconveniencing them; that's how it worked, wasn't it?—but now something worse was descending, gravid with dark possibilities.

The chopper touched down at the far end of the parking lot. To her uneducated eye it looked huge and menacing, studded with doors and odd protuberances. (In fact, it was a regular police Black Hawk, an ex-military transport chopper rigged for urban search operations, with cameras and satellite drones to augment its cyclopean searchlight stare.) The side doors opened and two men and a woman climbed out, ducking involuntarily beneath the *swoosh* of the slowing blades overhead. After a brief conference with the officers clustered around the incident control van, one of the men peeled off and walked toward the cruiser. As if it was a prearranged signal, the driver up front climbed out, walked round to the passenger door, and casually tugged her to get her moving.

"Get the ties off her," said Jack, holding an ID badge where the uniforms could see it. He sounded disgusted. "Is this some kind of Masshole thing or do you always arrest kidnap victims?"

"Wait, she's a suspect pending identification, we caught her hanging around—"

"Yeah, right; who do you think phoned in the incident?" He slid his badge away before Rita could read it. The cop ducked his head, unusually compliant, and stepped behind her. Jack moved to face her. "Unless you object, I'm going to take you into protective custody. We can start you on witness security tomorrow; right now it's probably too dangerous for you to go home."

Rita finally found her voice as her wrists came free: "What the fuck is this about?" Her voice rose: "You set me up, didn't you? You and Gomez!"

"Hey, calm down." Jack stepped close, lowering his voice. "We didn't know they'd move this fast. Just plain lucky I was on a direct flight right after you. We didn't expect anything like this. Not so soon."

"Like what?" Rita pointed to the taped-off area, now crawling with cops—both the uniformed kind and crime scene officers in overalls. "Who are they and what are they doing?"

"I'm not sure." Jack looked uncomfortable. "Walk with me." He turned toward the helicopter and Rita followed, uncertainly. One of the cops trailed after them with her handbag and suitcase. "If I had to guess, I'd say they work for a faction opposed to your, uh, DNA donor. Your birth mother."

"My . . . why . . ."

"Isn't it obvious? The world-walkers want you dead, Ms. Douglas. We got a lead on them, chatter on some of their channels, and ran ahead of it. Luckily for you, as it turns out. If you're asking why they want you dead, well, I'm sorry but we don't read minds. On the other hand, we're not in the business of letting terrorists murder our people, and you're our best lead on them: this just confirmed they're serious about you. So we're going to try and keep you alive, and try to catch the bad guys and discover where they're coming from. Then we're going to deal with them."

It was all too fast and too slick, moving like a Hollywood production on well-greased runners. Rita was tired and hungry and shaking with cold-sweat fear, and still she didn't believe him. "But they—" She stopped, her inner censor clamping down. *Could have grabbed me and carried me to another world then cut my throat,* she realized. *Why didn't they do that?*

"They employ ordinary criminals to do their legwork," Jack continued. "Those guys were just hired muscle. You managed to bail before they made it to their handover point. But we'd better get you to a safe house before they try again. What do you say?"

"I, uh, I . . ." She trailed off, nodding. "Yeah. Yeah, whatever you say." What she really wanted to do was to phone Mom and Dad, reassure them that she was okay, then go and hide under the bed or take a long bath and not leave her home for a week. But her comfort zone seemed as far away as Pluto. "Whatever you think," she said, surrendering to the inevitable. "Just get me out of here."

"Deal," said Jack. He held the helicopter door open for her; it felt curiously flimsy after the trunk lid of her car. "Let's fly. My boss wants to talk to you tomorrow: I think you'll find what he has to say interesting."

BALTIMORE, MARCH 2020

FEDERAL EMPLOYEE 004930391 CLASSIFIED VOICE TRANSCRIPT

DR. SCRANTON: Well. What a mess.

AGENT GOMEZ: I *knew* we should have fridged her adopters instead.

COL. SMITH: And I remind you we don't do that sort of thing these days.

DR. SCRANTON: Please don't squabble; it's giving me a headache. I've got to work out what kind of spin to put on this. It's not a matter of shoving it under the carpet . . . there isn't enough carpet in Persia to cover up this mess.

AGENT GOMEZ: The hired help were deniable assets.

DR. SCRANTON: And may I remind you, the Massachusetts State Highway Patrol, the Boston PD, the local branch of the FBI, a bunch of hick security goons from Dorchester, and probably the MIT Campus Police and the Marching Band of the Massachusetts Rotary Club all got a slice of this cake? The folks upstairs are going to have a fit trying to keep the lid on it tomorrow. And guess who's going to have to brief them? So you people are going to help me assemble a story, a narrative that holds water and explains just what we were trying to achieve and why this happened. And you'd better hope I can spin it convincingly, because it's not just my job that's on the line if we get it wrong.

COL. SMITH: Right. So how about we run through the facts one more time?

AGENT GOMEZ: Go for it.

COL. SMITH: I'll start. Subject: Rita Douglas. It was decided—

AGENT GOMEZ: By this team *collectively*, let's get that clear—

COL. SMITH: Shut up. It was decided by this team that in order to expedite the voluntary recruitment of the candidate we should subject Rita Douglas to a motivational scenario. Frightening but basically harmless.

DR. SCRANTON: Only it turned out she had bigger balls than expected.

COL. SMITH: A pair of stringers were commissioned via a blind cutout to conduct the exercise. Small-time thugs. There's no back-trail to us that doesn't equally plausibly point at the adversaries.

AGENT GOMEZ: Hell, it's the sort of thing they do. We just stole a leaf from their playbook. If they'd identified her themselves they'd probably have done it for us—

COL. SMITH: Don't interrupt. Your concerns are noted and will be taken into account. Let me remind everyone who we're dealing with here: Miriam Beckstein's daughter.

AGENT O'NEILL: Who was raised by total strangers, is an inactive carrier of the world-walking trait, and who is a Generation Z underachiever who works as a booth babe at trade shows.

COL. SMITH: But who, despite being tased and shoved in a trunk, correctly evaluated her situation and turned the tables on her kidnappers. She did serious physical damage to one of them: subdural hematoma and major abdominal bruising. His condition is listed as critical by Mass General, by the way.

DR. SCRANTON: Where did she get the blackjack?

AGENT GOMEZ: It wasn't a blackjack, it was a tire iron. And she had it in her car trunk. Under the carpet, where the muscle didn't spot it.

DR. SCRANTON: Lovely. Do please continue, Colonel.

COL. SMITH: She called the cops. Why did it get through? I thought we had a divert on her phone?

AGENT O'NEILL: We did indeed have a divert: it didn't work. Turns out the hired goons took her handbag and phone off her—they weren't idiots, and somebody forgot to hand them that part of the script. Turns out she had a survival kit in the trunk—blankets, first aid kit, tire iron, and a prepaid phone for emergencies—and nobody thought to search her car before she got to it, so we never found it.

AGENT GOMEZ: If we're parceling out the blame, I'd just like to note . . .

DR. SCRANTON: Don't bother. I'm not going to let this turn into a scapegoating exercise. Just stick to the story so that I know *what* I'm covering for.

AGENT O'NEILL: She took down one goon and ran for it. Then because she got through to the real 911 service, the state police dogpiled the scene. Which made goon two lose his shit and light up one of their drones. And it all went downhill from there.

DR. SCRANTON: So we can point to the goon going off-script by taking her bag, and her unusual degree of preparedness in having an emergency kit in her trunk. So my next question is, did she swallow the narrative? Have we spoiled her by accident? It'd be a real shame if all this mess was for nothing.

COL. SMITH: That's a good question. I don't think we're going to learn the answer to it until I've had a chance to talk to her myself, tomor—later today.

AGENT O'NEILL: I make it 50/50. If she buys it, we might be able to recover and acquire a useful asset; I mean, she showed initiative and courage under pressure—that's got to be a plus. But if she doesn't buy the scenario . . .

DR. SCRANTON: We'll worry about how deep to bury her if and when that eventuates. Hopefully it won't. Meanwhile, I call this a wrap. Let's go and get some sleep. Tomorrow morning I'll brief the folks upstairs. In the meantime, when Rita's had a bit of time to think about things Sonia and Patrick can take her in and Eric can pitch her the offer. We'll take it from there.

END TRANSCRIPT

BOSTON, MARCH 2020

The helicopter spirited her away into night and mist. After a flight lasting less than thirty minutes, it landed in a distant corner of an airfield where the gray shadows of military transport aircraft lined the runway. Jack led her to a van with blacked-out windows, and it took them to a hangar. Then he led her inside, to a corner where a stack of modular prefab offices formed a multistory complex, completely invisible to the outside world. One of these was tricked out with another bland motel-style room with no windows and no handle on the inside of the door. Rita was unsure whether or not to feel grateful for the locks and the dog-sized six-legged robots with grenade launchers patrolling the darkness outside. She was beginning to suspect that perhaps the only foolproof way to tell the difference between a fortress and a jail was by the attitude of the guards to the inmates.

She held herself together while she showered and unpacked enough of her personal effects to pretend that this room was yet another hotel suite rather than a fancy prison. But then the day's events hit home. Curling up beneath the comforter, she clutched her phone, her traitorous link to the world, and hit up the local news sites, mindful that everything she surfed would be as transparent as glass to her custodians. There was, she discovered, absolutely no word of a lethal shoot-out near the interstate south of Boston. Nothing. She hadn't been expecting to be the talk of the town, but the totality of the media blackout was chilling. Everybody understood that this sort of thing happened, that the First Amendment had to take a backseat to the requirements of national security from time to time. But witnessing the thoroughness with which everything from street cams through Twitter feeds fell silent before the demands of the Dark State gave her an eerie sense of detachment. It was as if she was coming adrift from her life, and all that was solid was melting into air. She began to shake; then the tears came.

Catharsis and sleep brought her to a better place by the time she woke early the next morning. The lack of manacles and orange jumpsuits was a positive sign. Her absent relatives might be enemies of the state, but the state had decided that she was not one of them. She forced herself to message her parents, flatmates, and a handful of friends, telling them she'd been delayed out west but was okay. She kept it to the sort of content-free fluff that would tell a censor nothing about her, and that might even be viewed as evidence of cooperation.

By the time there was a knock on the door, she thought she'd managed to compose herself. But she learned she was wrong the hard way, as her heart pounded wildly. "Come in," she said, as if her consent meant anything.

The door opened. It was Gomez, her gaze as judgmental as before. "Get your stuff together; you're coming with me," she said. "Five minutes." Then she stood just inside the entrance at parade rest, watching as Rita hastily flung her toothbrush and spare clothes into her bag.

"Where are we going?" Rita asked.

"Breakfast. Then an interview." Gomez spoke as if words came at a price. She led Rita along a narrow corridor, then into a windowless ready room equipped with a metal sink and bare tables. A couple of bagged McDonald's breakfast muffins and oily, bitter cups of coffee awaited. Rita managed to eat under Gomez's stern gaze; *is it the world-walker thing that bugs her so much?* she wondered. *Or is it my skin?* Maybe the two were too deeply intertwined for Gomez to suspend her prejudice: Rita could have passed for Middle Eastern, and if Gomez saw her as a wanted terrorist's left-behind baggage . . .

Gomez drove her out of the prefab into the overcast morning light, steering an unmarked SUV under manual control. Her manner robotic, she scanned the rearview display constantly; perhaps she expected to be tailed by terrorists or attacked by world-walkers at any moment. She drove past a taxiway and a ramp studded with parked blue-gray drones, then hung a right into a tightly spiraling underpass leading to an underground parking lot. At the bottom, a security booth and barrier blocked her path.

She halted, wound the window down, and presented an ID card to a uniformed security guard.

The guard peered at the badge, then at Gomez—then stared at Rita, huddling in the passenger seat. "ID, please," he said.

"Agent Gomez with Candidate Red," she told him. "Candidate has no ID but should be on your list. I'm signing for her on my cognizance."

"Yes, ma'am." He eyeballed Rita again, comparing her with an image on his glasses. "Look directly at me, ma'am."

Rita looked. Saw a Homeland Security uniform, a sidearm, warning notices, and thumbprint locks on the kiosk behind him.

"Spit here," he ordered, proffering a glass tube.

Rita spat on demand, then she and Gomez waited for a couple of minutes as the guard processed the sample.

"You're cleared to proceed." The barrier rose and the tire-height caltrops retracted into the concrete beneath it. "Have a good trip, y'all."

"A good—?"

"Later." Gomez's tone was sharp. Another sharply spiraling ramp took them down another level: then another barrier retracted into the ground. Ahead, the ramp funneled them into something like a truck-sized freight elevator. Gomez inched forward, following directions on a large screen at the far side of the elevator car, then switched off the SUV's motor. "You may need to swallow a couple of times to clear your ears," she told Rita as the elevator door rose behind them.

"Swallow?" Something flickered behind Rita's eyes and her inner ears tightened painfully, as if she was in a rapidly descending airliner. "Uh, what was that?"

Gomez said nothing until the elevator door opened again; then she backed the SUV out into the parking garage. It was brightly lit now, much too bright—

Rita glanced up through the car's glass roof and saw wisps of cirrus drifting across a blue sky overhead. She froze. When they'd driven in, the sky had been slate-gray with heavy cloud.

"Welcome to time line four," Gomez said drily. "Ever wondered if a new life awaits you in the off-world colonies? Because now's your chance for a preview."

NEAR BOSTON, TIME LINE FOUR, MARCH 2020

There was no airfield here. No underground parking lot, just a ramp leading down to a half-buried blockhouse surrounded by a razor-wire fence. There was a road (a one-lane blacktop with no sidewalk), a guard checkpoint with cameras, a couple of parked gunbots, and a flagpole flying the Stars and Stripes. Beyond it, Rita saw nothing but forest.

Gomez drove slowly past the checkpoint, then along the road between the trees. "We're still inside the outer perimeter of Camp Graceland," she told Rita, losing some of her chilly reserve. "It goes on for miles."

"We're in another time line," Rita thought aloud. "That wasn't a freight elevator, was it?"

"Nope." She caught Gomez's withering sidelong glance, and the thought behind it: *Are you* really *that stupid?*

"The, uh, world-walkers. They don't know about this time line, do they?"

Now Gomez looked at her properly, a slow appraising stare that would have made Rita nervous if they'd been driving much faster than the posted ten-mile-per-hour speed limit. The DHS agent looked back at the road. "Assumptions are dangerous, Ms. Douglas. I could tell you that we don't think the Clan know of this world, and I might believe it too, but that doesn't automatically make it so."

"The Clan? You mean, the world-walkers?"

"The Clan is the organization we consider the States' most lethal threat to national security. They're world-walkers, yes."

"But." Rita checked her assumptions. What she knew about world-walkers was drawn from the news media, and as Kurt had carefully taught her to see, the news media were often deliberately misleading. "You mean there's more than one kind?"

"Do bears do their business in the woods?" Gomez glanced at her again, then back to the road. It curved around a thick stand of trees, roots forcing the asphalt up into wrinkles on one side. A fork came into view and Gomez turned left. A minute later they arrived at a broad clearing, where a windowless metal and concrete building squatted in the middle of a clear-cut apron. Something buzzed in the distance, like a lawn mower or a weed whacker. Gomez parked between a Jeep Wrangler and a late-model Humvee, then opened her door. "End of the road, girl. Out and walk."

Somehow that one belittling word rankled, hurting more than all the fear and craziness of the past couple of days. Rita kept her face impassive as she climbed out and collected her bag from the backseat. "Why did you bring me here?"

"There's a man who wants to see you."

"What about? You bugged my phone! You already know everything that happened to me yesterday—"

"Job interview, Ms. Douglas. Unless you want to go back to a zero-hours contract for a failing games SFX start-up, with the Clan looking for you?"

Rita stopped mid-stride. "You have got to be kidding."

"The US government does not *joke*, Ms. Douglas." Gomez's eyes narrowed. She carried on walking. "This is the best offer you're going to get. If it was up to me . . . Come on, let's get this over with."

The front door of the building opened onto a very unwelcoming vestibule, watched over by cameras in armored mountings; the inner door was positioned on one side, out of direct line of sight of the outer door, and clearly armored. Gomez had Rita stand on a pair of painted yellow footprints so she could look at one of the cameras, while she called someone on her glasses. What unnerved Rita most was the lack of visible guards. Guards meant human interaction. Narrow slots in the walls and ceiling meant something much less pleasant: bullets, or gas.

After a nerve-wracking wait, a concealed loudspeaker crackled. "Rita Douglas and Sonia Gomez, you may now enter the secure zone. Please proceed to briefing room G11. Ms. Douglas, do not step across any red lines you see painted on the floor. Use of lethal force is mandated."

Gomez led Rita through a guardroom staffed by four soldiers in body armor, who watched them unblinkingly. Then came a door that led into a much more normal office suite. More doors blurred past until they came to G11. Gomez opened it without knocking.

"Rita Douglas." The man behind the desk stood. Crow's-feet wrinkles around his eyes and a salesman's outstretched handshake welcomed her.

He looked about fifty, physically fit but balding, and wore an open-collared dress shirt with his suit. "Have a seat, please. Sonia, if you'd like to wait elsewhere while I discuss the situation with Ms. Douglas?"

Gomez virtually jumped to attention, then fled hastily. Rita looked around, perplexed. Apart from the lack of windows it could have been just another slightly dingy government office. Cheap carpet, institutional desk, and a flag in the corner of the room. There was absolutely nothing to show that it was part of an ultra-secure secret compound in another time line.

Rita was beyond diplomacy. "Who are you people, and what do you want with me?" she asked, trying to ignore the slushy fear in her belly. "Why am I here?"

"Sit down." He didn't sound annoyed, exactly, but Rita suddenly found herself sitting, in a visitor's chair that was slightly too soft and slightly too low. "That's better. Can I offer you a coffee? With or without caffeine? This is going to take an hour or two so you might as well be comfortable."

A couple of minutes later the door opened again: it was one of the guards, bearing a cardboard coffee cup and a breakfast muffin. Just for her, apparently. "You can call me Eric," he told her, smiling diffidently. "I also answer to 'Colonel Smith,' but that was in another land and long ago. I'm now officially retired from the Air Force." His smile faded slightly. "You're here because you came to our attention before the Clan managed to abduct you. Which was lucky, because if things hadn't happened in that order you'd most likely be dead. And if not dead, you'd be in their hands. The questions you probably have are, why did that happen? And how can I stop it happening again? Am I right?"

Rita nodded. "I was told, uh, I was given the impression, that you think my birth mother may have something to do with it."

Eric looked at her with disconcertingly bright eyes. He seemed to be about the same age as her father, she realized, but had the demeanor of a much younger man, full of a dangerous energy. "Yes. We've been monitoring you since you were eight," he added, then waited for her to react.

The enormity of it refused to sink in. Why would the DHS monitor an eight-year- old? It seemed flatly implausible, beyond even the paranoia of the Bizarro-world she'd glimpsed through Gramps's rambling tales of East Germany. "This *is* about my birth mother, isn't it?" She asked. *Gomez and Jack said she was adopted, too,* she remembered with a pang. It was an annoyingly humanizing fact: the first hint of a human face behind a silhouette she'd been trying to ignore all her life. She didn't like it. "Why? Did you think she'd show up again after all these years? Like a wicked fairy in one of the Grimms' tales, come to steal me back?"

Eric shook his head. "Nothing so simple." He put his coffee cup down, then picked up a hand exerciser ball. "What do you know about world-walkers?"

"What everybody knows. They blew up the White House? They're out there somewhere in the multiverse, and unlike us they don't need machines to move between other time lines?" Everyone knew a bit about para-time, after the bombing. They'd discovered their enemy had come from another version of this world, where history had diverged from ours. There were an infinite number of such time lines out there. The US had machines that could transport both people and machinery between universes.

But it was irrelevant to everyday life—unless you had the bad luck to be caught in the blast radius of a terrorist nuke planted by bombers from another time line, or had relatives who had been in India or Pakistan during World War 2.5. All you really needed to know was that they were the enemy, and that overthinking things aloud in public was a bad idea.

"Yes, I get that one of them gave birth to me, once upon a time. But I'm not a—"

"No," Eric agreed. "You're not a member of the Clan. And I'd like to distinguish between world-walkers—people with the inherited ability to think themselves from one time line to another—and the Clan, an organization of people with that ability. Like the difference between ordinary Muslims and members of Al Qaeda. The important thing is, one of your parents *was* a member of the Clan. That didn't matter until recently, but . . . things have changed."

"What kind of things?" She didn't even try to keep the frustration out of her voice. "What's this got to do with me?"

Eric picked up a tablet and began to read. "Let's see. Rita Douglas, age twenty-five. Adopted and raised by Emily and Franz Douglas, in Boston and then New Jersey. Attended UMass, a major in history, a minor in drama. Languages: Spanish, some German. Then a succession of dead-end jobs while trying to pay off student loans and build a career in acting." He smiled at her, a flash of teeth: obviously he found something amusing in this. "No criminal record, not so much as a parking ticket." The smile vanished. "Congratulations. You're very clean. You'd pass a background check for government service with flying colors." He put the tablet down. "But it never occurred to you to apply. Any particular reason?"

What the fuck? Rita stared at the ex-colonel, then used the too-hot container of too-bitter coffee to buy herself a few seconds. "I'm not the type," she said cautiously. "I'm not interested in the military." She'd heard too many horror stories from Libya and Bangladesh vets. And she'd had friends who'd enlisted, then dropped out of touch. "I really wanted to get into a graduate studies history program, or find a solid stage role, but that's just not happening in this economy." The post-2003 climate wasn't terribly conducive to historical introspection. And as for the stage, a momentary twinge from the implant inside her left elbow reminded her what was wrong with *that.* "What is this about? Why am I here?"

"You might want to put the coffee down."

She took a mouthful, swallowing hastily and burning the roof of her mouth. "Yes?"

Smith looked straight at her, and she had an uncanny feeling that he could see right through to the back of her skull. "Speculate wildly, please. Why do you *think* you're here? Why do you think I brought all that stuff up?"

"I don't know. You're going to offer me a job? Because you've suddenly got a need for world-walkers who speak foreign languages and can act? What is this, *Mission: Impossible*? I'm not a spy and I'm not a world-walker—"

"I agree." The Colonel nodded. "You're neither of those things. But we can fix that." He waited politely for Rita to finish spluttering before he continued: "Here's the proposition. We—by which I mean the organization I work for; you don't get to meet anyone else at this point—are empowered to offer you a job, with strings attached. If you take it, you'll spend most of the next two years going through induction and training. You'll learn necessary skills to bring you up to speed, and be thoroughly evaluated along the way. It'll be a lot like being in the Army, but without the uniform, the shouting, the saluting, and the shooting.

"If you wash out, well, the pay's decent and maybe you'll take away some useful skills. If you pass but don't have quite the right aptitude, you can quit or we can find you a job within DHS that's suited to your abilities—interrogating Latino theatrical troupes or something, a safe office job with a pension at the end, if that's what you want. But if you pass and demonstrate the right qualities, then, once you're a probationary federal agent, we can talk about the other stuff."

"But I'm *not* a world-walker!"

Smith smiled at her again, a Cheshire cat grin that froze her in her seat. "Like I said, that can be fixed." He leaned forward: "And it's the one sure way you can guarantee that the Clan won't be able to touch you. But it's only going to happen *if* you accept this job offer and give it your best shot. And maybe not even then. So. What do you say?"

In a moment of crystal clarity Rita realized two things, one very good and one very bad. It was the best opportunity she'd had in years, if ever—and she wasn't sure she'd be allowed to turn it down. So she licked her suddenly dry lips and gave what seemed to be the only safe answer: "I'd like to see the fine print, please."

Spies

"I think it's quite simple. To use an analogy from US history in my time line, imagine this is Cape Canaveral and we're their captured Nazi rocket scientists," Miriam Beckstein told her audience.

It was hot inside the crowded wooden hut, which was a small mercy. There was little enough fuel this winter, in the wake of the revolution that had brought down the British imperial crown in the Americas. But the privileged detainees in this hut had a stove and a supply of good Appalachian coal; droplets of water condensed on the inside of the windows, forming slug trails rather than freezing to the glass.

"That's an ambitious proposal." Helmut ven Rindt was doubtful. A chunky fellow, formerly part of the Clan's security organization, he was efficient if given a goal. But he wasn't the most imaginative of leaders. "It seems to me we've got more immediate problems." He raised a bushy eyebrow and looked round at everyone—the dozen or so members of the surviving Clan leadership who'd made it this far. "Like being imprisoned, and our families being held hostage. Just to start with."

After a rogue Clan faction had bombed the White House and Capitol, the US nuclear counterstrike had utterly destroyed their home country, the Gruinmarkt, in time line one. The survivors had sought exile here, in time line three, but the situation had been complicated, to say the least, by the recent revolution. Helmut continued, giving voice to the complaints Miriam had heard only whispered quietly so far.

"This isn't our home. In this new time line, we have no power and no future—unless we take action." Helmut stood as he spoke, emphasizing words with gestures, fist striking palm in vehement emphasis. "Nor are the radical rabble well-disposed toward our kind. We should do better to seek exile in the French Empire and reestablish our trade on the other side of the Atlantic—"

By "trade" he meant paperwork-free shipping: the Clan had become phenomenally rich by smuggling narcotics into the United States via their home time line. Miriam suppressed a shudder. She'd been given a leather trench coat by their captors: a gesture of privilege for the leader of the Clan refugees. Worn over a cable-knit sweater and heavy wool skirt it was at least right for the climate. Now she pulled it tight around her shoulders, as if against a sudden draft. The old trade—smuggling—was how the Clan had gotten into trouble in the first place, and if Helmut thought restarting the trade was a good idea, so must a whole lot of other relatives.

"We can't go back." She shook her head, denial personified. "They'll be on the lookout for us everywhere in time line two: everybody knows about us, thanks to those idiots. Trying to restart the traditional smuggling trade in Europe or China is a nonstarter. Also," she added, almost as an afterthought, "the American government will come after us if they see signs of suspicious activity."

Helmut wasn't dropping it: "Look out there!" he said, angrily gesturing at the iced-over window. "This is where they've put us!" Beyond the window, rows of snowcapped barracks huddled together in chilly solidarity within high brick walls topped with broken bottles set in hastily applied mortar. Guards with bolt-action rifles patrolled beyond the wall. These were the Special Prisoner quarters, given over to the world-walkers, asylum seekers from a parallel universe where history had taken a different course. "It's insupportable! I know you sought alliance with the revolutionaries, but they treat us like—"

"Stop your foolishness!" Iris Beckstein erupted. She looked older than her sixty years, and she was slowly dying. Hunched inside the hood of the half-broken invalid chair their captors had donated, she shuddered briefly, then glared at ven Rindt with a death stare she'd clearly inherited from her mother, the dowager duchess. "Pursuing the old trade is what put us in this camp, in case you've forgotten. And we're not doing badly compared to the neighbors."

The rest of the camp was full of Politicals—captured Royalist troops and members of the aristocracy who hadn't made it onto the refugee ships in time to escape the revolution that had toppled the British Empire in early 2003. After the civil war, the Politicals didn't rate heating and full bellies in the famine-struck winter of the Emergency. Almost two feet of snow lay on the ground outside the huts. Prisoners working under guard removed the frozen bodies from the Politicals' side of the camp every morning. The Clan refugees, in contrast, had fuel for their stoves and food for their children.

"It can't be worse than—"

"For once in your life, just shut up and *listen*," Iris grumbled, then subsided in a fit of coughing.

"Mom? Are you all right?" Miriam asked anxiously.

Iris waved away the offer of help: "'M surviving," she said hoarsely. "Been better. Carry on."

Helmut, possibly due to some residual respect for authority, was momentarily silent. Miriam took advantage to continue her urgent pitch. "Helmut is absolutely right that we've got no power or influence here. But I think we can remedy that. Our new goal must be to make ourselves indispensable. And the easiest way to do that is to give them information. We can give them technological and industrial know-how—knowledge this time line won't discover themselves for many decades."

"Are you suggesting industrial espionage as a business model?" asked Huw. Gangly and inquisitive, he was one of Miriam's most reliable allies within the Clan. She could count on him for an easy prompt. The downside, though, was that if the majority didn't feel that their concerns were being adequately addressed by her plan, more and more of them would sign on with Helmut and drift back to their old ways. Before the exile, the Clan's members had been held together by fear and a ruthless internal police organization; now that the worst had happened, Miriam really had no way of compelling them to follow her.

"This goes a lot further than industrial espionage," she said gratefully. "We aren't going to feed them isolated tidbits—we're going to promise a whole new way of life. What we need to do here is what I tried and failed to do in the Gruinmarkt—accelerate social development for all." The Gruinmarkt, one of the eastern kingdoms of North America in time line one, had barely medieval levels of technology: the privileged few with Clan connections had been able to import US tech by means of world-walking, and had rejected attempts at modernization for the masses. "Here in the Commonwealth they've just conveniently smashed their aristocracy: there's nobody with entrenched privilege to defend. That's an opportunity for us to exploit, if we're smart enough."

"Just how are you going to go about that?" Helmut asked acidly. "From inside a prison camp?"

Miriam reined in her annoyance; she responded badly to provocative sarcasm: "We need to somehow get the Commonwealth leadership to commit to full-scale industrial development and modernization. Right now, the USA is about sixty years ahead of anyone in this time line. But I think the Commonwealth can close the gap completely in less than forty years—maybe thirty—with our help. And if they can do that before the USA discovers us here, we'll be infinitely safer. Make no mistake—sooner or later, they will find us. And even though we didn't kill their president, they'll expect us to pay the price."

"Is it even possible for a society to progress that rapidly?" asked Brilli-ana, who was usually loath to disagree with her leader. She perched on a desk in the corner of the room, keeping one wary eye on the door. (As Miriam's first-sworn bodyguard, she took Miriam's security personally.) "It's 2003. Let's say the USA have a sixty-year lead now. In thirty years it'll be 2033. You're talking about catching up to a ninety-year lead in thirty years, not a sixty-year lead. Are you sure about your projections?"

"Yes. That's why I said it might take nearer to forty." Miriam's shoulders slumped slightly. A forty-year plan: that was a lifetime's work, a daunting project for anyone. "But it's not impossible. Look at the Korean Peninsula in time line two. North Korea and South Korea started out level-pegging in 1953. They were both oppressive dictatorships with flattened cities and superpower sponsors, and they were still pretty much even as late as 1973. But today, South Korea's got a higher GDP than Japan, while in North Korea they've gone backward.

"Folks, this is it. This is the time line we have to live in. We don't get to go home to the Gruinmarkt, in time line one: it glows in the dark. Even if we could, would we want to? I will remind you that the only things that made the Gruinmarkt tolerable were enormous local wealth and access to luxuries imported from the United States. We don't have the local wealth and we can't import stuff from the USA anymore—we're not welcome there, in case you'd forgotten." Any Clan member trying to make a life in the United States risked ending up in a supermax prison for the rest of their life—or at least until their date with a federal executioner.

"We're stuck in time line three, stuck in the Commonwealth here, unless you think striking out at random in search of something better is a solution. At least here we've got the ear of the First Man," she said, referring to the founder and head of the Radical Party, who had consolidated power in the wake of the Revolution. "We can work with that. But running away again isn't an option unless our backs are up against the wall. I don't know about you, but I don't want to go and live in a cave somewhere, or a drafty castle with no antibiotics and no general anesthesia. I happen to like civilization, and this is the nearest thing we've got."

Miriam looked round at her audience. She'd taken care to ensure that half of them were women, and she could tell at a glance that she had their attention. The state of civilization in the Gruinmarkt had been medieval, except where world-walkers had traded in US goods, such as the imported medicines that meant they didn't have to endure repeated risky pregnancies and bury half their babies before their fifth birthday.

"My plan, which I intend to sell to the First Man, is to turn this camp into the Commonwealth's source of miracle technologies and scientific insights. We're going to engage in knowledge transfer on a historically unprecedented scale, acquiring and disseminating the necessary skills and ideas to enable the Commonwealth to play catch-up with the United

States in time line two. Then, once we get ourselves out of this camp and into strategic positions within their economic and industrial planning apparatus, we'll be able to move mountains. We can turn this time line into somewhere we're proud to live, a place where we're safe from the US government. And there's one more thing: once we have official government backing for the project, we're going to skew it to suit our own agenda."

Suddenly Helmut looked interested. "And what is *that* going to be, as you see it?"

"Revolutions typically run their course in a generation." Miriam had been doing a lot of reading about revolutions. "Our job is to survive this one. Things look chaotic right now, but eventually there's going to be a new normal, and I intend us to get back all the stuff you're complaining about losing. Power, influence, wealth, a place in the sun."

"All well and good," said Helmut. "But how are you going to make our captors follow your agenda? Unless you can do *that*—" He sat down, clearly feeling that he'd made his point.

Miriam stared at him, perplexed: what more did he want? "We're going to catalyze disruptive technological development—" she began, just as Iris cleared her throat. "What, Mom?"

"The problem is political, as usual. You youngsters never make sufficient allowances for that. You especially, Helmut; your tool of choice is the club, not the olive branch." Then she looked at her daughter. "I found that book of the First Man's writings most interesting. If your friend Erasmus can get me anything else by Sir Adam, or more reading matter of that kind, I'd be most grateful. And keep your own eyes open for useful signs in Sir Adam's writings too. But I assure you, your plan will only work if he is willing to learn from the mistakes of other revolutions—and is receptive enough to contemplate a New Economic Policy."

Miriam frowned. "What do you mean?"

"Isn't it obvious? You've been focusing on the idea of technological development. But you've been doing it in isolation, looking at means without considering the ends."

"But I have—the ends are the development of civilization—"

"Sir Adam Burroughs won't see it like that!" Iris snapped. "You are thinking like a technocrat. But Adam, the First Man, is not a technocrat, he is a revolutionary. He has a vision of what should be, of a shining city on a hill, which is based—if I read him correctly—on the rights of man and woman. A vision that went out of fashion long ago in the United States. It was probably doomed by the failure of the First International, in the world you grew up in. Your late father would set you straight."

Miriam flinched: Iris had raised her in exile in time line two, marrying Morris, an idealistic but ultimately ineffectual political activist. The kind of guy who had walked out of the Revolutionary Communist Party because they didn't do enough charity work, feeding the sick and clothing the poor. "No, Miriam. We need to prove ourselves to Sir Adam by giving him tools that he considers *useful*, not what *you* consider important."

"And what would these tools be?" Huw asked, intrigued by the turn the conversation was taking.

"Political levers, not shiny scientific toys." Iris's eyes twinkled. "That's not to say that they cannot be the same thing, but presentation is all. Sir Adam has just led a revolution. The first successful democratic revolution in the history of this world. Forget technology for the time being: you have a crystal ball! It is your duty to bring him dismal tidings—all the myriad ways in which revolutions can come to grief. Your first job must be to produce a comprehensive report on all the failed democratic revolutions of time line two, with specific analyses of how and why they failed to achieve their objectives.

"Show him that, and then—if you can—show him a revolution that succeeded. Show him he can learn from it and use it as an object of emulation—and he'll listen to you. In fact, if you can do that, he'll give you everything you ask for. Which is how you go about setting up your, uh, para-time industrial development program. But before all else, you need to demonstrate your usefulness. And the easiest way to do that is to show him all the ways to fail that he has not imagined, so that he can avoid them."

Brilliana nodded, then grinned at Miriam. "It's the oldest trick in the book, isn't it? Work out what they'll get hooked on, then give them the first hit for free . . ."

NEW YORK, TIME LINE TWO, MARCH 2020

Hulius Hjorth was about to start his very last courier mission—although he didn't know it yet. There was a standardized protocol for world-walking agents entering a hostile surveillance zone: the goal was to do it quietly and anonymously and stay one jump ahead of the surveillance cameras. He'd been doing it for more than twenty years, from his first teenage outing as a Clan messenger to his current status. These days he was a major in the Commonwealth's Department of Para-historical Research—and he was good at his job. Unfortunately, the adversaries were getting better, too, and it was harder to stay ahead of the enemy every year.

Hulius entered time line two via a quiet side street in Brooklyn. It was lined with red-brick warehouse conversions playing home to start-up businesses and specialist mail-order supply shops. Few people lived here, and some of the buildings were empty, their windows boarded up as their owners waited out the slack in the business cycle. After 8 p.m., as twilight descended, a certain quiet fell. And it was then that the door of one such boarded-up building opened.

An onlooker would have seen a tall, heavily built man in his late thirties or early forties step out, glance up and down the street, and wheel a bicycle onto the sidewalk. With horn-rimmed spectacles, drainpipe jeans, plaid shirt, and knitted cardigan, he could be mistaken for a hipster. He bore a capacious messenger bag, an obscure name-brand item chosen to harmonize with the rest of his outfit. He checked carefully for cross-traffic, then locked the warehouse door and pedaled up the road, wobbling slightly.

(The warehouse itself was empty, seemingly abandoned when the business that had previously occupied it went bust. Only a rectangular area on the stained concrete floor, marked out with duct tape, would tell an informed observer that there was anything out of the ordinary about it. That, and the fact that anyone reviewing the previous day's camera footage of the front and back of the building in search of Hulius's arrival would have a fruitless task.)

Every stage of this type of insertion was hazardous. The warehouse might have been let to a new tenant in the week since the preliminary reconnaissance designated it as an entry point. Or some unfortunate event might have attracted unwanted police or DHS attention. Once one was out of the entry building, the risks continued. Unable to use a trackable phone or GPS device, Hulius had memorized the neighborhood—a good solution, but only effective as long as he stuck to known territory. And he had to keep moving confidently, for he couldn't stop and consult a paper map. If his motion kinematics seemed weird, software running on the sensors embedded in the street signs on major roads would notice and call the cops. He'd then face a search for alcohol or drugs. This could not be allowed.

In this world-walker-aware city, there were cameras with motion tracking firmware at every major intersection. They were designed to spot a sudden appearance out of thin air: so transfer had to be effected inside a disused building. Hulius's managers back in the Commonwealth didn't think the DHS was capable of monitoring every doorway in the United States for foot traffic: only federal buildings and security zones like airports had that level of surveillance. But sooner or later the feds would start clamping down on pedestrians and cyclists who had no radio-frequency devices like phones or ID cards. It would make covert operations infinitely harder. At present it was still possible for a courier to dip into the quiet backstreets of a big city for a couple of hours without courting disaster, but the end of Commonwealth intelligence operations on US soil was clearly in sight: the USA was already a harder nut for foreign infiltrators to crack than the Soviet bloc had ever been.

At the end of the street, Hulius stopped at the four-way and diligently checked for oncoming traffic. Most New York cyclists didn't bother—it wasn't necessary, now that anticollision radar was mandatory on cars and trucks—but he was patient. An accidental collision with another cyclist or a hot-wired car would be a mission kill at best. If it put him in the back of an ambulance, it would most likely prove fatal: he'd have to use the suicide capsule he carried in a false wisdom tooth.

He pedaled on across an avenue and took a left, then wobbled slowly uphill along the main road for a block. A few streets later, he reached his destination and dismounted. He linked the bike to a railing and pretended to arm the bike lock, then (after looking for passersby) turned his reversible jacket inside out and put it on again. Pocketing his conspicuous glasses, he walked round the corner and straight into a cheap local diner.

His contact was waiting in a seat facing the front door, toying with the wreckage of a burrito and a bottle of juice. The bottle was positioned to the left of her plate: a simple sign that meant, *I am not under duress.* She was around fifty, thin-faced, her black hair scraped back in a severe bun: she looked like a tired office worker. Hulius paid her no obvious attention, and she gave no sign of recognition. Instead, he walked to the counter and bought tostadas and a root beer. He turned to casually survey the diner as if looking for empty seats, then carried his portion over to her table and sat down facing her.

"Good morning, Ms. Milan."

She nodded politely. "Always a pleasure to see you, Mr. Jefferson. How did the ball game go?"

"We won, 4-2." He'd noticed no sign of surveillance on his way to the meet. The set of her shoulders relaxed infinitesimally. "We have maybe fifteen minutes—no longer. It's not safe: they're rolling out more and more networked cameras." The safe duration for contact was narrowing all the time.

"Damn." Her expression was pinched. *Too much tension there,* he thought. He'd known Paulie for years, almost since before the Clan survivor's exile in the Commonwealth: she'd been a protegé of Miriam herself. "That's not good. I'm not sure I can cope if it falls below five minutes."

He took a mouthful of soda. As ever, it tasted oddly alien—almost familiar, but not quite right, too sweet. It was the high-fructose corn syrup they put in everything, he decided; it tasted weird if you were used to cane sugar. "You don't have to. You do a good and valuable job here, but if you think they're onto you, or if it's too stressful, all you have to do is say so: we can arrange an extraction to time line three whenever you want. There's no reason for you to risk detection."

She shook her head, very slightly. "I have family. Two nieces and a nephew who just married." She paused. "Also, this is my country. It's been good to my family, and good for me: I can't just leave."

He put the drink down, allowed his bag to slide down to the floor by the side of the booth. "Nevertheless, the offer remains open. *She* said I was to remind you that extraction is the lesser evil, compared to spending the rest of your life in a supermax prison cell for assisting supposed terrorists." He paused. "I don't like to be the bringer of bad news, but the risk level is becoming unacceptable. We're going to have to stop meeting like this soon, possibly in as little as three months. We can work out another protocol for risk mitigation in the short term that'll keep things going a bit longer, but . . ." He shrugged.

"I don't want to relocate if I can avoid it." She twitched: her expression was haunted. "I know how stupid that sounds. I ought to take you up on your offer: if I was sensible, I would. I mean, you're winding down your operations over here, aren't you? But part of me keeps thinking it's about me. That I'm too old and unstable and you're just saying this to cut me loose gently."

"Eighteen million lives," he said. "That's what the antibiotic factories bought us." The factories whose plans she'd researched and packaged for her world-walking employers, years earlier. "You asked last time, so I went and looked it up. Paulie, we're not firing you. We owe you too much."

She relaxed very slightly. "You're just flattering me now."

"There is a faraway land where you are known and honored as a hero of the revolution." He didn't have to fake sincerity. Then force of habit prompted him to glance at his antique windup wristwatch: "Nine minutes left."

"The shopping bag is full," she said. A moment later he felt something nudge against his ankle: a messenger bag, identical to his own, but considerably heavier. "I was unable to obtain a couple of the items on the list: I hope the substitutions are appropriate."

"Thank you," said the spy, reaching down to move her bulging bag closer to his feet. "They almost always are; you should know that by now." Paulette was a *very* experienced supplier: she knew exactly what interested Hulius and his bosses. He nudged his own bag toward her. It was empty but for a block of increasingly useless $20 bills and the usual burner phone, battery physically disconnected, with a shopping list stored in its memory. When she got home she'd turn it on and use the stored credit in it to purchase items on the list, whereupon she'd arrange for delivery to a friendly local bodega. When the job was done she'd turn the phone off again for good, using a hammer. Once sterilized with acetone, the fragments could be safely flushed down a storm drain.

"They've discontinued the specific power supply model required for item eleven. I ordered a replacement device," she said.

"Thank you." He smiled for her and tried to put some warmth into the expression. Isolation took its toll on the sanity and sense of self-worth of the long-distance agent. "I really mean that. What you do here is making a huge difference. More than you can imagine."

She sighed pensively, picked up her glass, and drained it. "I should go now," she said.

He checked his watch. Four minutes remaining. "Yes, I think so." He stood up and shouldered the messenger bag: it was far heavier than the one he'd walked in with. "The next rendezvous is in memory. Queens, I think. I'll take the front entrance, you take the back."

"Goodbye, Hulius," she said, sounding sad. "Give my best to Miriam."

"I will," he replied. "Good luck, Colonel." He stood and left, heading toward his bicycle.

The spy watched through the window for a couple of minutes, until she could stand the tension no longer. Rising, she walked to the back of the diner and then through a door, the exit into the alleyway behind. The cameras overlooking the dumpsters had been carefully tagged with graffiti the week before: blinded by paint. Nobody saw her leave.

Fifteen years of my life for eighteen million lives, she thought. From anyone but Miriam's messenger she wouldn't have taken it: she'd have sneered. The offer of extraction and a fresh start in a new world felt like a cynical joke. Who would she be, over there? A fifty-year-old spinster with no family and no life, just a pension and a medal to wear at alien parades: a life sacrificed on the altar of an undeclared war. Whereas this was her country: it had taken in her great-grandparents, the GI Bill had put her father through college, and she'd grown up and lived her entire life here. The thought of moving away was almost unbearable. Then the claustrophobic threat of exposure, the fear of omnipresent surveillance, closed in on her once more. Sometimes it felt like a noose around her neck, threatening to strangle the breath in her throat. Sometimes she wanted to scream. *Is this all there's ever going to be for me?* Paulette wondered. *Where did it all go so wrong?*

PALACE OF THE PEOPLE'S DEPUTIES, NEW LONDON, TIME LINE THREE, JULY 2005

Forget musketry. Forget aviation carriers. You're going to need washing machines. Lots of washing machines.

There's a saying that goes something like this: "Lieutenants study tactics, colonels study strategy, generals study logistics, and field marshals study economics." But economists—the smart ones—study education. We've got three hundred and eighty million people on two continents, and another thirty to fifty million overseas, and these people are the foundation on which you are building your Commonwealth. Half of them are women. Of those, more than half are of working age . . . but they typically spend fifteen hours a week slaving over washboards or banging cloth on rocks, and another five to ten hours a week sewing.

That's a hundred and ninety million women, a hundred million workers, spending a third of their working time unproductively. Roll out free laundry services inside every factory gate and you gain the equivalent of thirty million extra full-time workers. Or you can use the time not spent on drudgery to upgrade those women's education by about one high school year per twelve months. If you do *that,* it is an investment that pays off in the future. No productivity gain for five years, but then thirty million extra skilled workers become available. Or twenty million skilled workers, and an army of teachers to educate the next generation. In military terms, that's enough to increase our economic base by about twenty percent. Enough to support a hundred divisions. Or a spare navy and a half. Or the nuclear—uh, corpuscular weapons program.

You're going to need the working women, because the United States is coming.

They have aircraft that can cross between time lines. They have corpuscular petards—atomic weapons, they call them. We face a development gap of roughly sixty years. That's how far ahead of us they are, in terms of science and engineering. It's not insurmountable, but there's more to it than just better nutritional supplements and technological toys: a lot of it is psychological. They have different ways of looking at things, better cognitive models for understanding certain types of problems. And they're vastly more efficient at logistics and training than we are. Unfortunately for us, their government is frightened and angry, and they have already incinerated time line one, the first other inhabited time line they discovered.

We can't afford to get this wrong. Sooner or later they will discover the Commonwealth: and they are a far deadlier threat to the Revolution than the French Empire or the remnants of the old regime.

If we don't deploy those extra thirty million workers, then we've lost a quarter of our workforce before we even begin. We also need to educate our people. Many of those workers could be teachers instead. We need those teachers to educate in turn the generation of skilled workers and specialists that we'll need in twenty years' time. And they will be vital to our tertiary education system, which will equip that next generation for the high-technology jobs that are coming. These in turn will be generated by the series of industrial revolutions we're going to embark upon.

Yes, I said industrial "revolutions." Plural. Technologies are not neutral: they come with attached agendas, with associated ways of thinking. Industrial revolutions are inherently political revolutions. Today's ironworkers and coal miners will find it hard to adapt to tomorrow's automated factories and thinking machines. It would be very difficult for an entrenched empire to survive such a series of revolutions without experiencing serious unrest, but you—we, gathered here today—are the party of revolution. Our whole raison d'être is to ride the tidal wave of change and use it to build a better future. This should not be beyond us.

If we try and make a sixty-year leap forward in, say, thirty years, we'll still be behind the Americans when we get there—they'll have moved another thirty years ahead of us. So what I'm proposing to do is to aim *ahead* of the target. Merely modernizing the New American Commonwealth on an industrial level should be achievable in thirty years, but we must also build in social structures that enable our successors to maintain the pace of progress, to make it an ongoing process. Modernization can become the engine of continuing revolution.

Radical citizenship and a universal franchise are a good start, but that's not enough. We need to produce an educated, skilled workforce, and to do that we need to deliver full female emancipation—for which family planning services are essential. Workplace nurseries are also essential. And health care and school support are both essential too. They are also popular with women who vote. And they will vote.

Next slide, please.

Some of you are thinking that if we need more workers, we should simply breed them. That all that's needed is to focus our efforts on reducing childhood mortality through inoculation campaigns and the new antibiotics. But the change I'm proposing isn't just about numbers, it's about quality. I'm proposing that we engineer a demographic transition, from a society with a high birth rate and a high death rate to one with a low birth rate and low death rate. Once we get there it becomes cost-effective to train and educate everyone to a high level, because we'll recoup the investment over their working life. That's one of the keys to rapid development: a transition to smaller families, much higher educational attainment, and new technologies. These factors combine to produce a generation that can work far more efficiently than their predecessors.

In time line two, this happened decades ago in the United States and Europe. It's happening right now in China and India. Their economies are growing at a sustained average of more than ten percent a year. In five decades they have gone from peasant agriculture to placing spaceships in orbit around Mars. But you can't do that with unskilled labor and a workforce that systematically excludes half the population. Or with ill-educated women who are too busy and too fatigued to give their babies the attention they need to stretch their minds, teaching them to learn how to learn.

Next slide, please.

Communications and information technology is the next key area where the USA is notionally ahead of us; arguably, this is the most significant area of all. Right now we're barely aware of its existence, but it's the main engine behind the recent runaway growth in the USA, amounting to a new industrial revolution. It has also led to a number of negative problems there, including increasing structural unemployment, a ridiculously hypertrophied police state, and fiscal instability. But forewarned is forearmed, and therefore I propose that we make an end run around their worst mistakes by setting up the security frameworks for our Commonwealth's communication networks a decade before we need them . . .

BROOKLYN, NEW YORK, TIME LINE TWO, MARCH 2020

To get to his exfiltration site, Hulius needed to take his bike on the subway for three stops. It was a calculated risk: his mission planners had decided it was faster and marginally less dangerous than requiring him to ride for fifteen blocks through Brooklyn, and if the weather was inclement it was clearly preferable. But this was where he ran into trouble.

To get to the subway station he pedaled uphill along a couple of residential roads, then turned onto a main street. It was an uneventful, if effortful, ride. He was in good shape for his age, but the way the Americans had taken to neglecting their road surfaces was shameful, and by the end of the trip he was glad for the front and rear shocks on the mountain bike. Every second he spent in time line two gave him a crawling gunsight sensation between his shoulder blades, as if one of the Americans' invisible flying killer robots was stalking him across the streets of the city. While his path took him past no fewer than nineteen CCTV cameras, most of these were domestic or commercial alarm systems: only one was connected to the municipal surveillance system, and that via the Department of Transport automatic number plate lookup system. Even in the United States, bicycles were not yet expected to bear plates.

But the entrance to the subway station took Hulius down a flight of drab concrete steps, into an underground vestibule with ticket machines and barriers, and here things changed. The city of New York had become extremely sensitive to terrorist threats since the turn of the twenty-first century, and the subway was seen as a primary target. Not only that: it was a highly efficient checkpoint—after all, almost everybody used it.

Entering the station, Hulius passed under the lenses of cameras on the staircase, of cameras fronting the ticket machines, of cameras watching the faces of everybody passing through the barriers, and, finally, of the cameras on the platform and on the subway train itself. These cameras had just enough onboard intelligence to match faces against a database of persons of interest, and to call for help if they scored a hit.

And, all unbeknowst to him, Hulius had become a person of interest.

It wasn't because he had been detected making contact with Paulette Milan on a previous visit. Hulius's tradecraft was watertight, his organization's doctrine as good as any. It wasn't because he'd been observed behaving oddly. It was simply that bigger memory cards made it practical to store more faces on each camera node, and in addition to the FBI's Most Wanted, the cameras now looked for a wide range of interesting people. Hulius was a person of interest because he'd been observed on numerous previous occasions and *never identified*. His face was known, his biometrics logged; but he was never associated with the same cell phone ID, or with RFID tags in an ID card (or the washing instruction labels in his clothing), or even with the same bicycle. Hulius was a blind spot in the surveillance network's purview, like the 600-mile-per-hour moving hole in the radar reflection of a rain cloud that betrays the passage of a stealth bomber.

And as he walked toward the back of the platform for a train to Forest Hills, phones began to buzz.

As it happened, Hulius didn't have to cool his heels for long: after just four minutes a 7 train screeched and rattled its way to a halt beside the platform, and he rolled his bike aboard.

The organization had run couriers through the city before, equipped with carefully configured sensors, programmed to record the distribution of monitoring cameras. They carried wi-fi receivers in promiscuous mode, sniffing for buried ubicomp cells. They also used jail-broken phones with baseband chips hacked to help them map cell towers. The results were alarming. In the past three years, the density of surveillance devices scattered through New York City had skyrocketed tenfold, and there was no sign that this increase would slow down until every square meter of sidewalk and road had its own secret police machine, vigilant for signs of subversion.

What the organization *hadn't* done was to run the same tests on subway trains.

Fortieth Street, Queens Boulevard. Three stations ahead, four Transit Police stopped what they were doing and paused, listening to their earpieces. Walking, not running—there was plenty of time—they began to converge on the nearest eastbound platform. (Two other cops, busy with a random search, declined the call.)

Forty-sixth Street station. Hulius had, over many years, developed an almost supernatural sensitivity to the signs and portents of operations on hostile soil. Right now, he wasn't on full alert; but he was never entirely relaxed when on a mission, and some instinct he couldn't name made him tense up and glance surreptitiously up and down the almost deserted subway car.

Too long, he thought, his skin crawling. The train sat at the platform edge, brakes ticking, transformer fans humming. *Something's wrong.* Ten seconds stretched into twenty, then thirty. *Uh-oh. It might just be a signaling fault,* he told himself; *that's probably all it is.* But the MTA had in-cab signaling these days, didn't it? They'd just completed a monstrously expensive upgrade to the entire network.

Hulius took a lurching step to one side just as the doors hissed and rattled closed. Cold sweat burst out up and down his spine. The train began to move. He looked around quickly. Reasons for delaying a train: (1) signal at red, (2) mechanical fault, (3) allowing someone to get into position ahead. *Scheiss, time to bail!* Maybe he was spooking at shadows, but instinct told him otherwise.

He unslung his messenger bag and slid the jacket off his shoulders. Inverted it again, other way out; pulled the spectacles out of their pouch and put them on before he picked up the messenger. A quick glance at the bike: *Farewell, trusty steed.* The train was already slowing. Nobody had looked up: nobody was watching him. He glanced at the ceiling, seeing the cluster of pinhead-sized camera pickups. Ops had assumed they were off-line recorders, just logging foot traffic and faces for digestion at the end of the day. But: what if that monstrously expensive network upgrade had been enough to carry live video streams of all the cameras on all the trains? A decade ago it would have been preposterous, but these days—

Hulius turned and ran to the other end of the car.

Fifty-second Street station. The train rattled and squealed to a stop: doors banged open up and down its length.

Two MTA transit cops entered the rear carriage, scanned the seated passengers with practiced eyes. A bicycle, shackled to a vertical rail, told its story. One of them swore under his breath as the doors closed again. As the train began to move, the door at the end of the carriage—the one giving passage to the next car along—squealed and banged open, admitting a rattle of tracks and a gust of stale subway air.

Hulius was already stepping onto the platform when the transit cops got on the carriage behind the one he was leaving. He kept his eyes down, shoulders hunched. Two more cops waited by the turnstile, heads cocked slightly to one side, listening to their earpieces as they waited for the handful of passengers to leave the platform.

Fuck, it's a sweep. Mouth dry and heart pounding, Hulius walked toward the barriers. Two on the train at the back to push forward, two on the gates to stop anyone from escaping—it'd be the same ahead, all the way to the end of the line. Subway trains were beautiful things right up until they turned into a killing ground. He mentally rehearsed what he'd have to do, but kept his hands free. Pepper spray in one pocket, drop knife concealed under the cuff of his right wrist. *I don't want to do this*, he realized distantly. They were just transit cops, doing a dirty and unrewarding job—

The turnstile buzzed. He walked through. An incurious glance, and they were behind him. Sometimes the oldest tricks are the best: they'd be looking for a man with a bicycle in a green jacket, and here was a guy in spectacles and a blue jacket, no bike. *Still.* He tensed, and lengthened his stride. *If the trains are networked then any moment now they'll hear that the mobile team found the bike.*

Escalator. Legs pumping, Hulius bounded up, shoving his way past an older man with a walking stick, a woman wearing earbuds. The cry came later than he expected: "Hey, you! Stop, police!"

Hulius ran.

They were near the bottom of the escalator, but he was almost at the top. There was more shouting—he didn't stop to listen—then he saw the emergency stop button. Punched it in passing, and a bright pain shot up his left hand. An alarm bell began to clang behind him, and he heard a loud mechanical grating noise, accompanied by indignant yelling. People falling down: *good*, under the circumstances.

He made it into the daylight, breathing hard, and kept running.

The surveyed return point was an alleyway that ran between a fore-closed house and a shuttered head shop, just around the block from the station. Hulius took the corner at a run, certain the cops were on his heels: they might be holding fire because of bystanders, but that was no guarantee of safety against New York's Finest. There was no time to check for witnesses: he was going to burn this site. Hulius ran to the spot beside the fire escape they'd surveyed on a previous mission, pulled on the elastic strap of his wristwatch, and flipped the device upside down, so that the crystal lay against his wrist and the back was visible. Engraved into the burnished metal of the casing was an interlocking knotwork of tail-chasing complexity. He focused on clearing his mind and stared at the pattern that would take him back to time line one, just as the first officer rounded the corner, gun in hand, and opened fire.

Hiatus.

FORT GEORGE, NEW YORK, TIME LINE THREE, MARCH 2020

It took two world-walking jumps in quick succession to return to the Commonwealth from time line two. Normally Hulius would take his time to recover between trips, find a fallen tree or something to sit on: but he was spooked, and took the second jump too fast. Pain spiked through his forehead as he dropped the messenger bag and bent forward, retch-ing, his ears still ringing with the echo of the single gunshot. He stood in the center of a large room, high-ceilinged and with whitewashed walls, his knees wobbling like jelly. *That was much too close,* he thought numbly. Painted markings on the floor corresponded to the layout of the alleyway. Helpful hands took the messenger bag, while others eased a wheelchair into place behind him. "Easy there, Major. Please sit down . . ."

"Thanks," he tried to say, tongue-tied. *That was a* really *bad mission exit,* he thought. *Just about the second-worst outcome possible. I'm getting too old for this shit.* In his late thirties, he was old for an agent—especially a world-walking agent running courier missions into a hostile high-tech surveillance state. The idea of shuffling quietly into a desk job and then a slow slide down to retirement usually lacked appeal, but right now he was experiencing a dizzying perspective shift. Retirement was a welcome prospect, compared with the alternative so recently on offer.

"Medic? Medic?"

He settled into the chair as someone slipped a blood pressure cuff around his left arm and began to inflate it. *Home again,* he thought. "Blood pressure's 165/116, sir. If you lie back, we'll get that down. This won't hurt . . ."

Hulius relaxed, feeling the familiar sting of a needle seeking a vein in his left forearm. Over to the left, the Forensics and Biologicals teams were taking inventory of the courier bag, checking for unwanted passengers. Everyone wore surgical masks and overalls. Access to the Quarantine/Arrival Room was via an operating theater–grade scrub and robing area. Nobody wanted to risk importing plagues or parasites from a parallel universe.

The doctor and paramedics crowded around his chair, waiting to slip their latest potion into his bloodstream: a cocktail of potassium-sparing diuretics and a fancy new calcium channel blocker, guaranteed to smack down post–world-walking hypertension within minutes. It was far better than the old prescriptions the Clan's doctors had fumbled together, back before they had a superpower's entire pharmaceutical industry to call on.

His arrival and reception had been recorded by the bulky cameras in the corners of the room, while technicians logged everything on the crude locally made computer terminals lined up against the far wall.

The Department of Para-historical Research was meticulous about data collection on these runs. Missions to the United States of America were extremely hazardous: nobody could guess in advance what might be of interest to the board of inquiry if a world-walker was lost.

"Open wide, sir?"

Hulius gaped for the dentist's forceps. A sharp tug and the man held up the false crown for inspection: "All clear." He transferred the crown to a labeled jar. "Hmm. I'd like to book you in for descaling and a regular check: there's a bit of plaque developing. Otherwise, you can go whenever Brian is through with you."

"I want to take another blood reading in five minutes." Brian, the doctor with the sphygmomanometer and the antihypertensives, was taciturn. "I'll sign you off for decontamination when it's back within sight of normal, but not a moment sooner."

"More than your job's worth, eh?" Hulius asked, joking. But judging from the medic's frown, it was no joking matter.

"If I let you go early and you suffer an apoplectic fit, it wouldn't just be my job that's on the line. With the flu doing the rounds, we've got only eighty-four walkers available for active ops this week."

"Eighty—" He swallowed a curse. *Of course.* Plagues could travel piggyback on a world-walker in either direction, and importing a nasty epidemic wasn't the only risk the Department of Para-historical Research ran when it authorized a transfer mission. The other time line was terrifyingly proficient at automated genome scanning and biowarfare defense. If a flu strain from the Commonwealth ever got loose over there, the US authorities would rapidly deduce the existence of the DPR's espionage program. Pinpointing exactly where patient zero had arrived would follow, and then—

The consequences would be bad. Starting with the enemy waking up and plastering Manhattan Island in time line one with sensors and killer drones, then going rapidly downhill from there.

Hulius waited while the medics fussed, trying to relax. As usual, it did little to speed things up. After a couple of inconclusive blood pressure checks and then a better one, Brian grudgingly pronounced himself satisfied and an unseen attendant wheeled Hulius into the robing area. He stripped, showered, and dressed himself in civilian clothes—every step following strict decontamination protocols. It was a soothing and familiar ritual. He'd performed it more than a thousand times in the sixteen years since he'd joined the Department of Para-historical Research, and in rudimentary form for years before that. It was far more elaborate and effective than anything the Clan had bothered with back in the old days: more like the routine his bright younger brother Huw had come up with for probing new time lines. But the DPR didn't dance to the same tune as the fractious families of merchant princes who had made their homes in the Gruinmarkt. Far from it.

The guards in the lobby of the building saluted politely enough, but kept a close eye on him. "Sign here, Citizen Major," said the sergeant waiting by the turnstile with a clipboard. Hulius nodded, signed. "Thank you," the sergeant continued. "You may leave the secure zone now." He gave no sign of recognition, even though he'd been on this posting for several months and had spoken exactly the same words to Hulius at least thirty times. Inter-service rivalry could be brutal in the postrevolutionary Commonwealth, and the troops were drawn from the Commonwealth Guard, a body loyal to the Party rather than the state.

Outside the squat, concrete shed, Hulius paused for a minute to take in the evening air. Then he headed toward the office block where he would make his report in person.

Fort George was still centered on a century-old shingle-roofed brick barracks, but it had lately been overrun by an infestation of concrete. There was fresh cement everywhere from the driveways to the new multistory office buildings, including the sinister hemispheres facing out toward the Atlantic coast, their embrasures concealing antiaircraft missile launchers. About the only new structures that *weren't* made of the stuff were the radar dishes and the flagpole.

The twenty-first century was definitely the age of concrete, Hulius mused. Concrete and blast doors and automobiles with floor-mounted gearshifts. Sidewalks and orange-glaring streetlights that turned the night to day, the gold to chrome. It was all horribly industrial, as far from nature as one could get. Computer terminals with chord-keyboards and green phosphor screens and magnetic cartridge drives: sometimes it seemed as if the Commonwealth was desperate to turn itself into an echo of the paranoid place he had just visited.

A growing shriek like the howl of a demented, mindless god split the sky overhead. Hulius glanced up in time to see a pair of silvery arrowheads disappearing into the eastern sky, trailing orange fire. A few seconds later double thunderclaps rattled the windows. They were probably off to protect the Commonwealth's airspace from encroaching French bombers. A job at which they were very good, although it was anybody's guess how effective such second-generation fighter jets would be if they were called upon to defend the homeland against the stealth drones and advanced electronics of the United States . . .

CAMBRIDGE, MASSACHUSETTS, TIME LINE THREE, SPRING 2018

Another day, another public opening ceremony. The Commonwealth public loved factory-opening ceremonies. Opening ceremonies meant jobs, money, and the white heat of a new technological revolution. Drama, television cameras, a news autogyro circling overhead to get the best shots of a vast new complex. They'd be highlighting the shiny new parking lots and monorail stations linking the factory to the planned workers' satellite towns. *I just wish I could hire an actor to stand in for me,* Miriam thought wearily as she adjusted her white gloves. Erica, her makeup assistant, fussed around her hair, making sure every strand was in place: "I want to matte your forehead some more, madame," she said. "Otherwise, the cameras will—"

"Certainly." Miriam sat still. Her legs ached. Her back ached. Sometimes it felt like she was a single ache held together by willpower: she was a year off fifty, and middle age was not proving to be fun, even without the cancer scare the other year. "As long as you're done in ten minutes."

"Don't worry, Minister." That was Jeffrey, her young new PA. Was it just her, or were PAs getting younger every year? And changing faster and faster? Hell, Radical Party Commissioners seemed to be getting younger by the day too, especially since she'd ended up running a ministry of her own—the then-unforeseen but retrospectively inevitable outcome of that prison camp meeting all those years ago. "You're looking wonderful, madame."

"Great." She kept her face still as Erica dusted her, brushes flicking. Fashions had changed slowly in the New British Empire of old, at least until relatively recently. Fabric and labor had been more expensive than in the United States, so clothing had to be made to last. The Revolution that had overturned the old monarchy and created the New American Commonwealth had done away with the baroque court dress of the old royal court—for which Miriam was sincerely grateful—but the outfits she was expected to wear, as a female Minister presiding over public events, were still elaborate compared with what she'd grown up with. It meant her entourage was large—dressers and makeup artists as well as bodyguards and personal assistants. "Do we have time for one last run-through?"

Half an hour later she was on stage, standing before a bouquet of bulbous microphones and a flicker of press camera flashes. Beside her were the Mayor of Cambridge, the Citizen Commissioner of Development for the Republic of Massachusetts, and a collection of local Party members and handpicked workers. Then it was time for speechifying:

"Today is a great day for Cambridge and Massachusetts—and more important, for the entire Commonwealth. The Commonwealth has made great progress in the past fifteen years, but many of our fellow citizens have yet to be exposed to the revolutionary potential of micro-electronics, much less the potential of automation, information technology, and computing that the microprocessor makes possible."

Before she'd discovered—or been discovered by—the Clan and learned to world-walk, Miriam had grown up in the United States. She'd worked as a tech journalist during the dot-com boom era. The hackneyed Silicon Valley rhetoric of revolutionary change came easily to her. But to ears raised in the New American Commonwealth it sounded fresh, exciting, and new: they'd barely had vacuum tubes when she arrived. "This factory will showcase the Watertown Semiconductor

Cooperative's first fully integrated fab line: a historic breakthrough. And one day in the future, we'll be able to put a minicomputer in every school and workplace across the Commonwealth"—not to mention eventually providing the brains for the secure terminals required by the People's Logistic Allocation Network, in every factory and warehouse and farm across three continents—"training our children for the computerized future they will live in . . ."

Keep it as short as possible was one of her guidelines: Miriam had sat through too many of these events, on the other side of the mikes and cameras, to enjoy abusing her captive audience. But: *Make it too short and nobody will notice anything you say.* And Miriam needed to milk every opportunity to be heard. It wasn't just everyday politics: it was vitally important to keep the master plan visible in the public eye at all times, gathering momentum, delivering the goods. Or in this case, delivering the first indigenous, crude, eight-bit microprocessors from the Commonwealth's first civilian semiconductor factory.

All because the USA was coming.

Finally it was time for the ribbon-cutting and confetti—the latter an imported prop, one that had been latched onto with enthusiasm by the locals—and the band struck up a jaunty revolutionary march. Miriam took her place at the end of the receiving line in the factory canteen, beside the union convener and the plant's magistrate. They were both old hands, deeply wary of each other and of her world-walking self: they clearly had no intention of burying their worker/management hatchet without some discreet external head-banging.

"Play nicely, now," she said, smiling at the magistrate over a glass of passable sparkling zinfandel: "We're in this to make life better for everyone, not just a select few."

"In my experience, the nobs don't settle for just their share of the cake if they think they can 'ave it all," said the union rep.

"You've got my office number. If you think the managers are overreaching, I assure you my staff will be very interested to hear about it. Just try to remember that my task is to ensure the best outcome for the nation as a whole." She smiled again to take some of the sting out of the words. "This plant isn't going to stand still and hammer out the same products for the next thirty years, you know. Today's chips will be obsolete in five years' time. The only constant will be change—"

The line shuffled forward while she shook hands, chatted over her shoulder, and exchanged smiles and the odd greeting with the people before her: they were into the workers now, mostly skilled technical personnel who'd been taken on to run the silicon foundry. She was glad she was wearing gloves: about one in four of them seemed to want to cripple her with their robust handshakes, but at least she wouldn't need to worry about picking up the flu.

A young man stood before her, wide-eyed. Something about him didn't seem quite right: it wasn't his clothing (a regular worker's suit, with a cravat after the modern style) or hair (curly, with flyaway locks escaping the grip of his pomade), but rather his curiously fixed expression. Somehow it reminded her of someone she'd seen before. "Hello," she said, smiling professionally, and reaching out to take his right hand, "how are you today—"

Danger. As he opened his mouth she remembered where she'd seen that look: back during the Revolution, or even earlier. He snatched his hand back from her offered palm, lips curling back in rage—

"Down!" It was Melvyn, her number one bodyguard, shouting over the hubbub. Miriam ducked without thinking and began to roll, realizing *This is going to hurt tomorrow*—

—then somebody landed on top of her, crushing the breath from her body and shoving her off to one side as the young man shouted "For God and Emperor!" and repeatedly pulled the trigger of the snub-nosed revolver he had somehow, improbably, smuggled in past the security guards.

Someone shrieked hoarsely, in an uncontrolled bloody-throated wail of pain. The crash of the gun, so close, felt like ice picks in her inner ears. A bullet struck the floor close enough to her face that she saw splinters. More screaming, and a bellow of rage. "—God and—"

Boots, stomping past her face. Different screams, with the shrieking of whoever had been shot a ghastly counterpoint. "Got 'im!"

Miriam gasped, trying to breathe. Her ribs hurt, and her left shoulder was a solid lump of agony. For a moment she wondered if she'd been shot too, but there was no blood. "Off me," she tried to wheeze. A second later the man lying atop her shifted, grinding her harder against the floor, then began to lever himself up.

"Sorry, ma'am. Clear?" The latter question was not addressed to her.

"Shooter down, stand down, stand down! Evacuate the Minister!"

Suddenly she was free. Miriam took a deep, moaning breath and began to push herself up on her right elbow. Strong hands grabbed her under the armpits and bodies closed in, carrying her backstage in a rush. Her chest heaved. "I'm all right!" she choked out. "Let me walk!"

Melvyn was insistent. "Madame, we have to get you out of—"

"I'll walk!" Her chest heaved. "How many gunmen?"

"Just the one, but—"

"Casualties?" She dug her heels in, turning to face him. Her body-guards drew in, facing outward, forming a human shield. "Who's hurt?"

"Madame, he hit Jeffrey in the stomach, an ambulant will be here just as soon as—"

"Who else?"

"His shots went wide, thank God," said the other guard.

"Right." She took a deep breath, then another, assessing the situation. "Lone gunman, one pistol, one injured, nobody killed. Secure the scene, Mel, I'm going back."

"Ma'am, I can't let you—"

"You can't stop me and you *mustn't* stop me," she shot right back. "Do you want to make me look like a coward? There are frightened people there—"

"But Commissioner—"

"*Fuck it.*" Miriam took an unsteady half-step forward. Her guards shuffled around uneasily, more shocked by her language than by the assassination attempt. "*Do* you want to make me look like a coward?" She glared at her escort. "Because if I hide, that's what I'll be." She drew herself fully upright, winced and gritted her teeth, forcing herself to ignore her shoulder. "I've a factory to open, and we're *not* going to let some little royalist toe-rag spoil the big day for everybody else. If he'd brought backup that'd be another matter, *but.*" She took another step, and they made way for her as she walked back toward the auditorium, which was in turmoil. The shrieking was subsiding, but the sound of sirens was still rising outside. Press flashbulbs flared. "I'm going back in there and I'm going to call for calm." She bared her teeth at Melvyn: "Because that's my job. Otherwise the terrorists have won: and that's not going to happen on my watch."

Politicians

Hulius found a surprise waiting for him at his destination. His boss, Colonel Jackson, had a visitor.

"Come in, sit down." Jackson gestured at a chair. "Major, I believe you've met Mrs. Hjorth already . . . ?"

Hulius gaped for a moment. "Yes, we've met," he said. Then he beamed. "Nice to see you again, Brill. Colonel, Mrs. Hjorth is my sister-in-law . . ."

Jackson kept a poker face as Brill smiled at Hulius: clearly he hadn't realized it was a family matter, even though they were both world-walkers. "It's been ages, Yul." Indeed, it had been: he'd barely recognized her at first. She'd cut her long blond hair much shorter and curled it after the current mode, and it was graying toward ash. She was also slightly dumpier than he remembered, and the crow's-feet at the edges of her eyes were deeper. She wore a fashionable shalwar suit: the very model of a modern female Party member. She extended a hand, and he shook it across his boss's desk, still startled to see her here. "How are Ellie and the girls?" she asked.

Hulius caught a very slight tension around Jackson's eyes, and caught himself before relaxing into informality—"Ellie's doing fine. So are Sophie and Mary and Rina: we really must get together properly! But I take it you're not here just to catch up?"

"Sit," grunted Colonel Jackson, looking rather put out. Hulius sat. "Mrs. Hjorth, before your arrival I was expecting the major to report to me about a matter I can't discuss in front of you. Hulius, if there are no special circumstances demanding immediate consideration, we can skip the verbal. Just have a final write-up on my desk by first thing tomorrow morning. Yes?"

"Yes—"

"Is this about the BRONX RESTART program?" Brilliana asked. Both men looked at her as if she'd grown a second head. "Because if so, that particular report is due to land on *my* desk on Friday morning."

Of course. Hulius felt like kicking himself. *Definitely* not a social call. Brill worked for Miriam: and this entire organization was one of her projects.

Jackson cleared his throat apologetically. "You may say that, but without confirmation I can't discuss it with you."

Brilliana, formerly the Lady Brilliana d'Ost, in the days before the Clan sought exile in the Commonwealth, frowned. It was an expression that struck fear in the hearts of braver men than Hulius. Now she turned it on Jackson. "The major has just returned from excursion AT-962, collecting this month's uncleared intel package from Paulette Milan," she said, speaking slowly and clearly. "His rendezvous point was the Blue Star Diner in Red Hook, New York. Colonel, your concern for operational security is noted, but you might want to bear in mind that to me, it's family. If you *really* want to go through the motions, you can query my clearance with the Minister right now, but that will delay us and drag her away from her dinner—"

Colonel Jackson raised his hands in surrender. "That won't be necessary!" he agreed hastily. "I'll go through the forms and get you added to my cleared list tomorrow. In the meantime . . ." He winced. "Can I count on your discretion?"

"Certainly." Brill's smile was bright and, reassuringly, walked things back to just the right side of frightening. "I note that the TRACAN forecasts for safe transfer windows have been narrowing rapidly in the past six months. Yul, in your opinion, is Ms. Milan showing signs of stress?"

"Is she—" Hulius instinctively glanced at the colonel for permission.

He nodded, almost imperceptibly. "Yes, she is. She's not requesting extraction, but she's clearly worried about detection."

"I see." Brill nodded thoughtfully.

Hulius felt an explanation was in order. "She has relatives," he said. "Nieces and a nephew." He shrugged. "Doesn't sound like much of a life to me, but it's her choice."

"Unfortunately—" began Jackson, just as Brilliana cut him off: "No it isn't."

She cleared her throat. "We owe her a huge debt, but the longer we run her, the higher the probability that the adversary's traffic analysis will identify her as a person of interest. She's already one of our longest-running agents. Part of my reason for visiting you today was to poll you about the practicality of arranging a voluntary or semivoluntary extraction—"

"Semivoluntary?" Hulius couldn't help himself.

Brill's lips pursed. "I can probably persuade her to cooperate, if I talk to her in person. Assuming we're not already too late. But I think we need to retire her. She knows too much."

Hulius shuddered. "It's going to be difficult. The details will be in my report"—he caught Colonel Jackson's eye—"but today was *extremely* difficult."

"How difficult?" Her eyes narrowed.

"I nearly didn't make it back." Hulius's shoulders slumped. "There's no indication that they're onto her, but they nearly caught me on the subway. I had to break cover and run."

"Oh hell."

"Well, that tears it." Brill frowned. "I've got to talk it over with the Minister and clear it with Oversight, but I believe we're going to have to end her residency."

Hulius paused. "I think you're going to want to use a different controller for that mission," he said reluctantly. "I'm pretty sure they made me on the station cameras."

Colonel Jackson was frowning too. "Just when we're shorthanded."

"Doesn't signify," said Brill. "We can't afford to leave a compromised agent behind in the United States, not with seventeen years of accumulated bread crumbs pointing to her front door. It would tell them altogether too much about our interests and progress. But it would set a really bad precedent—a terrible one—if we liq—no, if we kill—a loyal agent for no fault of her own other than being at risk of apprehension by the adversary. 'Trust is a two-way street' and all that." Hulius recognized the words: she was quoting the Minister, Miriam.

"We can lay the groundwork for an extraction," Colonel Jackson said warily. "But I'll need a written order."

"You'll get it tomorrow."

"Is that all?"

"No, it isn't." Brill leaned back in her chair. "Feel free to correct me if I am laboring under a misapprehension, but Hulius isn't due to visit Ms. Milan again for another twenty-seven days. Am I correct? And he's going to have to be reassigned anyway, now that he's apparently on their face recognition database?"

"That's right."

"Well then. Can you spare him for the next six months, Colonel?"

"What?" Jackson sat bolt upright. "You've got to be joking—"

"Let me rephrase that, Colonel. I'm in need of Major Hulius Hjorth's unique combination of abilities, so I'm going to requisition him. You can have him back temporarily if it's essential to pull Paulie out, but I need him on an ongoing basis for an operation vital to national security. I'm afraid this comes from the top: resistance, as they say, is futile."

"I'm sure you can make it stick," Jackson grumped. "But you realize that Hulius runs nineteen other US-based agents? Not all of whom live in the middle of a camera hot spot. We've been hit hard by this damned flu pandemic—"

"Your sleepers have a protocol to follow in the event of a no-show," Brill pointed out. "This is going to cause temporary disruption, yes. But I really need Yul."

"May I ask why?"

"Because we need him for a little trip to Europe in time line two. And he has—or used to have—a private pilot's license . . ."

PALACE OF NEW LONDON, MANHATTAN ISLAND,
TIME LINE THREE, SPRING 2018

Three days after the abortive assassination attempt—only the second in the past two years: the Minister was unsure whether to be relieved or offended that she was held in so little esteem by the enemy—Miriam found herself back in her office in the capital, chairing yet another meeting. Revolutions (she'd long since learned) ran on committees just like any other government, once you got past the screaming-and-shooting stage. The price of leading a faction among the winners in the postcoup dog pile was an office in a government ministry and, by and by, a daily briefing that, in digest form alone, was several inches thick. However, an assassination attempt still merited a meeting with her head of security.

"On the subject of your assailant, my lady," said Olga Thorold. Her aristocratic youth in the Gruinmarkt time line still colored the style of her private speech, even though it might have been seen as counterrevolutionary backsliding: only her position enabled her to get away with it, unquestioned. "I have a report from Internal Security on the background of the would-be assassin." She reached into a side pocket of her wheelchair with one shaky hand and pulled out a slim document file, its edge striped in the yellow and red indicating its security classification level. She slid it carefully across Miriam's blotter. "I find it disturbing by implication."

"Summarize for me, please?" Miriam slid her reading glasses down, then pinched the bridge of her nose tiredly. "Eyestrain again," she muttered apologetically.

"Think nothing of it: at least my eyes still work."

Miriam winced. When she'd first met her, Olga had been a willowy eighteen-year-old, to all appearances a naive noble lady of the Clan. Her role in life was apparently to make a good marriage and provide the linked families of world-walking merchant princes with a fresh brood of aristocratic couriers. But it had been a creative lie. Working as an agent of the Clan's internal security organization, Olga's real role was far from passive. Subsequently she'd acted as Miriam's head of intelligence during and after the escape to the revolution-racked new home in time line three. But the multiple sclerosis that ran in the Clan's bloodlines and had taken Miriam's mother now had its claws into her.

"Just the talking points will do, Olga."

"Certainly. Your shooter was a Mr. Michael Buerke, age nineteen, born and raised in Boston. By employment, a postal sorter. Unmarried, no children, second youngest of six siblings, father deceased. No criminal record to speak of." Olga shook her head. "We had no warnings about him, which is disturbing. He left his previous job as an assistant railway signalman nine months ago and his whereabouts were unknown for two months afterward, before he sought work with the post office."

"Hell." Miriam closed her eyes. "Any leads?"

"Hard to say. Mr. Buerke was not an associate of any known royalist clubs or debating societies. I cannot swear to his reading habits at the library, but he certainly did not subscribe to any questionable periodicals, and none such were found in his room when SCEP raided it. And they're cooperating with my people about as well as you can expect."

Miriam winced again. The Special Counter-Espionage Police were not her favorite people.

"I can't help thinking this sort of trawl would be easier if we had hot and cold running Internets, cameras on every street corner, and carte blanche to wage a war on terror." Miriam paused: "Probably just as well we don't, come to think of it. If the previous regime had such tools we wouldn't be here, would we?"

"You might think that; I couldn't possibly comment." Olga's frown was eloquent. But then her expression brightened: "I had enough leverage to learn that the Specials found a ticket stub in his room," Olga continued. "The return half of an open railway return from Philadelphia. The issue dates match when he was missing."

"What are they—"

"SCEP are proceeding on the assumption they're hunting for a sleeper cell. There's a certain stench to this that suggests careful organization, not a lone wolf. They said they'll let me know if they uncover anything, and for once I'm inclined to believe them." An attempt on the life of a Minister was too serious to sweep under the rug, and SCEP would risk serious blowback if they didn't keep Miriam's own security team updated on the threat. "I have a contact there; for now, that will be sufficient. But it looks as if the royal court may finally have worked out who their real enemies are."

"Ouch." Miriam frowned. The King-in-Exile in St. Petersburg, capital of the French continental empire, was slow on the uptake when it came to matters mechanical; with the arrogance of hereditary aristocrats, they had paid far more attention to the Commonwealth's navies and armies than to their ministry of washing machines and higher education. But it seemed that he—or one of his advisors—had *finally* realized where the Commonwealth's economic and technological progress was coming from and decided to do something about it at source. "Do I have anything to worry about?"

"I'm doubling your bodyguard and putting them on twenty-four/seven alert, my lady. And notifying your husband's department. Other than that, nothing immediate. Once we get confirmation, Brilliana and I will come back to you with some concrete proposals to teach them the unwisdom of playing games with us."

"All right. Other matters . . ."

"Yes." Olga straightened painfully, levering herself up against the back of her wheelchair. "Do you want the weekly update on operations in the United States first, or—"

There was a push-button phone to one side of Miriam's desk, equipped with a bulky transistorized scrambler unit. Right at that moment it began to buzz angrily. "Hold on?" She glanced at Olga, then back at the phone: "You can stay."

"Certainly. Who is it?"

"External, long-distance, encrypted." She frowned. "Wait—" Her direct secure line wasn't public, but government phone directories were quite extensive. She picked up the receiver. "Miriam speaking."

"Miriam?" The voice was familiar, and welcome. "I have a sitrep."

"Huw!" It was Brilliana's husband, the Explorer-General, head of the department's exploration force based in South America—and of various other exotic assets, which were also based as close as possible to the equator for reasons of orbital dynamics. Her chest suddenly felt hollow.

"What's happening at your end?" Across the desk from her, Olga leaned forward eagerly.

"I thought you might want to know before it makes the evening news—Rudi just called. Test five was a complete success." His voice was shaky, as if he was finding it hard to control himself. "Dawn One is in the correct orbit, and we're receiving telemetry from the payload!"

"What?" She realized she was clutching the phone as if it were trying to escape. "It worked?"

"One hundred percent!" Now he sounded triumphant: "We finally made it!"

"Oh my. Oh my." The butterflies made it hard to breathe. "Who else have you notified?"

"You're the first. Rudi's calling the First Man's office, and I believe Director Kemp is on the phone to the Communication Ministry—"

She could barely believe it. The long series of launchpad fires and explosions seconds after liftoff had been a never-ending embarrassment, even though they'd only been trying to place satellites in orbit for a couple of years—and were barely twenty years on from fabric-skinned biplanes. "I think I can scare up a news crew this evening. Do you have a prepared statement you can wire me?"

"*I* don't, but Rudi does! I'll get the propaganda office to e-mail it over immediately."

Huw cut the call short: intercontinental trunk calls were still hugely expensive. "Well!" Miriam looked at Olga.

"Was that what I think it was?" Olga gripped her armrests.

"Yup." She took a deep breath. "They did it. Dawn One is in low Earth orbit and talking." Dawn One wasn't just this world's first satellite. They'd gone for broke: the four-ton behemoth was actually the prototype for what would, one day soon, be a manned vehicle. (And then there was the other, more radical space program: but that hadn't launched anything yet . . .)

"Sorry, Olga, I'm going to have to cut this short." She picked up the phone again. "Hi, Galen? Can you round up a news crew? They're going to want to interview me just as soon as they hear what's just happened . . ."

Yes, the USA is coming. Let them come: we'll be ready.

NEW LONDON, MANHATTAN ISLAND, TIME LINE THREE, SPRING 2020

Two years later, Miriam was thinking back to that momentous phone call as her limousine—one of the clean, efficient diesel cars that were replacing the steam vehicles of yesteryear—pulled up in front of her current New London residence. As a senior Party member, she merited a grand brownstone town house on Manhattan Island, within a mile's radius of the First Man's mansion. The mansion itself was the Manhattan Palace: it squatted at the southern end of the fortified inner city of New London, near the southern end of the island. The city had been renamed multiple times, most recently in 1759 when the British Crown moved to the Americas in the wake of the French invasion of England. Miriam's brownstone was sited midway along a curving avenue, almost exactly where Washington Square Park was located in that other Manhattan.

"We're here, ma'am," the ministerial chauffeur said redundantly as she yawned and gathered her papers, shoving them into her briefcase. It was half past eleven at night: it had been a long day. "Jack's getting the door."

"No need to wake everyone up for me." The door opened and she slid out, stretching. She'd caught the newly electrified express train down from a plenary session in Boston that afternoon. The trip had taken just two hours, but the evening reception and the rides to and from the stations had eaten the night. The air was warm and damp, the faint sweet-sick open sewer stink from the Hudson River fighting with the honeysuckle bushes lining the front of the terrace of state houses. "That's all for now. Just make sure someone's here to collect me at eight tomorrow before you go off shift."

She climbed the front steps slowly and the door opened for her. Jenny the housekeeper had stayed awake. "Ma'am? He's still up—in the lounge." Jenny seemed uncharacteristically anxious.

"Thank you." Miriam nodded. "How is he?"

"Much the same." Jenny closed the front door and threw the bolt. "Will you be wanting anything?"

"A mug of chocalatl, if you don't mind. Unsweetened." Miriam paused outside the lounge doorway as Jenny took her coat, and heard an outbreak of coughing from behind the closed door. "Damn."

"Are you all right?" she asked as she entered the room.

"I'm"—more coughing—"fine." Her husband, Erasmus, was sitting in a wingback armchair, putting his handkerchief away. "There's no blood, if that's what you were wondering."

"I was." She sat down carefully in the armchair opposite him. "It still worries me. And if you don't promise you'll see the doctors about it this week, I'll keep nagging you."

"It's not the phthisis." *Tuberculosis*, she translated mentally. He briefly closed his eyes, and for a moment looked a decade older than his fifty-five years. "It's just a winter cough—the humidity disagrees with me. I know the white death well. If it was coming back—"

There were two piles of document folders on the occasional table: one tall, one smaller. She picked the top item off the taller pile. "Progress Report, State Committee on Metropolitan Optical Fiber Cable Infrastructure, March, Year 17," she said lightly. Year 17 of the Revolution, or 2020 AD, in the old style. "Just think how they'll manage without you if you die of tuberculosis through self-neglect—thanks to staying up after midnight reading reports!"

He glanced sidelong at the briefcase by her chair: "I'll give up when you give up, dear."

A dizzying sense of drifting perspective seized her. "I'll give up when the Americans—when the United States—when we're safe—"

"In other words, never." He spared her a sad smile. "You can't lie to me: I've known you too long."

Another dizzying look down from the pinnacle of the present into the yawning canyon of the past. "I can't believe it's been eighteen years already."

"But you only said 'yes' to me fourteen years ago." His tone was light, as if he was trying to make a weak joke of it, but the years weighed heavily on them both.

"I was still gun-shy. You would be too, if your previous marriage was anything like my two." Her fingers tightened on his hand. "Tell me what your schedule is for the rest of the week and I'll tell you what to drop so you can make room for a doctor's appointment. Please?"

"You're going to blackmail me now, aren't you?"

"Yes. I want you to get your lungs checked out. Erasmus, I make a terrible widow."

"On one condition, then: I think you've been working too hard. If I get my lungs fluoroscoped, will you agree to take a nice quiet vacation with me, my dear?"

The door opened. It was Jenny, bearing a tea tray with two steaming mugs, which she deposited on the table before tactfully leaving them to it. Miriam picked up one of the mugs of chocalatl. "Have you taken your pills?"

"What? The—yes, I have." Erasmus picked up his mug and blew on it thoughtfully. "Thank you—and I *will* see the doctor. After the cabinet meeting tomorrow morning. I expect in the afternoon I'm going to be drawing up policy guidelines for how we spin our latest satellite launch. Such is the lot of the Commissioner for State Communications. I should have been more careful what I wished for."

"Space: the final frontier," Miriam suggested. "Rockets are exciting, Erasmus. And for propaganda purposes, rockets that don't kill people are even better than ones that do."

"Our adversaries are still terrified, though. Wouldn't you be, in their position?"

"Yes." She put her mug down and rested her chin on her right fist. "The technology gap is widening all the time—we're at least ten years ahead of them, more in some areas. They've barely begun to develop battlefield rockets beyond the gunpowder stage. They're testing a turboprop bomber; they've got atom bombs. But we've got nuclear submarines and sea-launched intercontinental missiles. They can't even shoot down our reconnaissance planes, let alone our spy satellites."

"Yes." Erasmus rubbed his forehead. "So I'm going to push the rockets-for-peace message as hard as I can. Otherwise we risk terrifying the French into starting a preemptive war—especially if they listen to our idiot exiles. Letting the former emperor and his family sail off into the sunset was, I fear, a long-term misjudgment on Adam and the Radical Party's account. It will come back to haunt us."

"I'm not so sure," Miriam countered. "What were the alternatives? Give him a trial and execute him? It would have created a martyr—"

"Another Charles the First, yes."

"No, it would have been worse. Charles the First was a nasty piece of work: the Rump Parliament only put him on trial and chopped his head off after the third civil war he started. He deserved what he got! But John Frederick isn't in the same league, and we want to reduce the level of violence in politics, not inflame it. Convince our public that it's possible to transfer power peacefully. I've seen your polling: half of them still don't understand the idea of a loyal opposition, even after fifteen years of explaining till we're blue in the face. Executing the King would have set us up for a counterrevolution. His son turns out to be an asshole who sends assassins our way, and he still wants a Monarchist uprising to put his family back on the throne over here. But he isn't covering himself in glory at the Dauphin's court, is he? If we hold our shit together for another ten years of building microprocessor factories and jet airliners, everyone's going to see him for the irrelevant throwback he is. As long as we manage to avoid starting a fourth world war."

"Yes, but in the meantime, he's inflaming passions at the French court, Miriam. A king-in-exile is a romantic cause, and he can promise the more entrepreneurial grand dukes a continental ransom. Especially if he auctions off that pretty young daughter of his to someone with ambitions. Meanwhile, they're terrified of us. We represent the peasants on the march—every noble's worst nightmare. Worse: they *know* we're not just a mob of pitchfork-wielding yokels. They've read Adam's books. They've read mine. They understand that this is an existential conflict between those who adhere to the monarchical system and those who honor the new social contract: equality before the law, liberty within the law, nobody above the law. They won't give up their privileges without a struggle, and they know it's a fight they're losing. Our satellites"—he pointed through the window, indicating the southern horizon—"are signs and portents in the heavens. It tells them who owns the skies. They can't ignore that. It's decades beyond anything they can do—" He paused. "How much stolen US technology went into the space program?"

"None. We were very careful about that."

"What?" The light was just bright enough for her to see his pupils dilate.

"Oh, we bought textbooks. *Lots* of textbooks. And it soaked up almost a quarter of our Skills Transfer Program for five years."

The STP recruited unemployed graduate researchers and teachers from time line two—their reach, in combination with ex-Clan world-walkers and the nuclear submarines of the Commonwealth Navy, was global—and made them an offer they couldn't refuse. "We hired rocket scientists by the double-handful, mostly from Russia and Europe. And Rudi made sure Space Force ate their own dog food: we didn't let them copy anything directly. We've got a launcher that looks like an R-7—the missile that evolved into the Russian Soyuz system—and runs on the same fuel, liquid oxygen, and kerosene. But it's entirely homegrown. We may have lost the first four launch attempts, but compared with the early days of the United States or Soviet space programs, Rudi's made amazing progress."

"Well, that's as may be," Erasmus grumped, "but I have to use it to enthuse our people without frightening the French into attacking us. And they're going to panic all over again when we tell them we're going to put an astronaut up there next month." They pondered the implications. "Tomorrow evening it's the Guild of News Editors annual ball, where I shall be expected to speak—and, oh, the invitation should be in your diary as well, because wives are invited—"

"Wait, what about the female editors—"

"Yes, and their wives are invited too." Miriam gave him a look: Erasmus's sardonic sense of humor could sometimes get the better of him. "The wording of the invitation assumes the membership are all men," he explained. "The guild is full of deadwood because we needed somewhere to store it where it couldn't do any more harm . . . Hmm. How would you like to borrow my bully pulpit to talk about equality? I'm sure they won't dare make a fuss. After all, the invitation was addressed to 'Commissioner Burgeson': they simply forgot to specify which Commissioner Burgeson they were inviting to speak—"

"Oh you!" Miriam chuckled. "No, dammit. Picking fights with newspaper and wireless editors is—" She glanced sidelong. "You weren't serious, were you?"

"Oh, I don't know." Erasmus drained his mug. "Sometimes I don't know my own mind. We are surrounded by bigwigs and stuffed shirts. I'd be delighted to see you tear into them, but . . ." He shrugged. "We'd never hear the last of it."

"Enough of them seem to hate us simply for existing."

"You're a constant reproach: a woman and a tireless overachiever. And I"—he spread his right hand above his heart, striking a dramatic pose—"am the henpecked husband! Merely the Commissioner for State Communications." In charge of what had once been the State Ministry of Propaganda: now with oversight of all broadcasting, film, and print media, not to mention the embryonic network of clunky mainframe computers that were destined to grow into the Commonwealth's Internet. "Miriam, you terrify them. The Ministry of Intertemporal Technological Intelligence scares *everybody*. What was that phrase? 'Creative disruption'? Nobody is sure that your organization won't make their own pocket empire obsolete tomorrow, but none of them dares move against you while MITI delivers the goods. Just don't"—he paused to examine his mug—"underestimate the attraction of a little bit of decadence to old revolutionaries who think they're due their reward."

"I don't," Miriam said tersely. She finished her mug of cocoa. "Now I'm tired. It's been a long day. Come to bed, Erasmus."

"All right, but only if you promise to consider a vacation."

She rose to her feet. "A vacation? We might be able to make some time for it next year—"

"No, Miriam, I mean this year. Next year we might not be here. Or there might be another crisis. One damn crisis after another: pretty soon you look round and realize you have no time left."

"All right," she relented. "Let's look into it tomorrow?"

"Tomorrow. But first, to bed."

Empire Games

Two vast concrete buildings sweltered beneath the noonday heat on the northern shore of Lake Maracaibo in New Granada, bleached white by sun and storm-driven spray from the Gulf of Venezuela to the north. Both buildings supported gigantic level platforms on their roofs. Bunkers and warehouses off to the west were linked to the platforms by gravel roadbeds. The complex was surrounded on all sides by razor-wire fences, patrolled by sweating soldiers from the Commonwealth Guard, who stuck to the air-conditioned interiors of their half tracks as much as possible.

On the far side of the isthmus, gleaming silver arrowheads waited beside a broad military runway, baking hot despite the canvas shades draped across their bubble canopies. The distant buzz of a trainer conducting touch-and-go landings on the second runway rose and fell periodically, disturbing the too-still air. But nobody ventured outside in the noonday heat without good reason.

Then, as if in competition with the somnolent drone of the trainer's engine, another engine note began to rise. It was the shrill jet-howl of a government courier plane, on final approach into the sprawling lizard-stillness of the Maracaibo Aeronaval Complex. The Explorer-General's wife (who according to persistent rumors was herself involved at a high level in MITI's para-time espionage program) was returning from the capital, two thousand miles to the north.

The Explorer-General himself was being fitted for a pressure suit when the telephone rang. He was standing in a sagging mass of fabric and artificial rubber, suspended by its shoulders from a scaffold while a pair of technicians worked on his inner helmet: "If it's for me, I'll be ten minutes," he said. "Oh, and find out who—" Only a very few people could get through to him while he was spending either of the two days a week he jealously clung to for practical work, as opposed to the endless meetings and administrative sessions that had eaten his life since he became a senior officer.

"Sir, it's your wife. She said to say she's landed and she'll meet you in staging area two in an hour."

"Oh." Huw nodded—or tried to, inasmuch as nodding wasn't terribly practical while wearing a rigid helmet with a raised glass visor. "Let's finish up with the helmet today and we can sort out the legs tomorrow—"

"Sir? Would you mind holding still for a minute?"

Huw surrendered. The pressure suit was a new model, loosely copied from a Russian Sokol KV-2 that Brilliana had somehow obtained for him by way of the DPR: a survival space suit, designed to keep cosmonauts alive inside their Soyuz capsules in the event of an in-flight emergency. It weighed only ten kilos: cumbersome, but far easier to move in than a full-up EVA-certified suit. Huw wanted it very badly. It was intended to keep Explorer Corps world-walkers alive during the critical minutes it might take before they could escape, if they found themselves trailblazing a time line with a nonbreathable atmosphere. But being fitted for any space suit was tedious—like all pressure garments, it had to be tailored to the individual wearer and adjusted for a good fit. And he'd insisted on seeing for himself, a decision he was now regretting.

Half an hour later the suit team allowed him to undress, their final set of measurements recorded. "We should have it ready for you by next Wednesday," said the seniormost fitter, "assuming they've got enough umbilical sets. There was a parts shortage last month."

"Fine," Huw grunted. The astronaut corps was greedy for all the space-rated kit. But it wasn't as if his part-time project was going anywhere in the next week anyway. "Send me a memo when it's ready." He pulled up his trousers. "See you on Wednesday."

The suit-fitting department was part of a clump of windowless, fiercely air-conditioned buildings along one side of the road leading to the staging platforms. Huw walked to the parking lot, surrounded by the clump of bodyguards, assistants, and factotums that seemed to adhere to anyone of any importance. The cars were waiting under a shaded awning, engines already running. "Take me to staging area two," he said, climbing into the back of the frontmost vehicle.

"Sir." The cars moved off in convoy, chillers roaring in the heat. Huw glanced out at the parched, browning vegetation. *Six days*, he noted. This was the sixth consecutive day in which the nighttime temperature hadn't fallen below thirty-seven Celsius. Daytime temperatures were in the death zone—without forced ventilation or HVAC, people couldn't work outdoors here. Global warming had already bitten this time line hard: its population wasn't any smaller than that of time line two, and they'd stayed on coal- and wood-burning fires longer than the more developed world. Another decade or two of rising sea levels and strengthening hurricanes and they'd probably have to abandon Maracaibo completely: even the desperate plan to switch the Commonwealth over to nuclear power in the next ten years would be too little and too late to stop the warming in its tracks.

The cars scurried like shiny-carapaced ants from shadow to shadow, until they pulled up beside a windowless door opening onto the second of the big staging area platforms. The guard in the front passenger seat jumped out and held the door for Huw: he stepped into the searing oven-heat of early afternoon. His entourage followed: a few seconds later they reached the lobby. The doors opened automatically; the guards saluted, opening the inner doors before them. "She said you can find her in Hangar B," said the sergeant on duty.

"Good." Huw nodded, then walked straight down the main access corridor, leading a cometary trail of followers.

"Sir, if you've got just a minute . . ." His secretary—a junior manager, in this continent's office culture—hurried to keep up with him.

"Yes?"

"It's about the corps task assignments for next week: according to my manifest we've just been assigned a new world-walker, a major on transfer from Fort George—"

Huw stopped dead. "A major?" The secretary nodded. "Would he by any chance be called Hulius Hjorth?"

"Yes sir, how did you—"

"Excellent!" Huw carried on, this time with a spring in his step. "He'll be with her in Hangar B," he predicted.

"Possibly, sir, I don't really—"

Huw barged through a side door, across a freight corridor, dodged a slowly reversing forklift truck, and walked onto the floor of Hangar B, pausing briefly for the security check.

The hangar formed a sports stadium–sized open space at the center of the staging platform. Right now, the domed roof was closed and the hydraulic elevator rested at ground level, safety gates down and payload area accessible. Cranes rolled back and forth above it on their tracks, deftly lifting twenty-ton freight containers from a line of flatbed railway wagons and stacking them carefully on the deck of the massive hovercraft that occupied almost the entire surface of the elevator platform. Meanwhile maintenance crews checked over the vast rubber skirts of the vehicle and refueled the engines that would, for a few brief minutes, lift the entire stack a handful of centimeters off the ground.

Minutes were all that it needed, minutes during which the world-walker on board would concentrate, focusing on a carefully tailored knotwork design that would shift them—and everything they were grounded to—to another time line with a leveled receiving area. World-walkers were a scarce resource, only able to make two trips per day on a regular schedule: but a world-walker using one of the staging platforms at MAC could transfer two thousand tons of freight at a time, and much larger carriers were on the drawing board.

Huw made a beeline for the site office beside the side entrance, marched in, and took the stairs up to the second floor two at a time. The door to the committee room was open: he charged in. "Brill!" He embraced her, then: "Bro!"

Hulius stepped forward. They hugged. "It's been too long."

"Far too long. How's Elena?" Huw caught Brilliana's look. "What?"

"Out." She waved irritably at the secretary who had just arrived, trailing slightly breathlessly behind Huw. "Shut the door. Where's the security light?"

Huw flipped the switch for the red SECRET light outside the door. "What's so urgent?"

"Yes—" Hulius turned to face Brilliana. "We're here now." He raised an eyebrow. "I see no *Anglisch* . . . ?"

"Speak hochsprache," Brilliana replied in the same tongue. It wouldn't guarantee secrecy, but it would place a major obstacle in the way of casual eavesdroppers. The Gruinmarkt's language was effectively dead, spoken only by refugees born in time line one. "Family matters."

"Family—" Hulius stopped. He dragged out a chair and straddled it, arms resting on its back. "I thought this was official business?"

"It is." Brill frowned. "Huw, are you up to date on the weekly intelligence assessments?"

Huw blinked rapidly. "I believe so. Why?"

"When I went north to collect Yul for the flight training project, I thought it was routine, but I caught up with the take from his previous month's dead drop just as he got back from the latest, and it looks like we've got a major problem. So major that I had to take time off to brief Miriam, who's going to raise it with the Survival Committee. They haven't met yet, but I'm telling you right now because I'm pretty sure they're going to order you to bring the project forward."

Clearly upset, she began to pace. "That *fucking* quack."

"Quack?" Hulius looked puzzled.

"Are we talking about *him*?" asked Huw.

"Yes." Brill nodded. "Dr. Griben ven Hjalmar, deceased and unlamented Gynecologist to the Clan and sometime would-be kingmaker before he defected to the dark side. We're pretty sure—from what the old Duchess admitted to—that he kept a copy of the database from that crazy breeding project Duke Angbard was running. Artificial insemination to breed . . . you know." Her lips wrinkled, cheeks tensing. "It probably fell into the hands of one or the other of the US government agencies that were stalking us, back in the day. Anyway, we had a copy, too, and, well, let's say my people have been keeping an eye on them via social networks like Facebook and Google, using throwaway overseas accounts and software running on rented servers in places like Indonesia and Turkey."

"Oh shit," said Huw, running one step ahead of her. "You mean they—"

"I'm getting to it, love. Give me a minute? It's not exactly the NSA, but our system is good enough to keep track of five thousand teenagers from a safe distance. It's all automated, using syntax analysis software to keep an eye on their prose style in case anything happens to them, then squirt a logfile to one of our stay-behind assets"—she shared a glance with Hulius—"every month. Anyway, up till now, nothing's happened. Our herd of little recessive carriers have been left to their own devices. Except, last month, the prototype went missing."

"The proto-what?" Huw sat down. "I thought they were all born over a six-month period." Dr. ven Hjalmar had, with the backing of Duke Angbard, the then head of Clan Security, used a fertility clinic in New England to distribute sperm samples from world-walkers to infertile couples. They'd kept track of the infants: the plan had been to offer the females good money a generation later to act as host mothers for babies that would grow up to be full-fledged world-walkers to supplement the civil war–depleted ranks of the Clan. (This plan had, like all of the Clan's operations in the United States, come to an abrupt end in 2003.)

"Well, that's not entirely true." Brill gave him a slow, appraising look. "There's an older one, born years earlier, who's listed on the database. Actually, she wasn't the product of the breeding project—she predates it—but was added to the list as an adopted-out carrier born in the US."

"Wait—born over there? In the US? But the child of a world-walker?" Hulius raised an eyebrow. "Whose bastard are they? Wasn't that sort of thing frowned upon strongly? Why didn't we—"

Brill raised a hand. "You don't want to know," she said, her tone curiously flat. "Trust me, you don't. Anyway, as of last month, her Facebook page has become curiously bland. No new photo sharing, and the word frequency metric has changed."

"That might not be significant." Huw thought for a moment. "Aren't those social network accounts prone to being hacked?"

"Not so much these days." Brill stopped pacing. "I raised an intelligence order: we should find out something more about this in the next month. It's amazing how many cameras they've got on the Internet over there that aren't properly secured, and how little it costs to get someone to go through their feeds looking for a face."

"Cameras?" Huw looked nonplussed for a moment. The Commonwealth had television now, even in color. There were closed-circuit cameras and videocassette recorders: but they were cumbersome tube-based things that drank electricity and vomited bulky and expensive tapes. Knowing that CCD camera chips and DVDs were possible was one thing: mass-producing them was still a decade away.

"Convenience stores, gas stations. I'm not talking about government surveillance here. We should be able to confirm if she's really missing soon enough. It's often as simple as paying a credit ratings agency or a skip tracer for a report. But the change in social profile is noticeable. Two months ago our prototype was desperate for a job. Now she's clammed up."

"It might be a coincidence." Huw took a deep breath. His pupils were wide: unlike Hulius, he'd obviously added two plus two and gotten the correct result. "She might have been murdered or something. Or just have landed a job that keeps her very busy or that she can't talk about." Another breath. "I'm whistling past the graveyard, aren't I?"

"Yes." Brilliana flashed him a brief, very tense smile. "It looks like the DHS have decided to pull her in, and there can only be one reason why they'd do that. We know they're better than we are at genetics and bioengineering: what do *you* think? My dear, the Survival Committee is going to shit a brick. I might be a little bit paranoid about this, but I think you should prepare to accelerate project JUGGERNAUT. We may be only weeks away from being knee-deep in world-walking spies."

Huw closed his eyes. Leave the political shit to Brill. *Oh what a mess.* "The first driver pits aren't due to arrive until next month, the boost stage tankage isn't even finished, and we've got a lot of testing to do before we're going anywhere. Rudi's flying test-bed was a huge help, but you realize how crazy-dangerous this is? Nobody's ever done anything like this before. At least, not outside Kerbal Space Program."

"Done what?" Hulius said. "Cuz, why *exactly* am I here? And where *is* here, anyway?"

Huw looked at him with mixed affection and exasperation. "You're a world-walker with a pilot's license. Or at least you had a license and you can requalify. What do *you* think you're here for?"

"Um." Hulius's brow wrinkled. "World-walking while flying?"

"Exactly!" Huw slapped the table. "But that's *another* of Brill's projects, and anyway, I'm forgetting my manners. You've just flown in from New London; you must be tired. How about I get Denis to show you to the officers' quarters and give you a chance to stow your kit? Then you must join us for dinner." He glanced at Brilliana. "Unless you've got other plans, we've got a lot of catching up to do . . ."

ST. PETERSBURG, TIME LINE THREE, SPRING 2020

In one of the more fashionable salons of St. Petersburg, in the upper stories of a grand hotel whose gaudily painted onion-domed towers echoed the long-bombed ruins of the Cathedral of the Protection of Most Holy Theotokos on the Moat, two crown princes egged each other on with wilder and more provocative toasts to the demise of their enemies.

"And here's to the extermination of the traitors infesting the Summer Palace in New London: long may their so-called First Man rot in his gibbet when you return at the head of your armada!" Louis, the Dauphin destined to be Louis XXVI of France and her Empire, raised his glass. He was the younger of the two, in his early thirties: blond, cherubic of complexion, with the athletic build of one who had devoted much effort to proving himself in military exercises.

"I'll drink to that," Prince John Frederick Charles of Hanover, by Grace of God heir to the Empire of the Americas, Protector of the Chrysanthemum Throne, and bearer of various other titles, responded laconically. He drained his shot glass of spiced vodka in a single gulp. In his mid-forties, he had gone somewhat to seed in the years of his exile. "Ahh." He held out his glass and a footman stepped forward to refill it.

"I still maintain," said the Dauphin, "that it is in France's best interests that this treasonous uprising be dealt with harshly, to set an example for the ages, and that furthermore the British Crown is the closest of allies compared to the filthy usurpers and their degenerate ideology. So"—he briefly covered his mouth as he hiccuped—"I am at your confidence, cuz, should you choose to confide in me as to how I might best help a brother monarch."

The current fashion in St. Petersburg was a collision of revival styles, the baroque competing with the classical. The two princes reclined on Romanesque couches in a modern and perhaps overelaborate re-creation of a triclinium, while their seven most-favored courtiers (and their mistresses) made elegant and humorous conversation for their edification. Swagged velvet drapes surrounded the gilt-framed floor-to-ceiling windows, beneath fans that twirled lazily overhead. At one side of the room, an imported Japanese stereoautogram played popular love ballads, recordings of a brass band with string accompaniment and drums. Perfumiers from old France used handheld fans to waft the lightest of scents toward their majesties. Belowstairs, in a refectory adjacent to the kitchen, young peasant girls sampled morsels beneath the gaze of gaunt-faced doctors before the courses were served upstairs; their vigilance came of knowing what would happen if a poisoned dish slipped through their guard.

"An uprising of serfs is best dealt with by the law of divide and rule," Prince John Frederick said slowly. A surprisingly studious, scholarly fellow—for a crown prince—he was reputed to have read far more widely than his disengaged father, and it was whispered that while his father had tinkered with clockwork for a hobby, the son had a soul of spring steel and gears that powered a mind like a mantrap. "You pay your Army to crush the rebels using the rebels' own property as fuel for the machine. But if the rebellion cements a new government in place, especially one that is popular, dislodging it becomes far harder. My father spent the last seven years of his life trying to convince hoi polloi that their so-called Revolution was a monstrous aberration that would eat them all in the end, but they didn't heed his warnings."

He raised his glass toward his lips, nostrils flaring as he sniffed the liquid. "But. *But.* It is the natural way of the world for men to seek a just and honest ruler. The ruler the revolutionaries chose was, by all accounts, austere and serious. But he is close to death. When he goes, there will be an opportunity to take advantage of the bickering among his followers. The most corrupt and untrustworthy of their number will seek to occupy his chair: they will discredit their own revolution, and I shall make use of the opportunity."

"I suppose your spies keep you well-informed of the bickering among the peasant clique?"

John Frederick met the Dauphin's gaze. "I couldn't say."

"Indeed not. Nor would you stoop to encourage disquiet among the usurpers by engineering acts of vandalism, either through your loyal supporters or by means of paid agents?"

"Of course not. What kind of monarch would I make if I were preparing a wave of civil unrest to follow the demise of the rabble's leader? It would be unconscionable. I must be seen as a sympathetic and emollient king, one whose return heals all ills and settles all grievances after years of misrule. And of course I must be a peacemaker as well."

"External as well as internal, I should hope?"

"Yes, cuz." The prince lowered his glass and frowned at it thoughtfully. "The corpuscular era renders the prospect of war between sovereign empires unthinkable, does it not?" He met the Dauphin's gaze steadily. "Tit for tat, they call their strategy. After the children's game. But the usurping peasants' strategic planners are not fools, however baseless their claim to power might be."

"I would like to propose a treaty." The French heir snapped his fingers. Deft hands stripped away the vodka glasses, then presented a silver platter and two goblets of fine pear brandy. "Once you are back on your rightful throne, our two great empires must take every possible step to make common cause, so that a war fought with corpuscular weapons becomes as unthinkable as the prospect of a revolution overturning the rightful reign of a monarch. Your daughter is going to be eighteen soon enough, isn't she? And unless your lady wife provides you with a son late in the day, Elizabeth will be your heir."

John Frederick's eyes widened. "I say, that's rather a big step!"

"Yes, but it would solve our dilemma, would it not? It would put an end to the persistent libelous rumor that you are my father's unwilling prisoner. *And* it would give me good and sufficient reason to demand that my father grant me command of the Empire's forces, to the extent necessary to assist you in retaking your throne."

"To place you on *her* throne," John Frederick retorted. "As Prince-Consort, as well as, in the due fullness of time—God save him!—your father's seat. Louis, why *now* and not ten years ago? Where did this half-baked idea come from? What has turned your head in the past week? Please do not ask me to believe that you dreamed it up on your own without benefit of ministerial counsel. Or that Liz has fallen in love with you and offered to elope."

"Of course not." Louis gave the English monarch a heavy-lidded stare. "And you're absolutely right. I haven't suddenly had my head turned by the ethereal beauty of your precious jewel of a daughter, cousin. She is somewhat willful—some might even say waspish—and I believe I need not inform you of her opinion of *me*, or of my mistress. But the times turn, and the seasons change, and the usurpers have proven themselves to be uncommonly ingenious in the mechanical arts, have they not?" He snapped his fingers and glanced over his shoulder: "Bring me my new toy now!" he called.

Back to John Frederick: "There have been more unwelcome developments, and I think some in particular that you need to see with your own two eyes." Behind them, a quartet of liveried servants pushed and heaved a television set into the room—a hulking piece of cabinetry fronted by a circular green glass disk—and positioned it at an angle convenient for the princes. "We are used to reigning as of right, cousin. But things are spinning out of control: the revolutionaries are ingenious, and I very much fear that unless we hang together and put an end to this nonsense as fast as possible, then dedicate our lives and those of our heirs to suppressing it, we will hang separately . . ."

PART TWO
FAST TRACK

Learning carries within itself certain dangers because
out of necessity one has to learn from one's enemies.
—Leon Trotsky

Training Mission

Two months after her abortive kidnapping, Rita was allowed a weekend trip home to visit her family. In fact, she was urged to do so. "E-mail and Facebook aren't enough," explained her supervisor, an affable African American named Patrick O'Neill who'd worked surveillance operations when he was in the FBI. "If you vanish off the face of the earth for weeks, then send them vaguely reassuring messages, your parents will worry that you've been abducted; it's entirely natural. But you've been through basic orientation and briefing now, and it'll make life a lot easier for us—and for them—if you go home and explain what's happened."

"Easier for you?" Rita asked dubiously.

Patrick shrugged. "Your grandpa's been rattling the bars. Your father's even talking about hiring a private eye, just to shut him up. It's not going to help anybody if they waste money on a wild-goose chase, and we figure they'll calm right down if they get a chance to see you in person. Regularly, even. So we've got a cover package for you that should hold up for a weekend, and we can work it into your training schedule. Think of it as a field exercise. We'll recycle the same cover when you go to Quantico for the National Academy course, so it'll help you bed in."

"Okay!" Rita resisted the urge to jump up and down. Eight weeks of grueling exercise and six-hour classroom days at the TSA's off-world Camp Graceland training center had begun to blur into a hellish cross between the Girl Scouts, college, and a prison.

Camp Graceland was a boot camp for spies. The teacher/student ratio was nearly 1:1, and except for her direct supervisor, Patrick, everybody knew her by a false name. They had started with medical tests (drug tests, epigenetic methylation scans: the usual), then rushed her through a bunch of interviews and security checks—some while being monitored by a polygraph, others with her head stuck in an fMRI scanner. She still remembered the Very Serious security officer's expression as he'd asked if she was now, or ever had been, a Communist: he'd been a sight. (The question was clearly the legacy of some paranoid congressional imposition on the national security apparat. "No, but my grandpa Kurt used to be one, and I send him photographs of government buildings via dead letter drop" clearly wasn't on the list of acceptable answers.) It had led to her explaining her geocaching hobby to him—and the idea that there was an entire subculture of folks who went on furtive Internet-mediated treasure hunts for buried objects using GPS and old-school spy tradecraft seemed to have caused him deep personal distress. Luckily for her, eccentricity was not yet illegal. So she eventually passed the checks.

The interviews and a swearing-in were followed by a weeklong basic organizational orientation course, then a stripped-down version of the training that National Clandestine Service people got. The upcoming course at Quantico was more conventional—it was the law enforcement leadership course the FBI ran for other organizations. Clearly someone upstairs thought it might help if she knew how to think like a senior cop . . . or a senior counterespionage officer. "When do I go?"

"You've got two more weeks on this segment," said Patrick. "We'll use the final week to work up your cover and establish operating procedures. Then you get to go on leave on Friday, using your cover while traveling. You don't need to use the cover while you're with your folks, but resume on Monday when you travel to Quantico."

"Huh." She paused. "How much can I tell them? How much do you want me to hold back?"

Patrick checked a file on his tablet. "You can tell them you landed a job with DHS; that's not a problem. If they know anything about your, uh, birth parents, you can hint that it's connected. But they don't need to know about Graceland, about anything that's happening here, or anything you've been told is classified or that you suspect is classified and somebody screwed up and forgot to tell you about. And if they don't already know about your birth mother's capability, they don't need to learn about it now. There's a cover story for them—a boring office job and some stuff you periodically get asked about. If they conclude that we've roped you in so we can keep an eye on you, that's perfect, because it's partly true."

"Right." Rita paused. "I don't like lying to my parents," she admitted. It went against every instinct of her upbringing: but then, so did opening up and telling Patrick what she was thinking. It had taken weeks of work on both their parts to get to the point where it was possible. Rita was independent-minded, suspicious, and somewhat antiauthoritarian. She'd have been a complete washout for a regular DHS job: but a human intelligence agent—or HUMINT asset, as the organization referred to them—required an entirely different profile. "It goes against the grain."

"We don't *want* you to lie to them. People are mostly very bad at lying, and good at telling when folks they know are lying to them. What we want is for you to tell them the truth—but only the safe bits. This way, you can calm them down and reassure them not to worry about you, and then you can stop worrying about them—which you have been doing, to the point where if you keep doing it it'll impair your ability to do your job." He raised an eyebrow. "Did you think we hadn't noticed?"

"No." Rita flushed.

"Kid, you're wound up tighter than a drum. We're training you for one of the most specialized and stressful missions; you'll do your job better if you're not looking over your shoulder the whole time worrying about your family. Anyway, we'll start on your cover briefing tomorrow. Right now you're due to start the Intro to Crypto workshop with Melissa from No Such Agency in about ten minutes: I'd get moving if I were you."

NEAR PHOENIX, TIME LINE TWO, MAY 2020

"Mom?"

"Rita! Where have you been?"

"Long story, Mom. Listen, is Dad around? Grandpa? What about River, is he okay—"

"Yes, yes, everyone's all right! Are you—"

"I'm about thirty miles up the road, Mom, driving a rental. I can be with you in an hour?"

"Oh my, oh my, yes. Come right over. Listen, are you in trouble?"

"Not exactly, but I've got a new job and things are complicated. Can it wait so I can tell everyone over dinner?"

"Oh! Yes, yes, you're right. Come right on over."

"Love you, Mom. Bye."

"Love you too."

Click.

Rita hunched over the steering wheel of the rental, breathing deeply for a minute, then slid her split-personality phone away. It didn't seem real, exactly: there was a sheet of invisible glass between her and the world now, unreflecting, intangible, but a barrier nonetheless. *And I'm not Rita. I'm Anna, until I get home.* "Anna Mittal," read the name on her Arizona driver's license. With an address in Phoenix, age twenty-four, a physiotherapist. Not: Rita Douglas, age twenty-five, Boston resident and driver's license, former nonunion actor turned DHS probationary employee with payroll records pointing to a back-office job vetting frequent fliers for the streamlined secure boarding program.

"It's a game," Patrick had explained during one of the briefing sessions. (Training doctrine called for the gamification of everything short of "wet ops"—assassination. Games were, after all, formalized play, and play was how young mammals acquired and then performed essential life skills.) "Your objective is to minimize your threat surface when exposed to a hostile environment; in this case, all you need to do to flip between Rita and Anna. There'll be a different protocol if we ever send you overseas, but these are the basics, and practicing on your family is a great way to upskill yourself. Just remember not to show Anna's ID card or SIM personality to your folks, or Rita's to any Hostiles, and you'll do fine."

The car did most of the driving for thirty miles, finally beeping for human supervision when it reached the main street leading to the

subdivision her family lived in. The suburbs were undergoing a mild re-
naissance, recovering from the gas price–induced real-estate wilt of the
noughties. Franz had followed a job out here, Emily joining him
along with her brother, River, another adoptee. They'd snapped up a
McMansion in a not-too-decrepit area for cash and extended themselves
on credit to adapt an adjacent house for Grandpa Kurt, on the not-
unreasonable theory that when Grandpa didn't need it anymore they'd
be able to turn a profit on it for the kids. Back when gas had been four
bucks a gallon, commuting from here would have been a real strain, but
with gas at eighty cents, thanks to imports from other time lines, it was a
different story. The neighborhood was rising: only the unnatural green of
the Astroturfed front yards hinted at the real cost of living large.

Rita didn't like Arizona. It was currently run by a Dominionist gover-
nor who rallied his followers with a dog whistle, with a creepy Save the
Babies/Defense of Marriage proposition on the ballot to amend the state
constitution at the next election. But it was where her family had moved:
if she wanted to see them, she could either visit Jesusland or use her
phone camera.

Rita pulled in behind a familiar SUV and parked. She swapped her ID
cards again, reset her phone, and hauled out her carry-on. She walked up
to the front door, smiling and waving at the camera: "Hi, Mom! It's me!"

The door clicked open. "Rita!" Emily hugged her. "We've been so
worried! Where have you *been*? Come in, let's shut the door." It was almost
a hundred Fahrenheit outside, seventy-five indoors.

"Long story." Rita dropped her bag in the hallway. "Ancient history
came looking for me, but I'm okay."

"Coffee first. Your room's waiting for you: I left the bedding off to air,
but it's same as always. River's in class but he'll probably be home by
six—"

"Gramps?"

"He's out, as usual at this time of day. He volunteers at a Goodwill
shop. Not Goodwill, a different charity, but you know what I mean." Emily
retreated toward the kitchen; Rita followed. She hadn't seen her mom in
three months. There was more gray in her hair, and her cheeks seemed
to sag more than ninety days could account for. "Don't worry, by the way,

I've finished all my work today. I was thinking about cooking up a feast for tonight, seeing we're a full family." She smiled. "Want to help me shop for food?"

"Oh, Mom. Yes, but you don't have to—"

"The hell I don't! First you're off to Seattle on that hand-to-mouth thing, then you disappear for a couple of days, and the next I hear is some horrible news—an attempted abduction? And we're visited by a couple of men in black who tell us everything is going to be fine, then you barely write, much less call, for weeks and weeks—"

Her mother's shoulders were shaking. Rita stared for a moment, then closed the gap and hugged her. "Listen, it's going to be *all right*. But—" She hesitated. "I'm going to have to ask you about my, uh, birth mother: everything you know about the . . . before you adopted me—"

"Oh, hon." Emily sniffed. "I was hoping you wouldn't ask me that. Or it could wait for another few years. Until everything was a bit . . . calmer."

"Calm." Only her mother would use that word to talk about the biggest national trauma of the century. "Mom. Listen, it's okay. They, uh, gave me a job. I think so they can keep an eye on me. The DHS, I mean. It's just that I need to know everything *you* know. For my own safety?" She heard a whine threatening to climb into her voice, made herself stop talking.

"I get that. Thing is, hon, we didn't *know* anything. No, that's not quite right. I mean, yes, Kurt suspected something. A bit. But we didn't put two and two together until after 7/16. We thought it was just the usual sort of problem, that your birth mother had just been unlucky and you could live a normal life. It wasn't until after 7/16, and the visit from the FBI, that we realized who she must have been." Rita let go and took a step back. "Well, I mean I, I never met her! It mostly went through the lawyers. But her mother—your grandmother, I guess—Kurt knew her, and he introduced us this one time and she seemed perfectly nice."

"Wait." Rita shook her head. It was too much to assimilate quickly. "A grandmother? You mean, I've got a grandmother?"

"Maybe. Maybe not." Her mom shrugged uncomfortably. "She was on crutches, Rita. She had MS. A few years later Kurt said he'd seen her and she was in a wheelchair. Then she disappeared. This would have been, oh, late 2002 or early 2003. A while before 7/16. Months, maybe a year."

"She disappeared? How come?"

"I don't know. Ask your grandfather; he might know some more. But Rita, you've got to understand—*we didn't know.* Nobody knew about the world-walker thing. Or the bombs. That all happened years later, and we only figured it out when the FBI came and interviewed us after 7/16. All we knew was that this nice lady, a friend of Kurt's, whose daughter had got in trouble at college, and was looking for adopters. And Franz and I were never going to have babies ourselves."

"Oh, Mom." The coffeemaker began to hiss, then clicked loudly. Rita moved instinctively toward the cupboard with the mugs. It was something to occupy her hands with while her brain tried to catch up.

"I hope you don't think I blame you for any of it."

"No, Mom. I don't. Fat-free or half-and-half?"

"I'm on fat-free again. I'm sorry. I thought you were better off out of it, not knowing. It wasn't your fault. I can't believe your birth mother had anything to do with it—or her mother, for that matter. I honestly thought it was all in the past and there was nothing to worry about anymore . . . until they came and started asking us questions about you a couple of months ago."

"Mom? Here's your coffee." Rita tried to conceal her disquiet: *of course* they'd have visited Emily and Franz as part of her background check. Why wouldn't they?

"Thank you, dear." With a visible shudder, Emily pulled herself together. "Then I need to go shopping. Come with me and you can catch up on all the gossip."

That evening, after an exhausting family dinner—almost a mini-Thanksgiving, with a distinct subtext of gratitude for Rita's delivery from whatever durance vile she had been consigned to by the DHS—Rita walked home with her grandfather Kurt. It wasn't much of a walk, but it put some distance between Rita and Emily's hand wringing, Franz's quiet concern, and River's brattish teenage-brother act. "Come in, come in," Kurt mumbled as he held the front door open for her. "Out of the heat."

It was hot in Kurt's abode too: he kept the upper floor closed off, sleeping in the downstairs den next to the living room and venturing up top only to shower. But it was cooler than the desert evening outside, and it was quiet, with only her usually taciturn grandfather for company.

"You must tell me the truth," Kurt said, "Over a beer." It came out like an order, a throwback to his youth.

"I'd rather not."

Kurt snorted, then pulled out his phone. He placed it inside a fleecy bedroom slipper on the boot rack by the front door, raised an eyebrow, and offered the other slipper to Rita. After a moment's hesitation, she copied him.

Kurt led her through the front hall to the kitchen and closed the connecting door. The refrigerator was well-stocked with imports that reminded Kurt of home—Schöfferhofer, Weihenstephaner, Maisel's Weisse—and a six-pack of Miller Ice for visitors. He ate most evenings with Franz and Emily; after Greta had died, he'd retreated into quiet introspection, his son and daughter-in-law and grandchildren the focus of his remaining social life. Rita had been worried by his withdrawal, but the news that he'd taken a volunteer job sounded hopeful.

Kurt pulled two bottles from the fridge, popped their caps, and carefully poured them into a pair of ceramic steins. "Drink," he told her. "I know you didn't tell your parents everything. Nobody ever does. Come into the living room and unwind. I'll tell you a story."

"What do you mean?" Rita followed Kurt into the living room. It was furnished mostly in shades of brown and orange leavened by outbreaks of ancient black leather, like a washed-up seventies bachelor pad, and it smelt faintly of stale cigarettes. Kurt had been giving up tobacco for as long as she could remember. He walked stiffly, wincing slightly: his hips were hurting again.

"When I was a young man, fresh out of the Volksarmee, let me tell you, it was a different world. There were seventeen million of us in East Germany, and over a hundred thousand secret police in the Stasi. Think of it—two and a half times as many *secret* police per person as there are ordinary cops in America! And ordinary VoPo—Volkspolizei—on top! But that's not all. The Stasi used informers, half a million of them.

Maybe two million irregular informers. One in eight people were snitches. You couldn't drink at a bar without drinking with a snitch. So we drank at home. *Prost*."

He raised his stein. Hesitantly, Rita raised hers in return. They'd been doing this since she was fourteen, although he'd had the sense to start her on the *alkoholfrei*. This wasn't Germany, after all.

"Of course, these days they don't need informers—your phone does it for you. So no need for nice Herr Staatssicherheit to buy you a beer, make you feel good, and offer you the life of adventure and secrecy and free goodies in return for playing spy-on-my-neighbor." Her grandfather raised an eyebrow at her. "That's not what happened to you, is it?" She shook her head. "Good. When they asked me to spy for them—I was your age—I was young and foolish, but not *that* foolish. I was listening to *Feindsender* and reading stuff I really shouldn't be caught with when I was in the factory. So maybe they thought, *ach*, I was a young tearaway but not so crazy I didn't fit in during my time in the Army, so they could use me: tell me to go to music clubs and listen to people who talk too much to people they really should not trust. And you know, in those days, if you do as they tell you and tell stories, you maybe get ahead, get promoted faster? That sort of thing."

"They asked *you*?" Rita goggled at him.

"Yes, the Stasi asked me." Kurt's face crinkled into a grin. "Them, asking me, made me ask some questions of myself, I can tell you. I didn't much like the answers. But as we used to say, the opposite of 'well done' is 'well meant.' I devised a way out, and the next evening I went to my local bar and got drunk. I told anybody who listened how the Stasi asked me to spy for them. And they never asked me again." He took a gulp of wheat beer and sighed happily.

"I'm not an informer," Rita said hesitantly. "But they made me a job offer. I wasn't allowed to refuse it." *So far so good.* "I think they want to keep an eye on me. A close eye."

"They can arrest you," Kurt said dismissively. "Why do you think they *want* you?"

Rita sat down on the edge of the sofa, opposite Kurt's recliner. "Tell me about my, my birth mother . . ."

"I never met her." Kurt sniffed. "*Her* mother, though, I knew her kind. An illegal, living under a false identity. I guessed she was on the run, had been involved with the Weather Underground or something like that. Wanted by the FBI. Anyway, she did not fit in on her own. Turned up in Boston and hooked up with a Jewish bookstore clerk, man called Beckstein. That was in '72 . . .'73? I met her later, in '91, through your grandmother. She was with a group of counterculture dissidents, optimists who didn't believe it was just the same shit on either side of the Wall. Anyway, in '94 her daughter gets in trouble at med school. Has to choose, career or *Kinder*. And Mrs. Beckstein asks me, your fine daughter-in-law and her fertility problem, does she still want a baby?"

Rita licked her lips. "Mom's problem was that early?" "Problem" was the family euphemism for uterine cancer. The ob-gyn had spotted it soon enough that the surgery was a complete success, but it had put an end to Emily's baby-making plans before she even got started.

"Yes." Kurt nodded. "So we talk it over, Mrs. Beckstein and your mother and me and your father, and we agree to work it out. Which is where you come from."

"Tell me about Mrs. Beckstein . . . ?"

"Why?" He looked at her sharply. "What do you know about her?"

Rita licked her suddenly dry lips. "She's one of the, the world-walkers."

"Right." Kurt nodded. No attempt at dissembling: *You knew,* she thought. "The FBI came calling when you were eight. You don't remember, of course; they are not idiots to arrest small children."

"But you, aren't you—"

"Appalled? That she's one of the people who blowed—blew—up the White House? Rita, she was a runaway! A refusenik. One who walked away, taking her daughter. You might as well blame me for the shootings at the Berlin Wall." Kurt sat up straighter. "You listen to me, girl: you must not be ashamed of her. All groups have dissidents. All groups have those who reject them, change their names—just like me, your grandfather Douglas: a good American name, no? I change my name because even after I come over here I do not want to make it easy for the GDR embassy to write to me. Now you . . . tell me. What do the DHS *really* want with you?"

"I—" Rita froze. "I'm not supposed to tell you. I'm supposed to spin a story about how they were following up records and ran across my, my birth mother. And offered me an office job where they can keep an eye on me in case the world-walkers come looking for me."

Kurt nodded encouragement. "Yes?"

"Well, I—" She licked her lips again, then abruptly took a mouthful of beer and put her stein down on the coffee table. "The world-walkers came looking. Kidnapped me and stuffed me in my car trunk. Luckily the DHS were there, and—" Kurt was shaking his head. "What?"

"Nothing. Go on."

"I'm *not* a world-walker," she said, crossing her arms defensively. "But they said the world-walkers appear to think . . ." She trailed off.

"Rita." Kurt peered at his stein, then shook his head: "They always lie to you. *Always.* It's the first law of *Staatssicherheit.* The American *Heimatschutzministerium* is no different from the Stasi in the old days, except they have more money."

"If you think it's so bad, why did you come here?" she demanded, hating her words the moment she heard them.

"Because"—for a moment he looked every one of his seventy-seven years—"we *knew* our government was lying to us about our glorious socialist system: so we thought they were lying about the evils of capitalism, too! Also, everything here was good at first. It was only later"—he looked wistful, or frustrated, or both—"it was only after the failure of actually existing socialism to deliver the goods that we learned they'd been telling the truth *some* of the time. Whenever it was convenient for them. And that the other side had been lying too, whenever it was convenient for *them*. The best kind of lie is one that is a selective version of the truth, leaving out the messy, sticky, embarrassing bits. They *all* lie—the difficult part is telling when they aren't. And even so, many things are still better here."

He looked round, miming confusion, at the shag pile carpet and the 72-inch TV. "Big houses, big cars, big steaks, big government. It's true: capitalism delivers the goods. It also delivers big police, the Internet *Rasterfahndung* . . . " He sighed. "They don't talk about that, though, any more than the Communists liked to admit that their less-unequal society was also poorer. For people so obsessed with freedom, they have a surprising number of police. But this is my home now, and I am too old to start over, and besides, Germany is not so different today. Unless you are a woman of a certain type, of course, in which case perhaps Germany is more welcoming."

He gave Rita a knowing look, then picked up his stein and took another mouthful. (Chugging the German import wheat beers in one gulp was inadvisable, as Rita had discovered the hard way some years ago.) "Remember this, Granddaughter: they lie to you, but you can learn the truth if you look for the silence between the lies." He paused for a moment. "If you were useless to them, they would ignore you. If you were a threat to them, they would put you in prison. So they must think you are useful to them."

"I told you, the world-walkers tried to—"

He cut her off with a gesture. "This happened right after the DHS spoke to you? How convenient!"

"But they tried to kidnap me—"

"Did you see them world-walk? No? Then how do you know they were world-walkers?"

"But one of them was shot by the police! I saw it happen!"

"So?" Kurt snorted. "A local lowlife is hired to abduct a woman—who cares what happens to him?"

"You're saying the DHS kidnapped me? And told me it was world-walkers? *Why?*" She was mustering her objections one by one, and Kurt was knocking them down, just as she'd been afraid he would.

He shrugged. "I don't know that that happened. And you don't know that it didn't, do you? It could be a way of making you say 'yes' to their job offer, couldn't it? Like the beer in that bar in Dresden that time, and the promises of adventure to a young man. Do you know why they want you?"

Rita shook her head, acutely aware as she did so of a growing sense of self-betrayal. "I have no idea," she lied, for in truth she *did* know: but she couldn't tell Kurt *They plan to make a world-walker of me* in a room that might be wired. "I need to find out, though, don't I?"

"Yes, you do. They will of course have told you not to discuss this matter with anyone. Especially your grandfather. So we have not had this conversation!" Kurt announced to the room. He emptied his stein. "Well, that's it for me for this evening," he said thoughtfully.

Rita set her own tankard down. It was still a quarter full. "I'd better get back home."

"You do that." Was that disappointment in his voice? Or just her guilty imagination?

"I'll see myself out," she said.

"Of course." As she walked to the door, he added, "if you ever decide to tell me the rest of your story, I'll be here. I'll trade you for more about your third grandmother."

He wasn't disappointed: he was amused. But of course, he could read her like a book. Rita slammed the door on her way out and stomped back to her parents' house in a foul mood. They, at least, seemed to believe what she told them. But then, they'd never played footsie with the Stasi. Whereas Grandpa Kurt—

—had taught her everything she knew.

On Saturday, Rita went to a ball game with Dad and River. On Sunday morning, she declined an invitation to go to church with her mom. Instead she went for a long walk with her fatphone and a geocaching Web site for company. She found and logged two caches, collected a travel bug from one of them ("Help me get to New Zealand!" it declared: having started in Anchorage, she figured a ride to Maryland wouldn't hurt), reported another cache as muggled (removed by noncachers), and went home. In the afternoon she hung out with Kurt at the thrift store he volunteered at, which was hosting some kind of local artists' event in support of their mission. She didn't apologize for lying to him and he didn't let her off the hook, but by tacit assent they avoided the subject and instead kept the conversation to anodyne matters like the game, a dumb sitcom, and Dad's work. It kicked the ball down the road a way, but it wasn't like she had to tell Kurt anything, was it?

The art display struck her as naive and a bit tacky, but the thrift store had a bunch of other stuff, ranging from ancient laptops and tablets through souvenirs and a couple of bookcases stuffed with musty-smelling old paper books. Kurt paused beside one, ran his hand along a shelf, then presented her with a dog-eared paperback, its cover missing. "You should read this," he said, handing it to her.

Rita held it between finger and thumb. "It's probably moldy," she said, nose wrinkling. "Why should I? What's so special about"—she checked the title page—"*The Grasshopper Lies Heavy*, by, uh—"

"It's out of print; you won't find it on Amazon," said Kurt. "Which is odd, because the author also wrote *Do Androids Dream of Electric Sheep?*, the book behind *Blade Runner*. You have seen *Blade Runner*?" He sighed when she shook her head. "Read this anyway—it is an excellent allegory for the totalitarian mind, and also nobody can examine your online annotations or page-turning habits on paper."

"Gramps, you're being paranoid! Anyway, it can't be any good if it's gone out of print, can it?"

Kurt merely turned away, his sardonic smile fading. Stung, Rita hovered for a moment, then took the yellowing block of paper to the front desk. "Oh, just take it," Allie the clerk told her. "They've been clogging up the back for years. Nobody buys those things anymore."

After lunch, Rita loaded up her rental and said her goodbyes, hugging Mom and Dad and promising to write more often. Kurt saw her out to the car. "Your birth mother's mother was a good woman," he said gravely. "Not one of the mad bombers. Remember that. Remember, too, you may work *for* the Stasi, but you do not need to be *of* the Stasi."

"Oh, Gramps." Rita shook her head. "Spare me the riddles?" She hugged him, but his attention seemed to be focused elsewhere, inward. So she closed her car door and became Anna Mittal again for the drive back to the airport, and the DHS highway checkpoint that nearly made her miss her flight.

CAMP GRACELAND, TIME LINE FOUR;
QUANTICO; TIME LINE TWO,
MAY–JULY 2020

The next ten weeks passed too fast for Rita to write to her folks, let alone take another weekend off work. The National Academy course was physically exhausting. While the Department of Homeland Security trainers at Camp Graceland had put her in the gym daily and begun working on her self-defense, most of the people attending the FBI course had military or police backgrounds, and everyone was expected to keep up. It was also mentally grueling, if not demoralizing. Some of her classmates had antediluvian attitudes toward women and people of Indian appearance, especially slightly built women of Indian appearance. It wasn't what they said to her, exactly, but what they *didn't* say.

She was on her own, without any of the peer support her classmates gave each other. There were lectures on law, behavioral science, forensics, and terrorism and terrorist mind-sets. The stuff about leadership development made her head spin. Rita did not do well in these classes, especially the areas that emphasized policing skills. "Not to worry about it," Patrick told her when he visited during week three: "You're not going to be a cop, and even if you were, this stuff isn't about basic entry-level police work that you could expect to pick up. Just go with the flow and try to get a handle on how senior cops think, because if you get to go out in the field these are the people who'll be looking for you."

"I guess." Her eyes narrowed involuntarily. "But about that: I don't think my cover's holding."

"What, has anyone accused you of being an impostor?"

"No, it's just that—I can tell—they know I'm not really one of them. Some of them are playing along deliberately, and a couple have cut me dead, but I'm *really* not fitting in. Not sure whether I'm being given the cold shoulder because I'm not a . . . not a typical cop," she said weakly.

Patrick's face hardened. "Any overt racism?"

"No, but—"

"Has anybody called you out, to your face . . . ?"

"No, I think it's more that they think I'm some kind of fake."

"Then it's not a problem. Drop it." O'Neill's tone was hard. "You're not expected to graduate top of your course. Or even in the upper half. You're here to learn how detectives think, what makes them tick." He thought for a moment. "We'll give you a second-level story. They already know you're DHS. If anyone challenges you, tell them the truth: you're undergoing deep-cover training. The spin is that you'll be infiltrating activist groups as a long-term informer. If you don't mention the world-walkers, nobody's going to look for that angle; it's too weird. If they think the DHS is running spies into activist groups, that'll keep them happy." He paused. "Racism is another thing. Official policy is zero tolerance, but you know what *that's* worth. If you get any trouble, call me and I'll get the Colonel to drop the hammer on them. That is all."

"What's . . . ?" Rita paused. "Yeah, I can do that." *Pretend to be exactly what I am. Tell Patrick if I get any of the other shit. Maybe they're not all assholes. Maybe that's why I got a non-Anglo supervisor.*

"Just don't volunteer any information unless you're directly challenged and you'll be fine."

"Apart from the bruises and the Marine assault course they expect me to pass!"

· Patrick snorted.

As it happened, nobody challenged Rita to her face. So after another week she deliberately slipped some tells into her classwork—showing more interest than was strictly necessary in the law surrounding under-cover informers, or in evasion techniques used by terrorists. After that, a couple of the guys who had been avoiding her started to nod in passing. There were even some brief, guarded conversations in the canteen. They thought they had her pigeonholed. It made life a little more bearable, which she came to appreciate as the physical regime and long classroom hours ground down on her. It didn't break the ice all around: for some people her skin would always mark her out as *other*. But it wasn't only her skin that was the problem—simple racism would have been stamped on, hard, by the instructors. By week six she was coming to suspect that the real problem was in her head.

Rita was lonely, an introvert exposed to an extrovert culture. She could fake it in the classroom and exercises by putting on a front, just like she could act on stage. But the continual effort over a period of weeks left her scant energy for socializing in the evenings; nor was the prospect of barroom bonding with sheriffs from small towns and lieutenants from big-city forces remotely appealing to her. The cultural chasm she perceived when she looked at her classmates was dizzying. They'd chosen a career in law enforcement. She was something else, so different that she felt like a fraud—not through any kind of criminal inclination, but because where they saw things in red and blue she saw an infinite range of purples.

The graduate-level coursework she could focus on; the fitness regime was a weak point. But if she failed at anything, it was the networking and team building.

Finally, after ten weeks, the ordeal was over. She said her abbreviated goodbyes to classmates who had remained strangers throughout, and slunk back to Camp Graceland with her tail between her legs.

"Good luck with your *Mission: Impossible* assignment, wherever they send you," said Martina, her course director, a grizzled FBI senior agent turned teacher. "You didn't fool anybody, by the way," she added with a smile. "But we don't mind. I just hope you got whatever your handlers sent you here for."

Surgical Intervention

BALTIMORE, TIME LINE TWO, MAY 2020

FEDERAL EMPLOYEE 004910023 CLASSIFIED VOICE TRANSCRIPT

DR. SCRANTON: I have some bad news for you gentlemen. We lost another drone to the anomalous time line yesterday. That's time line 178. Situation's escalating.

LIAISON, CENTRAL INTELLIGENCE AGENCY: Fuck.

COL. SMITH: Louis, what can you tell us about it?

LIAISON, AIR FORCE: Mission three was flown by an RQ-4 DarkStar. It departed from Wright-Patterson AFB at 1620 local time, then headed south until it crossed over water, topped up from an Air Force tanker, and climbed to flight level 700. Once at cruise altitude it triggered its ARMBAND unit to take it to the destination time line via time line one, and that's all we know. It's more than a day past its minimum fuel reserve time, so we're calling it a definite hull loss.

COL. SMITH: Wait a minute. If this was mission three, what were the first two?

LIAISON, AIR FORCE: We followed the usual protocol for newly opened indirect-access time lines: a ground-level atmospheric sample-return box to confirm the presence of air and gravity, then mapping using MQ-1 Predators. They fly in daylight at medium altitude, with cameras set up to perform a wide-area survey of the eastern seaboard area. They were expecting business as usual: an uninhabited wasteland or, at most, Paleolithic hunter-gatherers. But neither of them came back, and after two hull losses in a row, some bright spark decided to up the ante. The RQ-4 is a high-altitude stealth drone, sort of an unmanned U-2 analog. And it's now overdue. Never showed up. Didn't activate its DOOMWATCH device, either—

DR. SCRANTON: DOOMWATCH?

LIAISON, AIR FORCE: It's a special ARMBAND unit—a world-walking machine—with a flight data recorder attached. It's switched on right before the drone transitions to its target time line and logs all the telemetry from the drone's flight control system and instruments. If the drone does anything unpredictable, DOOMWATCH ejects and transitions back to the home time line immediately, then pops a parachute. That way, if there's no breathable atmosphere or the UAV encounters a thunderstorm or some other irrecoverable situation, at least we get an idea of what happened.

DR. SCRANTON: So you got a positive for atmosphere and gravity using the preliminary sample return box, but then lost three drones in a row. The last of them a high-altitude stealth machine. But the Air Force aren't totally stupid—

COL. SMITH: Thank you!

LIAISON, AIR FORCE: Indeed. So this morning we sent up a sacrificial Tier 1 UAV, a Gnat 750, programmed to bounce over to time line one, continue to time line 178, buzz around at five hundred feet for a while, then phone home. The first three drones were real aircraft, things that need a runway and ground crew; the Gnat is a toy with a ten-foot wingspan that you launch off the back of a jeep. Anyway, it came back bang on schedule. Its meteorology package said conditions over there were fine, too.

LIAISON, CENTRAL INTELLIGENCE AGENCY: Shit.

COL. SMITH: The scatological commentary is getting old, Barney.

LIAISON, CENTRAL INTELLIGENCE AGENCY: Sorry. It's been a bad week.

DR. SCRANTON: If you've quite finished?

COL. SMITH: Sorry, sir. Please continue.

LIAISON, AIR FORCE: Well, we picked up something interesting from the Gnat. They sent it up from McGuire AFB in New Jersey, not Wright-Patterson, and it hedge-hopped around Pennsylvania for an hour, and here are some of its holiday snaps.

LIAISON, CENTRAL INTELLIGENCE AGENCY: Holy—sorry.

COL. SMITH: Well, isn't *that* interesting.

DR. SCRANTON: The cat is out of the bag, gentlemen.

LIAISON, AIR FORCE: (pointing) That's a railroad switchyard. And here's some kind of industrial plant—a factory, we think, but this is preliminary. That definitely looks like an ore conveyor, though—

COL. SMITH: Yes. So we have heavy industry for sure, and we can infer the existence of air defenses. Possibly even defenses that can take out an RQ-4. (pause) Has anyone briefed NCA yet? NSC? The Joint Chiefs?

DR. SCRANTON: There's worse to come.

COL. SMITH: Oh dear.

LIAISON, AIR FORCE: I hadn't got to the air samples yet. They show a surprisingly low level of PM10 and PM50 particulates, which mostly come from diesel engines. This tends to suggest that they use all-electric traction on their railroads. But then there's the radiation issue.

COL. SMITH: Radiation . . . What did you find, Louis?

LIAISON, AIR FORCE: I'd like to remind everyone that you can get some radioactive isotopes in your air just from burning too much coal. We're going to have to give the eggheads more time to chew it over, eliminate other possible causes . . . but we are seeing isotopes like Cesium-133 and Iodine-131, and the radioisotope mass/yield curve suggests they came from prompt—not thermal—fission of Plutonium-239, and a bunch of thermal-neutron-induced fission of Uranium-238—

LIAISON, CENTRAL INTELLIGENCE AGENCY: What does that mean?

LIAISON, AIR FORCE: It's fallout from an atmospheric H-bomb detonation. The Plutonium fission fragments came from the initiator and spark plug, the U-238 products come from the hohlraum. They—or someone on their time line—set off one or more thermonuclear devices quite recently. Less than a month ago, in fact, and it was probably in the hundred-kiloton-to-five-megaton range. This *might* indicate an active aboveground H-bomb test program. But the timing is right for them to have nuked our drones out of the sky.

DR. SCRANTON: We're playing it close for now, gentlemen, but the White House is aware of the situation. A decision has been made, for better or worse. (pause) As of now, we're treating this time line, time line 178, as a high-tech threat. It gets its own code name: BLACK RAIN, a hat tip to the fallout. While a National Security Order has been drafted and SAC are migrating a para-time-capable B-52 bomb wing armed with nuclear-tipped cruise missiles to Thule *just in case*, the President has made it abundantly clear that this is a defensive posture only, not preparation for a first strike. She's been briefed on Camp Singularity and is fully aware of the implications. She wants to play this very low-key, until we can provide some intel context on what we're dealing with in BLACK RAIN. She doesn't want to risk whacking a hornet's nest with a baseball bat unless there's no alternative.

COL. SMITH: This is what you were priming us for, isn't it?

DR. SCRANTON: Yes, Colonel. I'm afraid we've run out of time. We're going to keep probing with Tier 1 drones and micro-UAVs, but they can only get us so far; we badly need human eyes at ground level.

LIAISON, CENTRAL INTELLIGENCE AGENCY: But she's not ready to deploy yet!

COL. SMITH: Leave that to me.

END TRANSCRIPT

UPSTATE NEW YORK, TIME LINE TWO, JULY 2020

That afternoon, Rita flew into Rochester on a Delta connection via Minneapolis. She was as tired and irritated as usual on arrival (she had been mildly disappointed to discover that her DHS staff ID card didn't give her the right to magically sidestep the airport security lines or the scrum at the checked baggage belt); all she wanted to do was rent a car and drive out to the transit facility for Camp Graceland. She was *not* expecting to find Colonel Smith waiting for her in Arrivals, looking impatient. "Your flight is late."

"Tell me about it, sir." She'd worked out early on that calling him "sir" put the Colonel in a more receptive frame of mind. "You aren't here just for me, are you?"

"As a matter of fact, I am. Walk this way. We need to talk."

Rita tried to keep up with him while wrestling with three months' worth of baggage. It was a futile battle, adding extra stress on top of her irritation and the layer of stifling paranoia added by the Colonel's arrival. *What does he want* now? she wondered. She knew she hadn't done well on the FBI course, but surely it would take something more important to drag the Colonel out of his office for the day?

Smith headed straight for the drop-off lane in front of the terminal, then paused for her to catch up. A gray government car nosed into the curb beside him; the trunk and doors sprang open. "Let me help you with that," he said, taking Rita's suitcase to her chagrin. "Get in—we've got a lot of ground to cover."

It wasn't exactly a luxury limo, but there was a privacy screen between the passengers and the driver up front. The Colonel climbed in beside her, fastened his seat belt, then rapped on the partition.

"You're probably wondering if this is about the course," he told her as the car moved off. "It's not. What's happened is—" He paused, then rummaged for a bottle of water in the storage bin the car featured in place of an armrest. "Want one? No? Okay. There's been a major new development, and I'm rearranging your training and operational preparedness as a result."

"New development?" Rita echoed.

"We thought we had a year to put you through the standard clandestine ops backgrounder. But events are outrunning us. The original plan was to certificate you for basic fieldwork, then assign you as a trainee analyst for a year or two, before looking into provisioning you for autonomous para-time deployment. Unfortunately"—he grimaced—"shit just got real. So we're rescheduling everything."

"What kind of shit? What rescheduling?"

Smith opened his water bottle and chugged it. "Sorry. You need to be able to world-walk. This may be a false alarm, in which case it's back to training as usual. But we need you ready for deployment at short notice. You're going to be in the clinic for a month—"

"Clinic? What clinic?" Rita realized her voice was shrill. "What does this involve?"

"No brain surgery." Smith flashed her a nervous grin, evidently startled by her response. "No knives, nothing like that. Just a couple of injections. Hmm. Well, actually there *is* some surgery involved—on your left arm. I'm assuming you're right-handed? It's an implant to control the ability. But my understanding is that it's pretty straightforward stuff, and once you're in control you can take some leave, or go straight back to studying Spook 201. It's just that it can take up to a month, and in a worst-case scenario we may not *have* a month in which to activate you when we need you."

"Worst—" Rita stopped. "You're going to turn me into a world-walker because you might need me at short notice?"

"Pretty much. Unfortunately I can't tell you precisely why at this point. Let's just say, we no longer have the luxury of giving you a lengthy training period. And for now let's leave a big fat question mark over *where* and *what* it's all about."

Oh great. Rita tensed. Her head was beginning to ache. "Is this optional?"

The Colonel's fey grin was equally tense: "Not really, no."

"Okay. Sir." She leaned back, closing her eyes. "Where are we going?"

"You don't need to know. Let's just say it's a private clinic in Connecticut, within chopper range of a bunch of high-end hospitals for backup if we need specialized help. First, you'll undergo a couple of brain scans, MRI and PET, and a lumbar puncture. Then you sit around for a couple of days; then there'll be some injections. Next you go into a special isolation suite, which is locked down to prevent you triggering by accident. After a few days they'll begin testing you with a particular trigger engram in a safe space: if you world-walk successfully, you'll find yourself in a mirror installation in the destination time line we're using for testing. Then, after a couple of weeks of tests and training so you know how to work your new ability, they'll implant you with an emergency beacon, show you how to use it, and that's it. Oh, except for the legal formalities, which we'll run you through before we activate you."

"Legal . . ."

"World-walking is illegal without a court order issued by a Foreign Intelligence Surveillance Act court; they amended the law in 2004 . . . So before we switch you on, we have to haul you up in front of a judge, confirm you're a DHS employee, and get you a shiny personalized certificate giving you carte blanche to commit a felony—as long as you do so on government business—that would normally carry up to twenty years in jail or an unlimited fine per occurrence."

"Oh." Rita fell quiet for a minute. "There's a lot here that I don't understand." *There's a lot here I don't want to ask you about,* she added silently. Over the past few months a claustrophobic cynicism had settled deep into her bones: *Trust no one, and verify everything,* it prompted. She hated it, but—

"Don't worry, I've got a classified background briefing document for you that goes into all the details in mind-numbing detail. You're cleared for it: just remember it's code-word-secret and *not* for public disclosure."

"How routine is all this?" Rita opened her eyes.

"You're the first," said Smith, staring out the window at the passing traffic on the other side of the highway.

"I'm a *guinea pig?*" She stared at him.

"How many *other* Clan orphans do you think we have?"

"I don't know, I—hell."

"Listen, we have been manipulating this stuff in cell cultures for nearly two decades now. We know all about how the process works. Most of the stuff you need to world-walk is already inside you: we're just going to repair the broken on/off switch. Yes, it's an experimental process. But you're valuable to us. You're not the only one, but people like you don't grow on trees. Professor Schwartz isn't going to tell her team to do anything if she doesn't think it's safe to proceed. And on the other side of the coin, think what the benefits are: you're going to gain a superpower and get an opportunity to use it to protect America. Doesn't that mean something to you?"

Sitting in the back of a government limo and listening to a highly persuasive secret police colonel, all Rita could do was nod, nervously: whether because she agreed with him or because it was the course of least resistance she herself could not have said. *They ask you to do one more unforgivable thing and you cannot back out,* Kurt had explained. At the time, she hadn't really understood, but now . . .

"I can cope," she lied.

SOMEWHERE IN CONNECTICUT,
TIME LINE TWO, JULY 2020

The first week went exactly as Colonel Smith had told her it would, except for one significant deviation: he hadn't mentioned the boredom. The clinic was located in woodland somewhere off a highway between Durham and New Haven, and there was sporadic cell service at best— and none in her room, which was underground. There was no cable TV, no high-speed Internet access, and if she wanted to update her phone or check her e-mail she had to go upstairs and hope for a signal. There *was* a small library of dog-eared books in the rec room, but it appeared to be policed by a member of the nursing staff who was both excessively friendly and claustrophobically evangelical. Consequently its contents were not to Rita's taste.

She was the only patient, although there were half a dozen beds. The clinic's main function, she gathered, was to perform surgery to change the biometrics of deep-cover DHS agents—bone-shim insertions to change gait and facial appearance, fingerprint and iris transplants, even experimental CRISPR genome editing of epithelial cells to spoof DNA sequencers. Rita spent her time in the break room, trying not to attract attention. Short of going for long walks inside the perimeter fence, it was the best entertainment on offer. Which was to say, very little.

"Good morning!" Dr. Jennifer Lane greeted her brightly on her first morning. "Call me Jenn? I work for Professor Schwartz, who runs the project here, and I'm responsible for your therapeutic regime. If you have any questions about the medical aspects of this procedure, I'm the person you need to talk to." Rita smiled, taking an instant dislike to the doctor, whose bright-eyed chirpiness reminded her of early morning lectures suffered in silence after student drinking parties. Not her greatest moments, but nevertheless . . . "I guess you want to know *all about* how world-walking works for walkers of worlds! Isn't that the case?"

Kill me now, Rita thought. "Yeah, but can I grab a coffee first?" She hadn't slept well—or at all, if she was perfectly truthful with herself. She'd spent the night wired up to a mobile EEG and an ambulatory blood pressure monitor, which by 4 a.m. had become an almost unendurable torture (for it woke her up with her arm in agony whenever it inflated, which was every half hour). "I'm not myself right now."

"Absolutely! Caffeine is safe at this point, so I'll just fetch one for you right now! How do you take it?"

"Flat white, extra shot, no sugar."

Rita slumped into the patient's chair in the doctor's office as Jenn bounded away in the direction of the coffee robot by the nurses' station. She yawned, scratched halfheartedly at the inflatable cuff around her arm, and tried not to doze off. The doctor returned regrettably rapidly, just as the blood pressure monitor ground its gears and the cuff began to inflate again, sending sparks of pain into her arm. "So!" Dr. Jenn bounced into her chair. "World-walking! Let's skip the physics for now, it goes off into brane theory, which nobody understands without a PhD in pure mathematics. Let's just say we live in a multiverse—a bundle of parallel universes branching off each other. The vast majority are identical but for some quantum uncertainty, and they keep merging and re-emerging. But there are sheaves of parallels where the differences add up to something we can tell apart. A huge number of such sheaves exist, and we call them time lines.

"The world-walking mechanism uses some intracellular machinery, self-replicating wet-phase nanotechnology with embedded quantum dots to ensure coherence of the wave function, that can bounce you—and anything electrostatically earthed with you—into another time line, as long as the Q-machines are all triggered together. The trigger event is a bunch of them going into the same state transition more or less simultaneously, and the easiest way to get this to happen is by hitting a bunch of neurons in your brain that contain Q-machines with a signal that excites all of them at once. The easiest bunch to trigger are in your lateral occipital complex, where your vision system recognizes images. We hit them with a unique image—a complex knotwork—and as you recognize it the Q-machines in that part of your brain activate.

"You're probably wondering how we control *which* time line you end up in. It's all in the knot we use. Different knots have different dimensional parameters and so they trigger different recognition groups, and this causes differential ensemble excitation in the Q-network—"

Rita raised a hand. "Whoa. This is too much." She smiled defensively. "I look at a knot, and it makes these Q-machines send me to another universe?"

Dr. Jenn smiled back at her. Patronizingly or sympathetically, it was equally annoying. "That's the gist of it! My, you're quick on the uptake this morning. Yes, but not all knots work in this way—only ones that follow certain geometric rules. And of course they don't take *you* anywhere yet because your Q-machines are inactive because of the missing link between your own central nervous system and the Q-machines." Rita's heart sank as she noticed Dr. Jenn gearing up for more neurobabble: "The world-walkers all carry a gene for a nonstandard postsynaptic glutamate receptor. It binds to the Q-machines and activates them. However, whoever designed the mechanism used a hack to switch production of the modified receptor on, and it turns out to be a recessive trait. You've got the gene for the receptor, but it's not expressed—actually making receptor proteins—unless both your parents were world-walkers, which in your case they were not."

Dr. Jenn paused barely long enough to draw breath. "We can fix that now, thanks to a big-budget top-secret research project called JAUNT BLUE. You've heard of the Six Million Dollar Man, or the Seven Million Dollar Woman? You're going to be the Half Billion Dollar World-Walker. That's inflation for you . . ."

"How exactly does this work?" Rita narrowed her eyes, annoyed by Dr. Lane's attempt at manipulating her through levity. "Genetic engineering? Stem cells?"

"No. That would be impractical and potentially dangerous. Instead, we do some tests to make sure that your receptor complex is inactive because of the stalled repressor function, then infuse a short interfering RNA sequence into your cerebrospinal fluid that gives it a kick. The only dangerous aspect is that if you start world-walking prematurely—if something triggers you—you can end up lost in para-time. Which is why you're sleeping in an underground bedroom where the only place you can go is a corresponding underground mirror room on a base in time line four."

"What? You mean I can end up buried underground or something?"

"No." Dr. Jenn shook her head emphatically. "You can't world-walk into a solid object. Nor can you move while world-walking. Actually, there's a lot about it that we don't understand yet: the Earth is moving through space, for example, so why do you move with it? What about the air in the time line you're going to, that you displace? We figure there are safety mechanisms we haven't decoded yet . . . but that's not *my* department: that's for the physicists to worry about."

"Oh." Rita thought for a bit. "So what happens is entirely controlled by my, my seeing some kind of, what did you call it—a trigger engram? A knot?"

"Yes. Whoever designed the world-walking Q-machinery was pretty careful about that. They picked a set of topological deformations in the visual field that don't occur in nature. And, believe me, this mechanism *was* designed: it certainly didn't evolve. It's very unbiologically straightforward. While they recycled the glutamate pathway and the recognizer networks from existing neural wetware, the self-replicating Q-dot machines have all but got patent numbers stenciled on them. They look a bit like mitochondria under an electron microscope, and they're self-replicating, like mitochondria, but they're a hundred percent engineered and there are additional mechanisms to ensure they get copied and packed in the acrosome during meiosis. It's high-grade nanotechnology, miles ahead of anything we can match yet. Anyway, you're *mostly* safe from running into a trigger engram by accident. But . . . you've flown recently? You saw the DHS notice when you signed onto the in-flight wi-fi? They only switch on the wi-fi above ten thousand feet, once the plane is airborne, and the animated background to the DHS logo—"

Rita swallowed. "It's some kind of knotwork design. Is that a trigger engram?"

"Yes. The theory is that if the Clan are sending world-walkers here and they try to catch a commercial flight, the plane will land with one fewer passenger than it took off with, which will flag it for us. The flight data recorders log the flight's GPS coordinates when the wi-fi is switched on, so we know where to look for the world-walker's body."

"But I—"

"Relax. There are a couple of ways of turning off your sensitivity to triggers. The simplest method is to close your eyes. If you need to switch off for longer, there are drugs that mess with your glutamate pathways and render you unable to world-walk for a period of hours to days. And we think there's a kind of meditation you can practice that will stop it from working on you, if you have time to put yourself in the right frame of mind."

"Where did you get that from?"

Jenn's smile slipped. "I can't tell you that."

"DHS has captured world-walkers. Right?"

Dr. Lane's smile turned cold. "You are not supposed to ask that kind of question. If DHS *has* captured world-walkers, it would be a very serious and highly classified project. Even asking about them without prior clearance would be a serious security infraction. Luckily for you I don't know the answer to your question so I'm going to *assume* that the answer is no, so your question is not actually a security infraction. But how about we agree that we didn't have this part of the conversation at all? It'll make life ever so much easier."

"Okay!" Rita surrendered unconditionally. *Good cows avoid the electric fence; there's plenty of juicy grazing in the middle of the meadow without risking any nasty shocks.* Not that she was taking the doctor's denial as anything other than confirmation, but some fictions were best preserved. "What do you want me to do today?"

"That's better," Dr. Lane muttered, apparently unaware of her vocalization as she poked at her tablet. Then, louder, she continued: "We've got a bunch more basics to go over this morning, then this afternoon we'll get you weighed, run a bunch of bloods, take your first baseline MRI, and start you fasting this evening. Tomorrow morning we'll do the lumbar puncture—then in the afternoon, we'll start the cognitive tests. And the day after tomorrow is your big day, starting with a visit from the judge who's going to swear you in and sign your court order, and then the second lumbar puncture . . ."

Off-white walls, gray plastic floor, recessed overhead lighting, and no windows.

A hospital bed, with fancy powered adjustable motors. A chirping bedside monitor with a fingertip clip to measure her blood oxygen levels and a display showing her ECG trace, relayed wirelessly from the skin sensors taped to her torso. An IV drip. In a wardrobe in the corner of the windowless room, her suitcase and clothing and personal effects.

There was, Rita thought, an ancient symbolism embedded in the modern pattern. The liminal soul suspended in the antechamber of death. First-dynasty Egyptian princesses would have recognized her situation, but wondered at the absence of canopic jars. Eighteenth-century plantation heiresses might have questioned the lack of leeches and cupping.

Not that Rita was doing too much thinking. The first day had tired her out, with a whiplash segue from Dr. Lane's high-velocity briefing into uncharted medical guinea pig territory. She'd given blood and urine samples, stool samples, weight and height and then 3-D morphological imaging measurements, and finally been subjected to a noisy, borderline-claustrophobic hour in a full-body MRI machine. For dinner, they gave her clear soup and coffee with no milk.

The second day started with a sedative, and went rapidly downhill from there.

On the third day, she'd awakened dizzy and lethargic, as if with a Valium hangover. They'd then put her in a wheelchair and brought her into an office. She'd haltingly echoed back an oath, with her hand on a book, to a hawk-faced man in a black gown. He asked her the questions Dr. Lane and Colonel Smith had told her to expect, then announced that he could see no reason not to issue the requested order. Then they stuck a cannula in the back of her left hand and her day dissolved into confused kaleidoscope memories of being swallowed by brain scanners and attacked by electrodes.

And on the fourth day she awakened in this white and desolate space, wondering if it had all been a terrible mistake and life was still waiting for her somewhere outside.

The implant in her left arm itched. Flinching slightly, Rita raised her right hand to scratch, then remembered she didn't have HaptoTech's motion capture implants anymore—the base clinic at Camp Graceland had removed them on her first day, packaged them up and returned them to her former employer. She rubbed the inside of her left elbow furiously, and the pain shifted to the back of her forearm. *Referred pain.* There was something there, embedded under the layer of fat beneath the skin, something the size of a long grain of rice. *An emergency beacon? A new implant?* she wondered as she lifted her arm. There was a yellow-green bruise below her wrist, and a cotton ball held down with micropore tape across the injection site. The familiar itch had fooled her into thinking it was in the usual location, when it was just interfering with the same nerve. *Implant. Fuck.*

She fumbled around until she could bring the bed's motor controller into her line of sight, then stabbed random buttons until, with a whir, the backrest began to rise. As she sat up, the vertigo began to subside. Now she felt a moment of nausea, but recognized it for what it was: hunger, gnawing at her guts with the insistent ache of two days' near-starvation. With that realization, a bunch of other irritating imps began jabbing their metaphorical tridents into her: she had a headache, she felt dizzy, and she was hungry. Her muscles felt as if she'd fought a bout with the flu, and the flu won. Last but not least, she needed the toilet badly—and she had no idea where it was.

There was a call button. Not feeling at all proud, she pushed it.

A minute later, she heard a door open behind her bed. "Oh, you're awake!" The nurse who bustled in, in green scrubs and gloves, was the friendly but religious one—Marianne—who ran the library in the rec room. "And how are we feeling this morning?"

Rita tried to smile. "I need the bathroom, but I'm dizzy, and—"

"Not to worry, we'll have you there in a second!" The bathroom turned out to be right behind her. It was a typical hospital unit with grab rails everywhere and a smart toilet primed to snitch on her eating habits every time she pooped. Was everything in this clinic a potential informant? Rita wondered as Marianne helped her out of bed and hovered until she had a solid grip on the rail. Quite possibly: after all, the health industry had been an enthusiastic and early adopter of the Internet of Things that Leak Personal Information, right behind the NSA in the queue.

Morning ablutions completed, Rita returned to her room, towing her

IV stand behind her. Marianne had brought in an armchair and a bedside table while she was in the bathroom. "What am I meant to be doing today?" Rita asked.

"Nothing." Marianne smiled. "Well, apart from eating three square meals and taking it easy! We've got a couple of tests for you. But you don't start the post-op workup until seventy-two hours after the activation shots. You may feel a bit feverish or unwell—that's expected with this treatment—but Dr. Lane will look in on you later this morning, and if you feel particularly bad, you can call at any time and one of us will come."

"Oh." Rita digested this information. "I've got a couple of days off?" Marianne nodded. "Can I go and sit outside? Or use the rec room?"

"Ah, well, there's a problem, you see." Marianne smiled, presumably with disarming intent: "You're not supposed to leave this suite. It's mirrored in another time line, for safety, in case you jaunt by accident or see a trigger symbol."

"Oh. Is there a TV?" The nurse shook her head. "Internet . . . ?"

"I'm sorry!" Marianne said brightly. "I can bring you some books if you like? But you're not allowed any visual media *at all* until Dr. Lane says so. No Internet, no TV, not even magazines or newspapers."

"Books." The prospect of spending the next three days cut off from the world did not fill Rita with unalloyed joy. Camping on a hiking trail in the wilderness was one thing; climbing the walls in a soothingly featureless hospital room was something else again. "Yes, please, if you don't mind?"

"Sure!" Marianne chirped. "I'll just go and let Catering know you're ready for breakfast . . ."

Breakfast was predictable: cereal, juice, an anemic boiled egg, low-fiber toast. Rita wolfed it down, then confronted the morning with a cup of weak coffee and growing boredom. Marianne returned, bringing a small pile of books and pamphlets with her: to Rita's dismay they consisted entirely of testimonials for Scientology.

Rita had nothing against religion as such. Kurt had grown up Lutheran; Mom and Dad had occasionally taken her to church and sent her off to summer camps run by them, but their approach to such matters was very much that it was a social club. Rita wasn't sure what she believed, beyond a vague sense that there was something Up There keeping an eye on things. Consequently she found Marianne's pamphlets disturbing in their zealous insistence that Dianetics, and only Dianetics, held the key to realizing one's full potential.

Spending the day reading advertorials for someone else's scripture lacked appeal. So she unpacked and stowed her clothing in the wardrobe, just for something to do. That was when she discovered the musty, coverless paperback that Grandpa Kurt must have stuffed down a zipped side compartment of her carry-on. Normally she had no time for elderly pulp novels: but at least it wasn't a religious tract.

There was nothing lightweight about *The Grasshopper Lies Heavy*. The combination of the author's paranoid outlook and his cautionary tale within a tale—set in a metafiction in which the Nazis had won the Second World War—made her head spin as she tried to understand it. But the lack of any alternative kept her chewing doggedly along until evening. Whoever had owned it previously had underlined a couple of passages in every chapter in thick, gray pencil, sometimes phrases or words and sometimes individual letters. Trying to make sense of the annotations gave her a little more to chew on, but ultimately that, too, was unproductive. Unfortunately it wasn't a particularly fat book, and she reached the end all too soon. The end pages were blank, and she was about to close the book when something caught her eye.

As she turned past the end matter she found herself confronted by a page covered in tiny, very precise handwriting. Squinting in the illumination of the adjustable bedside lamp, she read the opening:

Dear Rita, if you need to talk to me in private, write by hand, trusting no keyboard. Use this book as your one-time pad, using the two methods described below—high risk, low content, fast; and low risk, high content, slow. I may not be able to help, but if you don't ask you don't get—Kurt.

Inscribed in the middle of the page, before the code instructions that followed, was a pencil sketch of a knot. As Rita looked at it, it made her feel oddly queasy: guts twisting, vision blurring. She blinked it away hastily, then covered it with her thumb, heart hammering. *Oh, Gramps, what have you gotten us into?* She began to read the rest of Kurt's message. Boredom was suddenly very far away.

BALTIMORE, TIME LINE TWO, JULY 2020

FEDERAL EMPLOYEE 004910023 CLASSIFIED VOICE TRANSCRIPT

DR. SCRANTON: Okay, so our pawn has just leveled up to queen. What's the state of play looking like now that our prototype is nearing deployment readiness?

COL. SMITH: Well, I think I've got a pretty good feel for her character, and she's not perfect but things could be a lot worse.

AGENT GOMEZ: Oh? What's not—

COL. SMITH: For starters, we are not dealing with a classic authoritarian follower personality: not even your typical Gen Z me-first narcissist with no patriotism and no loyalty. Instead she got your full-on liberal, nurturing, question-authority upbringing, with an added dose of extreme political cynicism from her grandfather. This *doesn't* mean she's useless—you can motivate anyone, given the right lever—but she's going to take some work. She's actually a lot better suited to the mission profile we're looking at than someone who obeys orders blindly just because they feel good when Daddy tells them what to do. The key issue is that she's an introvert. Self-contained is a job requirement for spies, especially solitary infiltrators. But it means she doesn't open up easily and tell us what she's thinking, and that will make it hard to manipu—motivate her. And it means she doesn't do well in all facets of training.

DR. SCRANTON: Are we talking about her National Academy session?

COL. SMITH: Yes. I had to pull strings just to ensure she scraped a pass. I didn't—I say I *didn't*—rig it; I just made sure she got some TLC. Extra coaching. Let's be honest: she's not a cop, much less an officer on the leadership inside track. She didn't belong on that course; she was a fish out of water. It's to her credit that she finished it at all, even with a bare pass. Putting a twenty-five-year-old introspective liberal female actor through a graduate-level course in policing and leadership populated by ex-Army county sheriffs and upwardly mobile municipality lieutenants was a big risk. But she, she survived. She nearly wiped out but it didn't break her. Which makes me think she's got what it takes to operate in an unsympathetic environment as well as having picked up the insight she needs for Evasion Planning. If we can earn her loyalty, we're gold.

AGENT O'NEILL: That's the hard part.

COL. SMITH: You know the old saying? "Set a thief to catch a thief?" We were trying a new angle. Train a spy in security policing to avoid getting caught by the adversary's secret police.

DR. SCRANTON: Nevertheless, it seems to me that failure would have had a significant impact on her morale, not to mention making it harder to keep this little red wagon rolling along. Oversight wouldn't like it.

COL. SMITH: I'd have pretexted her out of there in an hour if I thought she was going to crack.

AGENT GOMEZ: So now we have this introverted liberal hippie actress chick with diplomas in police leadership skills from the FBI, Espionage 101 training, and, and DRAGON'S TEETH capability? In what way does this get us closer to our objective?

COL. SMITH: We ran out of time. You're on the distribution. You got the memo about BLACK RAIN.

AGENT GOMEZ: Yes, but I don't see how—

COL. SMITH: She was set for another six months of Clandestine Ops School, then two years pushing a desk with Operational Analysis before deployment. Under constant scrutiny, of course, and we were going to take the time to weld some handles onto her to make her easier to move around—

DR. SCRANTON: What did you have in mind?

COL. SMITH: Boyfriend, girlfriend, whichever way she swings. Background says she dated boys in college but didn't have anyone serious. Meanwhile there was a female BFF in high school, lots of tears when she moved away. So it's not entirely clear which way she leans. But it doesn't matter: if we can get her emotionally attached to someone, we have a handle. Or if we find something she's afraid of, we have a handle. Or if she gets religion, same deal. Or if we get her to imprint on her colleagues—the Small Unit paradigm—that works too. She may be an introvert, but she's not invulnerable: we just need to get her to open up.

AGENT GOMEZ: We can use her without a handle if push comes to shove, can't we?

COL. SMITH: Yes, but it's less reliable. Humans are social organisms. We want her to feel protective toward *us* as a society, before we send her out among *them*. Otherwise there's the risk of Stockholm Syndrome.

DR. SCRANTON: We don't need that. Termination Expedient is all very well as a policy, but not a sensible option for unique assets. Too much risk of making the wrong call.

AGENT O'NEILL: So you want her to fall in love, get religion, discover patriotism, discover team loyalty, or learn to fear us. Okay, so noted. But why has everything come so far forward?

DR. SCRANTON: Because of BLACK RAIN. We've lost three drones and detected fallout in that time line. People in high places are beginning to ask questions, and it falls to us to provide answers.

COL. SMITH: Once is happenstance, twice is coincidence, but three times is enemy action.

DR. SCRANTON: Exactly.

END TRANSCRIPT

In the Valley of the Shadow of the Gate

They started Rita's training three days, four MRIs, and one swearing-in after her last subarachnoid injections. The evening before, they began to cut back on the bad head meds. In the morning Rita, feeling a lot less mind-fuzzed and mildly irritable (if not stir-crazy), climbed out of bed and dressed in her own clothes before Marianne wheeled in her breakfast. "Well, we're feeling better, are we? Great! Dr. Lane will be so pleased. I hear y'all have a visitor coming this morning . . ."

An hour later, stomach full and nerves buzzing with caffeine—it was the first mug of coffee she'd been allowed since the course of injections—she was in another windowless white room full of unidentifiable medical equipment, with a large display covering most of one wall. This one had markings taped out on the floor in various colors, like a basketball practice court that had accidentally shrunk. And she did indeed have a visitor, tapping his toes with Dr. Jenn. The Colonel smiled. "How are you feeling?" he asked.

"I feel fine," she said noncommittally. She had a gut feeling that Colonel Smith wouldn't appreciate her true feelings—a layer cake of resentment at being railroaded into this isolating situation, unease and disquiet at being treated as a medical guinea pig, and a glaze of boredom on top. He probably wanted something more positive: excitement, a sense of adventure, maybe a dose of unreflective salute-the-flag patriotism. "Is this the big day?"

"Yes, I certainly hope so!" Jenn interjected. "Yesterday's bloods were looking good so—"

"I thought it would be best if I came to witness the first test jaunt," Smith said easily. "It'll be a major landmark."

Rita nodded seriously. *Landmark for what?* she wondered. "But you've got the para-time machines . . ." She noticed Dr. Lane glance briefly in Smith's direction, and his twitch of acknowledgment.

"They're not very flexible," he said blandly. His movements as jerky as a small bird's, he stepped to one side. "Doctor, if you'd like to begin your orientation?"

"Sure." Jenn smiled at Rita again. "Rita, because we cut back on the suppressors, you should be sensitive to trigger engrams now. So what we're going to do here is try a very simple test run. First, we're going to ground you—that should prevent you from jaunting by accident—and use the EEG and EKG to see what happens when we expose you to an engram. I'll need to take bloods, too. Then this afternoon we'll do it again, only without the grounding straps and using ambulatory biomonitoring."

"Ah." Rita stared at the marks on the floor. "What will happen?"

"This is a mirror room; there's an identical facility in the time line the engram we're using is keyed to. And there's a transporter cell next door. What *should* happen is that you'll jaunt over there; then we'll use the transporter to come over and confirm you're healthy before you make the return jaunt."

"Jaunt? You're using that word—"

The Colonel shrugged. "We lifted it from an old SF novel. It's short and descriptive and differentiates what you'll be doing—jaunting—from what the transporters do—para-time traversal." He seemed to be mildly amused, if slightly tense. He turned to Dr. Lane: "I've got a meeting with Professor Schwartz now; message me before you proceed with the actual jaunt test." He nodded at Rita and departed.

Rita stared at the door, then looked at Dr. Lane. "What now?" she asked, feeling hollow.

Jenn pointed her to the examining table. "Take a nap. Marianne should be here—we need to start by wiring you up. This is going to take a while, I'm afraid."

Rita lay down and stared at the ceiling. "Does Colonel Smith visit often?" she asked.

"Is that his name?" Dr. Lane shook her head. "I wouldn't know." Her tone dropped slightly. "You're asking questions again. Bad habit."

"Sorry. I get bored easily."

"Try not to." Dr. Lane stood. "Back in a minute." She disappeared, leaving Rita alone with her unanswered, stifled questions. More than a minute passed before she returned, Marianne and another paramedic trailing behind. "Okay, showtime! First, we're going to wire up the EKG harness. You'll be wearing it for the rest of the day, so if you wouldn't mind stripping down to your underwear . . ."

The morning passed in a blur. Wired into an itchy tangle of electrodes, Rita sat through most of it staring at strange knotwork designs on the big screen on the wall opposite. Jenn and her assistants bustled around, discussing their test equipment readings as if Rita weren't there.

"Okay, I've got another series of knots for you," Jenn told her. "Ten coming up. Press the button if you feel queasy, have any visual disturbances, or feel unwell in any way—that shouldn't happen, but it's a precaution." The button was attached to a long cable leading to one of the racks of equipment behind her. Rita clutched it nervously, thumb hovering. What appeared to be an elaborate sailors' joke appeared in the middle of the screen. "Next one coming up."

The knot dissolved, replaced by a similar, but somehow different tangle of lines. Rita stared at it, vision blurring. Somehow it didn't want to come into focus. "How many more—" she began to complain, as the lines writhed and another knot condensed out of the pointillist flickering on the screen. "Hey, your monitor's broken."

"Broken?" Dr. Lane looked up sharply. "Okay. Let's try the next."

The disturbance went away, as another knot appeared. "Hey, it fixed itself," said Rita.

"Uh-huh. Next." Something about Dr. Lane's tone had changed.

"Was that it?" Rita asked.

"Listen, why don't we get through the rest of this sequence then break for lunch," Jenn suggested. Rita, knowing a diversion when she heard one, nodded and kept watching the screen, and herself for sudden headaches. *That was it*, she realized. *That was a trigger engram.* But she was grounded, electrostatically earthed, the Q-machines she still only half believed in blocked from entering their excited state. Somehow it barely seemed real.

After lunch—another bland burger in the staff canteen—Rita slouched reluctantly back to the test room with Dr. Lane. She was even more enthused than usual: babbling about procedures and test protocols and blood pressure monitoring for some reason. Rita nodded politely and let it all flow over her. The reality was that she didn't much want to be here, but there was no obvious way out. And the morning's tests had reassured her slightly that whatever they'd stuck in her hadn't had any obvious bad effects. She could live with an itch in her left forearm and the inability to focus on a particular odd-shaped knot. "After you're jaunting controllably we'll switch on your engram generator," Jenn told her. "But not until the day after tomorrow at the earliest."

"Engram generator?"

"The implant in your left arm."

"Huh." Rita squinted. Her left forearm was a little sore near the wrist, where she might have worn a watch if she were so inclined, and the fine downy hairs were missing. "I can feel something there."

"Really? It should be almost unnoticeable. Come over here now—"

They hung a shoulder harness on her, with slim medical data loggers connected to the EKG and EEG pickups, then stood her on a black plastic mat where the chair had been that morning. "Okay, Rita," said Dr. Lane. "I want you to just relax and look at the engram when it shows on-screen. That's all. Don't move from where you're standing."

Rita glanced over her shoulder. Colonel Smith had arrived, was standing quietly at the back of the room, watching her intently. Another middle-aged man stood behind him, balding and self-important in a white coat. Rita assumed he was the elusive Professor Schwartz. "Are you sure this is entirely safe?" she asked.

"Quite sure." Jenn moved aside to one of the control tablets. "Look at the screen . . ."

Rita looked. Something shimmered, and she tried to focus on it, then staggered slightly. "Dr. Lane, I don't feel—"

She stopped. Jenn, the Colonel, Schwartz, and the nursing orderlies had vanished. So had most of the equipment racks and the examining table. There was a different table on the wrong side of the room, and the screen on the wall had shifted sideways minutely and gone blank. Her ears ached; she swallowed, and they popped.

"What. The. Fuck?" Rita glanced up. Tiny insect-eyed webcams watched impassively from the corners of the room. *Oops.* She turned round. A sign on the inside of the door read:

"Welcome to Nova America four, Rita!"

Wow. Just wow. She swallowed again, just as the door opened and Colonel Smith, followed by Dr. Lane, rushed in, calling congratulations and questions—"Excellent!"; "How do you feel? Any headache? Visual disturbances?"

"I'm fine," Rita said. She swallowed again, her throat dry, and rubbed her left forearm. "Just a bit . . ." She didn't want to say *freaked out* in front of them. They'd take it the wrong way, like the trainers after she'd fallen off the wall when she tried the assault course at Quantico. Or her seventh-grade teacher, Mrs. Stewart, the time she'd forgotten that Mrs. Stewart was easily upset by others' failure to share her religious beliefs. "Slightly shaken. I knew what to expect but it didn't feel real . . ."

"You'll get used to it," Smith said. He was breathing fast, as if he'd had run to catch up with her, but he sounded pleased. "Once Dr. Lane's checked you out and confirmed everything's all right, you can jaunt between here and the clinic until Dr. Lane's satisfied you can control it—and avoid jaunting by accident whenever you see a trigger. Tomorrow, Dr. Lane will switch on your key generator implant and you can try programming it. Then we head back to Camp Graceland."

"Wait up!" Jenn raised a hand. "I thought I had her for the next four days? We've got commissioning tests to run, and biofeedback training, and—"

Schwartz cleared his throat. "Prioritize the basics. You've got one and a half days. If there are holes in her training, you can travel with her and finish the job on-site."

Rita looked between them. "What's the sudden hurry?"

Smith's crow's-feet wrinkled. "Remember what I told you during your last briefing? Stuff happened."

"Oh. Yeah." Rita nodded, trying to hide her frustration. *Stuff happened*, and she had to jump to attention without knowing what.

"We've got some final orientation to hurry you through," Smith said, downplaying it, his tone dismissive. "Nothing you can't handle in your sleep after your last three months."

"Uh-huh." *Final orientation?* That sounded ominous.

"So if you'd like to jaunt back over to the clinic?" Jenn's lips tightened in something like a smile.

"How?" Rita asked. Then she saw something on the screen, out of the corner of her eyes. "Oh—"

And they were gone again, in another round of interdimensional ping-pong. Dr. Lane kept her busy until dinnertime and exhaustion brought an end to the day's training: and Rita didn't have a chance to ask Colonel Smith what his *final orientation* involved.

BALTIMORE, TIME LINE TWO, JULY 2020

FEDERAL EMPLOYEE 004910023 CLASSIFIED VOICE TRANSCRIPT

DR. SCRANTON: So, what progress are we looking at with our JAUNT BLUE subject?

COL. SMITH: She's nearly ready. I mean, Schwartz's group hasn't activated her key implant yet, but she's already able to jaunt at will if given a trigger engram, and reject inadvertent triggers if she recognizes them in time. Dr. Lane only managed to get her to jaunt by accident once, in the lab, and she came back instantly. The stability is phenomenal compared to the observed capabilities of captured enemy couriers. The blood pressure problem just isn't there at all—I mean, she made multiple jaunts in a fifteen-minute period and her readings were within ten percent of median. If the key generator works properly, so we can dispatch her to surveyed time lines at will, we're onto a winner.

AGENT O'NEILL: Can you tell me about this key generator?

COL. SMITH: Sure. It's a very neat bit of engineering—a subdermal implant. Part of it is an ultra-low-powered computing device powered by a fuel cell running off blood glucose. The other part is a color e-ink display embedded just under the skin. Basically it's a programmable tattoo. Properly equipped operatives like Rita—once we've recruited them from candidates among DRAGON'S TEETH—will be able to use the pressure-sensitive switches in the tattoo to feed the key generator the parameters of a trigger engram. Then it generates the knot and displays it on the skin of her forearm. It fluoresces under UV light, so she can see it in the dark if necessary. Or she can blank the display, in which case the adversary would need to X-ray her arm to realize she has an implant. I'm sure we'll be able to do better in time, but for now it means she can access any time line for which she has a set of knotspace coordinates.

AGENT O'NEILL: Knotspace—

COL. SMITH: The trigger engrams resemble complex knots with a couple of standard topological deformations. Vary the deformations and you vary the destination time line. There's some kind of quantization function, but basically the key can generate engrams for anywhere we've ever been and several billion time lines we haven't visited yet.

AGENT O'NEILL: Sounds dangerous.

COL. SMITH: Yes, it is, in multiple ways. She could get lost in para-time—although the implant retains a stack-based memory of past engrams, so she can jaunt backward as well as forward. But there are other dangers. She could miss a digit and end up somewhere with no breathable atmosphere. There are some safeties—she can't jaunt inside a solid object—but experimentation is discouraged. On the other hand, we can now send Rita to any time line we've visited.

DR. SCRANTON: And she's a lot less conspicuous than a Predator C or a Rivet Joint aircraft.

AGENT GOMEZ: Doesn't burn as much jet fuel either, I'll bet.

COL. SMITH: Human intelligence has been the Cinderella of the intelligence services ever since the early 1960s when we were up against the closed societies of the Communist bloc. Look at the National Clandestine Service's budget compared to the NSA's, and weep. But ELINT and SIGINT won't get you *anywhere* if the targets haven't invented the vacuum tube yet and are still coordinating by smoke signals or semaphore. We've nearly forgotten how to do old-fashioned spycraft, let alone motivate Generation Z slackers to stay loyal to an abstraction while they're in the pressure cooker. But the best-quality agents can deliver more and better intelligence than any given billion dollars' worth of network sniffers. And that's before we start thinking in terms of executive ops—

DR. SCRANTON: Let's not go there, Eric. We're not in that business anymore. I hope.

AGENT O'NEILL: But, but that assumes we're looking at an adversary, doesn't it? I thought all we'd found so far were Stone Age head-bangers? And the stuff in time line four, of course. The archaeological stuff.

DR. SCRANTON: BLACK RAIN.

AGENT O'NEILL: But we don't know who they are yet! I mean, you talked about closed societies, like the Soviet Union—running agents in there always ended in tears. How is this any different?

COL. SMITH: The big difference is that Rita can jaunt. It's very hard to trap a world-walker who's expecting trouble: she can just click her heels and not be in Kansas anytime she wants.

DR. SCRANTON: The only way they can nail her is if they know about world-walkers and are expecting one. Now, it's remotely possible that BLACK RAIN is where the Clan survivors have gone—but they've historically shown a strong preference for working under cover. So the chances of the BLACK RAIN people being able to grab her are slim. I'm more concerned with how *we're* going to hang on to her, once she realizes she can go anywhere she likes.

COL. SMITH: I think we're going to need superego handles.

AGENT O'NEILL: What?

DR. SCRANTON: Do tell.

COL. SMITH: We've got her relationship with her family. That's a subconscious drive; call it her id. We've got her organizational relationship with us—ego level, she knows we trained her and pay her. And there's a bit of idealism going on behind that carefully controlled shell—if BLACK RAIN *is* a closed society, I think we can count on her basic loyalty to bring her home. But to cement it on top, I want to give her a superego drive. A rational long-term explanation for why she *should* stick with us and not defect or desert. So I'm going to run her through the Valley of the Gate, give her the dog and pony tour, and see if the implications spook her as much as they spook everyone else.

AGENT GOMEZ: This is your motivational big stick, huh? It's a bit limp—

COL. SMITH: On the contrary. Once she knows about the Valley, she'll know rationally that she can run as far as she wants but she can't hide. She can hide from us, but she can't hide from *them*.

AGENT GOMEZ: Tenuous, very tenuous.

COL. SMITH: You really think so? Listen, I've spent some time with Rita now, and I think I've got her measure. She's a high-functioning introvert, so she doesn't open up easily—this is a good profile in a HUMINT asset. It means she's deceptively compliant, even slippery. But she's not a perfectly spherical human-shaped object of uniform density. Beckstein's meddling counterculture mother picked the adoption family well. What Rita's *really* about is her grandfather. She pretty much worships him, and my team finally worked out why Beckstein *mère* picked him—

AGENT O'NEILL: This is Kurt Douglas we're talking about, yes?

DR. SCRANTON: We already investigated him.

COL. SMITH: Yes, I expect the FBI checked him out when he first arrived here. He came from the German Democratic Republic—over the Wall, or rather, over the fence—in the late sixties. After his compulsory military service he volunteered for the *Grenztruppen*, the border troops, just to get into a position to defect. He deserted—drugged his unit's dog team—then figured out his way through a minefield. Stole a map, as I recall.

DR. SCRANTON: Yes, that showed a lot of initiative. The FBI backgrounder was quite positive about him . . .

COL. SMITH: Well, I detailed a couple of people to do some digging, because I thought it was a bit suspicious, and I was right. The *Grenztruppen* weren't like our Customs and Border Protection. CBP are cops; the GDR's border troops were military, and elite military at that. If they'd caught him in the act, they'd have shot him. If he survived, he faced five years in jail and probably espionage charges on top. He claimed to be a motivated political dissident, but back then everyone did. It went down well with the FBI and they rubber-stamped his Green Card and didn't flag him when he applied for citizenship. What caught my attention is that he left family behind. His mother and father, grandmother, two sisters, plenty of cousins.

AGENT O'NEILL: Huh? He broke his handles?

COL. SMITH: That's what got me wondering.

DR. SCRANTON: What are you suggesting?

COL. SMITH: He had a plan, he had the means—why didn't he bring them with him?

AGENT GOMEZ: What did you dig up?

COL. SMITH: I put through a request to our friends in the BfV, the German security agency, to look for signs of Kurt Douglas in the archives they inherited from the *Hauptverwaltung Aufklärung*—the Stasi's foreign intelligence division. They didn't find a case file *as such*, so there's no evidence that he was a spy, but it turns out that Kurt wasn't just a border guard either. He was a member of a Pass and Control Unit—the special troops who controlled crossing points, not just securing the border itself—and the Pass and Control Unit troops were all members of the 6th Main Department of the Stasi.

AGENT O'NEILL: Ouch!

AGENT GOMEZ: So Kurt is ex-Stasi? That means his immigration status is—

COL. SMITH: Don't say it. You're thinking we could use this as a handle on Rita, aren't you? Threaten her beloved grandfather with deportation if she steps out of line.

AGENT GOMEZ: Yes, but—

COL. SMITH: Deportation to that well-known starving hellhole and backwater, Germany.

AGENT GOMEZ: Oh.

COL. SMITH: Where he has relatives, will be received with open arms as one who turned against the GDR for moral reasons, and can probably claim a pension.

AGENT GOMEZ: Isn't lying on your naturalization form a felony? Or, or, we could nail him for conspiracy to act as an agent of a foreign government without notifying the US Attorney General—

COL. SMITH: We'd have to convince a judge to play along. There's no positive evidence that Kurt was a sleeper, and in any case the GDR collapsed more than thirty years ago. It's ancient history.

DR. SCRANTON: FISA has plenty of judges. We could pick one who lost relatives during the cold war, if we really had to.

COL. SMITH: But it'd be better all round if we didn't. I can't think of a better way to break Rita—to make her hate us—than threatening her family. The reason I brought this up . . . Rita imprinted on a guy who clearly had some exposure to tradecraft at an early age. Beckstein Senior probably picked the adoptive family precisely because she was looking for someone with the right skill set, and she hit the jackpot. Do you realize what this means?

DR. SCRANTON: (slowly) We've won the lottery on a rollover.

AGENT GOMEZ: You're saying she—

DR. SCRANTON: Our prototype candidate doesn't match the personality profile for a world-walking intelligence asset by accident. She matches it because she's been trained for it since birth! Trained by a professional paranoid who learned how to operate in a totalitarian police state. Trained to keep her head down, trained how to avoid attention. Admittedly she was trained by a role model with limited experience of a modern ubiquitous computing panopticon, but—

COL. SMITH: We don't need DRAGON'S TEETH—and JAUNT BLUE—equipped agents to get us intel on adversaries who have Facebook and Google. We have full-spectrum infowar dominance in that sector. We're trying to develop a world-walking intel capability targeting adversaries who are old-school.

DR. SCRANTON: Handle her with kid gloves, Colonel. It takes a generation to breed a resource like this—they don't grow on trees. You were absolutely right to draw this to my attention. Give her the Valley tour if you think it'll help motivate her: hell, give her anything she wants, if you think it'll make her love us. But you don't have a lot of time. We need to get this show on the road.

COL. SMITH: How long do I have?

DR. SCRANTON: A week, Colonel. Just one week. Then you need to start her mission training.

END TRANSCRIPT

BALTIMORE, TIME LINE TWO, JULY 2020

Two days later they discharged Rita from the clinic and drove her down to Brooklyn in the back of a van with blacked-out windows. The day after that, they put her on a train to D.C., with orders to overnight in a hotel room, then report to an office in Baltimore the following day. The e-mail came attached to a DHS-backed credit vCard for her fatphone, and stern instructions for how to record subsistence expenses. *Traveling on the government's tab: I've come up in the world,* she realized. *Shame it's economy class all the way.* (Except on the high-speed train, which was business class only.)

Being at semiliberty felt strange after months on a training course and two weeks in a clinic, like release from an unusual incarceration. On the train, she whiled away a couple of hours catching up with her FB friends: seeing who'd changed jobs, married, gotten ill, had babies, gotten cats. But there was something curiously distancing about observing her ex-classmates from college and high school at this remove, as if she were watching them in a zoo, from the other side of a wired glass window. It felt dishonest. *I'm on my own,* she realized. When she'd been struggling for acting gigs and casual employment, she'd just been another Generation Zer. But now she was locked into something much larger, a cog in a huge, invisible machine. Even if she broke security and tried to explain herself to her friends, most of them wouldn't understand: they'd be like dogs barking at a lecture on the semiotics of Shakespeare. If they *did* understand her, it would be even worse. It would mean they were wolves in the night, hunting for security leaks.

When FB got old, she logged on to a couple of geocachers' boards. But then second thoughts arrived. She had a job that involved working for professional paranoids. It had been bad enough explaining geocaching during that polygraph interrogation: what if they were watching her? Worse, what if the watchers didn't know it was harmless? Geocaching had gotten started as a popular hobby that mimicked old-school tradecraft. Then—as group activities tend to over time—it had gotten more complicated. These days, teams competed to muggle each other's caches and intercept cyphered communications in travel bugs; it looked so like the real thing that the risk of coming to the attention of people with absolutely no sense of humor whatsoever could not be discounted, just as one who works for the post office might want to rethink the wisdom of using photographs of their coworkers as targets on the firing range.

Rita was beginning to realize that the DHS had inadvertently dropped a neutron bomb on her social life, destroying her personal relationships—even her hobbies—but leaving the bare-walled buildings of her experiences and skills intact. It didn't hurt: like waking up to a tooth with a dead root that hadn't succumbed to infection yet, the pain lay in the future.

The next morning, she repacked her bags, checked out, and headed for the office address she'd been given. It turned out to be located in yet another anonymous concrete ten-story cube, part of the constellation of government buildings that had sprung up in Baltimore as government overflowed from the downtown D.C. fallout zone.

She wasn't sure what to expect of her posting at first. What she found was an office building shared between a bunch of DHS back-end divisions: everything from procurement services to HR and IT support. But there were uniformed officers at the front desk, sitting under a huge gold-fringed flag, and they were expecting her. "Please spit here, ma'am," said one of the guards, proffering a tube. Rita spat to order. "Thank you. Please take a seat and wait over there while we authenticate you, ma'am. Bags go on the belt."

There were DNA scanners everywhere. Fly's-eye arrays of webcams goggled from the corners of the ceiling. The turnstile led to an area with X-ray belts for bags and T-wave booths for bodies. Her phone rolled over onto a red FEDERAL OVERRIDE network ID instantly. Nobody

wanted terrorists to be able to bring phone-controlled bombs into federal buildings, not after 7/16. Not that smartphones or fatphones had existed back then, or that the terrorists who nuked D.C. had used phones
of any kind at all, but—Rita flashed back to her own kidnapping and felt
a sudden spike of remembered terror and pain.

"Ma'am?" Rita looked up, broken out of her reverie. "Your badge is
ready." She approached the desk. "Fingerprints, please." She spread her
hands on the glass plates. "This is your visitor badge. Wear it at all times
and go where it tells you. If you lose it or it's taken from you, report to
security immediately. You may now proceed to security screening, then
go to room W4. The badge will show you the way. Do not cross any red
lines on the floor or try to enter any doors the badge shows in red."

Rita took the smart badge and lanyard, looped it round her neck,
and managed a weak smile: "Thanks." She flipped the badge so she could
see the animated arrows on the map display on its backside, and followed
them down the rabbit hole. At least the security checkpoint here was less
overloaded than the ones at Penn Station.

Room W4 turned out to be a conference room on the fourth floor. As
Rita let herself in, her phone vibrated. She stared at the message from
Colonel Smith: *Running late, be with you in 30.* "Huh," she said under
her breath. There was nobody around, just a conference table and a side-
board with a coffee vending machine. *Hurry up and wait.*

Smith took closer to an hour than thirty minutes to show up. "Sorry
I'm late: I was in a meeting with the boss." He glanced at her suitcase.
"You'll need that. Everything packed? Excellent, let's go."

"Where *are* we going?" Rita asked, hurrying to keep up with him as
he headed for the lift to the parking garage.

"It's called Camp Singularity, and it's in time line four." Elevator doors
closed around them. She saw herself and the Colonel in the walls of the
lift, reflected to infinity by a wilderness of mirrors. "You'll be staying
there for a couple of days."

"More training?"

The elevator doors opened onto concrete and cars. "Not exactly: more
like a background briefing. Stuff we want you to be aware of."

"Stuff."

"Stuff we shouldn't talk about outside of a secure conference room—
or outside of Camp Singularity." A Mercury winked its sidelights and
rolled out of its parking bay, turning toward them. Doors slid open. "Get
in." They sat in the back as the sedan made its way to the exit, steering
wheel spinning eerily under the fingertips of an invisible AI driver.
"We've got one more body to pick up, then we'll go—"

The car stopped at the top of the ramp, and the front passenger door
opened. A few seconds later, Julie from HaptoTech climbed in. "Reporting for duty, sir! Hi, Rita." The smile she sent Rita was just faintly
apologetic.

"Make yourself at home," said Smith, ignoring Rita's frozen face.
Julie's door closed; a second later the car moved off, heading for I-83.
"Transit point's about an hour out of town. Julie, you've seen the Valley,
haven't you? Why don't you fill Rita in on it."

"Sure! Prepare to have your mind blown, Rita. Uh, sir, I assume
she's . . ."

"She wouldn't be in this car if she wasn't cleared." Smith closed his
eyes. *He looks tired*, Rita realized. *Like he's been up all night.* "Tell her
about your first time out." The car turned onto Charles Street and ground
to a halt in the sudden snarl of traffic. "I'm going to catch thirty winks."

Rita wasn't exactly feeling receptive. She fumed quietly behind a polite mask as Julie prattled on about the mind-expanding experience of a
trip to some archaeological site in a capital-V Valley, somewhere over the
rainbow. *You set me up*, she thought grimly, not sure whether to direct
her venom at Julie, who was merely a pawn, or at the Colonel, snoring
quietly beside her, his mouth disarmingly ajar, whose will was almost
certainly the one in question: *You set me up.* There was no other plausi-
ble explanation for Julie to surface as a DHS undercover agent reporting
to the Colonel. *You had me under observation all the time I was at HaptoTech, and you want me to know it!* But why?

"—Climate in time line four is a lot cooler than here, because it's in
an ice age right now. The climatologists say it began about two thousand
years ago because of anthropogenic change caused by an, uh, nuclear

winter—" Julie was surreally lucid. For the trade show in Seattle she'd done a convincing impersonation of a bottle-blond bubblehead. Since then she'd lost the perm, dyed her hair back to a more natural chestnut, and acquired a set of rimless aug-reality specs. In office-casual she was almost unrecognizable. But she still wore a gold pin on her lapel, a hieroglyph of a scarab beetle. "They had a nuclear war back when the Roman Empire was at its peak. Freaky, no?"

"I'm sorry?" Rita shook her head. "I didn't catch that."

"I'll show you when we arrive." Julie gave her a worried smile. "Is he asleep?"

Rita glanced sideways. "Yes for now." Smith was in fact out cold, but she was not prepared to share a dust mote more than was strictly necessary with Julie right now.

"I hope you're not sore at me. I was just following orders—nobody even told me to keep an eye out for you!"

"Well, that makes it all right." Rita kept her tone even. "You don't need my forgiveness, anyway." *Just the Colonel's paycheck.*

"Like that matters? Listen, in this organization you go where you're told and follow orders. That's all I was doing. No need to make it something personal!"

Rita nodded, reluctantly. Julie had a point: once you took the agency's coin you couldn't really blame anyone else for the consequences.

"Anyway, the Valley we're going to really *is* a headfuck because those people were so far ahead of us it's not even funny—"

"Wait." Rita struggled with the phantoms of her distraction: "People? We're talking about another time line here, right? One that was nuked?"

"Yes." Julie was beginning to sound just slightly impatient with her. "That's what I've been trying to tell you."

"But . . . hang on. I've been to time line four." The safe room in the clinic had been located in that time line. So was Camp Graceland. "Isn't it uninhabited?"

"Yes! At least, it's uninhabited *now.* We're going to Camp Singularity, in the Valley."

"But if they're—are there ruins?"

"You bet," said Julie, her voice rising slightly to match her fervor. "It's every archaeologist's dream, and more besides. You won't believe your eyes!"

CAMP SINGULARITY, TIME LINE FOUR, JULY 2020

Camp Singularity was another DHS installation, a grim little cluster of prefab buildings huddled behind fences and surveillance cams that straddled the ridgeline of a forest valley. The trees were mostly conifers, dark green and spiny, and the weather was chill. A New England autumn transplanted to the latitude of Baltimore in early summer.

By early afternoon, Rita had been checked in and assigned sleeping quarters, and had caught a late lunch with Julie—not a terribly sociable affair, despite the latter's attempts at conversation. As Rita deposited her tray at the collection point, Julie was checking her glasses. "Come on," she said. "Time for the tour."

There was a compact SUV waiting outside. Julie swung up into the driver's seat; Rita took the passenger side. They bumped off toward the edge of the asphalt apron, then onto a dirt track that meandered toward the radar dishes and guard tower at the gatehouse. Rita finally cracked. "Is it far?"

"Just a couple of miles, but it's a bumpy ride."

"Why not put the camp on top of, of whatever it is we're going to?"

"You'll see."

They bumped and jounced down a narrow trail between trees. Once Julie had to back up, then pull over to let a returning pickup truck swagger past, its load bed tarped down and bulging with something or other. The driver, Rita noted, was wearing battle dress and body armor. She suddenly felt underdressed, unprepared. She'd surreptitiously bookmarked the knotspace coordinates of the para-time transport facility back in Maryland, but this chilly, heavily wooded valley worried her. There was no telling whether she'd be able to jaunt back to Earth prime from this place if . . . if anything went wrong, God forbid.

Finally the track widened and turned out into a clear-cut dirt vehicle park. A low-loader bearing a huge generator squatted at one side, suckling on a fat pipe. "Okay, end of the road. We walk from here." Julie parked beside a row of other cars. Rita climbed out and followed her to the checkpoint. The guards here were armored up, their helmet visors mirroring her approach. "Dr. Straker and Rita Douglas for Colonel Smith," Julie called, holding up her ID badge. After a second, Rita followed suit.

"Approach and ID, ma'am." The guard was politely impersonal, but kept his rifle ready and didn't blink until Rita and Julie lit up green on the inside of his network terminal. "Okay, you can go right in." He waved them past the barrier. "Ms. Douglas hasn't been here before, have you? You'll need to take her through the robing room, Dr. Straker."

"I'll do that," Julie promised.

"*Dr.* Straker?" Rita asked, looking at her askance.

"Yes: archaeological science. Camp Singularity is my main posting. It's where I did my PhD. Unfortunately my thesis is classified, otherwise I'd give you a copy . . ."

It was too much to absorb: bubble-headed blonde to DHS agent to scientist in one hour flat. "What was that about a robing room?" Rita asked, trailing after her.

"We need protective gear before we enter the dome—"

"The *dome*?"

Julie grinned at her. "I said there were ruins, didn't I? I just didn't say what *kind* of ruins."

"But—a dome?" Confused visions of cathedrals and igloos spun in her mind.

"Yes: a high-tech one. *Ancient* high-tech, and still contaminated with long half-life fallout. It's okay—we just use disposable overshoes and bunny suits. But you don't want to eat or drink anything in here."

"It's *radioactive*?"

"Yeah, but it's not as bad as the sarcophagus at Chernobyl . . ."

The path wandered between trees and came to an abrupt terminus in the shape of a three-story stack of prefab container offices, behind which loomed a white concrete dome the size of a football stadium. "What the f—hell?"

"Welcome to the dome!" Julie was annoyingly smug. "Let's hit the robing room and get you set up. Then I can show you around."

CAMP SINGULARITY, TIME LINE FOUR, JULY 2020

As Julie and the Colonel had intimated, the dome was a headfuck. Worse: as it all sank in, Rita found it raised more questions than it answered.

"Who built it?" she asked Julie.

A shrug. "Nobody knows. Not us, not anyone from our time line. Sure as hell wasn't the Clan world-walkers, though. We call them the forerunners, because they were building nuclear reactors back when the Romans were building water wheels."

"Are there any"—she swallowed, staring at the carefully gridded-out archaeological excavations around the trashed buildings that lined the northern quadrant of the dome—"people?" *Remains*, she nearly said.

"Yes." Julie's expression through her faceplate was somber. "There were. They were all moved to the forensic lab years ago, though. This is just about a museum-quality preservation site now. The real action is behind the curtain wall over there."

The curtain wall looked recent, illuminated in merciless shadow-free detail by the huge floodlights the excavation team had suspended from the roof. The Camp Singularity archaeologists had installed it to surround something within. Julie referred to it obliquely as the capital-G Gate while they were robing up in their antiradiation suits. The suits were white plastic, with canned air supplies to protect them from any dust that might have been kicked up by human activities here. "What's it there to contain?"

"It's the security cordon around the Gate airlocks. Which are there to hold in the air." Julie lumbered round to face Rita. "When they first found this place, the entire valley was full of mist. I mean, clear blue sky above and freaky thick fog down below, like something out of a Stephen King movie. The first crew into the valley found the air pressure dropping. When they got to the dome, there was a gale blowing through the crack in its side"—the dome had been breached by some long-ago catastrophe—"and the air pressure was well below half a bar. The first job they had was to figure out how to plug the Gate before it sucked the entire atmosphere away."

"Wait—a gate? What kind of gate?"

"You'll see for yourself," Julie said. "But anyway, that was twelve years ago."

"They found this place twelve years ago?"

Julie nodded clumsily, emphatically. "C'mon. It's really quite something." She led Rita forward, delivering a running commentary all the way.

"The dome has no entrance as such. It was a perfect sealed sphere until it was cracked open like an eggshell. We think what did it was some kind of directed orbital gamma ray strike, about two thousand years ago."

Rita looked around, awed by the age of the site. The floor inside the dome was flat, unnaturally smooth where the excavations had swept aside nearly two millennia of dirt and muck that had blown in or grown in.

"It's concrete," Julie explained, "but reinforced with graphene fibers. And there are embedded semiconductor chips all through the top few millimeters—synthetic sapphire substrate, powered by ambient light and microwave radiation. And I mean *all* through it—if you scraped up a cubic yard of the top layer, it'd contain more processing power than Google's biggest data center. They don't work anymore, though. Burned out centuries ago. They're just junk, electronic waste."

"What were they *for*?" Rita asked.

"We don't know. The usual ubiquitous computing stuff, maybe: looking for and fixing cracks, monitoring the micro-environment, fly's-eye optical sensors on the surface-dwelling chips, sniffing the ambient microbiological genome for biowar threats. Who knows? Radiation damage killed them after the dome breach. Ion migration over the centuries since then has blurred the surface features so badly that the geek squad can't reverse-engineer them. It's pretty cool stuff, but nothing we won't be able to do ourselves within the next decade or two—if anyone wants to pour concrete that costs a million dollars a cubic yard. But that's just one of the puzzles."

They walked across the floor of the dome toward a cluster of white-walled buildings. Steel scaffolding surrounded them, stabilizing and providing ladders to the upper-story openings. "We think this was a barracks," Julie continued. "There were external catwalks but they'd collapsed. Damaged in the attack, again. We think maybe they were fire escapes, if anyone made fire escapes out of 3-D-printed titanium alloy."

"This was a military base, wasn't it?" Rita asked.

"Probably, yes, and it'd explain the exotic metals: mil-spec suppliers seem to be a universal constant. But there's other weird stuff you need to see. This is building 102. C'mon upstairs?"

Rita followed Julie up the aluminum stepladder that the DHS archaeologists had used to replace the fallen fire escapes. They entered on the first floor. "Where's the light coming from?"

"The ceiling is wall-to-wall pixels, and while the display driver died centuries ago the backlight still works just fine. Although it took the PaleoComp people a couple of years to figure out how to power it."

Rita looked around the structure. It was a room: as rectilinear and vacant as any other she'd seen. Which should, she felt, be a sign of something. The walls were lined with rows of what looked like bunk beds, layered three high. Yellowing polymers had crumbled away to reveal metal frames within. They had individual shutters to block out the light, high-density kit lockers between the head-end of one unit and the feet of the next. "It looks . . . efficient."

"We think it was refuge accommodation. You'd see the same in any nuclear emergency bunker today." Julie gestured around. "Tell me what you don't see."

"There are—" Rita blinked. "Where's the bathroom? Where are the doors?" Suddenly the room made no sense at all. "You're telling me they had to go out on the fire escape and downstairs and into another building to use the restroom?"

"It's worse than that." Julie gestured at the door they'd entered through. "That was an emergency exit, not an entrance. The ground floor is full to ceiling height with what seems to be a filtered HVAC system, bottled air for a day or so, and water tanks."

"But how did they go to the bathroom?"

"Imagine they were world-walkers. How do *you* think they went to the bathroom?"

Rita stared at Julie for a few seconds. "The bathroom is in *another time line?*"

Julie nodded. "Very good: that's what George—he's our site director—thinks." She turned slowly round, taking in the entire room. "They built a para-time fortress because they were being hunted by a para-time-capable adversary. We think it consists of several installations scattered across identical geographical locations in several time lines. They'd use some of the installations for offensive operations, others as logistics depots or hospitals and other rear-echelon facilities. All in the equivalent location, but in different time lines. Without having a knotspace map of the facility, the enemy couldn't roll them all up. *This* one was the air raid shelter—passive, no emissions, hidden as well as they could. The entire outer shell of the dome is riddled with smart dust. We think it was stealthed to the point of optical and infrared invisibility, using the ground underneath it as a heat sink. If they came under attack, they could just jaunt in here for a few hours or until they could find an evac route. Eat ration packs and shit in a paper bag until it was time to leave."

"Wow." Rita looked around. "It's the bomb shelter under—inside—a five-dimensional Army base? What killed them?"

"Our best theory is it took a gamma ray laser. Fired from low orbit, pumped by a megaton-range hydrogen bomb. But c'mon, let me show you the Gate. It'll top anything you've seen so far." Julie waved her toward the escape hatch/doorway and the ladder beyond.

Rita followed her, duck-walking laboriously in her protective suit. *World-walkers with death rays and H-bombs.* A hollow sense of dread gnawed at her sternum. *What could top* that?

CAMP SINGULARITY, TIME LINE FOUR, JULY 2020

On the other side of the cinder-block wall that bisected the floor of the dome, there was another dome. It was a dome within a dome, Rita noted, but this one lacked the strangely smooth curves and textures of the forerunner ruins. A bunch of modular buildings nuzzled up around its rim. Beyond them the excavation area on the dome floor took on a chaotic, jumbled geometry, as if the forerunner installation had been badly damaged there. "That's where the mach wave converged," Julie explained. "When the forerunners' adversary cracked the outer dome the radiation pulse created a shock wave of superheated air. It expanded, hit the inside of the dome, and rebounded, focusing on this area. If you were standing anywhere else on the apron when it hit, you'd have been fried and blasted: but at the focal point you'd have been crushed instead, just by the overpressure."

Rita shuffled along behind her in mild shock, her thoughts whirling. "What's in the, the small dome?"

"That's ours: we built it. Follow me and I'll show you." Julie led her along a reverberating metal catwalk that spanned a ten-meter-wide excavation site. The arachnoid shapes of archaeology robots crawled back and forth below their feet, ablating and recording everything as they drilled slowly down through the wreckage. "This is where I work most of the time," Julie added brightly. "It's an archaeologist's dream job."

"Most of the time? What else do you do?"

"Write reports and position papers. I don't get to play at spy stuff except when something unusual happens, like when the Colonel roped me in for that thing with Gomez and Jack because he needed another body with all the right clearances. The talent pool's tiny when you get down to it." She sounded irritated.

"So that's why you were along with HaptoTech?" Rita asked, biting back her instant angry response. *Was the entire trade show job a ploy to get me into a sandbox, surrounded by DHS agents?* It seemed excessive, even knowing about the JAUNT BLUE technology.

"Partly. We use their motion capture implants for driving bots around, some of the time." Rita couldn't be sure, but she thought the other woman was shaking her head inside her bulky headgear. "Come on, we need to de-suit before we can enter the clean room."

A door gaped open onto another white space, a NASA-esque vision of a space station airlock vestibule. A bench ran the width of one wall, occupied by empty suits with their backs docked to small hatches. Julie helped Rita sit down and showed her how to lean back against the suit-lock. "Duck down to get your head out from under the helmet rim, grab the overhead rail, and swing yourself out," she advised.

After a minute of mild claustrophobia Rita managed to worm her way down and out through the back of her radiation suit. She found herself in a cramped robing room. "Ms. Douglas?" A lightly built man was waiting for her. He wore a skintight but weirdly quilted outfit that left only his face bare. "You haven't been here before so I'm going to have to authenticate you. Hi, Julie, you can go in, but you'll need to help Ms. Douglas suit up for the Gate."

"The Gate?" Rita looked from face to face. "Is that radioactive, too?"

"No, but you need vacuum protection. I'll hang around, Jose."

"Wait—'vacuum'?" It was one too many surprises for a single afternoon: Rita was beginning to feel petulant and resentful at the way it was all piling up.

"Yes, like I said, all the air in the valley was being sucked out through the Gate when we found it."

Jose took Rita through the increasingly familiar DNA sample and password authentication routine. "Okay, in the next room Julie will help you into one of these," he explained, pointing to his own outfit. "It's a mechanical counterpressure suit—it compares to a normal space suit the way a wet suit is to an old-school canvas diving suit. Keeps you from blowing out in vacuum because it's elasticated and squeezes you, while a regular NASA suit is an airtight bag. The reason we use them is we have to work in confined spaces beyond the Gate, and ambient pressure suits are too bulky." He raised his left arm and pointed to an intricate tracery of red seams stitched across the fabric around his torso. "Got to get it skintight first, though."

Rita swallowed. "What *is* this Gate?" she asked, trying to keep a plaintive note out of her voice.

"They didn't tell you?" Jose stared at her. "It's the *Gate*. Uh, it's a paratime portal. The one that nearly vented all the air in this time line into vacuum, except we caught it before that happened and it's small enough that it would have taken tens of thousands of years anyway."

You have got to be kidding me, Rita thought as Jose, with Julie's assistance, strapped her into a space suit that felt like an inch-thick body stocking, hung a slim life-support vest around her, and screwed a helmet onto the steel ring that hung around her collarbone. *I'm going to wake up any moment now,* she told herself uncertainly. *This is just crazy.* World-walking she could handle: she could do it herself. But she'd never heard even a hint that the government was sitting on top of some kind of gate between time lines. She felt numb. The implications of what she was being shown today were too big to get her head around: she ought to be freaking out, she felt, but over what particular aspect of the whole shocking secret?

"I'm monitoring your vitals remotely," Jose added. "In event of a pressure emergency the helmet will seal automatically; there's a short-range voice channel over infrared: the transponder's on top of your head." Julie, already suited, raised a hand and tapped a protrusion on her helmet that Rita had taken for a headlight.

"What about Mission Control?" Rita asked.

"I *am* Mission Control. We requisitioned this stuff from NASA—space station spares and prototypes they never flew—but we don't have their manpower. Or their budget."

"But what"—Rita turned to face Julie—"do you need *me* for?"

Julie waved her forward, toward a rectangular metal door at the far end of the robing room. "Jose? You don't need to hear this."

"Gotcha. I'll be in the office; page me if you need me." He ducked out.

"This way," Julie said.

"You haven't said why." Rita stood her ground, stubborn.

"The Colonel told me to give you the dog and pony show." Julie momentarily looked mulish. "If you want to know what this is *really* about, you'll have to ask Colonel Smith: I'm mostly just a researcher here." She looked around warily. Rita couldn't be sure—the humming aircon and the muffling effects of her helmet liner messed with her hearing—but Julie seemed tense. Almost as if she was afraid of being listened in on.

"I'm not arguing, but—" Rita stopped. "You've got a script, you've got a dog and pony show to give me, I get that, but do we need to do this drip-drip thing? Why couldn't you show me the video or something instead of dragging me out here?"

"Because the Colonel wants you to see it with your own eyes," Julie said snippily. "You wouldn't believe us if we just showed you a video. This stuff's real. It's also so crazy that most people go straight into denial unless they see it for themselves." She took a deep breath. "If I had to make a guess—this is just a guess, you with me? I don't *know* that this is what's happening—I'd guess that he's worried about your commitment. But you're not stupid or crazy, so he's giving you enough of the background to make up your own mind."

She pointed at the door. "On the other side of that airlock there's a walkway into the Gate. It's a gate into another time line. One where there's no Earth. We built a receiving area and laboratory on the far side, but there's a risk of micrometeoroid impacts, hence the suits. Part of the dog and pony show is that the Colonel wants you to use your magic JAUNT BLUE thing to log your knotspace location before you step through the Gate, and again on the other side. You're not to try and jaunt there, you understand— you'd die, with or without a space suit. But he wants to see if you can log it, and if it agrees with readings we've taken using other devices."

Her heart pounded. "But why? I mean, couldn't they just map the knotspace location anyway?"

"He wants *you* to do it. So that you get to see what's on the other side of it."

"But what's so hazardous? Apart from vacuum?"

"There's no *there* there. The lab is anchored to the Gate and there's gravity, but there's no surface, just a point mass several thousand miles down. Because on this side the Gate is sitting on the surface of the Earth, the far side is being carried around the point mass at a few hundred miles per hour as the Earth rotates. That's well below orbital velocity, so if you jaunted through to that time line you'd fall below ground level really fast. Best case, if you didn't fall right into the center, is that you'd eventually drift up: in which event, if you jaunted back at *exactly* the right moment and had a parachute, you might survive. But if you drifted too far down, or got too close to the center—"

"Yeah, I get it." Rita's mouth was dry. "So the Gate's in two time lines at once, isn't it?"

"Yes. That's why it's a gate." Julie pulled the heavy airlock door open and walked inside. A red line painted along the floor of the room continued up the far wall, bisecting the door opposite. "Come on in. I've done this dozens of times—it's routine as long as you don't screw up."

"Okay. Just a minute." Rita paused on the threshold and squeezed her left forearm, hoping she'd remembered the multitouch gesture correctly and that it would register through the padding of her skinsuit. Then she followed Julie into the chamber. "I'm ready now."

"Don't let the airlock hit you on the ass." Julie pulled the door closed and dogged it. "Hold the handrail and follow me." Demonstrating, she walked across the red line. "Come on, nothing to it."

Rita followed her. A faint wave of nausea gripped her stomach as she stepped over the red line, but it had to be her imagination. There was no way her inner ear could register her sudden departure from the universe of light and air and gravity, was there?

"That was the Gate. Easy, wasn't it?" said Julie. She paused before the opposite airlock hatch. "Pressure's equal. I'm opening up." She rotated a handwheel and pulled the door open. "Come on inside." Julie left the airlock; Rita followed, marveling. She'd seen the old movies *2001* and *Apollo 13*: *Okay, so now I've fallen into a sci-fi flick* she thought dizzily. It was a giant leap too far: all disbelief faded, burned out like an overloaded fuse. They were in a dimly lit corridor, lined with velcro pads and cable ducts, with drawers on all four walls. A docking node at the far end contained sealed hatches to either side. Inset in the floor, a cluster of windows like the nose of a Second World War bomber opened onto starry darkness. "That's the cupola," Julie told her. "It's a duplicate of the one on the international space station." Rita drifted toward it, fascinated.

"Why is it here?" she asked.

"We need to study the singularity. Right now there's nobody posted here—they're all in their regular weekly team meeting back in the dome. But we've usually got a crew who keep an eye on it: astrophysicists, mostly, but also the life-support engineers who keep the whole thing running. Unlike the international space station, we can feed it power and air and hydraulics through the Gate and commute home daily. So we ripped out a whole lot of stuff NASA would have needed. But it still takes a lot of TLC to keep it running and safe to work in."

"What's the singularity?" Rita asked as she peered through the big circular window at the bottom of the cupola. There were stars. As her eyes adjusted to the semidarkness, she saw more and more of them. Centered in it was a dim, glowing blue cloud, about as big as the full moon but fuzzy around the edges. A violent pinprick glare at its heart illuminated it from within.

"It's a planetary-mass black hole. The glow you can see is coming from the accretion disk around it. The hole itself is only about a centimeter in diameter, but it's still chowing down on all the gas and debris that leaked through the Gate before we plugged it. Stuff heats up down there due to friction and tidal drag as it falls in. So that glowing dot is actually at about a billion degrees, putting out as much energy as a ten-megaton nuke every second. Luckily it's eight thousand kilometers away, or we'd be toast. We're not in orbit around it: we're effectively hanging off the end of a bridge to nowhere, the other end of which is anchored back in the dome. We think"—Julie paused—"it's all that's left of the Earth in this time line. After the forerunner adversaries crushed it."

Rita stared. "The Colonel wanted me to see . . ."

"Yeah." Julie was silent for a few seconds. "Whoever did this could still be out there, Rita. Somewhere in para-time."

Rita swallowed. "They crushed the Earth down to a black hole?"

"Just like the Clan world-walkers nuked the White House."

Julie was watching her, Rita realized: wearing her DHS agent hat. Doubtless she'd write up a report for the Colonel. A horrible realization struck her. "This Earth, the one that was crushed—it was inhabited, wasn't it?"

Julie shrugged, the gesture almost invisible in her space suit. "Probably. Who can tell?"

But why would anyone destroy an uninhabited *planet?* Rita thought, sickened. "But if they're still out there . . ."

Julie completed the thought for her: ". . . it's our job to make sure this doesn't happen to *our* time line."

Deployment

Miriam was deeply asleep, dreaming of an earlier life in another world's Boston, when the red telephone rang.

Once upon a time she'd been a go-getting business journalist, working for a high-profile magazine that covered the BosWash tech community. Her particular beat was the Cambridge/Boston biotech start-up sector, but she'd covered other businesses too, until her investigation into the connection between a chain of secondhand car dealerships and a medical clinic had cost her her job—and nearly her life.

That kind of journalism didn't exist anymore in the United States. Caught in the crossfire between the Internet's corrosive impact on advertising and the burgeoning security state's disapproval of unauthorized snoopers and unembedded media, it had died out a decade ago; and in any case her path had taken her unimaginably far from there. But she still dreamed of it from time to time, oppressed by a vaguely claustrophobic sense of nostalgia for her youth in a land of opportunity, when she'd been driving toward goals she'd long since outgrown. These days her objectives were so huge, shimmering in the distant heat haze of the future like a Mosaic vision of the promised land: she no longer expected to live to see them.

It was three in the morning, and she was dreaming that she was on a conference call in the *Insider*'s offices, waiting on the line to speak to a source in a monoclonal antibody start-up while an inexplicable earthquake rumbled. The telephone began to ring, louder and louder. It wasn't the single long ring of an American phone, but a sequence of three short trills, then a pause, then three more. A Commonwealth telephone, summoning her to—

She rolled over and, barely awake, reached for the handset on the nightstand. "Burgesons. Miriam here." Beside her Erasmus thrashed and snorted loudly, stopped snoring, and sat up.

"Commissioner? This is Commonwealth Crisis Command, I have General Benn on the line for you. Is Commissioner—the *other* Commissioner—Burgeson with you? This is an all-ears Cabinet flash."

The bedside light flickered on. Miriam rolled on her back and pushed herself up against the headboard. Her husband looked at her: "Flash message for both of us," she said.

Seconds passed as Erasmus untangled the telephone cord on his side of the bed and other Commissioners joined the party line. Miriam waited, heart pounding. The cobwebs of sleep were fading, replaced by bone-deep fatigue and apprehension. *Is it the French?* she wondered.

"Citizens?" A new voice came on the line: "This is Colonel-General Benn, watch commander at Triple-C. I am calling this Cabinet flash because Air Defense Command has just reported the shoot-down of a high-altitude radar-occult aircraft, sixty nautical miles off the New England coast. A capital weapon was used to complete the interception. Air Defense has had a system-wide alert in force just in case the intruder was French, but observation and backtracking suggests the intruder materialized out of nowhere—it was traveling out to sea when ADC lit it up—and was well within the Capital Defense Zone. In accordance with standing orders, we are declaring War Condition Two. The Continental Bombardment Force is scrambling its petard carriers to their dispersal stations. The Continuity Authority has been activated, and I am now notifying Commissioners and Senators of the crisis. Thank you for your attention."

The line crackled for a couple of seconds, then a new voice spoke. "Commissioners Burgeson and Burgeson? The First Man is on his way to his designated location. He has asked for you to join him for a meeting at nine."

Miriam made eye contact with Erasmus. He grimaced and mouthed a quiet obscenity. "We'll be ready to go in fifteen minutes," she told the caller.

"Excellent, ma'am. A rotodyne is on its way to collect you. It will touch down on the near end of Soldier's Field shortly."

Erasmus was already pulling on yesterday's trousers as Miriam put the phone down and shoved the bedding aside to stand up. He coughed horribly for a few seconds, then straightened up. "This can't be good."

"No." Feeling shaky, Miriam opened her wardrobe and pulled out her emergency go-bag. There was an appropriate outfit folded neatly in a paper bag atop it, a ladies trouser-suit not unlike a shalwar kameez. She dressed rapidly, then rang the service bell. "Erasmus and I have been called away suddenly," she spoke into the intercom. "We'll need help with our luggage."

"I'll send Jack up to carry it, ma'am." It was Jenny the housekeeper; she sounded sleepy and confused. "How long shall you be gone?"

"No idea," Miriam said tersely. Her knees ached and her hair was a rat's nest. Even so, Erasmus looked worse, his shirt rumpled and his neckcloth unfastened. "We need to be out at the double, on our way in ten minutes."

Soldier's Field public park opened off the far end of the crescent their house faced. It was flat and level and the size of several football fields, surrounded by a border of neatly manicured trees. The huge rotodyne descended onto the grass with a screeching roar from the ramjets on the ends of its rotor blades, landing lights glaring. The rotors kept spinning while it squatted on the field, doubtless waking the dead across a radius of miles. The rotodyne was a triumph of brute-force engineering over subtlety, a heliplane—halfway between a big transport helicopter and a turboprop troop carrier—the product of a road not taken in the US due to noise and fuel-thirst, but effective nonetheless.

Lights were coming on in homes all around as Miriam and Erasmus duck-walked toward it, guided by a pair of airmen. Doubtless radios and televisions were coming on too. The news that the Air Defense Command had just shot down an unidentified intruder nearly seventy miles out past Cape Cod using a corpuscular weapon couldn't be kept quiet.

The distant flare of the two-megaton warshot would have been visible all the way from Boston to Baltimore.

It was too loud to talk inside the aircraft as it spun up to takeoff power, but once they transitioned to level flight and the tip jets throttled back, things were no worse than on any other military turboprop. Miriam managed to make herself heard: "How long are we going to be airborne?"

"Only forty minutes, ma'am; we're making nearly two hundred knots. We'll have you inside the designated location within the hour."

Miriam frowned and glanced at Erasmus. He nodded, his face ashen. The New American Commonwealth didn't—yet—have anything like the USA's airborne command posts. The metallurgy for efficient high-bypass turbofans—engines that could keep a drone or a jumbo jet airborne for days on end—was tantalizingly close. In the meantime, the Commonwealth leadership had a radically different protocol for maintaining command during a nuclear war.

"I'm going to dose up," she told her husband. "They might need me to jump—"

"Not on my watch," he said firmly. "Not unless the petards are falling. We need you lucid, not moaning from a killer migraine."

"Thanks." She squeezed his hand. "Still dosing up, mind." The small bottle held two gelatin capsules: a devil's brew of antihypertensives and painkillers. They were the Commonwealth's best self-administered solution to the effects of world-walking.

The rotodyne screeched on through the night, props and rotors thundering. Fifteen minutes into the flight the radio operator came aft, saluted, and handed Erasmus a teleprinted message. He skimmed it, then passed it wordlessly to Miriam.

INTRUDER DETECTED 0219 HOURS
RADAR CONTACT LAT 41°40'16.92"N LONG 69°24'32.15"W
    ALTITUDE 64,400 FEET BEARING 066°58' GROUND SPEED
    590 MPH
FLIGHT PLAN ABSENT BREAK FOE IDENTITY FAILED BREAK
    HAIL UNANSWERED BREAK
MISSILE INTERCEPT PLAN ISSUED AT 0230 HOURS

MISSILE BATTERY ENGAGED TARGET AT 0234 HOURS
INTRUDER PRESUMED DESTROYED BY ZEUS-IV MISSILE AT
  0237 HOURS
LAST CONTACT AT LAT 41°43′51.32″N LONG 68°18′9.44″W
  ALTITUDE 64,800 FEET BEARING 066°58′ GROUND SPEED
  582 MPH

"They didn't mess around," Miriam muttered, heedless of her throat mike. Zeus-IV was a long-range surface-to-air nuclear missile. It was unguided and unjammable, but able to reach out and swat an enemy aircraft with a two-megaton warhead from over a hundred miles away. Brute-force weapons like the old Nike-Hercules had gone out of fashion in the USA during the 1970s, as sensitive electronics proliferated. A Zeus strike would burn out every unshielded microprocessor within fifty miles. Luckily unshielded microprocessors were a rarity in the Common-wealth, and would remain so thanks to MITI-dictated national shield-ing standards.

Miriam was still shaken from learning a nuclear weapon had just been fired in anger for the first time in nearly twenty years. And at a stealthy intruder capable of flying as high and fast as a U-2, that had appeared out of thin air. "This wasn't the French," she said in a thin voice. "They don't have the tech and they know better than to tug our tail like that. No, this is an escalation over last month's incidents."

The earlier American drones had popped up in controlled airspace far to the south-west, flying fat and happy at medium altitude. Air Defense Command had scrambled their shiniest missile-armed supersonic inter-ceptors and used them for target practice. Afterward, DPR's analysts had identified the recovered wreckage as coming from MQ-1 Predators, obsolescent unmanned turboprops so embarrassingly outclassed that even the French could have shot them down. This new contact was a much more potent adversary.

"The sooner we get to the Redoubt the better." Erasmus sounded no happier than she felt. Sick terror twisted her stomach, until she feared she'd need to reach for the bag under her seat. She hadn't seen the bombs fall on the Gruinmarkt, but her mother had. Iris had described them in morbid detail, and suffered from nightmare flashbacks for the rest of her life. (A row of distant flashbulbs, their sullen heat refracted through cloud, popping in the distance. Then another row of hell-sparks, detonating closer. Ripples in the bloodstained sky as the overlapping shock waves tore apart the cloudscape. Panic as the burning rain crept closer, deceptively slowly, dripping from a storm front of bombers traveling just below the speed of sound.) They'd sent scouts to the Gruinmarkt shortly afterward—wearing dosimeters and protective clothing, and keeping a low profile in case the USA had monitors in place. When Miriam had seen the photographs, she'd thrown up, then slept badly for a week.

"It's too soon. We're not ready; the JUGGERNAUT program is nowhere near ready—"

He looked at her tiredly. "We can't use that thing."

"No, but if we demonstrated we had a superweapon of that caliber they'd have to back down. Deterrence works, love. Game theory doesn't lie. It worked for half a century back in my—in the old world. It's working for us on the French. When JUGGERNAUT is complete and we've made overt contact, nobody will be crazy enough to attack us."

His chest rose and fell, wheezing. After a few seconds he reached into his coat pocket and removed a small metal aerosol inhaler. After he used it, the panting slowly subsided. A minute later he could speak again. "Your faith in psychology is wonderfully strong, dear." He gave her a crooked little smile, clearly more worried than he was prepared to admit. "Right now, we're boxing blindfolded with hand grenades taped to our gloves. We need intelligence; we need to know who and what we're up against."

"I've got people working on it," Miriam reassured him as the engine note of the turboprops shifted, heralding the start of their descent. *I just hope they deliver before it's too late.*

BALTIMORE, TIME LINE TWO, JULY 2020

"What do you want from me?" Rita tried to keep a whine of frustration from creeping into her voice. "I don't understand where this is going."

Smith looked at her disapprovingly from across the expanse of his desk. "Rita, calm down. It's not about you." The tension in his shoulders said something like *God give me strength.* "We have a problem. A very special kind of problem. One you might be able to help us with, if you can stop acting like a drama queen for five minutes."

I'm not—Rita managed to hold the words back, with an effort. Familiarity was making it too easy to open up to Colonel Smith and his team of handlers. She needed to focus harder if she was to keep a grip on herself: even surrounded by increasingly familiar faces she felt lonely and defensive. "I'm listening."

"You're listening—what?"

"I'm listening, *sir.*"

Smith nodded, stiffly. "That's better."

"I don't remember joining the services, *sir.* Sorry. I *do* know a, a sandbox when I'm in one. I'm not a mushroom; I don't thrive in the dark on a diet of bullshit."

"No, I don't suppose you do." Smith's lips were thin. "None of us do. And you're perfectly right, you didn't swear the oath. And you're right we're keeping you in a box. But the less you know about the rest of the Office of Special Programs and DHS, the less you can give away."

Give away. "This is the run-up to a covert deployment, isn't it? You want me to spy for you."

"Yes, but"—Smith leaned back and stared at the wall behind and above her head—"I'm having some second thoughts."

"Why? Sir."

Smith glanced down to meet her gaze. His eyes were pale blue; she found his stare disturbingly intense. "It's premature. Rita, in all honesty, you're nowhere near ready for this. The usual recruitment and training structure for a clandestine operative is for us to sound them out in college, security-clear them before hiring, then deploy them on an analysis desk for years of intensive immersion—often with added language training—in the target culture. We evaluate, assess their progress, identify their shortcomings, and assign them more training until they're perfectly acculturated for the destination. *Then* we generate their cover identity and background material and inject them.

"Modern biometrics and DNA databases mean that a clandestine asset gets just *one* home run in an entire career. If they're really lucky, if there are two different target nations with a shared culture that don't get on well enough to share their frontier databases, they might get a second outing under a new identity: but one is the rule. After their covert identity is retired they come home and teach the next generation of agents, or retire to the analysis desk. But they can't operate in the field again—two different names on passports with the same genetic fingerprint and facial bone structure will start alarm bells ringing. So we don't deploy agents lightly. We only send the best of the best, and we train them for years first, to make sure we get the most bang for our bucks."

"But you—" Rita paused for a moment, assessing her next words carefully. "You grabbed me at zero notice and I've only been training for a few months. Did something go wrong? Or were you watching me before?"

"Yes to both." Smith leaned forward. "JAUNT BLUE is very new. You're the first recipient. It only works on non-world-walking descendants of the, the Clan. And we don't have many of them. If we'd known we'd have it five years ago, you'd probably have been contacted in college, steered toward the right degree. And we'd still be sitting here right now, but you'd be fully trained and cognizant of the reasons for what we're doing. As it is, though, you're barely one step above a raw recruit. To make matters worse, we're completely in the dark about the target society. So we desperately need clandestine resources. You are all we've got, and some people I report to who you do not need to know about *do not believe we can rely on you.* I'd like to prove them wrong, but not at the cost of a blown operation and a dead agent. That would be you."

It hit her like a bucket of cold water in the face. "There's no one else yet?" He shook his head, lips pursed. "How long until . . . ?"

"Three years, minimum."

"But I'm—" She stopped. "Why so long?"

"We have a very limited pool of JAUNT BLUE candidates, Rita. You're the oldest."

"I'm the *oldest*?"

He spoke slowly at first. "Your birth mother and her mother were Clan runaways. There may be other deserters, but despite looking hard we haven't found them yet. As for the rest . . . there's a pool of inactive Q-machine carriers. The Clan were using a fertility clinic in Massachusetts to breed children carrying the trait by the thousand. We found a copy of the breeding program records: but the oldest of the cohort are just turning twenty-one now."

"So that's why you sank all that money into JAUNT BLUE?"

Smith nodded. "Spending half a billion dollars on one agent wouldn't make much sense, would it? But if as many as five percent of the Clan's breeding program clear their background checks and join up, we'll have the nucleus of a decent clandestine para-temporal intelligence service in five to ten years' time."

"But I'm a, a prototype?"

"Yes."

"And the Clan tried to snatch me off the street because of my birth mother."

"Yes." Smith paused for a fraction of a second too long. *Gotcha*, Rita thought sourly. "It's the first hint we've had in seventeen years that she may have survived."

"Survived what?"

His gaze focused beyond her again, on some unseen vista of historic failure: "Let's just say, mistakes were made in the lead-up to 7/16."

Rita froze, riveted. "Does that mean what I think it does?"

Smith refocused on her. "The CIA were in contact with Osama bin Laden before 2001, you know. But that doesn't mean they were responsible for 9/11. Nor were the Clan an accidental creation of ours. They didn't give us any concrete demands or try to negotiate before they bombed the White House: I want you to be very clear on that. We stumbled on them and tried to shut them down, and they attacked us with stolen demolition nukes. Escalated straight to mass murder. They left President Rumsfeld no option other than to respond in kind."

Rita shied away from thinking about it too hard. There'd been rolling video footage for weeks all over the TV and Internet when she was eight. First, the Washington Monument toppling on a shock wave, a fiery cloud rising where the White House had been. Then a month later, the horrors of New Delhi and Islamabad: when the news of world-walking broke, the cold war between India and Pakistan had abruptly turned nuclear. World War 2.5 they'd called it afterwards. Finally, unrolling beneath a camera mounted in the tail of a high-altitude US Air Force bomber, the TV news brought home the US government's revenge on the world-walkers' home time line. A field of ghastly flaming mushroom clouds had risen in parallel lines, spanning the horizon and bisecting the pale neck of history like a blow from a headsman's axe.

"You've seen Camp Singularity, and the dome and the Gate," Colonel Smith nudged her mercilessly toward the precipice. "What happened there was even worse than 7/16. Rita, the forerunners may be dead, or they may still be out there. *We don't know.* They may be connected with the Clan world-walkers. Again, we don't know. The JAUNT BLUE Q-machines didn't evolve naturally, that's for sure. What we *do* know, via mitochondrial DNA studies of captured Clan members, is that they all share a common ancestor who lived less than two and a half centuries ago. From what we know of the Clan's world they could no more build Q-machines than Benjamin Franklin could build an H-bomb. So all the evidence points to a high-technology para-time civilization that was active in the recent historic past. We think the Clan may actually be descended from a deserter or runaway from that civilization—like your birth grandmother—but as I said, we just don't know for sure."

Without realizing she was doing it, Rita had raised her left fist to her mouth: now she found herself gnawing on her knuckles. "So you found them. That's what this is all about."

"We don't know," Smith said gently. "We want you to find out."

"If they're the Clan's ancestors? Or, or the forerunners? Or their enemies?"

"They might be any of the above, or something else entirely. We *don't know.* All we know is that we opened up a new time line recently. This one was accessible via those parts of time line one—the Clan's former

home—that don't still glow in the dark. Which suggests a Clan connection. We lost three reconnaissance drones in rapid succession when we
started trying to map it. But the fourth drone survived and brought back
some highly-suggestive photographs."

"Another dome?"

"Nothing so high-tech. It looks like a big railway freight switchyard,
near the site of downtown Allentown on our time line. On the outskirts
of Philly. There are buildings and probably a city as well, but it's not
ours."

"Railway freight—" Rita frowned, puzzling over the drip of data. "But
so far all the time lines we've found have been uninhabited or Stone Age,
haven't they? Apart from Camp Singularity."

"Yes." Smith gave her an encouraging smile. "Pretend you're a fully
trained analyst. What does that tell you?"

"The forerunners built the Gate. They had unimaginable powers.
Still, it's hard to see them building railroads, isn't it?"

"Carry on."

"But . . . a freight yard?" The dust of history classes stirred in her
memory. "That means they're industrialized. They've got steam locomotives, at a minimum, and enough factories and stuff to need heavy rail
freight? And we still use rail freight for shipping goods around. Hang on.
We lost *three* drones?"

Smith nodded again, seeing the horror dawning in her widening eyes.
"Carry on."

"You found an industrial civilization that can shoot down high-altitude
reconnaissance drones? With stealth technology? Oh sh—" She bit her
knuckles again to stifle the curse.

"Stealth isn't a magic invisibility cloak. It's more like camouflage: it
works best from certain angles. And it doesn't work at all if your opponents
are sneaky enough. It's no good being invisible to radar if you fly through
a storm by mistake—the bad guys can look for the hole in the rain that's
moving at six hundred miles per hour. We've spent so long snooping on
jihadis in the tribal territories on the Afghan border, or rock-bangers with
flint hand axes in undeveloped time lines, that we've forgotten how to deal

with a real threat. So now we've got this headache time line and we're having to relearn old skills fast.

"Now, we *might* be looking at a Victorian level of technology, given those railways—but it's highly unlikely that we lost three UAVs by accident. It's much more likely that we're looking at, at a minimum, a time line with 1950s technology. That's radar and surface-to-air missiles. Nuclear weapons are a distinct possibility. Which is why your superiors and mine are quietly screaming for intelligence that simply doesn't exist. They're looking in a mirror that's showing them their own response to first contact with another para-time civilization, and they don't much like what they see. Especially as there's a risk that this time line is more developed than we are. Or that they're being watched by the forerunners. *We don't know.*"

"Oh Jesus." Rita stared at Smith, her mind whirling. "So, um. That's what you want me for, isn't it? You think a mid-twenties female with acting skills can sneak in and quietly look around and report back on . . . everything?" He didn't need to nod this time. She continued: "It's not going to be quick. We don't know what language they speak, do we? Or what they wear? What they look like, whether I'll stand out because of my appearance?"

Smith nodded again. "If you take it on, it's not going to be easy. In fact, it's potentially extremely hazardous. If we had more time, I'd send you on courses in social anthropology and ethnography first. Also for training with field anthropologists. Not to mention more work on personal self-defense and espionage tradecraft, because you're going to be unarmed except for your JAUNT BLUE ability. On the other hand, if you agree to do this for us, we'll give you all the support we can provide. Clothing, money, covert recording instruments—"

"Money?"

"Well, assuming they use money and you can get us some samples, we have friends in the Treasury Department who spend all their time examining forgeries. This will be a nice change for them, don't you think? And you've got another huge advantage over a conventional clandestine agent: you can choose your insertion point. It could be virtually anywhere, as long as nobody's watching."

"Wow." It was an enormous picture. Assuming it was true, it also shed a new light on his willingness to manipulate her. And despite having hard evidence that he'd lied to her in the past to railroad her into this position, she couldn't imagine why he might want to lie to her about this now. "It's huge, isn't it?"

"Yes, Rita, it's an enormous responsibility. It's the sharp end of a mission that, done right, could save us from a nuclear war. Done wrong—you don't want to think about that."

She bit her lip. "When do I start? And where?"

"Tomorrow morning you're going to an installation outside Philly—as near as we can place it to that railroad yard. The Unit is setting up a forward support site right now, and once you're checked in we'll begin drafting an operational checklist and insertion plan. *If*, that is, you're volunteering?"

The Unit. It had an ominous ring to it. Yet another sandbox, to keep Rita hemmed in and ignorant of what was really going on. "I don't feel ready for this. There's no alternative, is there?"

Smith spoke haltingly: "I am not . . . going to . . . strong-arm you into saying yes. If there's one thing worse than having no agent, it's having an agent who is scared out of their wits and doesn't want to be there. So, uh. You are allowed to say 'no,' if you really don't think you're up to it."

"But if I say no . . . there's no one else who can do this job, is there?" she asked, deliberately pushing him toward another lie. *Go on, tell me the truth, just this once.* She knew it was foolish, but she found his evasion inexpressibly depressing.

"I wish there were. I really wish there were. But we're out of time."

Rita nodded reluctantly. So she *was* working for an unscrupulous liar. Worse: one who didn't see anything wrong with lying because his motives were entirely pure. *What should I do?* she wondered. Then, *What would Grandpa say?*

PHILADELPHIA, TIME LINE TWO, AUGUST 2020

"Rocks," Rita said disbelievingly. "Really?"

"Yup. Rocks." Patrick, her supervisor from Camp Graceland and now, it seemed, her field officer, hefted a chunk of misshapen pink granite a couple of inches long. "Like this one."

"What's so special about them?" Rita shifted her weight. The cheap conference seat creaked unfairly beneath her. *I'm not that heavy!* she complained silently. Like everything else on this site—an office suite attached to a light industrial unit in Allentown, on the outskirts of Philly—it was secondhand and had seen better days.

"It's instrumented. The batteries are good for seven days, during which it will continuously record meteorological conditions and high-definition video—optical and infrared—whenever anything moves around it. It can report over Bluetooth if you go within a hundred feet of it while carrying an active transponder that's paired with it, but it doesn't broadcast its presence. *This* one"—Patrick picked up another object, which resembled a battered length of two-by-four—"has a six-month life, and inertial sensors. It works with a transponder disguised as a different rock. You drop the transponder in the switchyard and toss the mobile unit on top of a caboose or a shunting engine and it builds a map of the track network as it gets pushed around, then calls in whenever it comes back to the same switchyard. Uh, you probably don't want to put it on a goods wagon, though. Not unless you want it to go on an extended tour of North America."

"Uh-huh." Rita stared at Patrick's rock and scrap collection. "So what's the plan?"

"The plan is to build out our knowledge of the target time line, starting with somewhere relatively safe. We know there's a railroad yard, so we want you to go through there at night and scatter sensors around a couple of key areas without being seen. The first mission will be a double-jaunt into the switchyard via a place you do *not* want to linger in. It'll be a quick in-and-out, fifteen minutes max. We leave the sensors in place for a day, then you go back to collect them. That gives us a preliminary site survey, so we can pick a better insertion site for the next mission, when you will plant hidden cameras and mikes on platforms and offices. We need to know a whole lot more—what language they speak, whether it's related to any that we know, what their writing looks like, what they wear, their ethnicity or physical appearance—before we can develop a covert program."

"An entire program?" It was a daunting prospect. "But I'm just one woman, what can I—"

"You're the spearhead for BLACK RAIN," Patrick interrupted. His expression was serious. "That's the code word for this operation, to investigate this time line. We need you to spy out the lay of the land. Your goal is to establish a toehold, learn the basics, and finally identify a safe location on the other side where we can drop non-world-walkers. Then they can take over the heavy lifting. Once we've established a transfer gate you won't be needed there again—but we'll probably want to do the same thing elsewhere. Maybe even overseas."

Rita stared at the rocks apprehensively. "What if they discover the rocks?"

"They'll be disguised as track ballast. Over here we lay three thousand tons of the stuff per mile of track. Even if they figure out there's a bug in the ballast, searching a switchyard for passive transponders would be like looking for needles in a haystack the size of Iowa. You'll only be able to find them yourself because we'll give you a signaling device that can make them flash an infrared LED for your night vision goggles."

"And if they have infrared floodlights and CCTV, like an Amtrak depot?"

Patrick shook his head. "Then you cut and run, and we have a very big headache. Rita, our number one priority here is to get you back safely. Never doubt that! Because you can tell us far more about what's going on than any dumb sensor."

Rita tried to make it work inside her head. "Okay, so . . . Say we've got a surveyed location. At the designated time I suit up, cross over to the, the switchyard, drop a bunch of rocks, plant a couple of bits of debris on suitable cabs if I see anything, then come back. Is that it?"

"Yes. It'll be a walk in the park—just like the Apollo astronauts had." Patrick seemed tired. To Rita's eyes he looked like he'd been working overtime for too many nights. "You'll be wearing body armor and a night vision system. And you'll have a bunch of cameras strapped to your helmet, along with inertial sensors—it'll be like one of those HaptoTech motion capture systems you worked with, so we can put together a virtual map of the yard after you come back. But that's about it. We've arranged for a trainer from the Federal Railroad Administration to come in after lunch to give you a basic safety briefing on what hazards you can expect in a switchyard. There are no guarantees that they do things the same way we do, but we can make some approximate guesses based on the photographs—their track and loading gauge, maximum track curvature and length of railroad cars—which tell us things like how fast and how heavy their trains are. Oh, and the switch layout and siding geometry tells us how they load and unload stuff. But I'd better leave that to the FRA guy. And then after his briefing I'm sure you'll want to sack out."

"Why? You're planning on sending me through tonight?" she asked, half joking: *They can't* possibly *be in that much of a hurry* . . .

"Yes. At three-fifteen precisely."

PHILADELPHIA, TIME LINE TWO; IRONGATE,
TIME LINE THREE, AUGUST 2020

At ten past three in the morning Rita shifted her weight uneasily from one knee to the other. They were standing around in the middle of a parking lot behind the windowless warehouse unit the Unit had appropriated. Rita, Patrick, a cluster of technicians, a pair of armorers, the peripatetic DHS agents Sonia Gomez and Jack Mercer—Rita had finally achieved a high enough security clearance to learn his surname—and a bunch of uniformed officers had established a secure perimeter around the entire block, thereby ensuring that every undesirable within a fifty-mile radius knew something was going down.

After the afternoon briefing on how not to lose life or limbs to a bump-shunted boxcar, Rita had crashed out until ten o'clock. But now she was awake, pumped high on bad coffee and strapped into a mall ninja's parody version of a James Bond outfit. The ensemble consisted of boots, black BDUs, armor, and a mad-scientist helmet that sprouted VR glasses, a lifelogger, and a pair of night vision scopes cantilevered off the front. She lacked only a scary-looking gun to fit the part perfectly—but although Patrick had asked if she wanted a pistol, she'd declined: "First, I don't know if I could shoot anyone, and second, if I did it would totally fuck the mission, wouldn't it?"

"Right answer," he'd told her. "If you see any sign of trouble, you jaunt away immediately. If we luck out, anyone who sees you will think they were hallucinating. But you don't want to be seen. Got that?"

"Got it." She'd nodded queasily, her head unbalanced by the helmet-mounted protrusions. Meanwhile the support team was laying out her planned ground track on the asphalt using crime scene tape. "Walk me through this again? Headset, capture map on."

That had been a couple of hours ago. Since then they'd run through endless checklists, made her replay her choreographed series of steps in the head-up display of her glasses three times (following them in real time so that it became a habit to step within her own ghostly footsteps), and updated the folks "upstairs," who were waiting with the Colonel in a committee room somewhere in Maryland. And now, Rita's bladder was embarrassingly full.

"This is going to sound stupid," she said apologetically, "but I really need to go to the bathroom."

"You need to go? Can't it wait—" Gomez sounded disgusted, but Patrick cut her off: "Let her go." He glanced at Rita. "Just don't take too long."

Rita scuttled through the open door of the warehouse unit like a black-clad cockroach, making a beeline for the ground-floor restroom. Her bladder *was* full: coffee and nerves were a potent combination. Her stomach was also full of butterflies. *I can do this,* she told herself, self-consciously self-aware. *It's just another role. Front of stage. Your name in lights.* "Today's late-night billing: secret agent woman Rita Douglas in, in . . . BLACK RAIN."

She made it back to the taped-out departure zone with two minutes to spare. "Stand there," said Gomez.

"System check."

Rita looked at the transparent cutout in the forearm of her left sleeve. She squeezed a now-familiar pattern, then switched on the ultraviolet light above her helmet visor. Phosphorescence glimmered against the darkness of her skin. "Test pattern works, GFP phosphenes work, black-light lamp works." She looked straight forward through her night vision eyepieces. "Night vision works." Her mouth was dry.

"One minute to go," called Patrick.

Rita looked around, then cued up her captured choreography in a window at the side of her glasses. She felt curiously trapped, hot even though it was a cool night. The moon had set—

"Thirty seconds. Twenty. Ten. Five—"

She focused on her trigger engram, and jaunted.

Rita stumbled among trees in the darkness. A night rain was falling, pattering off leaves overhead: the air smelled overwhelmingly green. *Damn: obstacles,* she realized. She'd been lucky to come out *between* them. Trying to jaunt into the same place as a solid object was impossible, but the shock it gave her was like brief contact with a live wire. Or the jolting sensation of falling on the edge of sleep.

In her ear, mingling with the leafy rustling and the dripping of rain on trees, she heard the clicking of a radiation counter. Time line one was still hot from the nuking of the Gruinmarkt. She took a deep breath of forest air, squeezed to summon the next trigger engram in the sequence— dim green phosphorescent fireflies glowed on the back of her wrist, shimmering as they shifted into a tantalizingly not-quite-familiar knotwork design—and she jaunted again.

This time she slipped, feet sliding on sharp-edged, rough pebbles. The air on her face was warmer. She looked around: a tall wall rose beside her. It was right in the path of her programmed dance step through the switchyard. She blinked, focusing. *It's a shipping container,* she realized. *A shipping container on a flatbed wagon. I need to capture this.* It looked, ironically, just like any other shipping container she'd ever seen:

forty feet of corrugated steel with twist-lock connectors at each corner. It loomed above her like a wall, with another container stacked atop it. The wagon bed rose above the bogies at either end.

"Shit," Rita muttered under her breath. The bed of the wagon left barely a two-foot gap above the track, and the man from the FRA had taken considerable pains to impress on her the un-wisdom of crawling around under a railroad wagon. She turned round. The next set of tracks gleamed empty in the starlight. "Headset, new capture map, on." She was about to step across the tracks when there was a dull thudding sound behind her, and the container jerked.

Rita dived for cover. Lying on her stomach, heart pounding, she forced herself to turn her head sideways. The train began to move, with a squeaking and squealing of steel wheels on rails and a clatter of chains. As it inched past, only feet away, she reached into her sling bag and found some of the false ballast. One she threw past her head; another she planted in the direction of her feet. Then she grabbed hold of the transponder rock, ready for the fake two-by-four.

A bogie inched slowly past, wheels grating harshly. Then another slid into view. She looked up. Lettering stood out in ghostly silhouette on the steel flank of the container: IRONGATE IMPORTS INCORPORATED.

Breathing deeply, Rita tried to control her shakes. The terror that had sunk its icy claws into her began to subside. A flash of blue-white light, bright as lightning, flickered in the distance above the track. She looked up and saw a gantry spanning six or seven tracks, with cables slung beneath it. *Electricity*, she thought dismally. *I could be electrocuted as well as crushed.* With a primal *bump-thump*, the stacked container wagon jolted across a track weld as it passed her. Another rolled past, then a third. Finally the end of the sliding wall of metal came into view. A small shunting locomotive, unlike anything she recognized from back home, pushed the string of freight wagons forward. It was small only in comparison to its gargantuan payload: the bottom of the cab door had to be at least six feet above the rails. A pantograph buzzed atop its roof, occasionally sparking. *I am so not messing with that*, Rita decided. As it slid past, she saw an opportunity to resume her aborted sequence of dance moves: so she stood up, and followed her ghostly footsteps across the switchyard.

She crossed six tracks, distributing surveillance pebbles. At the next track she landed a prize: another of the shunting engines sat stationary and dark, pantograph lowered. She cautiously reached up and slid the two-by-four with the concealed mapper atop the walkway around the loco's transformers, then looked around. "I'm out of targets," she told the lifelogger. "I'm going to have a look-round. Countdown timer for five minutes, please."

Standing in the shadow of the shunter, she slowly scanned the visible horizon of the yard. Strings of container wagons lay parked in sidings. The train she'd seen before was rolling steadily now, clattering across points. A long, low maintenance shed blocked her view in one direction. Another parked train concealed the other horizon, but for a control tower looming above it. Lights burned in the distance: blue and green and red. Farther off, amber floodlights splashed a bright sodium-glare across the tracks, almost washing out her sensitive night vision goggles.

Rita felt a sudden, vertiginous wash of perspective. Had she world-walked at all, or merely teleported to another location in Pennsylvania? It was hard to tell. It was—

A momentary thought struck her, lodged quivering in her mind. *That's odd*, she thought. *The tracks are too far apart, aren't they?* She looked in both directions carefully, then stepped between the nearest rails. Kneeling, she stretched her right hand out to touch the inner edge of the track on that side. "Lifelogger, bookmark this. Headset, new capture map, pin to right hand." She held her arm out, stiff, as she touched the rail, then swung round until it touched inside the other rail. "Lifelogger, bookmark this. It should give us the track gauge, near enough. Next time I'll bring a tape measure." She stood again, feeling momentarily dizzy, just as the timer she'd set beeped softly for attention. "Okay, time to go home now."

She retraced her steps and jaunted twice in succession, confident that her first mission had been a success.

BALTIMORE, TIME LINE TWO, AUGUST 2020

FEDERAL EMPLOYEE 004930391 CLASSIFIED VOICE TRANSCRIPT

DR. SCRANTON: So what did we learn from our first HUMINT foray into BLACK RAIN? Colonel?

COL. SMITH: We got lucky.

LIAISON, STATE DEPT: Why, was there an unanticipated risk?

COL. SMITH: Yes. We nearly lost Rita. Stumbling around a railway switchyard at night after the moon's set is a risky business! She put a good face on it, but I replayed the motion capture log and she came *this* close to falling under a moving freight train.

LIAISON, STATE DEPT: Jesus.

DR. SCRANTON: No oaths, please. We're on the record.

LIAISON, STATE DEPT: Sorry.

COL. SMITH: Thank you. Luckily for us she made a good recovery, and after the train passed she distributed the sensor nodes exactly as instructed. Afterward she went for a ten-minute stroll to get her bearings, then came back. She stayed within the remit of her instructions at all times. I'm entirely satisfied with the way she conducted herself.

DR. SCRANTON: Okay. Findings?

COL. SMITH: This is where it gets disturbing. Firstly, they use intermodal freight containers just like ours. They're *too* like ours: for one thing they're labeled in English—

LIAISON, STATE DEPT: That doesn't sound possible. You're sure?

DR. SCRANTON: Yes, definitely. Rita didn't get a close look at much, but her helmet cams picked up stuff she missed. All the text in the frame uses the Latin alphabet and conforms to anglophone spelling rules. There wasn't much of it, mind you, and it was night. But there was enough evidence.

LIAISON, STATE DEPT: Could it be another version of our, our time line? A close cousin?

COL. SMITH: That's what we thought at first. But Rita's a smart kid. She thought there was something wrong with the tracks, so she knelt down and used her motion capture instrumentation to measure the gauge— the gap between the rails—exactly. We run on standard gauge—four feet, eight and a half inches. Rita measured their gauge at five feet, one inch, plus or minus an inch or so. Now, that might be Pennsylvania broad gauge—the Pittsburgh and West Penn Railways ran on a five-foot, two-and-a-half gauge—but we've *never* used those for container freight lines. Those railroads went bust in 1952 and 1964, respectively. So even if this is a kissing-cousin time line, it almost certainly diverged more than sixty years ago.

DR. SCRANTON: Good work. What else do we know?

COL. SMITH: They use overhead current and electric traction for freight shunters. So they electrified their heavy rail freight network, like in Europe or the new Chinese and Indian systems. But there's more. Rita glimpsed what we presume to be signal lights, but they don't follow the usual color convention—red, yellow, and green. These used *blue*. Nobody we know uses blue light signals.

LIAISON, STATE DEPT: Oh sh—sorry, gentlemen. This changes everything, doesn't it?

COL. SMITH: I don't see why. If they haven't got world-walkers, they can't touch us. And if they *do* have world-walkers, then as soon as they learn about us they'll infer our ability to generate a second-strike retaliatory capability: a bomb wing of B-52s out of Thule should be enough keep them from getting frisky.

DR. SCRANTON: That's above our pay grade, gentlemen. What else have we learned?

COL. SMITH: A lot of fine detail about the layout of a rail freight switch-yard near Bethlehem, Pennsylvania. Nothing else, as yet. Unless you say otherwise, I'm sending her back over again tonight. Mission objective this time round will be to do an initial data retrieval from the sensor net she installed, then to plant optical imagers and audio pickups somewhere more useful. I want to target the station platform and offices. We want to confirm that they speak English, and if so what sort of accent they have. We want to get a good look at their clothing, demographics, and security protocols. It's all essential legwork before we send Rita on an actual undercover mission: basic know-your-enemy stuff.

DR. SCRANTON: Do you have any recommendations you'd like to add, Colonel? Anything for me to pass up the chain?

COL. SMITH: Yes, I do. These people might be our long-lost cousins, but they've had *at least* sixty years of divergence, and they've got nukes, and they've shot down three of our drones. They're dangerously competent, if not just plain dangerous. Imagine how *we'd* respond if parties unknown began probing us with drones, then sent world-walking HUMINT assets to check us out. We'd shit a brick, assume the worst, and reach for the big stick.

DR. SCRANTON: So you're saying we should exercise extreme caution.

COL. SMITH: That's exactly it, ma'am. Because if we don't, someone's going to get burned, and it might be us.

END TRANSCRIPT

NEAR PHOENIX, TIME LINE TWO, MAY 2020

The federal government took justifiable pride in the comprehensive scope of its communication traffic monitoring activities. It was, without doubt, a best-of-breed program. Every phone call's end point was logged. Every e-mail was tracked. And quite possibly the NSA's vast server farms were converting those phone calls into text and indexing them for future recovery. The Internet was totally surveilled, and the Internet of things—everything with an Internet connection, from toaster ovens to televisions—was also surveilled. Every fatphone's or cell phone's location was monitored as its owner moved around and it switched between cell towers for better reception. Every automobile and truck and bicycle notified the Federal Highway Administration of its location, the better to prevent interstate commerce crime. And every city block in every town with more than ten thousand souls boasted a high-definition webcam on every street corner, monitoring pedestrian and vehicle traffic.

Kurt Douglas, for his part, found it a never-ending source of wry amusement. The diminishing marginal utility of information had been a vexatious nuisance to the Stasi—the East German secret police—back in his youth. The more you knew, the more chaff you had to process with your wheat. The more true positives you had for dissent, the more false positives you had to eliminate. False positives who were good citizens falsely accused would, even if cleared, be ruined—their hearts dead to the cause. Subtle secret policemen walked softly and exercised a feather-light touch until they were certain of their prey; unfortunately by its nature the profession offered an attractive career to crude authoritarians.

The soul of the American surveillance machine was just as drab and bureaucratic-gray as the East German system he'd grown up under. And it recorded *everything*. For example, every parcel and letter and postcard passing through the USPS network was photographed digitally, sniffed for drugs and explosives, pinged for illicit memory chips, and scanned for radio-frequency ID tags. Quite possibly they were also shotgun-sampled for matches against the National DNA Prime Suspects Database.

But there were blind spots on the panopticon's retina. The Post Office, for example, still offered prompt, reliable delivery of data—and it was possible to defeat the NSA and DHS data mining if you understood how to use it. It wasn't rocket science. All you had to do was leave your phone at home, dress in clothing from which all the RFID washing machine instruction tags had been stripped, and go for a walk. You had to make sure you passed two or more postal boxes while carrying a suitably sanitized letter—addressed to your recipient by name but showing the address of a neighbor the recipient was on speaking terms with. The panopticon couldn't distinguish between mail pickup boxes, and a misplaced digit would disguise the destination. Network analysis—looking for friends-of-friends relationships—would eventually crack a postal ring, but first they had to know there was something to look for. And to muddy the waters, there was always geocaching: the old tradecraft practices of dead letter drops, cutouts, and codes, turned into a hobby for the masses.

Until the authorities got around to putting RFID chips in every stamp, or banning cash transactions completely, the loopholes would remain open. Cypherpunks and paranoid libertarians might loudly swear that they would never! never! surrender their encryption keys to The Man. But in Kurt's view, there was a lot to be said for quietly archaic tradecraft.

It was mid-afternoon, and Franz was at work. It was Emily's day off, but she was on a grocery run—she used shopping as an excuse to get out of the house—and River was in college. Kurt ambled to his front door, locked it behind him, and stepped out into the street. There was no sidewalk, but it wasn't dangerous. Most everyone who lived here had up-graded their wheels to self-driving in recent years to avoid the insurance premium hike for manual. Shuffling slowly, he passed the dividing line between his lot and his son's. It was almost invisible—they'd pulled out the white picket fence when they bought both houses—but the grass on his side was slightly greener even though he never watered it. It was as-troturf, as artificial as this strange lifestyle he'd fallen into in his twilight years. He shook his head, then approached the driveway. The flag on the mailbox was up. He stopped to rummage, retrieved the contents, briefly finger-checked for magnetic travel bugs on the mailbox's underside—there were none, as was usually the case since Rita had left—then walked up to the kids' front door and let himself in.

He sorted the mail quickly and stacked it on the breakfast bar. There wasn't a lot: random junk flyers from local businesses, a package from Amazon for River; bills and banking were mostly taken care of online these days, except by old-timers. But in among the gravel there was gold dust, in the shape of a letter with a handwritten address and an honest old-fashioned self-adhesive stamp. And it was addressed to K. Douglas. Kurt smiled, tucked it inside his shirt, and headed back to his house.

It was Kurt's habit to regularly take an hour-long afternoon nap in his bedroom. Lights out, phone left downstairs. He climbed the steps patiently, with scissors, pencils, envelope, and a pad of paper in hand. An hour and a half later he came back down, a pensive frown on his face, carrying the envelope, its enclosed letter, and the page he had laboriously transcribed from its contents. A lidded saucepan, a few drops of cooking oil, and a match would erase their troubling contents. After a trip through the dishwasher this evening there would be nothing left save memories to trouble his sleep, and that of his circumspect correspondent.

"I am going to have to tell her the truth," he told himself unhappily, as if trying on a prisoner's orange uniform for size. "Sooner or later I will be compelled to tell her, eh?" He gave a sad-dog sigh. "Later rather than sooner." He opened the fridge door and pulled out a beer. Drinking alone in the mid-afternoon, he made the picture of a sad old widower. *Too bad*, he thought, *that Greta couldn't live to see this day.* The pang of loss was a pro forma emotion, barely registering any more than a phantom pain from the stump of a long-amputated limb. *She'd have laughed herself sick.* His long-dead wife had been glorious in irony, back in the day. She could see the funny side of everything.

"What a strange age we live in: history repeats itself, first as tragedy, then as farce . . ."

Switches

They were out of the side door as soon as the rotodyne stopped bouncing on its shock absorbers. The rotor disk high overhead was still shrieking
as a squad of Commonwealth Guards rushed them to a squat blockhouse,
checked their IDs, and led them into an elevator. The door concertina'd
shut just as the aircraft began to spool up again, vacating the pad to make
way for the next aircraft to land under the barrels of the point-defense
guns.

There was nothing terribly subtle about the Redoubt, where the First
Man and half the cabinet would take shelter from the gathering nuclear
storm. Thousands of tons of concrete and rebar had been poured into a
hole in the ground, forming a cradle around a sunken bunker that sat
atop a platform suspended on huge shock absorbers. Nearby hills supported a forest of antennae; radar dishes twirled continuously overhead,
tracking everything in the sky and feeding constant updates to the guns
and missile batteries emplaced around the headquarters.

But the Redoubt had one unique twist that placed it in a class of its
own, unlike anything ever built in the United States by anyone . . .
except the Clan. The entire four-story command complex sat atop an air
cushion; and hollow doppelganger Redoubts, identical save for a hole in
place of the command complex, had been built in three neighboring
empty time lines. With a world-walker permanently on station, ready to
move the entire core of the Redoubt to safety, there was no need to drill

a cathedral-sized bunker under Cheyenne Mountain for protection from a hard nuclear rain. Only a first strike executed in parallel in multiple time lines would stand a hope of succeeding—or so the designers hoped.

Over her years in government, Miriam had developed a bitter hatred for nuclear command bunkers. She'd spent more than her fair share of time holed up in them, taking her turn as Commissioner for Continuity of Government—a euphemism for Queen of the Smoking Aftermath, in her opinion. Bunkers stank of failure. They smelled metallic, their bottled air pumped through particle filters and monitored by Geiger counters. The corridors were unpleasantly narrow and the ceilings low, the walls painted a nauseous mustard yellow and the floors battleship gray. Hard, narrow bunk beds (space being at a premium) and ill-lit, cramped meeting rooms surrounded by men (and, increasingly these days, women) with drawn faces and bags under their eyes, all of them hoping that the axe wouldn't fall: even if they survived, their families would be left behind on the surface.

The First Man's Redoubt was larger, but no different in kind. So at nine o'clock, with only a couple of hours' sleep behind her, Miriam found herself bellied up against a conference table with her back almost touching the wall behind her. She was drinking bitter coffee and reading a steady stream of incoming reports in the vain hope of staying alert, in a meeting room full of People's Party Commissioners and general staff officers, waiting for Sir Adam to arrive.

The door opened. A woman in the uniform of one of the nursing orders shuffled in backward, pulling a wheeled chair: Miriam blinked her eyes into focus before she recognized the hunched figure within. She glanced sideways, caught Erasmus's shocked look and rapidly suppressed reaction.

"Good morning, everybody," husked the First Man as his nurse turned him to face the table. His smile was watery, his skin sallow and drawn tight across the bones of his face. "I see we are all present and correct."

Miriam forced her hands into immobility to avoid betraying herself by raising them to her mouth in shock. She had last seen Adam four weeks previously. He'd been walking, then: clearly increasingly frail, but not exceptionally so. She'd read the carefully coded memo: *The First*

Man is not currently accepting new public engagements due to nervous exhaustion. He sends his best wishes and urges everyone to carry on regardless. But *this* wasn't nervous exhaustion. Sir Adam looked at her, and for a moment his gaze carried its old weight, striking like a rod of iron. But then he faded as she watched.

"General Josephus. Your latest update, please?"

"Certainly, sir," said Josephus, his delivery polished. "Current prevailing winds are blowing northeasterly off Cape Cod, and as you know the Zeus-IV petard was designed to produce little radiative residue. So the fallout plume is blowing offshore. Unfortunately this means that the French will detect it within four days—possibly sooner if their spy trawlers on the Grand Banks are equipped with detectors. Even if they didn't spot the first light, this will provide confirmation of an air burst off our coast. We therefore anticipate increased French diplomatic and espionage activity within the week, even in the absence of other engagement."

"What about the target?" asked Sir Adam. "Is anything known about it?"

"We can't be certain, sir. There is only a very remote possibility that the French have acquired the capability to build something like this. Coming two weeks after the previous US intrusion—confirmed from the wreckage—we can reasonably assume that they have upped the ante. Published sources suggest that the target matched the profile of a Tier Three unmanned autonomous drone—a long-range, high-altitude strategic reconnaissance probe."

"Thank you, General. Mrs. Burgeson, do you have any insights?"

Sir Adam stared at her, his head lolling slightly to one side. *Weak neck muscles,* she noted. *Generalized cachexia. Muscle wastage. Looks like stage IV, probably liver or pancreatic cancer. Oh shit.*

"Miriam?"

She blinked. "I'm sorry," she said automatically. "If it isn't the United States, we've had the supreme misfortune to have come to the attention of another Class Two para-time civilization at the worst possible moment. But it's almost certainly the United States. Their standard protocol seems to be to send over a black box—just to check for atmosphere on the other

216 of CHARLES STROSS

side—then a medium-altitude mapping drone. Air Defense Command shot down the first, so a week later they sent another. It's not unknown for them to malfunction or crash. But ADC shot down the next one, and two hull losses on consecutive flights are statistically improbable, so this time they sent a bigger, faster, higher-altitude drone with wide-angle cameras." She knuckled her tired eyes. "And ADC, bless their little cotton socks, shot it down *again*. So if they didn't know we were here before, they certainly do now."

She looked round at a circle of dismayed faces. "The good news is, we're still alive," she said. "Either they're off-balance, or they're not on a war footing at all. We have some breathing space—although I have no idea how much."

Sir Adam opened his mouth. For a moment she was terrified that he would be unable to speak, but after a false start, almost a stutter, he followed through. "I will not order a preemptive strike by means of capital weapons." He spoke into the sudden silence. "None of the reports I have read from the DPR suggest that their current president is a sociopath. I expect her to behave similarly." ("Sociopath" was one of the most useful concepts that Miriam's Memetic Engineering Task Force had imported from the United States: Erasmus's Propaganda Ministry had been working overtime to raise awareness of it as an Anti-Democratic Problem: "People who think People are Things." Sometimes she thought that educating the Commonwealth about social psychology and teaching them about cognitive biases, authoritarian personality types, and game theory had done more good than all the STEM research they'd imported. Enlightenment was an uphill struggle, but if it reduced the likelihood of wars and reigns of terror it was well worth the cost.)

Miriam cleared her throat. "They tried it on the Gruinmarkt," she said. "It didn't succeed."

Scott Schroeder, the assistant Commissioner for Defense, snorted. "Obviously they should have tried harder." Miriam looked at him sharply for a moment, trying to discern any hint of ironic intent. "Just playing devil's advocate," he added.

Miriam shook her head. "Imagine if the French dropped a megaton-range capital weapon on this bunker right this second, killing us all—Sir Adam included." Eyes instinctively turned to the invalid. He watched them right back, calculatingly passive, guarding his remaining vitality. "How exactly would our people respond?"

"They'd—" Schroeder stopped. "I take your point."

"The United States started out as a revolutionary republic, just like our Commonwealth," Sir Adam said, a faint smile tugging at the corners of his sunken eyes. "They may have succumbed to the twin corruptions of oligarchy for the elite and bread and circuses for the masses, but their Deep State still has sinews of steel. Moreover, their form of government is extremely resilient. They are no more capable of surrendering than we are. War is unthinkable. If it is unleashed, the conflagration will spread until all are consumed."

He paused for a few seconds. "As you can see, I am indisposed." He looked at them across the table, deliberately making eye contact. "So I delegate this task to you who are assembled here. You are to devise a strategy for engaging directly with the government of the United States. I want you to lock them into a dance of, ah, I believe the term they will understand is, 'Mutually Assured Destruction.'" He smiled directly at Miriam: a fey, frightening expression. "It will give them the comfort and certainty of a well-thumbed rule book for avoiding the holocaust. And then"—he paused for a few more seconds, until Miriam was about to ask his nurse to intervene—"once the immediate situation is stabilized, you are to investigate ways and means of bringing democracy to the United States of America."

PHILADELPHIA, TIME LINE TWO, AUGUST 2020

Rita's first foray to the switchyard had taken place at 3:15 a.m. on a Thursday. It had taken six minutes, and she'd spent the next six hours being debriefed no less than three times, first by Patrick and then over a secure video link by Colonel Smith and a tired-looking posse of senior agents, all of whom were presumably going to brief their various superiors over the following days. Then they stuck her in a box with a tablet while she wrote up everything she remembered. A transcript of this would be carefully embalmed with the telemetry dumps from the equipment she'd been wearing. It would then be buried so deep in the Office of Special Programs' vaults that she herself wouldn't be able to retrieve it.

One committee briefing would inevitably lead to another, and by the time the ripples had spread out into the organization it was Friday lunchtime. The head-scratching over when to schedule her next jaunt to the switchyard then commenced. If it had been up to Rita, she'd have gone back over in the small hours of Friday morning, but Patrick told her that the Colonel couldn't authorize another trip without obtaining a consensus from his supervisors. "The BLACK RAIN discovery has rattled teeth all the way up to cabinet level. He wanted to send you out tonight, but he's got the Homeland Security Council breathing down his neck. OSP doesn't usually get this level of oversight, much less at his level—"

"He's a colonel, isn't he?" Rita frowned. "I thought that was pretty senior . . ." She trailed off.

"He's not a colonel, he's a *retired* colonel," Patrick said. He paused to take a mouthful of coffee. He winced: too hot or too bitter. "A colonel would be a pretty junior officer to be running this sort of operation; colonels usually command a battalion or an Air Force squadron. Eric isn't a colonel, he's a spook, and it's all alphabet soup. He may have started out in the Air Force, but he moved sideways into NSA, was assigned to the FTO in the early days, FTO became the OSP, OSP did a reverse-takeover of the DHS, and then he set up the Unit as his personal project. That's us, the human intelligence arm within what used to be the OSP, which used to be the FTO, which is what happened when the federal government discovered parallel universes and went WTF. Colonel was his rank when he retired from the Air Force; these days he punches above Major General."

"Um." Rita shook her head. "So he's called a Colonel but is actually a Major General?"

"Never mind." Patrick grinned suddenly. "Don't worry about it. Let's just say he's extremely senior. This started out as his personal hobbyhorse, but it's suddenly attracted the attention of a lot of even more senior people in the administration. He's not going to risk giving anyone an

excuse to take his toy away from him, so nothing is going to happen before Monday. Hurry up and wait, in other words. You might as well take
the weekend off: I'll clear it for you. You've earned some downtime."

Rita yawned. "I'm in the wrong time zone," she complained. "My
family are in Phoenix, most everyone I know is in Cambridge, and I'm
stuck in a motel in Allentown. What am I going to do?"

"Go get some beauty sleep, then pretend you're a tourist visiting
exotic Philadelphia."

"I guess . . ."

Rita drove back to the motel, lost in thought. Back in her room she
started by phoning her parents: her usual weekly sonar ping was rendered slightly stilted by the certainty that everything she said would be
transcribed and forwarded to whoever the Colonel had assigned to monitor her. She'd been on the inside of DHS for only a matter of weeks, but
that was enough to be certain that there was no way in hell an organization like the Unit would trust a newbie like her with a key technology
like JAUNT BLUE without putting her under surveillance. It was probably Gomez, she guessed: Gomez was a hard-assed bitch and had been
on her back since the beginning. If not Gomez, then Jack, the good cop
to Sonia's bad cop.

"Your grandfather's here," River told her when the idle big-sis/little-
brother chat began to bore him. "Wanna talk to him?"

"Yeah. Hi, Gramps."

"Hello, Rita. Are you well?" he asked gravely.

"I'm fine, work's fine," she said happily. "I can't talk about it, though."
"Talk" was their prearranged code word: it meant everything was indeed
fine. "Discuss," in contrast, meant "Send help," and "mention" was not
to be mentioned save in extremis. "That book you lent me was weird.
Are there any others like it?"

They chatted about trivia for another five minutes, until Kurt tired.
"Why don't you look up your old school friends, see if anyone lives
nearby?" he asked. "I'm tired; I need my nap."

"Yes, Gramps, I'll do that," she said, and hung up. Hearing Mom and
Dad and River and Gramps's voices had given her a brief boost, but the
chill of isolation began to descend again. Rita could feel alone in the

middle of a crowded party; being stuck in a hotel room in the middle of nowhere with a bugged phone and monitored Internet feed was beyond lonely.

Catch up on friends indeed. She hit Facebook, skidding across the frozen river of all the lifelines she'd crossed. *Do I know anyone who lives in Allentown?* she wondered. A quick search later, the answer came back: to her surprise, she *did* have a friend in Philly. And it was Angela, of all people. Or rather, Angie: she'd suddenly acquired a serious hate on her name . . . when? When she was fifteen?

Rita hadn't seen Angie since they'd been in the Girl Scouts in Massachusetts, a decade ago. They hadn't been *very* close at first, but they'd done a couple of the special summer camps the parents of girls in Wolf Troop sent them to, the ones with the language courses and orienteering and the other stuff. Then teenage kicks and tentative self-discovery happened and for a year they'd been inseparable. Not to mention fizzing bundles of anxiety at the possibility that one of their schoolmates might see them together and realize what they were to each other. This was back during the second Rumsfeld administration, when Congress was busy defending marriage from girls like them. It had fizzled out tearfully when Angie's folks had stayed in Boston and Rita's moved to Phoenix, but Angie herself had enlisted and then somehow ended up here . . . and she was on chat.

Rita procrastinated for almost a quarter of an hour. There were idiotic arguments to chip in on, after all, and five things she really needed to know about vaping that would totally change her life, and sundry clickbait to distract from the burning question, *How will she remember me?* Angie's face had sat frozen in her FB feed for years, unlooked at—Rita couldn't bear to think of herself as a stalker; it was undignified and creepy—but also undeleted. And Angie didn't update her wall very often, anyway. Like Rita, she clutched a thick veil of privacy tight around her online life.

But here she was, online for chat—and nearby, not thousands of miles away.

Finally, Rita ran out of excuses. *This is stupid*, she told herself. *She'll have found herself a cute blonde, settled down, and forgotten me. Or—*

Somehow, while she was spinning her gears, her fingers began to move without her conscious volition.

> Hi, Angie?
>> Rita? Been ages! Sup, Sis?
> I'm in Allentown. Work. Weekend. Bored.
>> Work!?! Permanent?
> Temp
>> Wanna meet up?
> Love to. When/where is good?
>> Lemme get back 2 U. Free 2 nite?

Feeling unaccountably hot and prickly, Rita stared at her phone for a minute. Angie seemed enthusiastic. Come to think of it, when had she last followed her? Angie lived so far away there hadn't seemed to be much point. She looked at Angie's profile status—single again—and bit her lip before replying.

> Y
>> Hot! Share Ur location & I'll be round at 8
> Y
>> L8R :-)

Oh my God, Rita thought dizzily. She hoped Angie wouldn't get the wrong idea. It had, after all, been a very long time.

PHILADELPHIA, TIME LINE TWO, AUGUST 2020

Rita had gotten close with Angie when they were both in tenth grade, gawky teens trying to figure out what interested them in life. They were both going through that phase of working out whether to try and scrape together the money to study, or to get a job right away: not to mention whether they were interested in boys or, or not. Rita: not so much, although, shy and introspective, she'd been unsure how her parents would cope if they found out. (A misplaced fear, as she subsequently learned.) Angie: back then she'd been a strawberry blonde with a bob and a smile, as devoutly Lutheran as her parents. Grandpa Kurt and Angie's parents shared a history back in the GDR that the girls were supposed to ignore, and for the most part they successfully did. When they'd first spent time together at summer camp Rita had pegged her for a boychaser who'd be married by twenty and pregnant by twenty-one. Then Rita had learned just how wrong first impressions could be, in a good way.

Angie's eyes were still blue and twinkled like the iridescent sheen on her nose stud and eyebrow rings, but her hair was cuprous green streaked with blue, and she walked with a swagger. Rita managed not to gape when she saw her across the hotel lobby. "Angela?" she called, momentarily forgetting. So much for the demure girl she remembered from high school days. On the other hand, Rita had been far from the only one who'd been kept in the closet for fear of bullying in the coldly repressive climate of the early 2010s. Times had changed, and in any case the whole wide world was not a high school diner: and Angie had blossomed.

"It's Angie, remember?" Angie hugged her. "And a five-merit-point fine every time you forget! You're looking gorgeous! Have you eaten? No? Let's roll, then."

Angie's wheels were recent enough to drive themselves, with a truck top and a fire-red paint job. "You're looking good, too," Rita said, trying to fill the silence. "Been keeping well?"

"It was hard at first, but I got my certification two years ago. You would not believe how much work there is for an electrical contractor in this town! Chariot, drive us to Emma's. Listen, Rita—"

The pickup's engine lit with a whine as it backed and turned out of the narrow parking lot, and Rita noticed, to her confusion, that they were still holding hands. *How did we even get in the truck?*

"You never called? Never even sent me a selfie bug?"

Rita swallowed. "I wanted to, but it kept getting harder the longer I waited. Then my folks moved and your folks moved—"

Angie leaned across the bench seat and turned Rita's face to hers and kissed her as if to hit "undo" on the last decade. "You do *not* leave it ten years next time, girl."

"I didn't mean to. Where are we going?"

"The best gay bar in town, not that there are many to choose from out here in the sticks. Uh, unless you're . . . ?"

"No, I'm fine." She tossed her head, then let go of Angie's hand long enough to shove her hair back. She caught Angie's eye. "There's a lot of catching up to do and I, uh, was hoping for somewhere private . . ."

"Really?" That smile. "Chariot, make all windows opaque." Angie's thumb clicked on her seat belt button as the outside world dimmed to night. Then the thumb clicked on Rita's belt button. "Will this do?"

Rita made a quiet *eep* of assent as Angie scooted sideways toward her. Then they kissed again as the steering wheel spun, unattended.

PHILADELPHIA, TIME LINE TWO, AUGUST 2020

Much later—after dinner and drinks and dancing, and a drunken auto-ride home—they sat together naked in the middle of Angie's bed, as Angie rolled another joint. Rita traced her finger across the tentacles of the Hokusai octopus. They trailed from its bulbous body, centered on Angie's left shoulder, coiling around her ribs, and rose to cup the underside of her right breast. She was luminous with sweat and sweetly aromatic with the new-mown-hay aroma of marijuana. "I feel like I've been living in a coffin for months," Rita said softly. "Too much work and no play makes . . ." Her fingertip lingered at the crinkling, stiffening edge of Angie's areola, then gently nudged the silver barbell.

"Too much of that and I'll spill the bud, girl."

"So I'll have to lick it off you, so what?" Rita leaned against Angie. "Like this."

She demonstrated. Angie tensed. "You never did say what brought you to town."

"Work." Rita paused. "I don't want to talk about it."

Angie raised the open cone to her mouth, ran her tongue along the seam of the papers. "If it's such a shit job, why don't you quit?" Angie asked as she rolled it between her palms.

"I'm not sure it's the kind of job I *can* quit."

"Mob?" Angie asked softly. "Because if so, listen, I know a cop who—"

"It's not like that. I, uh, I work for the DHS now. I'm not at liberty to discuss it."

"Oh." Angie fell silent for a minute, until the gathering sense of dread nearly convinced Rita that she'd confessed to something inexcusable. *Working for The Man.* They both understood—it was expected of them, like marriage and babies to so many other young women—but even so. "Okay." Angie's tone fell oddly flat. "Thought I'd heard the end of that when I got out of the Army." She extended her arm and placed the joint on the bedside unit. "Phone."

"What?"

"Phone."

Rita looked over the edge of the bed, picked up her purse. "What?"

"Give it here." Angie took it, flipped it upside down, and popped the battery. "Glass?"

"Don't wear it."

"Okay." Angie reached over her side of the bed and picked up her own phone. She held it where Rita could see it as she popped the battery. Then she pulled a thickly quilted craft bag out from under the bed and swept the phones and batteries into it, then closed it and shoved it in a bedside drawer. "I don't *think* they could have done an in-and-out here while we were gone. Wouldn't bet on it in future, though. So I think we're alone now. Just us and the stars above, like back when we were in camp."

Rita shivered. They'd been in the same Girl Scout troop: sent to the same weird summer camp down in Maryland, with other girls whose folks had serious faces and didn't talk about what they did. "You know we were nearly the only girls there whose parents didn't work in Spook City?" Spook City was the huge, formerly NSA-only compound at Fort Meade where the CIA and a bunch of other secret agencies had moved after 7/16. It had taken her years to figure that out: why she and Angie and a couple of others had perpetually felt like they didn't quite fit in.

"Little lone wolves," Kurt had jokingly called them when Rita told him about it.

"Of course." Angie sniffed. "I just want to be able to talk to you without the NSA on the party line." It was an old joke: *We're the NSA. We love to listen. We're the only branch of government that does.* Alternative version: *We're the phone company. We don't listen. We don't have to: we've got the NSA to do it for us.* She placed a hand on Rita's shoulder. "Do you need help, Rita?"

"I need—" Rita licked her lips. "No, I don't think there's anything you could do to help. Not right now. No, wait, yes there is." She reached out awkwardly, groping for Angie's shoulders. "I had no idea you were here. Or that you still wanted me."

"A happy accident." Angie pulled her close and nuzzled up against her neck. "Stay with me?"

"Always." Rita clung to her: a drowning woman who had just discovered a life raft. "And this time I mean it."

PHILADELPHIA, TIME LINE TWO, AUGUST 2020

Angie lived in a one-bedroom condo on the outskirts of Philly, in a suburb that was fitfully trying to redevelop. Rita spent the weekend with her, happier than she had been in years. The apartment was sparsely furnished. Angie's parents hadn't quite disowned her when she came out, but things had been tense. With the GI Bill benefits paying her way through her night school classes and electrician's apprenticeship, she'd scrimped and saved every spare dime to pay off the mortgage early. The walls were mostly bare, except for the framed certificates holding Angie's electrician's license and her honorable discharge (Private First Class, 704th Military Intelligence Brigade). There was a stack of old dead-tree books in the bathroom: Rita was amused by the discovery that the sole reading matter they had in common consisted of dog-eared copies of *The Grasshopper Lies Heavy* and a handful of government security manuals.

On Saturday night, Angie insisted on glamming up with Rita and taking her clubbing. On Sunday morning they lay in, Rita aching from unaccustomed exertion. There was a bittersweet edge to it. "I'm not sure how much longer I'm going to be on assignment here," Rita told her.

"We'll sort something out." Angie leaned against the headboard. "You don't get to escape again, girl." Her grin was wicked, inviting complicity. "What were we *thinking*?"

"We were thinking guilty thoughts and trying not to get caught making out. Typical fucked-up teenagers." Rita squinted, casting a judgmental gaze upon her earlier self. "I don't know if we would have clicked if we'd tried dating back then. Too young, too much external pressure. I had a bunch of growing up to do. Also"—she shrugged—"it gets better."

"You've changed for the better, too." Angie tugged her close. "I can't believe you were single—"

"Like I said: I had a bad breakup, then the whole DHS thing happened. I was being single, and then I was being kept busy."

"Do you still feel single?" Angie asked, and kissed her slowly.

"No," Rita said, when she caught her breath again. "I don't feel single."

"My girl." Angie giggled briefly.

"Yeah," Rita said fondly, and tangled her fingers in Angie's hair. A thought struck her. "Listen, just do me a favor and don't change your relationship status on FB just yet." Angie froze. "I mean, not *yet*, not in public. People are watching. I've got a feeling."

"Have I been misreading this?"

"No. But my, uh, employers might. Listen, how about the day after tomorrow? Wait that long? So I can, uh, so I can report the contact, so they don't think I'm hiding anything. Otherwise they might think it's a security infraction . . ."

Angie unwound very slightly. "Your employers are bastards."

"Some of them are Fundamentalists. The spooks love that kind of straight-arrow puritan programming. I am not exaggerating: only a few years ago they'd have been telling me I'd burn in a rather hot place for this, or require an extra-strong course of aversion therapy or something. If they were following their churches' doctrines, that is. Most of them aren't *that* crazy, but you can never tell." She kissed Angie again. "So, like, because of security I've got to report this, but I've got to be discreet. Don't be surprised if you're doorstepped by a couple of MIB in the next week or two. Background checks."

"I'll pass." Angie made a wave-off gesture. "Remember the twitch-your-toes trick for spoofing polygraphs? I'm current. Anyway"—she smirked—"I can always mistake them for Mormon missionaries, can't I?"

"You—" Rita sighed. "I should be getting back."

"Are you sure you can't stay longer?"

"No, like I said, I'm on call from midnight. Like being on watch. I have to go back to my hotel room before then or I'll turn into a pumpkin or something . . ."

"I'll run you over, then."

"Would you be a dear and do that? If it's—"

"Of course I'd do that! And listen, if they give you any time off mid-week, you call me, you hear?"

"I hear you. *Mm-hmm.*" Rita leaned close and kissed her again. "And that status update? I'm going to update mine on Tuesday."

PHILADELPHIA, TIME LINE TWO, AUGUST 2020

Rita got back to the hotel at eleven thirty. As she entered the lobby arm-in-arm with Angie, she spotted Sonia Gomez sitting on a sofa at one side, reading something on her fatphone. As Gomez glanced up Rita turned and squeezed Angie's hand, then gave her a swift peck on one cheek. "I'll be in touch," she whispered.

"Who's she?" Angie asked tensely.

"My problem, not yours. Internal security. Go home, now. Thanks for, for everything."

Rita waited for Angie to leave before she approached Gomez, with a spring in her step that the agent's sour expression couldn't banish. Gomez, for her part, didn't meet Rita's eyes but instead focused on Angie's departing back.

"Well, isn't *that* a special piece. Got one in every port, have we?"

Fuck you too, Rita thought, but kept the words to herself. "I'll be updating my relationship status the day after tomorrow." Rita gave her a shit-eating grin. "Or is having fun against your religion?"

"You didn't check in." Gomez hissed like an angry cat, positively bristling.

"I carried my phone, didn't I? And the Colonel's little helpers could have told you who I was talking to and exactly where I was at any time."

"That's not the *point*—" Gomez's fingers curled. "Fuck, you don't get it, do you? Come on." She grabbed Rita's elbow, gripping it painfully, and marched her toward the elevators. "You may not be needed over the weekend but you do *not* go off-base during—"

"Fuck you, Patrick told me to take a weekend leave!" Rita shook her arm free and glared at Gomez.

"Patrick—" Gomez glared back at her. "I'm going to follow this up. He shouldn't have. If you were needed at short notice, if anything happened while you were putting out like a two-bit hooker—"

"You'd have been sent to fetch me, wouldn't you?" Rita pulled her arm away. "I was in Philly, Sonia, catching up with—I hadn't *fled* the country. I have a life, you know?"

"Could have fooled me up till now," Gomez muttered under her breath. The elevator stopped. "Come on. Briefing's on in twenty minutes. The Colonel's come here *specially* to see you. Wipe that smirk off your face."

Rita's face was still stretched in a rictus grin when they approached one of the hotel conference rooms. The rest of the conference floor seemed curiously empty, bereft of weekend sales conventions and the like, but they'd passed a handful of armed DHS cops on their way. "What's going on here, Sonia—did he book the whole hotel?"

"Yes he *did*. Are you beginning to see where this is going, yet?"

"Mushroom, remember?" Rita waggled a couple of fingers in the air. "You keep me in the dark and feed me shit, you can't expect me to make a *positive contribution*."

"Well, try not to fuck up, child. It's not just the Colonel today, and these guys play at the high-stakes table."

Rita looked at Gomez sharply. "You know what? I'd be more inclined to listen to your advice if you didn't do such a good job of hating on me."

Gomez snorted. "It's not *you* I hate." She gestured at the closed conference room door ahead. "Go right on in—the lions are hungry and waiting. I'll be back for you with a mop and a body bag when they call me."

The door led into a large conference suite, with an outer office. Patrick was waiting there. "Had a good weekend?" he asked.

"Yeah." Rita found it impossible to keep a smile off her face. "Thanks for the time off!"

"Is she an old friend? Or a new one?" He stood up.

"We were in the Girl Scouts together." Rita forced her expression back to bland. "What's this about? What's going on?"

Patrick paused with his hand on the inner door. "Everything blew up about six hours ago. Until then, it was *hurry up and wait.* Now—" He shrugged. "You ready?" His glance reminded Rita that she wasn't exactly dressed for the office: hair tousled, clothes casual.

"They'll just have to take me as they find me," she said, her assumed levity only half false.

"Good." Patrick ushered her in.

"Hello, Rita." The Colonel smiled like he was putting a brave face on a toothache.

There were a couple of other men around the table, overformal in black suits with small gold lapel-pin crosses. Recalling her conversation with Angie, they reminded Rita of Mormon missionaries, except they were too old and senior for that. Their body language showed a subtle deference toward the third interloper. She was a middle-aged woman, her wavy dark hair sprinkled with gray. Rita would have pegged her as an HR manager first or an accountant second, but for the escort. *Uh-oh,* she thought as Patrick pulled out a chair and motioned for her to sit. "Is there a problem?" she asked quietly.

"Yes, but you're not it." The Colonel's smile was unreassuring.

Okay, I'm not in trouble yet *but he's about to throw me in it* . . . "It's nearly midnight," she pointed out. "I thought we were going for Tuesday?"

"Yes, well so did I." She caught Colonel Smith's brief sidelong glance at the woman. "Rita, I'd like you to meet Dr. Eileen Scranton. Dr. Scranton is the deputy assistant to the Secretary of State for Homeland Security. "

"Pleased to meet you, Doctor," Rita managed to say without stuttering.

Scranton smiled back graciously. "Likewise, I'm sure."

"Eileen is in my immediate reporting chain, two levels up," the Colonel added. *Two levels up from Major General equivalent,* Rita translated internally. *What does that even mean?* "She reports in turn to the Homeland Security Council and, thanks to the miracle of matrix management, to the National Security Council. The HSC being DHS and the NSC being the Defense Department."

"Uh—uh—" Rita tried not to hyperventilate. *Where does the President come into all this?* She had a horrible feeling that the ladder of government didn't have much headspace above the Homeland Security Council. Suddenly Gomez's paranoid live-wire act was looking less like an overreaction and more like justifiable caution. "I'm honored. Um. What can I do for you, Doctor?"

"For me personally, nothing." Eileen smiled self-deprecatingly. She glanced at Colonel Smith. "I'm just sitting in as a monitor. Ensuring that the Homeland Security Council and National Security Council are fully informed."

Informed by a first-person witness, Rita decoded, *in case the Colonel is an inaccurate correspondent.* Smith looked as relaxed as he ever did, which corresponded to somewhere between overcaffeinated and hitting the crystal meth in normal-person terms. But he certainly didn't look stressed out or upset, as he might if his superiors were investigating him for running a rogue operation.

"We've become something of a sensation over the weekend." The Colonel smiled tightly at her. "The Secretary of State was briefed on Saturday, and on Sunday we made headlines in a very small way—on the President's Daily Brief." Rita swallowed, queasily nervous. That document was more usually preoccupied by Chinese nuclear battle group maneuvers in the Yellow Sea, or the geopolitical consequences of fluctuations in the price of natural gas in Europe, than by the fifteen-minute foray of an agent blundering around a railway switchyard in the dark. To Rita, who'd grown up carefully keeping her head down, making it onto the Daily Brief felt *wrong*. "Dr. Scranton is here to ensure that the White House is kept fully informed."

Rita dry-swallowed. This was like something out of a bad Hollywood adventure game. "Okay, I guess. I'll do my best—" She realized her mouth was in danger of running away from her, and forced it into silence.

"We're still on for 0300 hours on Tuesday," Smith added. "Patrick, do you want to take it away?"

"Um, yeah." Rita took heart. Patrick was putting a good face on it, but she knew him well enough now to recognize the small signs: he was at least as unnerved as she was. "Our current mission plan repeats and extends the Mission One baseline from Thursday last, adding additional elements that extend the sortie duration to two hours. As before, there will be go/no-go checkpoints and emergency exits at each staging point. The objectives are to revalidate safe insertion protocol, check for signs of adversary awareness, collect uplink data from distributed surveillance nodes, then insert additional surveillance devices . . ."

One of the suits who'd blown in with Dr. Scranton raised a hand as soon as Patrick paused. "How exactly are you going to check signs of activity on the part of an adversary you have not yet characterized?"

Rita stifled a groan: *It's going to be one of those meetings*, she realized. Not so much micromanaged as nanomanaged, every footfall to be structured for maximum carefully contrived defensive ass-covering on the part of the stakeholders. Her unique status as the only JAUNT BLUE operative meant that everybody was simultaneously shit-scared of losing her and eager to put their own grubby fingerprints all over the intelligence assessment that would be read by the woman in the Oval Office.

It was simultaneously fascinating and tedious, like sitting in on one of HaptoTech's marketing meetings before the trade show. Only Clive would have fired the fingerprint hounds on the spot. *I should have stayed over with Angie*, Rita realized. Except that, as an opportunity to be a fly on the wall at an intel operation that had just leveled up to Boss, this was unbeatable. Historic, even. The other girls at Spy Camp would have been slack-jawed with envy—and so would their parents.

PHILADELPHIA, TIME LINE TWO; IRONGATE, TIME LINE THREE, AUGUST 2020

It was nearly three in the morning and a light rain was falling when Rita climbed out of the trailer—actually a TV production unit's mobile dressing room that someone had sprung for—and clumped over to the taped-out transfer location. Her back sagged under the weight of all the crap the committee had insisted she carry. *This is just nuts,* she thought. Tired and irritable, she wished she were brave enough to throw a quiet tantrum.

Sunday night's meeting had bled over into the small hours of Monday morning, then reconvened over coffee and cronuts at two in the afternoon, then run on again until eight. This deprived her of the chance to do more than catch a quick shower and call Angie—just for the blind reassurance of hearing her voice, a tangible reminder that she hadn't imagined her life taking an extraordinary swerve for the better.

She also managed to fit in an hour-long nap—one troubled by disturbing dreams of abandonment. Upon waking, the surreal sense of disconnection resumed: *Why am I even here?* she asked herself. *Why can't I just take the week off?* The emotional flash flood, pouring across the rock-hard plain of a life baked by months of drought, made concentrating on what she was supposed to be doing almost impossible. She was besieged by the resurrected ghosts of unquiet memories: hiking together on the Appalachian Trail, lying awake at night in a crowded tent listening to the girl next to her slowly breathing, and wondering—

For Mission Two, there were three times as many bodies clogging up the parking lot and getting in the way, most of them apparently bag carriers for rubbernecking bosses who couldn't force themselves to let well enough alone and allow the people who knew what they were doing to get on with the job. Which was basically her, with Patrick for instructions and the DHS armorers and sysadmins for tech support. The Colonel had come along to keep a nervous eye on the teeter-tottering hierarchs who had descended from above, as if to watch the launch of a new long-range missile or something. People in expensive suits kept bugging Rita to talk to them, made her repeat herself endlessly until her cheeks were tight from nervous smiling. Even that bitch Sonia Gomez was trying to make nice in her direction. And the floodlights—

Rita finally cracked. "Will somebody kill those floodlights, please?" Half a dozen mobile telescoping masts with lights on them lit up the parking lot so bright that Rita was beginning to feel the need for sunblock.

One of the rubberneckers called, "We need them for the cameras—"

"They're going to ruin my night vision!"

Colonel Smith heard her plea and took mercy. "You heard her! Everybody get ready for lights out at T minus five minutes! She needs to adapt to darkness before showtime! Who's in charge of lighting? You, yes you, I want the floods *out*, out at T minus five, all of them . . ."

The lights began to dim, fading finally to a pointillist sparkle of isolated LEDs that simulated moonlight. It was still too bright, Rita fretted, but her eyes were beginning to adapt. "Are you okay?" Patrick asked quietly from behind her. "Anything you need?"

Yes: get rid of the circus, she thought. "There are too many people here. Isn't that a security issue?"

"Yeah. I'll have a word with the Colonel. If we're lucky he can convince Dr. Scranton to lock it down again after this run, but she's under a lot of pressure from stakeholders who want to get an eyeful of the promised land."

"Who do? I mean, what? Why?" *Promised land?*

Patrick looked bone-tired. "The Mormons and the Scientologists are duking it out again. They'll take any excuse: you just have to roll with it. Can I get you anything else? Can of Pepsi?"

"I don't want to need a restroom while I'm out there. Have a coffee waiting for me in debrief when I get back?"

"Good girl." He patted her shoulder, misjudging the weight of her pack, and she staggered. "Oops. Try not to, uh, break a leg."

"Check."

"T minus one minute," some idiot intoned into a bullhorn, fancying himself the ringmaster.

Rita flipped her night vis goggles down, then squeezed her left forearm carefully. *Oh Angie,* she thought, *please let it not just be my imagination that you—*

"Thirty seconds—"

She forced herself back into focus. "Lifelogger, go to maximum bandwidth, record everything, and journal to backpack," she muttered into her throat mike. "Over." Then she jaunted, twice in rapid succession.

This time she thought she knew what to expect of the rail yard. So she kept her balance, swung her helmet-mounted glasses round in a circle to take in the tracks, recording everything like a good Girl Scout.

There were trains, but none of them were moving. Dim starlight gleamed off a distant fence. A faint breeze raised whispers in the overhead wires, and the station buildings formed indistinct black silhouettes on the far side of the tracks. "Headset, new capture map. Bookmark current." She squatted, then hit the release on her backpack.

A hefty Peli case thudded to the ground behind her. She turned, squatted, and flipped it open. Dim LEDs began to blink as the data logger began to ping the scattered surveillance devices she'd planted before the weekend. Now she opened the flap covering the other half of the case. Four gunmetal bird-shapes nestled within like legless, beakless pigeons with synthetic sapphire eyes: Raytheon birds that laid Rockwell eggs. She lifted them one at a time, unplugged their charge cables, and ran through the checklist on her head-up display, then stood back as they spread their carbon-fiber wings and lofted into the night.

Once the micro-UAVs had flown, Rita did another 360 turn. There was nobody in sight: it was as quiet as a graveyard. She flipped the Peli case closed, then armed the dead man's switch. If all went to plan, she'd pick it up on her return journey. If not, it had a world-walking ARMBAND unit of its own and would jaunt home in two hours. "Set timer to one hour forty-five."

She didn't like to think about what they would do if the base station went home without her. She'd tried to ask Colonel Smith, but he'd flatly changed the subject, not even bothering to evade. "You know better than to ask questions like that." He'd looked pained, as if she'd turned up to a test without studying for it.

She'd swallowed. "You know I'll come home on schedule unless, unless for some reason I can't. Aren't you supposed to offer me a cyanide capsule or something? In case I'm captured and tortured?"

"You won't be," he said, with calm reassurance that in retrospect gave her the cold shivers. "We're monitoring you via the telemetry return module. And your wearable diagnostics"—the harness of electrodes taped to her skin, under her clothes. "If you glimpse someone, you jaunt home. If you fall and break a leg, you jaunt home. If someone shoots at you, you jaunt home. If the locals capture you—and they won't if you've done the other things right—you jaunt home. Your only excuse for not jaunting home is that you're dead, in which case the JAUNT BLUE program is suspended. The question of what happens after that is one for the National Security Council. It's not my job or yours to second-guess them."

Casting around with her grainy noise-speckled green starlight scopes, Rita discerned no signs of motion. Looking down, she stepped across the first track, knelt, and used the right angle and laser range finder from her right thigh pocket to measure the interrail gap. Five feet, two inches precisely. Keeping her feet on the stony ballast between the sleepers, avoiding contact with the rails, she made her way across the switchyard toward the darkened signal house. Hulking transformers buzzed quietly in a fenced-in cantonment not far from the building, stacked insulators feeding fat cables up to an overhead gantry. Smell of damp wood, oil and ozone, distant trees. Odor of dirt, a slight sulfurous tickle at the back of the throat. An external wooden staircase ran up to the entrance to the signal box on the second floor. It was built of red brick, stained black with soot, and the paint around the window frames was peeling.

She scanned her environs again, then carefully checked the wall outside the signal box. Telegraph wires led under the eaves, or maybe they were low-voltage power cables—not the heavy traction current from the substation behind the fence—but there were no obvious signs of external alarms. The door at the top of the stairs was wooden, paneled, and secured with a bulky hasp and padlock.

"This isn't a forerunner time line," she said quietly, trusting the telemetry return module to capture her words for posterity. "Use of wood, brick, and natural materials. It's closer to—"

There was a sign by the side of the signal box door. Without thinking, she climbed the steps until she was close enough to read it. It was made of embossed metal: rust spots showed through the enameled paint surface.

"Sign in English. Lifelogger, bookmark this." She peered closer. "Eastern Imperial Permanent Way Rules and Regulations. Employees only. Trespassers will be Att—Attaindered. Maximum penalty, uh, squiggle fifty slash dash." Excitement—*I can read this! They speak English! Sort of*—vied with disappointment—*Oh, I can read this, it's just English.*

She hadn't brought a lock-pick kit, and she wasn't proficient enough to waste time fumbling around in the dark with a padlock on a semi-derelict-looking building. She contented herself by gumming a webcam up against one of the panes of glass in the door, where it would have a decent view of everyone working in the building by daylight (and the glass could act as a resonant surface for its mike). Then she descended the stairs and made for the platform with the station office, four tracks away. Her blood was humming in her ears: quick darting glances told her she was still alone.

The station building was a long, low, single-story structure with a gently sloping roof, sitting on a raised platform island between two tracks—it was clearly designed for passenger trains. Rita guessed its length at about five hundred feet, short by US standards per the briefing from the FRA guy. *Do they use it to bring in the switchyard crew,* she wondered, *or do they run short commuter trains?* Daylight and webcams would tell. She duck-walked along the track bed, checking for signs of activity in the building, then climbed the steps at the end of the platform. It was the work of a minute to climb atop some kind of low retaining wall sized for trolleys or supplies and to stick a couple of webcams to one of the supports of the long station canopy. Then she worked her way along the platform.

Rita came to what looked to be a waiting room or ticket office, shuttered against the night. There were posters on the wall outside in glass-fronted frames, just like a station at home. There was a timetable: she scanned it carefully at close range, trusting that the list of unfamiliar destinations would be meaningful to some back-office analyst. Other public information notices. She forced herself to glance at them quickly, but not allow herself to become absorbed. Some were strikingly familiar, as if they were a glimpse of home as seen through a semantic fun-house mirror. DEMOCRACY IS ENDANGERED: IF YOU SEE SOMETHING, TELL SOMEONE. That could *almost* have come from home. But then she came to another: LONG LIVE THE REVOLUTION! EQUALITY, DEMOCRACY, LIBERTY. And below it, in smaller lettering, DOWN WITH ROYALISM.

Hang on, she thought, her perspective expanding dizzyingly, *the rusting sign on the signal box door* . . . It had said something about an "Imperial Permanent Way." And now this: DOWN WITH ROYALISM. *What does it mean?*

She came to another locked platform door, beside a window. And for once the window wasn't shuttered. It was an office, looking out on the platform. Rita peeped inside: there was no sign of life. With her low-powered flashlight, she lit up the room within until her night glasses could see clearly—barely a single lumen sufficed. There were swivel chairs of heavy wood and brass with leather seats, and green metal-topped desks. File cabinets loomed against one wall. A tall electric fan with villainously sharp-looking blades hulked over the largest desk like a frozen mantis. The desk was crowded, with several in-trays and an old-school computer. *Paydirt*, she realized, and climbed atop a platform bench seat to affix another webcam to the glass, looking in.

Then she glanced down at the desk and realized what she had seen but not registered.

There was a *computer* on the desk. It was an old-school bulky beige box with a metal cover, not a tablet or a flat display panel. A keyboard you could club someone to death with sat proudly in the middle of the blotter, but something about it didn't quite look right. She fumbled for a moment with her webbing, then managed to pull out the super-zoom camera. "Come on, damn you," she muttered under her breath. The autofocus didn't want to work in darkness. She glanced around, nervously, then switched the flash to automatic and squeezed her eyes shut as she depressed the shutter button. Then she zoomed in on the image she'd captured. It was a keyboard, all right, but the key layout was all wrong. The keys weren't staggered; there were too many columns and not enough rows. *I guess we're not in QWERTY City anymore,* she told herself.

She was still boggling at the museum exhibits when the platform light came on.

PART THREE

DARK STATE

History repeats itself, first as tragedy, then as farce.
—Karl Marx

Extraction

Miriam and Erasmus spent a night in the bunker waiting for the bombs to fall, drinking bad coffee and grinding through a crisis agenda inconclusively.

Elsewhere, hundreds of pilots spent the night keyed up and sleepless in the cockpits of their nuclear-armed interceptors, wondering if this time the French were finally coming. And they were not alone, for the Commonwealth War Command responded to the uncertain threat in accordance with the age-old syllogism of the uncertain; something must be done, *this* is something, therefore *this* must be done.

Petard carriers—bombers—and their escort tankers scrambled, then flew out to orbit their hold-back points in the howling darkness above the Arctic Ocean. They flew armed and ready for the deadly one-way dash to the enemy capitals: to London, Paris, Cairo, Beijing, Bombay, and the heart of the enemy empire itself, Royal St. Petersburg. Across the flat prairies of Lakotaland, flight crews descended into their silos and pumped liquid fuel aboard their bulbous first-generation ICBMs. In the oceans, submarine captains received their low-frequency alert codes and brought their nuclear-powered vessels to periscope depth while the missile teams readied their birds. But it was an exercise in impotence: none of the bombers or ICBMs or SLBMs carried the world-walkers who were a necessity if they were to engage the real threat.

By dawn of the day after this deathwatch, it became clear that the sum

of all fears had not come to pass. The high-altitude drone was not the har-
binger of Armageddon. Across the New American Commonwealth's three
continents and scattered territories, the unsleeping Air Defense forces saw
nothing else unusual. After twelve hours of intense concentration—for, as
Dr. Johnson had so memorably observed, nothing concentrates the mind
like the knowledge that one is to be hanged—the Commonwealth War
Command began to draw down their forces unit by unit, backing slowly
away from the brink of a nuclear war with the only adversary they knew
how to fight.

All except for JUGGERNAUT, of course. But the JUGGERNAUT
superweapon was behind schedule and over budget. It might never be
ready. And even if it *was* viable, it was anyone's guess whether it would
work. After all, the Commonwealth war planners knew that bombers
and ICBMs and ballistic missile submarines worked: they'd supped at the
fount of dark wisdom supplied by the Ministry of Intertemporal Technological Intelligence. They'd studied the Cuban Missile Crisis, the
emergency at the end of the Yom Kippur War, and the ghastly intersection of Operation RYaN and Able Archer 83 that had brought the Soviet
Union and the United States to the edge of nuclear annihilation in the
mid-1980s. They'd majored in cold war studies: Hiroshima and Naga-
saki and New Delhi and Islamabad were on the syllabus of the staff college at Rochester. But nobody in any time line they knew of had ever
built anything quite like JUGGERNAUT, much less developed doctrine for using it . . .

NEW LONDON, TIME LINE THREE, JUNE 2020

"How long has he got?" Miriam asked bluntly.

Dr. Porter, the oncology consultant, looked tired. He'd probably answered the question sixteen times before breakfast already. "It's anyone's
guess," he said unhelpfully. "The Lord will know his own."

Miriam glanced sidelong at her husband. Erasmus appeared to be paying more attention to the writing pad on his lap than to her interrogation of the doctor. It was an old habit of his. "I know cachexia when I see

it," she said. "I also know acute spinal degeneration secondary to meta-static tumors, and peripheral neuropathy—"

Dr. Porter's eyes widened. "I see ma'am is up to date on the new foreign literature," he said.

Ma'am is actually very out of date indeed, but Miriam decided not to mention her uncompleted premed to him. She merely smiled tensely. "What's his prognosis? Days or weeks?"

"Ah, well." Porter looked faintly relieved. "*Well,* the First Man may not be as close to death's door as you believe. You met him at his worst last week. He's currently responding well to a combination treatment— fluorouracil and cisplatin—and radiation as well. I will not mince words with you: his prognosis is terminal. But while one can never rule out sudden setbacks, he might hang on for as long as six months."

Fluorouracil and cisplatin were 1970s chemotherapy drugs, but the Commonwealth was nowhere near ready to begin production of monoclonal antibody and epigenetic interference therapies. And Adam himself had refused, point blank, to consider a discreet trip to a private Brazilian clinic in time line two. "It is my duty to stand by my people and, if necessary, to suffer as they do," he'd pointed out to Erasmus when they'd come to visit his bedside the day before. "If there's an easy escape for the likes of us, when will we ever develop the indigenous technology"— he'd glanced at Miriam, eyelids fluttering—"to rescue our people?"

Sixteen years ago, Sir Adam had swallowed her two-phase proposal completely—so completely, he was willing to die by it. She'd lobbied to establish a ministry to use world-walkers to import knowledge and ideas and spread the spoils via educational establishments. But it was essential that they use these tools only to develop native infrastructure, from schools and universities to research establishments and factories. The Commonwealth must stand on its own, rather than becoming addicted to a steady drip of illicit imports from another time line, as the Gruinmarkt had. It had seemed like a really good idea at the time, she thought— not without bitterness—until the saintly Father of the Nation decided they were words to live *and* die by.

"'Setbacks.'" Miriam tried not to scowl, not entirely successfully. "Well, Doctor. While I appreciate your doing everything within your capabilities to help keep the First Man going, I was . . . shall we say, taken aback? As you might understand, the state of his health ultimately affects my commission. And my husband's"—it *still* felt strange calling him that, even after fourteen years—"duties, too, as Commissioner of Propaganda. We both have necessary and sufficient reason to be added to the distribution list for his daily updates."

"Um, ah." Dr. Porter looked unhappy. "If the First Man consents, of course. Otherwise power of attorney in respect of his physiodynamic needs rests with the Secretary to the Inner Party."

Oh hell. Miriam failed to suppress a twitch this time. Nor did she miss the tension that suddenly appeared in the set of Erasmus's shoulders. "Then I will take this up with the secretariat," she assured Dr. Porter. Standing, she turned to her husband: "I think we've heard enough, dear." Erasmus rose, and offered her his arm. "Thank you, Doctor."

Dr. Porter, too, rose, and bowed and ushered them out of his office with old-school formality.

"Well, *fuck*," Miriam whispered as they passed through the waiting room, which was crowded with no small number of Deputy Commissioners, Secretaries, and a handful of nursing orderlies and junior doctors. The Manhattan Palace was sprouting medical facilities, as if engaged in a bizarre bid to rival the teaching hospitals of New London. "We'll have to soft-soap Adrian," she confided in Erasmus.

Her husband's face was a closed book. "I trust our friend the Secretary as far as I can throw him," he hissed.

"Can't be helped. Have to confront him sooner or later. Better now than in cabinet when Sir Adam's too sick to keep up the pretense anymore."

Outside the palace medical center they picked up their respective retinues of clerks and administrative assistants, and proceeded by common consent toward what had once, before the Revolution, been the Empress's Chambers. They walked together: two distinguished-looking politicians, formally clad in the subdued version of the finery that courtiers had once deployed—austere gray and black tailoring over white silk—rather than the prerevolutionary efflorescences of crimson and purple over explosions of lace. Like magpies surrounded by the crowlike figures of their attendants, they made their way toward the center of the web ruled by the Party Secretary, Adrian Holmes.

Holmes was indeed home this morning. They passed through an outer office, in which clerks rattled the keys of no fewer than six computer terminals (wired, no doubt, to one of the municipal government mainframes that formed the beating heart of the Commonwealth Cybernetic Agoric Allocator, the real-time central planning system that ran the state). Then they were ushered into the windowless inner office, and the presence of the New Man himself.

"Ah, the Commissioners Burgeson!" Adrian Holmes hauled himself to his feet, beaming with a bonhomie Miriam suspected he cultivated only for high-ranking visitors: he could certainly switch it on and off like a lightbulb. A tall man, dour of disposition, he was also a supremely effective administrator. Which was why Adam had elevated him to the Party Secretariat at such a young age—he was barely forty.

("A bloody *Robespierre*," Olga had spat when she heard the news. Miriam had pretended not to notice, but over time she'd come to suspect that her younger protégé might have been right when she'd said, "You mark my words, my lady: give him his head and he'll reap all of ours, even if he has to build his own guillotine." Erasmus had not quite agreed. "Not a Robespierre," he'd said gloomily, "but he might grow into Stalin's shoes.")

"And what can I do for you today?"

"It's the boss," Erasmus said, affecting a slight nasality in his voice that elevated his tone but left it just short of a whine. It made him sound slightly stupid. He'd developed the trick, Miriam had learned, while on the run before the Revolution—as a way of convincing the political police he was harmless. "Nobody *told* us . . ."

"We want to be added to the daily distribution list for Sir Adam's medical status," Miriam added. "Our commissions have definite need to know."

"I'm sure they do," Adrian agreed affably. "Propaganda and industrial espionage—defending the indefensible, eh?" He beamed, then continued: "I'll see you're added to the list right away. Can't think why you weren't on it to begin with, honestly." He sat down. "Will you stay for a while? I'm not busy, and it's been too long since we've had a chance to chew the cud."

More likely he meant, *It's been too long since I had a chance to pick your brains.* Adrian was often in the office for eighteen hours a day, burning the midnight electricity. He had a mind like a mantrap, a superb memory, a grasp of the tiniest minutiae, and a pleasant demeanor. Miriam would have been entranced by him, and even considered him a possible suitable successor for the First Man, if she hadn't also suspected him of being as ideologically flexible as a rubber band. A courtier's courtier, rather than a man of integrity. "We really ought to get together some time." Miriam smiled at him. "Unfortunately I've got to chair a meeting of the Joint Intelligence Committee this afternoon, and Erasmus has— what do you have, dear?"

"Contingency planning." Erasmus gave Holmes a fey smile. "Black crepe, martial music, state funeral with gun carriage and cathedral, and then what, eh? It's coming, Ade. Someone has to manage how we are seen in our hour of grief, an' all that."

Don't rub it in too hard, you moron! Miriam wished, not for the first time, that marital vows conferred spousal telepathy: at times like this it would have been more than handy. "What he means to say is that, strictly speaking, the dismal contingency facing us is going to dominate the news cycle for weeks, and he's already in the throes of planning for it."

"Well, don't let me keep you." Adrian grinned at her, or bared his teeth—it was much the same expression. "But we really *must* talk soon, you know. Before we're overtaken by events."

"You must come round for dinner sometime next week," Miriam offered. "Have your people talk to my people: I'm sure we can sort out a quiet tête-à-tête, just the three of us."

"Absolutely," he said, his tone pleasant. "I'll see when they can fit you in. My diary's filling up rather fast, I'm afraid. Ciao!"

It was a dismissal. Not so long ago, a dismissal of that kind, in that tone, would have been the prerogative of the First Man and none other— you simply did not dismiss two People's Commissioners of cabinet rank. But thanks to a freakish piece of medical bad luck, time was running out for the First Man. And it was anybody's guess who would pick up the reins when the driver left the carriage for the last time.

PHILADELPHIA, TIME LINE TWO; IRONGATE, TIME LINE THREE, AUGUST 2020

The lights along the railway platform switched on without warning. There were dozens, maybe even hundreds of them. Hot, pinkish-white tungsten filaments sheathed in frosted white glass.

Rita jumped down from the bench she'd been standing on and ran, shielding her glare-bruised eyes. Behind the station office, the side facing the brick wall was unlit, the shadows around it thick and deep. *It's just this platform,* she realized as she flattened her back against the wall. She checked the time in her head-up display: *three forty-nine.* The rest of the switchyard was in darkness, but now she heard a rattle and a click, footsteps walking along the front of the building she'd taken shelter behind. *Scheisse. The tracks.* The tracks between her and the survey point for her jaunt home gleamed in reflected light. The switchyard floodlights were out, but up the line she saw signal lamps switch from red to blue. *Night train coming.*

She licked her suddenly dry lips and took stock. *I'm above ground level.* The platform was about five feet above the track beds. She whispered: "Maps, inertial, display current-equivalent location." The head-up display delivered. She was about a third of a mile away from the Colonel's big tent revival camp. If she jaunted home, she'd come out across a highway, maybe in someone else's parking lot, maybe inside a shuttered Target. A sickening sense of relief turned her knees to jelly and threatened her with blackout. She'd risk a sprained ankle, but so what. The telemetry box could look after itself, in a pinch. One-shot ARMBAND units cost only a few tens of thousands of dollars these days, according to Patrick. She took a deep breath. *So let's stay and see what's going on . . .*

More footsteps, then male voices, gruff and muffled by distance and corners. They were just at the edge of hearing, their accents strange. "Aye

Bill, that wert right clever." (Inaudible reply.) "Well youse can jist get thy-self across to tha' signals and set the track block to am-pass. Oh, an' light up the yard. They're due in ten minutes."

A rattle of keys in a lock: more footsteps, then a heavy thud and a crunching of boots on ballast as someone—Bill, at a guess—jumped down onto the tracks and headed away. The light changed, brightening slightly: possibly because Bill's interlocutor had entered the station office and turned on more lamps. "Video feed, last node," Rita whispered.

A grainy video window sprang to life in her head-up display: the interior of the station office. A middle-aged, overweight man with bushy side-boards and comic-opera headgear—*Is that a tricorn hat?*—flopped down behind the computer terminal, punching laboriously at the keys with meaty index fingers. His coat or cloak or other outer garment (it was hard to tell: ruffles and frogging obscured part of it) hung over a hook on the back of the open door. Without looking, he reached sideways and picked up an antique telephone handset that trailed a pigtail coil of wire. "Station mate's office," he said (his voice tinny but completely audible through the glass and the webcam pickup), "Eugene hailing." (A pause.) "Yes, you should have a good signal in another minute." He hung up.

Rita felt, rather than heard, a faint rumble, followed by a hiss and shimmer of tracks rubbing against their tie-downs. She looked sideways and saw the lights of a train, then heard a deep rumble and the crack of a spark as it approached, pantograph flaring momentarily against the over-head power cables. It was, she saw, a short passenger train. Like a commuter train, it had multiple doors spaced along each of its five carriages; but like a European high-speed express, it was streamlined and bullet-nosed. The windows were lit, showing an indistinct mass of people in dark coats sitting and standing within. Brakes sighed as it rolled along-side the platform and drifted to a standstill; then the doors opened with a hiss to disgorge a torrent of bodies onto the front of the platform.

Rita shuddered, wrung out on an adrenaline spike, and slid farther into the shadows. Doors rattled elsewhere in the station as the crowd stamped and shuffled their way toward an unseen exit. In her head-up display she watched as the stationmaster—station *mate*, she reminded herself—picked up his phone and pushed buttons on a blocky console below it: "Eugene hailing. The four o'clock shift change multiple is discharging onto platform two now. Prithee let the night shift in as soon as you sight the discharge? Thanking you kindly."

There was more rumbling elsewhere in the switchyard. A long, slow freight train hove into view behind an oddly quiet locomotive. It hummed as it approached, a deep sixty-cycle thrumming sound that carried even over the voices and echoing feet of the men from the passenger train. They were spreading out like an ant-trail leading into an open doorway just visible from one of Rita's other webcams. *There have to be three hundred of them,* she realized. *Maybe more.* There'd been standing room only on the train. Men and women in coats or overalls, indistinctly glimpsed in the harsh station lights. She tried to get a look at them. Acquiring some idea of local fashions, Patrick had pointed out, was important in laying groundwork for future infiltration missions. But all she could really tell, without stepping out from her hiding place, was that most of them wore shapeless berets or caps and hats. She'd have to rely on the webcams for detail.

The swarm of small-hour commuters didn't seem to be slackening, but now Rita noticed a new trend: people drifting back up the platform in ever-increasing numbers. They walked tiredly, stoop-shouldered as they climbed aboard the train. *Going home,* she noted. *A four o'clock shift change.* The train emptied out and refilled over a five-minute period. Increasingly edgy, Rita fumbled with her super-zoom, switching off the flash and diverting its output to her glasses.

Then (taking her courage in both hands) she slowly eased the barrel lens around the corner of the building to record the last stragglers in more detail. Men and women in long woolen coats, cut almost like dusters. They wore dark clothes underneath, suits or in some cases knee breeches and hose on the men. The women wore long skirts or Indian-style shalwar outfits—side-split tunics over loose trousers. Their faces were creased and rumpled by long, sleepless working hours. *Factory workers,* Rita speculated. Bethlehem's bones were built on iron and coal and the first steelworks. Was it any surprise there was heavy industry here, too?

As the crowd thinned, she pulled back deeper into the shadows. An electric bell clanged harshly above the squeal and thud the freight train made as it crossed a sequence of points. Then the doors on the shift change train hissed shut, and with a buzzing whine it glided back the way it had come.

Looking past the empty platform, Rita saw flatbed carriages rumbling and squealing past. Tarpaulins covered most of their loads, but there was something ominously familiar about the hunchbacked shapes beneath. A coy glimpse under a hem of oilcloth finally forced another dizzying perspective change upon her. She followed the edge of a track wrapped around a toothed drive wheel, the outline of hull, then turret and horizontal protrusion—*Are those tanks?* she wondered.

"Hey! You! You missed your shift! Dinna you ken the—hey!"

Rita spun round. It was the station mate, waddling along the platform toward her, waving. Without thinking, she'd stepped forward toward the freight train, and now he'd seen her. "Abort, abort, abort," she said aloud, trying to ignore her stomach churn. Raised her left forearm, squeezed for the return trigger—

"Hey, you! Let's see your pass—"

She jaunted in a panicky moment, falling hard onto soft grass and going over on her left hip. Falling hurt, but she pushed herself upright immediately and jaunted again, this time into an empty parking lot on the other side of the highway from her starting point.

I blew it, she realized dismally. *I totally suck at spying.* And then the true implications of what she'd witnessed struck like lightning. Tanks. High-speed commuter trains. Computers. *My God, what have we stumbled across?*

BALTIMORE, TIME LINE TWO, AUGUST 2020

FEDERAL EMPLOYEE 004930391 CLASSIFIED VOICE TRANSCRIPT

DR. SCRANTON: The way I read this action summary, we're burned. She's not going to be able to go back there again. Colonel? Anything to add?

COL. SMITH: We learned a lot, and I'm not sure it went as badly as you think.

LIAISON, STATE DEPT: Yes, but our JAUNT BLUE asset was exposed! She could have been killed! As it was, she barely escaped by the skin of her—

COL. SMITH: Nonsense. Don't overdramatize.

LIAISON, STATE DEPT: But she could have been shot!

DR. SCRANTON: (wearily) Gentlemen. As you were saying, Colonel?

COL. SMITH: Rita aborted the mission early, but completely in line with her instructions: do not risk confrontation, avoid exposure. The telemetry capsule auto-returned on schedule, as expected. The mission was truncated but we made a full recovery, and we learned a lot. Let me go over the pluses and minuses—

DR. SCRANTON: Please do.

COL. SMITH: First, the pluses. She retrieved the logs from the Mission One nomadic surveillance nodes. She released the Mission Two micro-UAV spy birds. She planted six webcams on two different manned installations. We got an *invaluable* look at the inside of a railroad office, and at some rolling stock—our analysts are still drooling over the take because it's gold-dust. And she got a look, up close with a telephoto lens, at a whole bunch of railroad employees and factory workers.

DR. SCRANTON: Analysis later.

COL. SMITH: Okay. The minuses: we weren't expecting the station to be busy at four in the morning, and Rita was just in the wrong place at the wrong time. The stationmaster—the station office video stream shows that he wasn't armed, so she wasn't in immediate danger. Nevertheless, she jaunted out of there. So we're left with a witness, singular, to a JAUNT BLUE departure at dead of night. The platform wasn't alarmed or surveilled, so it's a subjective eyeball account only. Which means that unless they're aware of world-walkers they'll probably write it off as a hallucination or a funny spell or something. So while I don't think it's advisable to send Rita back to the switchyard, I don't think she's blown. In fact, I'd recommend bringing Phase Two forward.

LIAISON, STATE DEPT: What do the analysts say? What did we get out of this?

COL. SMITH: Lots. They've got computer terminals in offices. Old-style cathode ray tube monitors with odd keyboards, but it's the real thing. And they use electric traction for railroads. That commuter train Rita witnessed is a big tell—it's an electric multiple unit with Jacobs bogies—

DR. SCRANTON: What are those?

COL. SMITH: It's a special wheel layout—French and Chinese high-speed trains use them. Saves weight, but means the cars can't be uncoupled. It's common on passenger trains that run upward of a hundred and fifty miles per hour. Not ours, in other words.

DR. SCRANTON: So it's fast?

COL. SMITH: They have a fully electrified wide-gauge railway network and use high-speed commuter trains to move people to and from industrial plants. Those low-altitude records we got from the Gnats? Lots of twelve-story buildings surrounded by foliage. The lack of suburban sprawl and highways is all consistent with a planned social housing infrastructure, built around apartment blocks and lots and lots of urban light rail.

LIAISON, STATE DEPT: You mean they, they live in apartments and commute by streetcar and train?

DR. SCRANTON: Yes. This tells us something about their financial system and economy, by the way. They're a rent-not-buy country, so their consumer economy probably isn't debt-backed and underwritten by an asset bubble. I mean, we might be looking at condominiums, but then we'd expect to see some McMansions as well, and suburban sprawl around highways. And we're just not seeing that. So either they're old-school Commies who live in state-run apartments, or they're like Germany or Japan, hardworking savers who don't mortgage up and whose real estate depreciates after it's built. Possibly they've got state land ownership.

LIAISON, STATE DEPT: That sounds pretty un-American.

COL. SMITH: Yes. And then there was the flatbed Rita spotted. I brought a print for you.

LIAISON, STATE DEPT: Jesus. That's a tank . . . Jesus.

COL. SMITH: A shift change at 0400 hours suggests to me that they're working round the clock, twenty-four/seven. The webcams got us an estimated head count of four hundred and eighty workers, plus or minus twenty. Now, they might have multiple staggered shifts, but even if they're swapping out five hundred workers every hour, that maxes out at four to six thousand in whatever factory they're at. And that train, well, our best estimate is that it was carrying about sixty main battle tanks. M1 Abrams class or similar, judging by what was visible of their hull box size, suspension layout, and turret design. Enough to equip the core of a mechanized infantry brigade.

DR. SCRANTON: Are they highly automated?

COL. SMITH: We might be wrong. The munitions train might have been a coincidence—but rolling out of the vicinity of Bethlehem? Appalachian coal and iron country? If you're going to start building heavy metal in North America, that's one of the places you'd begin. If they're producing tanks there and the factory only employs a few thousand people, then that implies highly efficient manufacturing. I mean, there might be other satellite stations serving the other side of a big complex, or maybe they run a reduced maintenance shift at night and those were the cleaners and janitors going home, but . . . I'm calling this a clear indicator of 1960s technology or later, just not *our* 1960s. We might be wrong about the housing and finance stuff, by the way. It might just be a local dorms-for-factory-workers kind of thing. We won't know until we get boots on the ground and noses in library books. But it looks like kind of a Soviet setup to me. Paranoid and heavily armed with nuclear weapons.

DR. SCRANTON: Okay, Colonel. Now here's a leading question: if this was your show, where would you want to take it? Feel free to brainstorm, I'm open to ideas . . .

COL. SMITH: Well, I don't think we're going to learn much more that's useful by having Rita stumble around a switchyard at night. For one thing it's dangerous, and for another, we got what we came for. What we need now is cultural intelligence—all the little details our future agents will need to operate in place. We also need large scale SIGINT and ELINT snooping programs, but that's a job for the National Reconnaissance Office. I imagine they've got ARMBAND-equipped spysats with capsule return systems like the old Keyhole series, or

254 ■ CHARLES STROSS

some equivalent. But we probably want to hold off on lobbing heavy metal into orbit until we know if these people have satellites of their own—we don't want to set off World War Three by accident. It's going to have to happen sooner or later if we plan to engage with them, but not yet. In the meantime, I'd strongly recommend pushing Phase Two: maybe into Philly proper. The social housing thing raises an added risk factor—fewer safe houses where agents won't be under scrutiny from the neighbors—but we've got enough video that our wardrobe department say they can knock off a costume that will stand up at a distance. And thanks to the webcams we should have enough dialogue for Linguistics to start working up a training kit in a week or so. And we can iterate. It gets riskier from here on in, but Rita's resourceful. As long as we give her as much support as she wants and as much elbow room as she needs, she'll do fine.

DR. SCRANTON: Right. So tell me how we're going to do it.

END TRANSCRIPT

Shell Game

Rita jaunted back into the real world, as she still thought of it, at seven minutes past four in the morning. By four forty she'd been through a decontamination shower, a medical check, three blood samples, and a humiliatingly random piss test. (Apparently someone was worried she'd spent her hour in the BLACK RAIN time line cranking up on crystal meth: the war on drugs might have ended in an armistice, but government employment regulations took a dim view of using recreational pharmaceuticals on the job.) So when Patrick materialized and shoved a steaming mug of Starbucks into her hand, it came as a blessed relief— until he shook his head. "Save it for the debriefing committees," he murmured.

"Committees, plural?"

"Yup."

"Oh hell. Sorry."

They let her take off her body armor and extract herself from the rat's nest of biomonitor electrodes before they sat her down and grilled her for eight hours. Her interrogators took shifts in strict rotation: Patrick and the Colonel, first and fastest, then two teams of suits from Maryland, one to perform due diligence and oversight on the Unit's reportage, and the other to perform due diligence on the due-diligence checkers. Patrick and the Colonel wanted her to walk them through her telemetry feed and provide commentary, giving them insights into why she'd done particular things. Suit Team One wanted to walk her through their checklist instead, and Suit Team Two seemed to want *her* to walk *them* through Suit Team One's checklist, while demonstrating all the flexibility of a gang of incredibly advanced animatronic department store mannequins.

Back in college old Prof. Hanshaw had explained the Second Artist Effect to her class: "The first artist paints the landscape they see with their own eyes. The second artist paints what they see in the first artist's exhibition. They can't show you a true representation, because they never saw the real thing in the first place." This, Rita was beginning to feel, was as true for intelligence operations as for any other art form—and so she spent a weary morning and early afternoon regurgitating endlessly chewed-over morsels of data for the third- and fourth-string hacks to squabble over.

The worst part of it all was that they mostly seemed to be intent on undermining each other, or the Unit's reporting, by digging dirt. She half expected one of the Men in Gray to stand up suddenly, point an emotional, accusatory claw at her, and denounce her as a double agent in the pay of Moscow Central. Or perhaps they were hoping to accuse her of summoning imps to sour milk, or of not complying with federal standards for hand sanitizer application during her restroom breaks. *If only they knew,* she told herself hopelessly, cleaving to the memory of the smell of the nape of Angie's neck in the early hours as if it was an anchor cable to reality.

At two in the afternoon, Colonel Smith broke in to rescue her. He'd enlisted reinforcements. Dr. Scranton trailed behind, her poker face frozen—like a thin rind of ice covering a lake of viciously dry amusement—as she sent the brigade of second-guessers scattering like tenpins. "Ah, Ms. Douglas." She nodded to Rita. "Ladies and gentlemen"—she glanced at the Suits from Maryland—"you've had your fun. Ms. Douglas, if you'd come with me, please?"

She turned and stalked away without waiting. The Colonel hung back and ran interference while Rita apologized to the swarm of third-tier interrogators and hotfooted it after the doctor. "Sorry about that," Scranton said offhandedly, then paused for Colonel Smith to catch up. "You were right, Eric."

"Right?" Rita echoed.

"You were being nibbled to death by . . ." Smith mopped his brow with a tissue. "What are those fish they use for pedicures? Doctor fish?"

"Diffusion of responsibility meets infighting," said Scranton. "Well, we left you in the pedicure pool for eight hours, until you were nice and wrinkled. They can't complain about being denied access."

"This is a rescue?" Rita yawned, too enervated to raise a hand and cover her mouth.

"First you came to the attention of important people, then you delivered an unexpected result." Scranton shrugged: her elegant suit jacket's shoulders rose as if padded with kevlar. Chanel couture for a D.C. bureaucratic quarterback. "They were bound to go apeshit looking for anything they can use as leverage. Do you think they found anything, Eric?"

The Colonel looked, if not haggard, then perhaps somewhat stale. He, too, must have been on the go since yesterday evening, Rita realized. "Not really, but that won't stop them trying to mix it. We'll just have to outrun them," he said. "My office, please. We should keep this quiet."

"What's this about?" Rita asked, trudging after him as he led the way to the elevators.

"Phase Two."

The Colonel's temporary office was a business suite on the top floor of the hotel building. An open door led to a bedroom. The main room was dominated by a conference table, a sofa suite, and a kitchenette where a coffee filter machine burbled welcomingly. Rita sank into a recliner and tried not to let her eyes close prematurely. Dr. Scranton took the sofa to her left, and spoke: "We're going to have to get rid of the leeches before they suck us dry."

"I don't really understand," Rita complained.

The Colonel placed a mug of coffee on the occasional table in front of her. "You're not supposed to. Do you want to bring her up to speed, boss? Or shall I?"

"Huh. Allow me." Dr. Scranton waited while he fetched her a coffee— *What kind of person has the equivalent of a Major General doing the fetching and carrying anyway?* Rita wondered. "We live and work in a panopticon, Rita. Everything you do, every breath you take, someone's watching over you. It's the price of doing business in a security state. The trouble is, you can be running a nice tight ship and if it suddenly starts delivering results, well, all those eyeballs turn inward. And their owners all start trying to figure an angle that'll let them take the credit for a job well done."

"But you're—" Rita struggled to sit upright. *You're a deputy undersecretary of state!* she wanted to shout. *What are you even* doing *here?* "Why are you getting involved? Isn't this below your level?"

"Eric petitioned me to help with leech detachment duty. You've waded into a swamp full of bloodsuckers and you can't reasonably do your job if you're carrying passengers. But nobody likes a rogue operation. So this week we're making sure that all the would-be stakeholders get a good look at the Unit, up close and personal. Then after they've had a look inside I'm going to slam the door in their face so that Eric can lock it down and get everything back on course."

She slid an etiolated, almost skeletal hand into her handbag and extracted a white cylinder, raised it to her lips, and sucked, hard. A blue LED glowed at its tip. "The stakes are escalating. Too high for this penny-ante house politics bullshit. My boss, he says *his* boss is counting on you. And the buck stops on her desk, in the Oval Office."

Rita watched, eyes glazed, as Dr. Scranton exhaled a stream of bone-white smoke. The undersecretary leaned back, then addressed Colonel Smith.

"The core need-to-know cell is going to be restricted as tightly as possible. Minimum threat surface. You will nominate a team of no more than four bodies to generate internal disinformation under top-secret classification. They will manufacture falsified mission transcripts and reports from Rita to support the appearance that operations in BLACK RAIN are proceeding nominally. Transcripts to be seeded with randomized tells in each distribution, so that your people can trace leakers. If any leaks are identified, those responsible will be either turned—if there's an organization behind them and they are cooperative—or detained incommunicado."

Rita noticed Smith's brief expression of unease. *Is that some sort of euphemism?* she wondered. "The disinform reports may include elements of legitimate intel if, and *only* if, we have no reason to redact it—the best lies are parsimonious. In other words, as far as the peanut gallery is concerned, JAUNT BLUE deployment and orientation in BLACK RAIN will continue as planned. In reality, we anticipate that Rita's tasking will increasingly diverge from the BLACK RAIN road map over time." The undersecretary turned her unblinking gaze on Rita. "What do you understand from all this?"

Rita's lips were suddenly dry. "Jesus." She tried to gather her scattered thoughts. "You're, uh, exposing the operation internally so that you can use it as cover for a deeper operation? In the BLACK RAIN time line?"

Dr. Scranton nodded slowly. Her face, no longer poker-still, was nevertheless serious. "They've got nukes, Rita. They're at least late-1960s in technology terms. They've got computers and tanks and the proven ability to detect and shoot down stealthed drones. In some ways they're ahead of us: they've got containerized multimodal transport, and they've also got electrified freight and high-speed trains. If you were in the White House, what would you be thinking?"

"I'd be thinking—" *Oh God, we're fucked. If they have world-walkers, we are so fucked.* "It's a good thing they don't have world-walkers, isn't it?"

Scranton nodded. Then she reached into her handbag and pulled out a tablet. "Watch this," she said, toneless as an executioner as she handed the device to Rita.

"Watch—"

Grainy CCTV video showed a sidewalk on a quiet city street. A middle-aged woman, her black hair scraped back, walked into a questionable-looking establishment, half diner, half bodega.

Cut to: red brick buildings, shuttered windows, locked doors.

A man dressed in last year's hipster uncool, with heavy-rimmed spectacles and urban sidewalk-warrior hybrid bicycle accessory, stepped out of a door.

"Brooklyn, back in late March this year," said Scranton. "Five months ago."

Under-eave cameras chased the cycle-hipster up an alleyway, along a street, up another alley, and into a wider avenue. Eventually he chained up his bike, shouldered his messenger bag, and approached the same diner as the woman.

"Everyone knows about face recognition algorithms," remarked Scranton. "They think wearing hoodies will conceal them. Somewhat fewer people know about ear recognition, but it's a big deal: ears are nearly as unique as fingerprints. And then there's gait recognition—you can't easily change the length of the bones in your legs, so we've got software that can identify people by the way they walk. You'll know it's gone viral when you start seeing news footage of bank robbers in veils and hoopskirts. And of course everyone knows their fatphone camera can recognize cats."

"What most people don't know yet is that we've got arbitrary package recognition," said the Colonel. He sounded amused. "*Bag* recognition software. Mulberry, Ted Baker, Hot Tuna. Or in this case, Crumpler. Twenty-liter capacity. The bag goes in thin, it comes out fat."

"Look at the woman, Rita," said Dr. Scranton. Something in her tone made Rita tense up, like fingernails on glass. "*Look at her.*"

Rita froze the CCTV stream, backed up, and pinch-zoomed on the woman as she entered the diner, blowing her up until the image pixelated.

"That woman," said Dr. Scranton, "Is a former coworker of your birth mother, Miriam Beckstein. Her messenger bag, when she entered, was bulging: when she leaves, it's clearly lighter. The *man*"—a bony finger stabbed at the screen—"we don't know who he is. The Transit Police lost him in Brooklyn. We dumpster-dived the trash after they both left. He's not on the National DNA Database, but we sequenced DNA traces off his meal tray, and they tested positive for the modified glutamate receptor required for JAUNT BLUE. Then we did a full workup. He's your third cousin twice removed, Ms. Douglas."

Rita froze, chewing her lower lip. She felt oddly unaffected. "So he's a world-walker. From the Clan. And she's a, a covert asset." She paused. "Why haven't you lifted them?"

"Because reasons." Dr. Scranton stood, clutching her coffee mug, and began to pace jerkily, her power heels digging notches in the deep pile carpet. "Like I said, we *nearly* lifted him on the New York subway. The more pressing question is Ms. Milan—that woman. The FBI investigated her shortly after 7/16; they concluded she was harmless: a first-degree contact, not an associate. It now appears that they were wrong and she was a sleeper. Now she's awake and she's supplying one of their couriers with . . . you don't need to know.

"Anyway, he hasn't shown up since that meeting. We're now monitoring her activities, and next time the Clan make contact we'll snatch them both. But the core takeaway we want you to be aware of is that enemy world-walkers are currently active in the United States—keeping a very low profile but conducting industrial espionage. And BLACK RAIN is one jaunt away from the Clan's old stomping ground. *Now* do you understand why we're briefing you on this?"

"You're afraid the BLACK RAIN people have world-walkers. And tanks, and computers, and nuclear weapons—"

"Yes, and we know *practically fuck-all* about them. Except that what we *do* know is enough to have the President climbing the walls—well, she's not, but only because she's got liquid helium for blood. She *is* pushing for results, Rita, so we need to move to Phase Two and Phase Three fast, to get safe houses established so we can install ARMBAND transporters and send regular clandestine specialists through to establish a presence. But the real problem is that we urgently need to confirm whether or not BLACK RAIN have world-walkers. World-walkers would make BLACK RAIN a deadly strategic threat to us. And especially if they're Clan revenants. Or, worst of all, if they're in contact with the forerunners. Meanwhile, we've got to proceed on the assumption that the Clan *are* still preying on us, that they've penetrated our security perimeter, and that if this operation leaks they'll be in a position to make us pay. Which is why I'm imposing the lockdown. I have a Presidential Letter authorizing me to set up an inner cell within the Unit, within the Department of Homeland Security's Office of Special Programs. And I am authorized to lie to everyone outside the cell, up to and including the National Security Council. Congress and the Supremes, if necessary.

"This is a matter of national survival, Rita. And that's why, sooner or later, on one of your missions into BLACK RAIN—not this one, but once

you've got the lie of the land and established a safe location for clandestine ops with ARMBAND units to transfer, and once we have some idea
of the political situation—we are going to 'lose' you.

"Because we need to open a back-channel for negotiations."

PHILADELPHIA, TIME LINE TWO, AUGUST 2020

After clocking off until the next day, Rita set her alarm for a three-hour
afternoon nap. She woke, showered, and checked her Facebook Friends
page. As promised, Angie had changed her relationship status from
"single" to "in a relationship."

She swallowed, heart pounding. With a tremulous feeling she couldn't
identify—somewhere between exultation and doom—she tapped on her
profile. Watched the page flicker as it reloaded. With a sense of reckless
abandon, she changed her status and tagged Angie as her partner. It gave
her a shivery sensation in the pit of her stomach. She hadn't gotten
around to doing this with Kate: she'd sheltered in the ambiguity of her
own emotional shadows, unsure about her own identity. And the uncertainty had eaten away at Kate's trust until, in the end, it proved insufficient unto the day . . .

To Rita's generation, tagging a partner on FB was as public a display
of commitment as wearing an engagement ring had been to her parents'.
(Minus the size of the stone, of course. Checkboxes came in a single size,
enforcing a social uniformity that left no room for carat-denominated
ego preening.) So she was tiredly unsurprised when her wall exploded with
distant tinny congratulations. And then, ten minutes later, her phone rang.

"Are you working, love?"

She swallowed. The monosyllable still stunned her with its implications. "I'm free tonight. But they want me tomorrow—I'm on day shift
for a while . . ."

"Great! I'll be right over!"

Head still foggy from a disrupted sleep cycle, but fundamentally, anom-
alously, almost distressingly happy, Rita barely noticed what she was doing
as she packed her suitcase. The checkbox on her soul was slower to re-

spond than the one on her Facebook profile, but it felt as if everything in her life was slowly rearranging around it. The idea of spending another night in this characterless, concrete commuter cage filled her with revulsion. Then the hotel phone rang.

"Hello?"

"Ms. Douglas? Front desk here. There's a Ms. Hagen to see you?"

Rita started. "Uh, send her up?" A minute later, the doorbell rang. She walked to the door, leaving her half-packed suitcase behind: "Hey, room service sent me an Angel!"

"Surprise!" It *was* her rustbelt girl. She opened the door, and Angie stepped inside. She opened her arms to accept her checkbox's reward and found herself, an hour later, lying in a twisted wreckage of hotel bedding and discarded clothes. "Hey, you fell on your feet, girl! This is some nice shit they're putting you up in."

"I, I was hoping to spend the night at your place instead?" Rita rested her head inside the protective curve of Angie's arm. "If you can cope with a roomie, I mean. I'm getting to *hate* hotels; I've been living out of a suitcase for the past year."

"I didn't know you were homeless." Angie sounded amused.

"No, I'm not homeless—well, not exactly." Her shared lease with Alice on the apartment outside Cambridge had expired while she was in Camp Graceland, and Alice had found a new flatmate. The Unit had kindly cleared Rita's possessions out and stashed her stuff in storage. Meanwhile, her modest pay was stacking up in her account faster than she could spend it. "I've got a job—they just keep sending me places so fast I've lost my center."

"No you haven't." Angie ran a fingertip down her spine, pausing at her coccyx and spreading a palm across her right buttock. Rita shivered. "You just temporarily misplaced it." Rita kissed her. It paused the conversation for a while. When they were ready to talk again, the sky beyond the floor-to-ceiling blinds was dark. "I wasn't expecting this, Rita. You're moving fast."

Rita had looked at Angie's time line that afternoon. She'd checked a long way back. "Ever got the feeling there was a hole in your life that suddenly got filled in?"

"All the time, baby, all the time." Angie sat up, leaned over, rummaged in her shapeless messenger bag, and pulled out a fancy e-cig. Chrome (or was that really silver?) gearwheels, implausibly meshed into immobility, cradled a transparent oil-filled chamber. She took a hit, leaned back against the headboard, blew white vapor back through her nostrils. "Why didn't I notice you earlier?"

"I was busy working. You were busy working. We lived too far apart." Rita shrugged. "All the old excuses for drifting out of touch." She pushed herself up, sat cross-legged, and glanced around the room. "It's not like I even had the time and energy for speed-dating."

Angie leaned against her and draped an arm around her shoulder. "Are you hungry?" she asked. "We could hit room service, but there's a diner I know—"

"I'm starving. Why don't we go there?"

"Yeah, let's do that."

They dressed, exchanging shy glances of complicity. Rita gathered her handbag, wrapping a sock around her fatphone for privacy before she tucked it away. Angie handed her a hotel notepad and pencil: that went in too. She hip-bumped Rita as she slid her room card key out of the light switch by the door. "I love you so much," Angie murmured.

Not holding hands, or sliding arms around waists and kissing as they made their way to the elevator, felt like a denial of self. But hotels were public spaces. The outraged were everywhere, disguised as ordinary people, but ready to show fangs and claws in an instant like so many werewolves of homophobia if their prejudices were affronted.

The culture wars had been in overdrive for a decade now, energized by the dreadful unknowns that had tumbled the entire nation into post-traumatic stress disorder nearly eighteen years ago. Civil partnerships were legal in some states, their relationship unremarkable among friends and family: but random public spaces were another matter, the risk of queer-bashing far from negligible. And that was in those states that weren't actively trying to turn the clock back to the seventeenth century. And so they stood just a few freezing inches too far apart until they reached the darkness of the parking lot doorway, whereupon Angie took Rita's hand to lead her to the pickup.

"You've been parked a while." Rita thought for a moment. "If you want privacy, you should know—they've got me on a very short leash. I know they bugged my phone: I wouldn't put it past them to have bugged your truck, too."

"Then we'll give them something to remember." Angie hugged her. "I'll drive manually." Then they climbed into the chilly truck cab.

PHILADELPHIA, TIME LINE TWO, AUGUST 2020

They ate at a pizza joint and spoke, somewhat disjointedly, of inconsequentialities: of mutual unfriends, of distant contacts, of hobbies and horses and hopes for the future. Rita caught Angie looking at her from time to time with the stunned gratitude of a lottery winner whose dream ticket had implausibly come true. It gave her a shocked frisson of delight and tenderness to realize that she could have that effect on her—she couldn't help seeing Angie as she'd been when they first met, over a decade ago, even though they were both grown up now, debauched by time and feeling the infinite weight of their mid-twenties adulthood upon them.

"Do you want to move out of that hotel? You're welcome to stay with me as long as you're in town, if this is just a few weeks. If it's longer, though, we might need to get somewhere bigger." Angie carved a slice of pizza, slurped its dripping tip into her mouth, and masticated as she continued: "And with more of an eye to privacy, if you follow me."

"I don't know how long I'm here," Rita told her, eyes disquietingly clear, concealing her mouth with a cup of Coke: "I don't really know what they want me for. Probably nothing good, but nothing good beats something bad, doesn't it?"

"Guess so. Let's take a walk?"

Leaving the remains of their food, Rita and Angie strolled around the food court and then out into the mall. It was safe enough to hold hands here, so they did, using finger squeezes for punctuation whenever the conversation took a turn toward more sensitive subjects.

"So you got a job working for the DHS?"

Rita nodded. "Yes, I sure did."

"OMG. Bet that makes you popular at parties."

Rita shrugged. *Yes.* "I can live with it. Before it happened I was look-ing for a job. At least this way I'm inside the tent."

"But your parents—"

"They're in Arizona. I haven't told them much. They might be okay with it, but I can't tell what the neighbors could think—Border Patrol's part of DHS, too."

"They think people like us hate America because 'freedom'?" Angie said, finger-waggling air quotes.

"Who the fuck knows?" Rita spared her a black-eyed look. "But they tell all cops it's a bad idea to let the neighbors know what you do. Just in case word gets around to the wrong ears."

"Well, no shit." Angie thought for a moment. "Bet your employer has a handle on you."

"Yeah."

"Can you talk about it?"

"It's complicated. Say, isn't that the exit?"

Contrary to TV and movie mythology, bugging people who move around a lot is difficult, unless they're carrying microphones with them and speaking clearly. As Angie and Rita left the air-conditioned confines of the mall, their phones were swaddled in socks and hidden inside hand-bag and backpack. Once out of view of the mall's own security cameras and mikes, and well away from bugged rooms and vehicles, they could finally speak openly to each other.

Rita explained the context of her adoption, the kidnapping incident, Kurt's suspicions: finally the world-walking elephant in the room. "There might be factions within the Clan, but they ignored me for my entire life. So my money's on a stupid-ass attempt by the Colonel's people to gaslight me. All I know is I've got this crazy ability and—"

"You don't know anything for sure." Angie squeezed her hand tightly. Rita saw fear and anger reflected in her eyes. "Fucking assholes get their ideas from the movies, like everyone else. Maybe it *was* your employers. Maybe they thought you weren't patriotic enough, didn't have that old-time/new-time/para-time religion. Maybe they wanted to put some iron in your belly. But it could have been the adversary."

"I'm pretty sure it was the Office of Special Programs," said Rita. "The Colonel's bosses are kind of desperate." Her eyes glanced sidelong into another space, as if reviewing something she'd seen.

"Whatever. You know what I think? I think you should ask your grand-pappy for backup. He knew your birth mother's ma. He's protective."

"Don't *say* that!" Rita's eyes grew wide. "If I drag him in, where will it all end?"

"Who better?" Angie tugged her closer. "Your watchers aren't going to take him seriously as a threat. Old guy, puttering around on a walking stick, chatting to his old-guy buddies. Give him something to do in his retirement."

"Angel, they did a *deep background check* on me. They've *got* to know about him. My entire family are at risk if—" Rita's breath caught. "You're at risk."

"So? That's my choice to make, girl." Angie shrugged, but Rita saw the tension around her eyes. What would she do if she woke up one morning and found spooks pressuring her? Just by wanting Angie in her life she'd put her in danger, added her to some kind of watch list for sig-nificant others, made her a target for some LOVEINT operation. Any creepy stalker with a security clearance could get at Angie, now. But be-fore she could say this, Angie went off on a tangent. "Say, *you* didn't run a deep background check on *me*, did you?"

Rita shook her head. "I don't have that kind of access. They want me for a sparkly clandestine asset. CAs get security-cleared, but we don't get to see anything—we live in a velvet-lined box so we can't give anything away if we're captured. Maybe if I get burned and have to retire to an analysis desk they'll give me the keys to the kingdom. But for now all I've got on you is whatever you put on Facebook."

"Oh, well *that's* okay, then. Because back in the day I'd have been through *your* profile like a ferret on crack." Angie smiled. "That was then, and today I'm just another vet. Listen, I'd like to write Kurt a letter. For old times' sake. I'll hold back if you don't want me to, but . . ."

"I shouldn't—" Rita stared at her. "Oh what the hell—you'll do it if you feel like it anyway, huh?" Her cheek quirked. "I'm not going to say don't—I don't want you to feel like you need to lie to me." Rita's eyes lost some of their sparkle. "But please don't take any risks on my behalf. It's not worth it. And for fuck's sake, please don't let Gramps go all James Bond on me?"

"Too late: I'm *already* taking a risk on you, and your grandpa will do whatever he wants. Where did I leave the truck? . . . I want you to come stay with me. Shouldn't I know what I'm inviting into my home?"

Angie drove Rita back to her place. Rita kept noticing her stealing furtive glances, and shivered. *Is it worth it?* she wondered, then realized she couldn't imagine life in any other way—a horribly, gratifyingly unexpected change to undergo in less than a week. *Then what should I do next?* There was no obvious answer.

The next morning, after dropping Rita off back at the hotel, where her employers wanted to keep her under their thumb, Angie stopped off at a big-box Staples and bought a couple of notepads and pencils and a packet of envelopes. Then, over her lunch break, she began to laboriously draft a letter to Ri's grandpappy Kurt. Once she got home she retreated under the comforter with a dog-eared copy of a paperback her parents had taught her how to use long ago, and the draft of the letter. She was very rusty: it took her a long time to transcribe it using a prearranged page in the book as the key to a one-time pad. But that was okay. Cipher skills came back once you started using them again, and she had a feeling that after Kurt wrote back with his instructions she'd be getting all the practice she needed.

PHILADELPHIA, TIME LINE TWO, AUGUST 2020

Evening, morning, a new day, a new headache:

"Walk with me," said the Colonel. Rita noticed the missing "please": attendance was mandatory. Smith led her into the open-plan area of the light industrial unit, past a temporary cubicle farm for the nonclassified workers, past the makeup, wardrobe, and props departments—the membrane dividing Hollywood production from Hollywood product was gossamer-thin in a short-term clandestine ops headquarters. They ended up at the door to the Faraday-shielded office trailer that served as a classified site office. Inside, the Colonel's own mobile office was barely big enough to hold two chairs and a folding desk. "We have a problem," Smith told her.

Rita tensed. "What kind?" *He said "we,"* she reminded herself. She clung to the choice of pronoun as she waited for him to continue.

Smith frowned at her, the rictus slowly deepening into a grimace of anger or frustration. His mood finally snapped like an overstretched rubber band: "Fucking *morons!*" He slumped into the chair behind his desk. "Siddown, Rita. I am"—he raised his hands—"*so* sorry I have to tell you this."

"What?" She sat, bewildered. She'd been nerving herself for a grilling about Angie for the past seventy-two hours. Things weren't as bad as they were during the crazy noughties, but there were still plenty of crazies willing to throw the Defense of Marriage Act in your face if you stood up to be counted. (Pro-marriage activists had moved on to trying to get the federal ban on sodomy laws revoked, now that they'd rolled back Roe v. Wade.) "Is it about my, uh, friend . . ."

Smith put her mind at ease: "Your new girlfriend isn't an issue." He waved a hand dismissively: "She held a Top Secret clearance back in the day. That ticks most of the boxes on the form. No, it's the . . . it's what Eileen was worrying about the day before yesterday. Too many chefs spoil the broth, and right now we've got sixteen different chiefs trying to run the kitchen. They can't even agree on whether it's sushi or McDonald's."

He pointed at the tablet on his desk stand: "O'Neill and Gomez had your third mission profile mapped out pretty much as I wanted it and we were ready to run you through it today. Then the shit hit the fan. From the Homeland Security Council, no less." Smith's frown turned thunderous, as if he were contemplating the wreckage of his midlife-crisis sports car, crumpled under the front fender of an uninsured pickup truck. "They've given me a Priority One tasking to look at the state of geological and paleontological research and confirm that BLACK RAIN was created in the Year of Our Lord 4004 B.C., just like our own time line."

"Huh?"

"That's not all." Smith looked grim. "Additionally, you're supposed to find evidence that BLACK RAIN has been visited by the Grays from Zeta Reticuli, and look for, uh, 'flying saucer secrets.' Someone else wants to know if the locals have located the Golden Plates of Moroni. Then there's a request for information on the state of anthropogenic climate change in BLACK RAIN, and *that* one actually makes sense, except it contradicts Executive Order 4603 banning use of federal funds for research into . . . You get the picture."

Rita closed her mouth. "What *is* this stuff?" she asked plaintively.

Smith rubbed his eyes and sighed. "It's open season, or silly season, or both. We've unintentionally created a honeypot for excitable whackjobs of every creed, and they're trying to piss all over the mission requirements with their own agendas." He tapped his tablet again. "Case in point: there's a Priority One tasking to locate the site of the Martian implant control station in upstate New York."

Rita closed her mouth. She opened it, and closed it again, speechless.

"You get the picture. We're in danger of turning into the ball in a psychoceramic football tournament." He looked at her pensively. "You're sure you're not deeply religious, Rita? No terribly deep convictions about anything?"

"I was raised Lutheran, kinda-sorta."

"Well, that's *something*. At least you're not going to turn missionary on me." His smile was disturbingly weak.

She shrugged. "Is that sort of thing common?"

"More than you might think. More than one idiot used discretionary funds to pay for their church outreach program under the guise of running a string of informers." Smith shook his head. "This game attracts kooks. Before my time, we used to have a real problem with swivel-eyed witch finders pointing and shrieking 'Communist!' back when there was a cold war to run. Then we went through the Great Muslim Panic—and look how well *that* turned out. Now we've got a multiverse to police, and no clear idea what's going on out there. So people with a clear idea of what they want yell the loudest and set policy. And we end up with terms of reference that are total *bullshit* . . ."

Smith raised a hand, took two deep gulps of air, deflated visibly, and gave a quietly unhappy chuckle. "You didn't hear this, Rita. You didn't see me lose my shit. Understood?"

She nodded.

"I think you need to know about the shit-storm upstairs, even though Eileen and I are going to do our best to keep you sheltered under our umbrella. In case of emergency, if I'm incapacitated and you can't contact anyone else, I'm going to send you a number in Baltimore that will put you through to Dr. Scranton or her boss. You get to use it *once*, no questions asked, and if someone is making trouble for you the White House will make them *go away*. But you only ever use it if you can't reach me. For the time being"—he shrugged—"the overt mission and the covert mission are still in alignment, 'kinda-sorta,' as you young folks say. I've made you *aware* of the priorities of our lords and masters, so I can check that off my list. Now, back to work . . ."

He spun his tablet round so she could see it. "We punched another couple of micro-drones through, too small and too low to light up their air defense radar. There's a city where Philadelphia is in this world, as you'd expect: it's smaller and denser, with more high-rise buildings and less suburban sprawl, but it's there. We've located a passenger railway station, too. These folks are big on public transport and streetcars, less so on automobiles. So we're going to put you through a quarter hour before dawn, and you're going to hang out and people-watch for a couple of hours. You'll be carrying a military inertial nav system. It works like a handheld GPS map except it's entirely self-contained, and we've filled it with lots of waypoints for safe jaunt sites. If there's any trouble, you just run away. How long you stay there is up to you—it's entirely up to your comfort zone—except the mapper only has a seven-day fuel cell charge. And we'd rather you came back the same day."

"Wait, but what am I going to do for clothes? Money?" Rita stared at him. "How will I fit in?"

Smith shook his head. "We don't know. That's why you're going walkabout. I suggest you study what people are wearing, how they talk, what they do. Wardrobe has run up an outfit based on what you video'd at the railhead. It should pass at a distance. If begging is legal, you could try and get us some cash to copy. Go window-shopping, see what things cost. Building a retail price index will tell us a lot about their economy, which in turn tells us a lot about the constraints imposed on their military by the funding envelope. If you get a chance to talk to people, take it—within reason, we don't want you running risks. Finally, back in 2003 we got a memo from the Office of Legal Counsel. The Attorney General approves the legal theory that people in other time lines are not subject to the protections and laws of the USA, even if they're in the equivalent geographical territory. We're not giving you a gun because if you find yourself in a situation where you might need to defend yourself you should jaunt *immediately*. But anything you do over *there* falls outside the scope of our laws over *here*, if you follow my drift: you have total immunity."

"Got it. Tomorrow morning, quarter before dawn—that's about six fifteen, isn't it? Walk around for a few hours. Not less than two, unless I'm in danger, not more than a day or you start getting edgy. See the sights, play penniless tourist. Anything else?"

"Yes." Smith nodded. "You're going to spend the rest of today in a wardrobe fitting, then with props—they'll orient you on the inertial map system. In particular we want you, if you get a chance, to log waypoints over there for a couple of different types of sites—abandoned houses or retail establishments in particular. Government offices, too. Then you're sleeping here tonight, I'm afraid. Four-thirty wake-up call for makeup." He rose. "Good luck and Godspeed."

Mission Abort

The Colonel, his staff in the Unit, their seniors in the Office of Special Programs, and everyone in the DHS who was aware of the JAUNT BLUE program and the BLACK RAIN time line assumed that Rita's aborted mission had been completed largely without consequence.

They couldn't have been more wrong.

Rita had been clearly seen by station mate Vance Schofield, age fifty-six. He was a forty-year veteran of the Irontown Regional Permanent Way and its successor, the Commonwealth Eastern Regional Rails, or the CERR. A sober-sided widower and abstainer from spirits, he had challenged Rita to display her ticket of travel: at which point she had vanished into thin air.

Aghast and worried that his eyes were failing him, Schofield had summoned his platform attendant, one Barnett Garrison, an Observer Corps veteran—who had also noticed Rita loitering near the end of the platform, but assumed she was merely a night-shift worker taken short and turned a discreet eye. Together they searched the platform and adjacent tracks. Returning with Schofield to the platform office, Garrison noticed an Unidentified Object attached to one of the windowpanes he had cleaned the evening before. And that's when Schofield recalled the electronic memoranda about Persons Vanishing in Broad Daylight, Unidentified Objects, and If You See Something, Say Something.

Ten minutes later Schofield laboriously pushed the SEND button on the teletype terminal that linked his office, via telephone line, to the powerful new time-sharing mainframe in Port Richmond (which the CERR had installed to coordinate their railroad network's back-office business just five years ago). Sixteen minutes later—the Commonwealth intercomputer network was chronically congested, the modems almost permanently engaged as messaging traffic grew by leaps and bounds— his message reached the in-box of one Inspector Alice Morgan of the Commonwealth Transport Police.

Inspector Morgan was in a morning briefing, so did not receive his e-mail at once. But half an hour after her return to a deskful of paper-work, she began to read—and the shit hit the fan. The Commonwealth Transport Police was responsible for securing a rapidly developing infra-structure network that had gone from steam locomotives and biplanes to passenger jets and high-speed rail in just seventeen years. They had been re-formed and trained along modern lines in the wake of the Revolu-tion, as one of the key security services of the Commonwealth Deep State. They were fully briefed on world-walking and its implications. And Alice Morgan had not risen to the rank of Police inspector (in a society that was, in many ways, still deeply conservative and unaccustomed to such newfangled ideas as women working and voting) without being something of an overachiever.

News usually propagates slowly, if at all, through any bureaucracy not built on advanced information technology. Of necessity, the faster chan-nels of communication are scarce and must be reserved for important bulletins. The Commonwealth's Deep State planners were aware of this. They were also aware of their most likely adversary's infowar doctrine (even though it relied on technologies that seemed like the most bizarre overextrapolation of current trends) and the vital need to get inside their decision loop. Inspector Morgan's subsequent on-site report, filed from Schofield's own railway network terminal using her priority key, went straight over the wire to the National Security Network, carbon-copied to the Force Commander and to the Director of the Department of Para-historical Research, flagged as a FLASH alert.

At three o'clock that afternoon, Miriam Burgeson took her seat at the head of a boardroom table to chair the resulting emergency briefing.

"Background first. What have we found, Commander?" she asked.

"Lots." Commander Jackson looked extremely unhappy—as he should have, under the circumstances. "I've had men combing the Irongate South satellite switchyard since ten o'clock this morning. So far they've identified four suspicious objects, believed to be miniature televisor cameras with attached storage devices: so-called webcams. The first was spotted by accident by the platform attendant who cleaned the office window it was adhering to the previous day. He retrieved it and after Forensics finished with it—taking fingerprints and surface samples for DNA matching—it was handed over to a DPR courier. The other three devices have been left in situ by order of the incident controller until we know what you want us to do with them. They are attached to the left upper door windowpane on Signal Box Two, the side of one of the support pillars on the platform awning, and above the northern side door of the supervisor's office on Platform Three.

"The switchyard is currently closed while my officers conduct a fingertip search of the entire yard, including the track beds. An hour ago, they identified another suspicious object: a device concealed in a lump of timber that had been placed on a walkway between tracks eight and nine. It's a small sealed weatherproof plastic container, and it radiates magnetoelectric vibrations." Jackson's terminology was archaic, a product of an education that predated the arrival of the Clan exiles and the deluge of new science and technology they'd catalyzed.

"So. Witness sighting of a person who vanished into thin air—from a normally reliable member of staff—and indirect confirmation in the shape of concealed monitoring devices." Miriam frowned. She wished she felt sufficiently at ease to relax her politician's mask and actually vent her true emotions—scream and shout, maybe throw something at the wall—but it would send entirely the wrong message at this point. *Deep breathing time.* "Ken. Analysis? What do your people say? Anything else?"

Ken McInnes, her deputy director in charge of Operational Analysis, shook his head. "We're still putting it together. There's been a marked uptick in UFO sightings in Pennsylvania in general over the past month, described variously as 'giant hornets' or 'tiny airplanes.' Air Defense Command confirms some anomalous sightings, both from the Observer

Corps and radar, but the objects were flying low and slow and nobody managed to get a lock. They scrambled interceptors for two of the sightings, but there was nothing there when the jets arrived. I would *speculate*—let me caution that this is uncorroborated guesswork—that the adversary might be using very small drones to conduct localized probes. If they pop into our airspace less than a thousand feet up, spend most of their time barely above treetop height, and hang around for less than fifteen minutes, we'll have the devil's own job spotting them.

"On the upside: there's no sign of activity anywhere else. Whatever's going on, it's highly local. We haven't seen any sign of UFOs over the Pacific Northwest or the Andes, for example. They're focusing on Irongate and Philadelphia, so I think what we may be seeing is airborne activity in support of a ground-based clandestine insertion."

Worse and worse. Miriam glanced sideways at the woman in the wheelchair. "Any thoughts?"

"Where did they get the world-walker?" Olga looked haggard. She had a bad tendency to insist on working even when she was too ill to do so productively. But as usual she asked the right question. "Do we have a defector, or is this something else?" She gave Miriam a penetrating stare.

"Defectors." Miriam rolled her pen between index finger and thumb. *Fuck.* She looked up. "Action this day: immediate roll call of all world-walking personnel, by order of the Commissioner in Charge, MITI. Make it so." She glanced at Olga again. The head of the Clan's own internal security force, such as it was, shook her head doubtfully. "What are the chances they unearthed that bastard Griben's database?" she asked.

"Database?" echoed McInnes.

"Low but not impossible." Olga raised a frail fist to cover her mouth when she coughed. She was only forty, but looked older than Miriam's early fifties: life's unfairness personified. "You're aware of Griben ven Hjalmar's position as the Clan's in-house doctor, back in the day?" McInnes nodded. Ven Hjalmar had thrown in his lot with the wrong side during the confused and turbulent aftermath of the Revolution— not the Royalists, but the quasi-Stalinists. He'd paid with his life. "He ran a fertility clinic in the United States, to help childless couples conceive."

Heads around the table nodded, uncertainly. The Commonwealth's demographic profile and medical technology was such that it still had a surplus of orphanages. "He was compiling a database of children conceived via this clinic—using seed harvested from world-walkers. The plan was to pay the resulting women—at adulthood—to act as host mothers. Producing a crop of active world-walkers, a generation down the line."

Heads were shaking, and a low undercurrent of whispering started. "Silence!" snapped Miriam. "Leave the commentary for later. Let her continue."

"Your mother assassinated the clinic's director and stole what she thought was the entire database of latent carriers." Miriam nodded. Iris had been an unholy terror, even in a wheelchair. "But her grasp of modern technology was sadly deficient."

"You think she left something?" Miriam momentarily forgot her own instruction.

"Don't know. Insufficient data." Olga's cheek twitched. "The first-generation carriers would be aged between seventeen and twenty-two at this point. But they'd be outer Clan—sorry, carriers. Not world-walkers themselves . . ."

"But you're thinking, if there's some way to activate the ability, the Americans have had more than fifteen years to work on it?"

Miriam looked round the table. No whispering. Just twelve pairs of eyes drilling into her as if her blood contained answers to their every nightmare question. "I don't know," she said. She felt like screaming, *Do you think I'm clairvoyant or something?* But she didn't: she knew what would happen. Half of them probably *did* think she was clairvoyant. The Clan refugees, since that tentative start in the freezing-cold prison camp in the winter of 2003–04, had turbocharged the embryonic Commonwealth with imported alien ideas. The Commonwealth had made as much technological progress in seventeen years as time line two had in three decades. But it had unfortunate side-effects. Everyone looked at her as if she were some kind of Albert Einstein / Marie Curie hybrid: they expected her to have all the answers, all the time.

"Let me repeat that: *I don't know.* But I think we should bear it in mind as a worst case. The United States knows about us—they've been sending drones, and we've shot down a few. *If* they've got actual world-walkers, then what we're seeing is an early attempt at clandestine insertion. Possibly supported by tactical drones. It's an information-gathering exercise, and our friend the station mate accidentally disrupted it." She shrugged. "Recommendations?"

Olga spoke up. "Keep looking for UFO sightings. Blanket those areas with watchers. That would be Irongate and Philadelphia, yes? Brief the regular beat police. Also perhaps ask the Commonwealth Guard to put boots on the ground. And move close-range air defense units into position. Hmm. A spy scare in the local newspapers would prime the locals. Remember to brief the cops not to use lethal force. Do they have tasers yet?" Electric stun guns copied from the American products were a new development.

Commander Jackson shook his head. "They're available but not issued yet. Men don't like them—the battery packs are heavy and they're no use against real guns—"

Miriam checked him. "Clandestine world-walkers won't stick around to get into a gunfight. They'll just leave. I want them taken alive for questioning, if at all possible. Shooting them may not stop them from world-walking, but if you tase them and get them blindfolded they won't be able to escape."

Jackson nodded, unhappily. "Tasers, blindfolds, and you want everyone briefed? It's going to cause chaos."

"Not necessarily." Olga looked thoughtful. "It is a first-contact scenario. Miriam, I believe you have some experience in this regard. Perhaps you could explain to the Commander here how a world-walker goes about making first contact with a new time line? Then he can focus his planning accordingly . . ."

PHILADELPHIA, TIME LINE TWO, AUGUST 2020

It was, Rita supposed, a sign of how urgent the operation was becoming that the chaos today was constrained. Rubbernecking was discouraged, and the guards were enforcing the guest list as sternly as bouncers at a Hollywood red carpet event.

But not everything was running so smoothly. "It makes me look like a hippie," Rita complained to Gladys Jensen, the wardrobe supervisor. "Are you sure it's meant to be this color in daylight?"

"That's what the analysts told me." Gladys looked apologetic. "That camera of yours is okay. It captured a decent spectrum from the lights, so we were able to calibrate a proper color balance and white point and extract useful color information from the people you photographed. This is what they wear in daylight. The pattern block is guesswork, and we don't know what fiber mix they use, but I'm betting on cotton and wool, natural all the way."

Rita looked at herself in the mirror. The dark gray smock hung to her ankles. And the accompanying blouse and jacket made her look like an extra out of a historical movie. *Dr. Zhivago*, maybe. "This really isn't my style."

"Tough. You were shooting at night, from cover, and the crowding on the platform obscured the detailing. Those baggy pant-and-tunic outfits are risky, unless you can bring me some more shots. If you find a dress-maker's shop, how about scanning some fashion plates or patterns for me? And get a bunch of daytime candid camera shots around the station, so next time you look more like a respectable citizen and less like you push a broom in a factory."

"Boots." Rita sat down.

"That's less of a problem. I'm guessing they use leather and go for du-rability. I'm assuming they lace up. I didn't see any obvious zip fasteners in your camera roll. So we got you a pair of regular boots with half-inch heels. Again, if you pass a cobbler or shoe shop, grab some images." Gladys offered her a cardboard box. Rita opened it, and gave black calf-high boots a grudging nod.

"Okay. What about headgear?"

"This." Gladys held out a hat with a floppy brim. "Off the shelf. It's a close enough match for one of the subjects. If it attracts the wrong kind of attention, ditch it. But only if you're sure it's not going to get found.

None of these items will stand up to examination—the fabric's going to be all wrong, right down to the fiber lengths, never mind the lack of labels and detail work. Any halfway-competent detective who gets their hands on you will figure out you're a clandestine agent in thirty seconds flat, just from your clothing. That's why we need coins to clone, and real local clothes, before we can begin to build out a reliable agent insertion protocol."

"Oh great." Rita sighed. "Gear bag? Purse?"

"We're still working on them," Gladys admitted. "The shift workers you shot mostly weren't carrying any—they probably eat at a diner in the factory. One of the women had something big, like carpetbag big, but we didn't get a good enough shot. Again: if you pass luggage shops or a department store, scans would be good."

"Scans." Rita sighed. "What with? I mean, if I don't have a bag, what am I meant to carry a camera in?"

"Check out the coat. See that seam? There's a concealed pocket in there. And more pockets, here and here." Gladys grinned. "It's a genuine old-school spy coat! If you invert it, it's fawn. This way out, it's charcoal."

"Ah!" Rita sat up. "So, um. I have a mapper"—Props had taken her through the basics of the milspec inertial navigation system earlier in the afternoon—"What about a camera?"

"You'll be using this." Gladys pulled out a compact slab of blackened aluminum. It sported a touchscreen on the back, and on the front a shuttered synthetic sapphire lens turret, beneath a rough patch where the rune CANON had been ground away. "It's a light-field camera. Saves to a memory card if there's no phone signal. The smarts are all in the adaptive optics and the light-field sensor—it's got a times-fifty zoom and infinite focal depth."

"Oh great." Rita turned it over in her hands. "Smile!"

"Hey, no!" Gladys protested before Rita could push the shutter button: "No way! That's going over to BLACK RAIN! You better keep it sterile!"

"Uh, okay." Rita put it down. "How am I meant to practice?"

"There's a manual." Gladys passed her a slim booklet, its cover labeled *Getting Started* in sixteen languages. "Memorize it or something. Or put the snapper on automatic and leave it to make all the decisions. It's probably smarter than you and I together."

"Great. So is there anything more?"

"I don't think so." Gladys looked her up and down. "If you get a chance to find out what they use for underwear, that would be very useful. And I want to know about men's fashion too!" Rita gave her a look. "But this is the best we can do for now. You should be all right at a distance. Just remember it probably won't stand up to close inspection."

"Thanks for all the hard work." Rita eased her trainers off and began to work her way into the boots. "I mean that. Sorry I can't wait around, though—I've got to go and see Ivan next. Last time he was threatening to break out skin-whitening creams, and God knows what he's going to want to do to my hair."

NEW LONDON, TIME LINE THREE, AUGUST 2020

Adrian Holmes, Secretary to the Central Commission of the Inner Party, ran his department from a small, windowless room deep in the former imperial palace. In place of a window, his office wall had a painting: a classic by George Stubbs, part of the Commonwealth State Art Collection: *Frederick, Prince of Wales, Arrives in Boston*. A fifty-two-year-old king to be, in white wig, hose, and red coat—not yet the ermine and crown and scepter of the emperor in exile—standing on a pier, graciously accepting the welcome of the city fathers. In the background, lurking, the engineer of the royal settlement and first Prime Minister of the New Empire, Baronet Benjamin Franklin—in Holmes's opinion, a beacon and an object of emulation.

Holmes was not happy. Neither, for that matter, were the two men standing before his desk. "Stop, please, and rephrase your report," Holmes said, staring at the older, shorter one of the two (silver-streaked gray hair combed back around his shining pate, a deeply lined face and a smashed nose souvenirs of a more exciting youth than his sober minister's tailcoat now suggested). "As succinctly as possible, if you will."

The younger man (skinny and bearing an air of perpetual worried puzzlement) sighed quietly and shifted from foot to foot, his hands clutched behind his back. He glanced at his elder, then back to the Secretary, who was younger than either.

"The Burgesons are active," said the older man. "The wife was summoned to an emergency meeting of a cross-departmental security committee the day before yesterday. Other attendees included Commonwealth Guard and Transport Police officials. Her director of espionage at the DPR then took off for Philadelphia with some handpicked officers, wiring orders ahead that stirred up the local constabulary and Guard barracks like hornets' nests. Something to do with alien spies of the world-walking variety. Meanwhile, Mr. Burgeson is holding meetings with every Commissioner who'll give him the time of day. Promising them a chicken in every pot and a pie on every plate."

"And the other thing?" Holmes turned his gaze on the younger man.

He dry-swallowed. "My correspondent within the Ministry confirms the rumor we caught wind of back in April. They are pursuing some scheme in great secrecy, on which account they have detached a Major Hulius Hjorth of the DPR—a world-walker—for special duty. The *new* information is that they're sending him to Berlin. In *great* secrecy.

"The correspondent in question has not yet been able to tell me what is happening, only that the assistant director of security at the Department of Para-historical Research is managing it directly, on Mrs. Burgeson's orders. And that Major Hjorth is a relative of hers. He went underground a few months ago, but we know nothing about what he's been doing except that they shipped him down to Maracaibo for some sort of special training."

"Lovely." Holmes looked away, resting his eyes on the painting. "The rats are scrambling." He looked squarely at the younger fellow. "Keith. I want to know more about this operation in Berlin." (Keith was not so young: merely in his early thirties. And not so puzzled and worried, unless it was the perpetual puzzlement and worry of the espionage-obsessed. Which was indeed the main purpose in life of Keith Pierrepoint, Holmes's rat-catcher-in-chief.) "It's out of their usual territory. I am distressed. Are you following the news from the enemy court?"

"The royal betrothal, sir?" Pierrepoint raised an eyebrow. "I gather the nuptials are to be delayed until the princess turns eighteen. Rather a late ripening if you ask me."

Holmes shook his head. "Big picture, man, follow the big picture." His tone of mild disappointment made Pierrepoint nervous, with good reason. "She is going to *finishing school,* Pierrepoint. Can you guess where?"

Pierrepoint's mouth made an O. He closed it silently, and nodded. "It falls somewhat outside my remit, sir, but I take your point."

"*Berlin,* Harry," Holmes said, looking now at the older man. "Commissioner Burgeson has suddenly developed an appetite for meddling in foreign affairs, just as we are called upon to confront the First Man's unfortunate decline. I do not believe this is a coincidence. I want Keith to find out more about Mrs. Burgeson's plans for the Pretender's daughter. I'm afraid we shall find evidence of treason: if not, *look harder.*" His cheeks tensed in an expression that might have been mistaken for a smile by an excessively naive onlooker. "As for her plan, whatever it is I trust Keith to disrupt it as embarrassingly as possible. If nothing else, she needs to learn to stick to her brief. I'm sure there are channels by which the French might accidentally learn of the presence of an agent in Berlin? But you, Harry, have the bigger job. I'm sure you can read my mind."

Harrison Baker, chief of staff to the Party Secretary, nodded lugubriously. "Leverage."

"Exactly." *Now* Holmes smiled. "A live boy or a dead girl in the minister of sanctimony's bed should be sufficient. Let Mr. Burgeson bluster his way out of *that.* Or something of equivalent magnitude. Something to sow distrust between the two of them. Something sufficient that any judge would grant a divorce on the spot. Or some other soot to spill across his spotless reputation. At a minimum, find enough to make his faction question his discretion and his fitness to lead in the months ahead."

Baker nodded again. "I am unaware of any singular vices attached to the man, sir, but I'm sure something can be arranged. Not certain it'll split him from *her*—they've been thick as thieves since before I met them—but it ought to be possible to isolate him otherwise."

"Good man." Holmes's smile faded. "You've both got work to do; don't let me keep you from it."

"And a good day to you, sir," murmured Pierrepoint as he accepted his dismissal and turned to leave. He might as well not have bothered. The Secretary's nose was already buried in the next of his briefings. Pierrepoint took a deep breath and released it as he and Baker left the claustrophobic inner study behind, passing the vigilant eyes of the outer office staff. An unaccountable sense of relief seized him: unaccountable, for he knew how little it meant to be out from under the direct gaze of the Secretary. Holmes had eyes everywhere.

If the Burgesons and other Party Commissioners were rats, scurrying about their urgent business with vibrating whiskers and beady eyes, lining their nests and tending their pups, Holmes was something cold-eyed and reptilian. A new ruler in waiting, coiled vigilantly in the cloaking shadows. And when the First Man finally departed, Holmes would ensure that there were fewer rodents in the palace.

PHILADELPHIA, TIME LINE TWO; IRONGATE, TIME LINE THREE, AUGUST 2020

The four-thirty wake-up alarm buzzed. Rita surfaced dozily from a melatonin-assisted warm bath of dreamless sleep to find herself in a bunk bed in a compact trailer. Stumbling and red-eyed, she worked her way through morning ablutions in the cramped bathroom, then dressed in the alien-hippie drag Gladys had set her up with. The camera and inertial mapper were fully charged: she stowed them carefully in her concealed pockets before opening the door. It was cold outside, with a predawn chill that hinted at autumnal weather to come. Beyond the security wall, agents in windbreakers moved around, prepping the convoy of vehicles that would escort her to the insertion site.

"You look like you need this." Patrick thrust an insulated mug of coffee into her hands. She nodded her sleepy gratitude. "Ivan's waiting. You've got about twenty minutes."

Incurably taciturn Ivan, exactly unlike anyone's stereotype of a male makeup artist, sat her down and examined her. "Huh. Your eyes are shot." He paused. "Good thing they're not big on bold statements there." He applied dull foundation powder and fill-in for the shadows, designed to make her look inconspicuous and pallid—at least by the standards of her natural skin tone. "That crowd was pretty white-bread, but we think you can probably pass for a deep suntan." He moved around and rapidly gathered her hair, pinning it up so that the hat brim covered it and shadowed her face. "That should do for now. Let's hope you're not noticeable. Try not to smile: your dentition is too good." He frowned. "Next station."

There was a big crew-cab pickup parked outside. The Colonel was waiting beside it. "Come on," he said. She climbed into the back and found herself the unwelcome filling in a Gomez-and-O'Neill sandwich. "Okay, we're just about ready," said Smith, leaning in through the window. "See you at the zone."

They rode in silence most of the way. Rita felt acutely uncomfortable, trying not to touch the prickly Gomez or cozy up too tight to Patrick. Nobody spoke. Eventually she pulled out the inertial mapper and tried to follow the route on it. It nailed I-476, as accurately as a satnav. "Huh," said Gomez, looking over her shoulder. "You want to put that away. Save the battery for later."

Rita blanked the backlit screen. "What are you even doing here anyway?" she asked.

"I'm guarding your sorry ass in case the Clan come after you." Gomez wouldn't meet her gaze, so she focused on the brooch the woman wore: two superimposed gold triangles, pointing upward. *Isn't that a Scientology symbol?* Rita wondered. "Just do your job and we can all go home happy tonight."

"The Clan isn't going to come after me." Rita shut her eyes.

"Rita"—it was Patrick—"don't go there, please."

"I am sick and tired of internal politics." She rounded on Gomez: "You've been on my case ever since we met. What is it with you? Is it my skin color or something?"

Gomez recoiled. "You're a spoiled bitch carrying a shitload of suppressive baggage around with you and if it was up to me you wouldn't be cleaning the toilets—"

"Ladies!" Patrick was clearly annoyed. "Not in public."

"Shit." Rita yawned, then caught herself. Gomez stared determinedly up front, to where a pair of uniforms Rita hadn't met were pointedly ignoring them. *So much for Patrick's offer of help,* she thought grimly.

"Keep a lid on it for another half hour." Patrick gave them both a look. "Try to play nice. Do you want me to ask Eric to arbitrate?"

Rita bit her lip. There had to be some other reason the Colonel was keeping Gomez in the Unit: hard-case cops were ten a penny. Hard-case cops with connections, maybe less so. Perhaps he wanted Gomez around because he *knew* she was leaking to one of the internal factions? Or perhaps he thought he needed to keep Rita on her toes, and didn't realize how badly Gomez was harassing her? But whatever the reason, it was stressing her out.

They traveled the rest of the way in silence. They turned off the interstate, drove through the darkened streets of South Philly, then across the expressway and into the Navy grounds near the river, and finally arrived at a parking lot close by the Office of Naval Intelligence. They weren't alone. A small gaggle of DHS crew-cabs and unmarked sedans clustered together. Traffic cones connected by crime scene tape cordoned off a square on one edge. Patrick opened his door. "Showtime," he said quietly. "Site survey says the other side is pretty much fallout-free. Break a leg."

Rita nodded. She no longer felt like speaking. She was simultaneously tired and keyed up. *Let's get this over with,* she thought wearily.

The Colonel was waiting in the taped-off area. "You know the plan," he said quietly. "Eyes open, mouth shut, free-form. Come back whenever you find yourself outside your comfort zone. Call me on this and we'll come fetch you." He handed over a tiny dumbphone, the voice-and-text-only variety that had a monthlong standby life. "And remember the real objective."

"Okay. If I'm not back in two minutes, expect me in three to eight hours." Rita grinned, then rolled back her left sleeve, squeezed her forearm, and clicked her heels. "There's no place like home—"

She jaunted.

The parking lot vanished. She stumbled in the dark, felt damp grass underfoot. It was colder here. In her ear, the clicking of a radiation counter. Time line one was still hot from the nuking of the Gruinmarkt, even this far south. She raised her wrist, cued up the next trigger engram, and jaunted again.

Noise assaulted her: a screech of metal on metal. She stumbled, felt hard asphalt underfoot, took a step backward, and nearly tripped over a curbstone. She managed to catch her balance on a narrow strip of sidewalk. The amber washout glare of streetlights cast multiple shadows in all directions. There was a windowless building behind her, concrete or stone. Steel rails gleamed as a streetcar rumbled and swayed toward the spot where she'd been. The narrow strip of paving she'd found was barely wide enough to stand on, and as the streetcar passed she saw more tracks beyond it, and heard the snap and crackle of overhead wires. *If it isn't one train station it's another,* she thought, dismayed, then kicked herself mentally. *No, it's a streetcar depot. The Colonel said they're big on public transport. I'm standing in the middle of the tracks.* She looked round at the wall. It vanished into the near distance, and high overhead there was a vaulting arch of metal girders supporting a dark ceiling.

The streetcar was slowing. Across four or five tracks she saw a low platform, notice boards that might have been timetables, and boxy station furniture that might have been ticket machines. *Did the driver see me?* she wondered. She'd nearly jaunted in front of the tram. *I could have been run over,* she thought with a sick feeling.

There was no platform in this part of the station, and no way out that didn't involve crossing several tracks. Swallowing, she glanced at her wrist and tried to jaunt again. She felt a silvery flash of pain, but nothing happened. "Ow!" She squeaked aloud, seeing the station still around her. She stepped sideways and tried again. This time it worked: she was back in the rainy nighttime forest. She closed her eyes, trying to remember how far away the station wall was. Took another step sideways, holding out her right arm to avoid obstacles. Stepped sideways once more. There was no tree in this direction. Now she looked at her wrist, squeezed to light up tired phosphors. "Come *on*," she murmured, focusing again.

She dropped almost a foot to the ground, landing hard. This time the wall was to her left. She stood on a broad sidewalk. Turning, she saw buildings opposite in a variety of unfamiliar styles. It was dizzyingly, achingly close to familiar: street markings that were somehow wrong, signposts bearing old-fashioned traffic directions but in a style nothing like the road signs she had grown up seeing. It was dark, the street lighting dim and the walls stained black with old soot. Half the storefronts were shuttered with metal grilles. The brick and stone of the buildings gave them a curious air of permanence, and they hunched close together. "Okay, I'm round the back of the downtown station," she whispered into the tiny mike in her lapel. She pulled out the inertial mapper and tapped a waypoint. "Let's see if I can find the front."

The station was, in some ways, comfortingly familiar: neoclassical in style, with the same stone columns and arches as many another nineteenth-century railway station. The surrounding buildings were less reassuring, though. There were few people about, although she spotted a man pushing a wheelbarrow slowly along a sidewalk, using long-handled tongs to pick detritus from the pavement. Mouselike, she scurried past behind his back. In front of the station there was a wide-open traffic circle, with many roads radiating away from it, like pictures she'd seen of Grand Army Plaza in Brooklyn. A huge plinth dominated the island in the middle, supporting a statue of a man on a horse. The color of the streetlights was somehow wrong, too orange for her eyes. They flickered slightly, and as she watched, one of them dimmed abruptly to a sullen neon red, then faded to dark.

There were one or two pedestrians out, bundled in long coats against the morning chill. Rita walked up to the front of the station and found metal gates drawn shut. A rattle of chains drew her eyes toward a uniformed man in an odd-shaped hat, the brim pinned up on either side. He was unfastening the gate at the far end, fumbling with a padlock. "Opening time," she said quietly. "They're just opening the public entrance now." She checked her wrist. "Zero six zero nine. Hmm. They're not early risers in the city."

She turned and looked across the circle. Picking a street at random—three lanes wide in either direction, with broad sidewalks and four- to six-story buildings on either side—she jaywalked across as fast as she could go without running. On the other side she found herself looking into the darkened windows of storefronts. For some reason they didn't seem to go in for big expanses of plate glass: the windows consisted of panes a couple of feet wide set in wooden or metal frames. Some things were constants, though. Proprietors' names were proudly emblazoned across doorways and on signboards hanging in front. Headless dressmakers' dummies swathed in odd-looking outfits loomed in the twilight. "Downtown shopping district, I think," she whispered.

Rita heard the unmistakable sound of a truck in the distance and spooked. The recessed vestibule of a shop offered her cover, gilt lettering on the door proclaiming it to be Barrow's Millinery. She stepped backward. The engine note was growing louder rapidly. Then the truck turned the corner. All she caught was a confused glimpse of a long hood and dark windows behind bright headlights. It pulled over on the far— left—side of the street. Doors opened, male voices called. Several men got out. Doors slammed, and the truck began to move again. She heard boots on the sidewalk, the men talking conversationally as they walked along the far side of the road.

Rita turned her face toward the shop's interior. *Let's try and look as if I belong here,* she decided. *They're probably just clerks arriving to open up shop . . .*

Something metal-cold shoved up hard against the back of her neck. "Dinna move," said the man behind her. His throat was hoarse, his voice deep. "I said, *dinna move,* woman. Dinna speak. Dinna even breathe."

Rita froze from the belly out. She'd been so focused on the carload on the far side of the street that she'd never even heard his approach. Her left arm hung uselessly by her side. Her head-up display could flash a trigger engram if she asked, but the finger wrapped around the trigger of the gun at her head would be faster.

"When I stop talkin' I want you to *slowly* turn an' face the wall. Hands up and brace yerself, lean *in.* Then go ter yer knees.

"I am placing thee under arrest by authority of the Commonwealth Guard . . ."

Contact

"I am placing thee under arrest by authority of the Commonwealth Guard. Slowly turn—now."

Rita did as she was told: turned, raised her hands, braced against the wall in front of her. *Please let him take the gun away,* she prayed. Her lifelogger was keyed to a single word: *bugout.* All she needed was a second—

"I said, raise your hands and lean in! Do it now! Kneel!"

Shit. Rita slowly lowered herself to her knees.

"Over here!" her captor shouted, deafening in the confined space. The cold gun barrel at the back of her head wobbled slightly but didn't withdraw. A handcuff locked around her left wrist. "Wrists together!" The gun barrel ground painfully into her hair. The other cuff closed. The one on the left covered the e-ink tattoo. Her initial terror was subsiding into an adrenaline spike and a sense of gnawing apprehension. *They're cops.* They were obviously on some kind of sweep. *What happens next?* She had a feeling that jaunting was going to be easier said than done.

The gun muzzle withdrew, but before she could react someone yanked a canvas sack down over her head. Panicking anew, Rita tensed and reared up. They kicked her in the ribs, slamming her face into the wall. For a while she lost track of everything but the pain in her face and the difficulty of breathing.

Shattered fragments of memory captured unpleasant sensations.

Being lifted and slung, hard, into the back of a vehicle. Motion, bouncing, and alarm bells ringing insistently above and behind her. Being lifted again and dragged through doorways and along corridors. The sack coming off her head in time for the final drop, facedown, onto a fetid, lumpy mattress that smelled of piss and terror.

By the time the cell door opened again, Rita had regained a tiny measure of control. Her head was sore, her ribs ached badly, and she felt nauseous: but she could think and assess her situation. They'd left her bound hand and foot. With the key generator behind her back, she couldn't jaunt. She was alone in a graffitied jail cell, the walls white and covered in tiles. The only furniture was the filthy mattress she lay on. The door looked to be made of sturdy wood bound in riveted strips of iron. A spy hole completed the dismal ensemble.

I'm fucked, Rita realized. *For the short term, anyway.* But they'd have to take the manacles off sooner or later, wouldn't they? And when they did, she'd be ready.

She rolled sideways, trying to work out if everything was still in place. They'd taken her hat. But the inertial mapper was in a concealed pocket . . . no, the inertial mapper was *not* in its concealed pocket. *Shit and more shit.* Alien technology would definitely flag her as an illegal. She shivered, flushing hot and cold. She could already see the Colonel shaking his head in pained disappointment. It was odd, she realized, how much this job had come to mean to her in so short a time. *They somehow caught me*, she realized, unsure whether she meant the police here, or the DHS, who had somehow managed to make her give a shit about the job, just in time for it to go horribly wrong.

She was still exploring this unwelcome new realization when then the door opened. "Up with ye." Hands gripped her armpits and heaved painfully. "Open yer mouth. I said *open* it, wummun!" A meaty hand clutching a cotton swab on a stick appeared in front of her face.

Rita opened her mouth hastily: the prospect of another beating, or worse, terrified her. The swab stabbed at her tongue, twirled nauseatingly, and withdrew just as she began to retch. The hands supporting her let go, and she flopped down on the mattress. She heard rattling and clicking behind her, and tried to turn her head, but the door slammed shut before she got an impression of anything other than navy-blue uniforms and odd-shaped hats.

It was cold in the cell, and they left her alone for nearly an hour. She was shivering, and uneasily wondering if she was going to piss herself, when the door opened again.

"Get those leg-irons off her!" The speaker was outside the door, beyond her field of vision, but the voice belonged to a woman and her tone of authority brooked no argument. Men in uniform moved in and tugged at Rita's legs. "You're not going to do anything stupid, are you?" the woman asked her. It was a thinly veiled threat. "These nice gentlemen are going to pick you up now. If you don't fight they won't hurt you. Then we can have a little chat." Her accent was half familiar, half strange.

"Who—" Rita cleared her throat and licked her lips. "Who are you?"

"I'm asking the questions. Boys, lift her." Two uniformed men—cops or jailhouse guards, Rita couldn't tell—raised her by her arms. After a second or two she managed to steady herself and turned to face the doorway.

The woman was blond, in her thirties, and wore minimal or no makeup; perhaps it wasn't a thing here. Her hair curled around her shoulders and she wore some sort of uniform, unfamiliar and strange. She held a leather attaché case or folio in one hand. "Bring her," she told Rita's guards, then turned and walked away. They nudged her along; after a moment she stumbled into motion, feet numb and head still sore and dizzy.

Rita caught more impressions of the jail as they marched her through whitewashed corridors with scuffed wooden floors. The overhead illumination came from long glowing tubes—*old-style fluorescent lights*, Rita realized, *not LED strips*. (She hadn't seen tube-lights in years. They were banned back home—something to do with mercury.) They came to a metal elevator. The guards crowded her inside, almost nose-to-nose with her would-be interrogator. The woman smelled faintly of rose water and sweat. She spared Rita a dry smile as she pushed a button printed with the digit 8. "I'd take you higher if we had any extra floors," she said, almost apologetically, as the elevator began to rise.

Rita swallowed. She had a sinking sense in her stomach, an intuition that the woman wasn't doing this at random. She *knew* Rita could jaunt.

Jaunting at ground level would have been safe. Jaunting from the eighth floor was another matter . . .

The guards hurried her along another corridor, with windows on one side looking out across an unfamiliar cityscape. Then she found herself inside a barely furnished room with a table and three wooden chairs. The table was bare but for a telephone out of an old movie, a box with pigtail wires and a rotary dial. One of the guards stood close behind her while the other closed the door. "Constable, please remove the cuffs." A tugging on her arms as the guard unlocked her wrists. "Have a seat," said the woman. Rita sat, apprehensive. "We've got a lot to talk about." Her interrogator unzipped the folio and removed a sheath of odd-sized documents. "At ease, Jeremiah. Bill, I'm sure our guest would appreciate a cup of coffee." She raised an unplucked eyebrow. Rita nodded. "Do you take it with milk or sugar?"

"Milk," Rita said reluctantly, then berated herself: *I'm* already *giving information to the enemy . . .*

"I'm Inspector Alice Morgan," said the woman. "And in case you hadn't guessed, this is the district headquarters of the Commonwealth Transport Police." She didn't smile. "I have a few questions for you. Starting with, what is your name, and what exactly were you doing in the Irongate South satellite switchyard at four o'clock in the morning last Friday?"

She reached into her folio and removed a small black sphere, then placed it on the table. Rita swallowed, her mouth abruptly dry. It was one of her webcams.

"Before you try to bluff, we found your fingerprints all over this device. Trespassing is one thing, but spying on an armaments factory is something else again. If I were you, I'd think very carefully before telling me any lies: we are willing to be lenient if you cooperate fully.

"So. Which agency of the United States government do you work for?"

IRONGATE CENTRAL POLICE STATION,
TIME LINE THREE, AUGUST 2020

The time Rita had spent in the FBI leadership course hadn't been completely wasted: it *had* given her some insight into how high-flying cops thought. Now, sitting opposite Inspector Morgan in an interrogation room on the upper floor of a police station, she couldn't fool herself: *I am so screwed.* In theory, she knew, she should give the appearance of cooperation while keeping her mouth shut and waiting for an opportunity to escape. But Inspector Morgan showed every sign of being one step ahead of her all the way. *Commonwealth Transport Police.* Did than mean she was in charge of fining fare-dodgers, or was it an antiterrorism role, like the investigative arm of the TSA? *Guess right, Rita,* she told herself uneasily. *She won't give you a second chance . . .*

"What's that?" Rita said brightly, and pointed at the webcam.

"I was hoping you could tell me." The inspector's expression was mild. "What's your name again?"

"Rita." *There's a fine line between disclosing operational intelligence and building rapport,* her trainers had told her. Building rapport was good. It looked like cooperation, and evidence of cooperation reduced the probability of beatings.

The door behind her opened and a flimsy aluminum tray landed on the desk. There were two oddly bulbous mugs of coffee on top of it. Ceramic mugs, she saw. *Odd.*

"Take your coffee," said the inspector. "Rita who?"

"Rita Douglas." Rita took the indicated mug, and the cop who'd brought the tray removed it. Thoughts piled up in a train wreck as she raised her mug and took a preliminary sip. It was coffee all right. *So they're going to good-cop me first, huh?* (It beat sleep deprivation or waterboarding any day of the week, but was no less an interrogation tactic. For one thing it helped build rapport, loosening the tongue. And when the coffee got to her bladder, a skilled interrogator could use the liminal leg-crossing unease to speed her along for a few minutes, then trade it in for more sympathy by allowing her a toilet trip.)

"Well, Miss Douglas." Inspector Morgan leaned toward her. "You're a very lucky woman. Unlike the driver of Streetcar 411 on the number 18 circuit, who I gather has been signed off sick for the rest of the week from the shock of nearly running you over."

"Shit." *Oops.*

"I'll take that as a nondenial," Morgan said drily. "The driver also testified that you were there one second, then vanished the next. Which, along with the gadgets found on your person—and the spy devices you distributed around the switchyard—tell us exactly what kind of person you are."

Rita took a mouthful of coffee, desperately trying to buy a few seconds to get a handle on a situation that seemed to be spinning out of control. "What kind of person would that be?" she asked.

The inspector's expression froze for a split second. "An evasive one. I suggest you start *answering* my questions, Miss Douglas. We know you are a world-walker sent by the United States government, and now that we've caught you we know how to keep you. All we have to do to neutralize your ability is keep you on an upper floor, or in a basement, or blindfolded. The question then becomes one of whether you cooperate willingly, or whether we have to do this the hard way." Morgan took a mouthful of coffee. "The hard way is easier for us, you know. We just do it by the book. Charge you with espionage, try you, lock you up, and throw away the key. Case closed. If you *really* want to spend the rest of your life chained to the wall of a cellar, we can make it happen."

Rita dry-swallowed. Her tongue felt like parchment and her heart was pounding. To stop her hands from shaking visibly, she wrapped them around the coffee mug. "What's the alternative?"

"You *answer my bloody questions!*" Inspector Morgan leaned across the table toward her, voice strident. Rita recoiled against the back of her chair. Morgan settled back, her tone moderating: "I don't care how you justify it to yourself. I don't care if you tell yourself you're worming your way into my confidence to gather intelligence before you escape and report home. Your motives are immaterial. All that matters is that you answer enough of my questions that I can tell my superintendent that you are in a cooperative frame of mind." She paused. "Do you want a minute or two to make your mind up?"

Rita knew enough to translate from cop-speak: *There's no pressure, this isn't a boiler-room operation, I just want you to do as I say* right now. But although she felt a mulish urge to throw it back in Morgan's face, the inspector really did hold all the cards. Unless Rita was willing to world-walk from the top floor, her only options were the ones Morgan was offering her. Life in a hole, or full cooperation . . . whatever that meant.

"Ask away," she said hoarsely, wondering if she'd be able to live with this numbness afterward. "What do you want to know?"

The inspector stared at her with unreadable eyes. "Let's start with: which agency do you work for, and when are they expecting you to report back next . . ."

PHILADELPHIA, TIME LINE TWO, AUGUST 2020

FEDERAL EMPLOYEE 004930391 CLASSIFIED VOICE TRANSCRIPT

AGENT O'NEILL: So our asset is now past her deadline. Gentlemen, ma'am, do we have any comments?

LIAISON, STATE DEPT: Colonel, is there any prospect—in your opinion—that she's defected?

COL. SMITH: What? No, absolutely none whatsoever. If you'd asked me three months ago I'd have said it was a low probability outcome, but since then she's seen the Gate and acquired a partner. She's solid, in my view.

LIAISON, STATE DEPT: So, she's either dead or captured?

COL. SMITH: (slowly) Those are the likeliest reasons, yes.

DR. SCRANTON: Have we had any signals since insertion? What about the switchyard?

AGENT O'NEILL: According to these transcripts, the last pop-up drone got nothing. It looks like they went through the rail yard with a fine-toothed comb—nothing answers when we ping it; all the relay nodes are unresponsive. Air Force sent another pop-up over the downtown station, but it got nothing from Rita's inertial mapper or the bug in her left shoe. They'd have had to get lucky to find her, but it's still worrying. The silence, I mean.

DR. SCRANTON: What else are we seeing over there?

AGENT O'NEILL: The drone we had overhead when we inserted Rita picked up her beacon in the central station. A few seconds later it disappeared and reappeared just outside the building. It's possible something inside spooked her, but not enough to abort the mission. Since then we've had zip. The five-minute restriction on how long we can leave a drone in the air over there means we have huge holes in our coverage. Rita disappeared in the middle of a ninety-minute blackout with no assets in place to track her.

COL. SMITH: I'd like to draw your attention to the ground activity around the station at that time. And in the downtown area in general. Lots of cars, lots of people on foot—too many for six a.m. She could have walked straight into a dragnet.

AGENT O'NEILL: What kind of dragnet could stop her jaunting?

DR. SCRANTON: There is a very unpleasant case that I'd like you to consider. We know that this, this Commonwealth entity, has extensive technological capabilities. Maybe they're not up to our level, but they're advanced enough to be extremely dangerous. We also know that they're one topological shift away from time line two, where we made hard contact with the Clan world-walkers—

LIAISON, STATE DEPT: Oh no, please don't—

COL. SMITH: No interruptions, please. Ma'am, if you'd continue?

DR. SCRANTON: Thank you. Our threat posture for the past seventeen years has been based on the assumption that, although we whacked the Clan *hard*, we had no conclusive proof that we got them all. And we've had indications of anomalous false positives in the national surveillance infrastructure that might be caused by visiting world-walkers. Not to mention recent evidence of a world-walker-assisted espionage operation in a major city. So the precautionary principle dictated that we conduct operations as if they were out there. Hence Rita, hence DRAGON'S TEETH, and hence a bunch of other contingency plans you don't need to know about.

I think we have to assume that the Clan—or other world-walkers— are *definitely* known to the Commonwealth, and that the authorities there know exactly what they're looking at when they see signs of world-walking. Just like us, in other words. The worst-case scenario is that the surviving world-walkers from the Clan are working *for* the Commonwealth. By repeatedly trialing a JAUNT BLUE asset at the same location we inadvertently alerted them to the presence of a world-walker, and they saturated the area with bodies who knew what to expect. We've gotten inexcusably sloppy: we need to relearn all the tradecraft we've forgotten since the Berlin Wall came down. And unless Rita shows up in the next couple of days we must assume the worst—that she's been captured and is being interrogated by people who know what she is. At which point I've got to have a revised plan ready for briefing that takes into account—Colonel?

COL. SMITH: There's a worse-than-worst-case scenario, I'm afraid.

DR. SCRANTON: What?

COL. SMITH: You asked, what if world-walkers from the Clan are working for the Commonwealth. But turn it on its head. What if they've got Rita and know everything she knows—and *the Commonwealth are working for the Clan?*

END TRANSCRIPT

IRONGATE CENTRAL POLICE STATION, TIME LINE THREE, AUGUST 2020

Even though Rita was cooperating fully with the inspector's line of questioning, it was clear that her answers weren't satisfactory. After a couple of hours, Inspector Morgan called a toilet break. But Rita's respite was short-lived. The inspector grilled her until late in the evening, then consigned her to a top-floor cell. She spent a bad night on a hard bunk, trying not to notice the periodic rattling of the inspection hatch. The next morning, everything started up again.

"So, let me see if I have this straight. You are Rita Douglas, age twenty-six. Previous occupation: thespian." (The inspector's language was weird—English, but with enough variant usage thrown in to suggest centuries of divergent evolution.) "You were inducted by an autonomous group within the Department of Homeland Security, in the wake of a kidnapping attempt by your long-lost world-walking relatives. The Unit is headed by a Colonel Smith, who reports to a Dr. Scranton." She paused. "What is a medical practitioner doing in this Unit, Rita? Do you have an explanation?"

"I don't think she's an MD. Nobody told me what her doctorate was in."

"Yet she uses the honorific—"

"That's not uncommon for people with higher degrees, is it?"

"I see." Inspector Morgan frowned, then stared at her with narrowed eyes, as if trying to recall the precise offense that applied. "Forget it." Morgan's lips thinned as she added another note to the book before her. The pen she used seemed to be a ballpoint of some kind, Rita saw, but everything here was a subtly different shape. "Back to the kidnapping. When and where exactly did it happen? Do you remember the date and time? I'd like you to walk me through it in detail."

"Um, yeah. Uh, it was March the twenty-first, a Friday evening in Boston. I'd just flown back from Seattle—"

"'Sea-attle'? Is that a city? Where is it?"

Oh God. "Um, it's on the West Coast? Between Vancouver and Port-land—"

"How do you spell 'Vancouver'? Is that another city?"

"Yes." Rita spelled it, then spelled "Seattle." "It's on Puget Sound, a deep bay way up the coast near the border with Canada."

"'Can-ada'? What is 'Canada'?" A five-minute detour taxed Rita's knowledge of eighteenth-century history to the utmost, before the inspector caught herself. "Let us pass over this for a while—it is of low significance. You were on the 'west coast,' and you *flew* to the 'east coast.'" The inspector sounded skeptical, as if flying was something too exotic to associate with the woman before her. "What happened then?"

"Oh, I caught the T—sorry, the commuter train—to the garage where I'd left my car. It was about eleven o'clock at night when I got there, and the place was nearly deserted, so I paid my parking ticket and went to my car when some guy tased me—"

"'Tased'?"

"A taser is, uh, an electric dart gun. Hurts like f—like a snakebite.

Worse. It paralyzed me and I fell over and two men picked me up and rolled me into the trunk of my car and—"

"A trunk is a baggage compartment, isn't it?"

A buzzer sounded from deep in the guts of the odd-looking desk telephone, rescuing Rita from a hellish spiral of ever-converging footnotes that served only to make her dizzy and irritable, highlighting the conceptual gulf separating this world from her own.

"Morgan here. Yes?" Inspector Morgan picked up the headset and listened attentively. Rita tried to overhear, but the speaker wasn't very loud. "Yes, I'm in the process of—no, you can't. I've already charged her and am interviewing the accused." (Rita sat bolt upright at that. *Charged?* she thought. *But she hasn't*—) "She's in Transport Police custody. No, you can't. This is a matter for the Police. You clearly have no standing in this case and I will thank you for not interfering in an ongoing Police investigation. Good *day.*" She slapped the handset down with sufficient venom to rattle the table.

Rita cleared her throat. "I couldn't help overhearing. You told whoever that was that you'd *charged* me. Are you supposed to read me my rights, or let me ask for a lawyer, or something?"

For a moment the inspector looked as if she was about to explode. She took a deep breath and shook her head. Then she looked Rita in the eye: "You didn't hear that conversation. You must have imagined it."

"Uh, I don't understand?"

"Because if I had not in fact charged you already, I would have been lying when I told the Specials to piss up a rope." Morgan looked past Rita's shoulder. "Jerry, I do not believe our guest here has made the delightful acquaintance of the Special Counter-Espionage Police."

The cop behind her shuffled nervously. "No, ma'am."

The inspector flashed him a toothy, indefinably uneasy smile. Then she turned back to Rita and explained: "The Specials are not a real Police force: they're a branch of the Inner Party apparatus. Politicals. The Commonwealth Transport Police is a national organization, working for the people. Our hands are bound by the law and the constitution of the Commonwealth. The SCEP men are not so constrained . . ."

Constable Jeremiah cleared his throat pointedly.

"Yes, well," Morgan said briskly, "Miss Douglas: by the authority vested in me as an Inspector of Constabulary in this force, I am officially charging you with trespassing on the permanent way, within the meaning of section forty-nine of the Public Transportation Regulation Act. I also intend to charge you with eight counts of littering, to wit, leaving objects all over the southern switchyard. And, ah, of being present on the platform of Central Station without a valid ticket. Witnessed, Jerry? As of an hour ago?"

"Oh *good*," Rita said weakly.

"You do not need to say anything. The charges mean that I can now hold you for up to a week for questioning. More importantly, they mean that Mr. Pierrepoint can't get his hands on you without first obtaining a bench warrant. Which he will no doubt hasten to do, but because I have both you *and* the evidence he would need to bring charges of treason and spying against you, we have a few hours' breathing space in which to prepare my report and get it in front of the right people."

"Who are . . . ?"

"The people who want to negotiate with your bosses before they do anything stupid, Miss Douglas."

IRONGATE CENTRAL POLICE STATION,
TIME LINE THREE, AUGUST 2020

Meanwhile, ten floors down, the sergeant on the station front desk was having a bad morning.

"Please tell Commander Jackson that Olga Thorold is here to see him," the woman in the wheelchair repeated firmly. This time she added: "*Immediately.*"

The sergeant, flustered, stared over her head. "The Commander is very busy—"

"If I don't see him within the next five minutes he will be even busier, boy!" The cop looked to be only a few years younger than Olga herself, but she was determined not to let him regain authority in this situation. "I'm here on official business of the Department of Para-historical Research. Call the Commander's office at once. It's urgent."

The word "urgent" seemed to galvanize the man: or perhaps it was the way Olga's attendant shifted his balance. She hated the wheelchair, but it gave her an excuse for bringing a bodyguard into places where bodyguards caused raised eyebrows, such as Police stations and military bases. Jack wasn't in uniform, but his posture bespoke his background—and the desk sergeant finally made the connection. "Who did you say you were, madam?"

"Olga Thorold, from the Department of Para-historical Research." A thumb over her shoulder: "He's with me. Commonwealth Guard, Security Section. Show him your warrant card, Jack."

Jack flipped a card wallet open and held it before the desk. The sergeant swallowed, then picked up his telephone receiver and dialed, hastily. "Front desk, visitor asking for Commander Jackson's office? A Missus Thor-old . . . Yes, sir, right away." He stared at her as if she'd grown a second head. "You're to go right on up. Sorry 'bout this—nobody said you was expected and you're not on the list—"

But Jack had already backed up and set Olga's chair rolling toward the elevator in the corridor beyond the front desk. She clung to the armrests. *I hope I'm in time,* she told herself. Her office had received the eye-opening transcript of Inspector Morgan's first day with the suspect late enough that Olga had been asleep when the phone jangled, pulling her straight into crisis mode. The arrest of a world-walker from the United States would have been sufficient to trigger a political earthquake on its own, even without the horrifying questions hanging over the identity of the spy in question. What little hope she had that the intruder was merely a common or garden-variety spy dwindled with every update.

She arrived on the fourth floor to discover the local Force Command Suite in a state of turmoil: majors and inspectors rushing around urgently, stenographers clacking away at their computer terminals and telex machines, a steady stream of messengers coming and going. "Where's Commander Jackson?" Olga demanded at the door.

"You can't see him," the callow young man on reception began. "He's in a briefing—"

"Aha! Miss Thorold!" The Commander bounced out of a boardroom door and came to rest in front of her, positively vibrating. "Excellent, we've been waiting for you!"

"About time," she muttered under her breath as Jack wheeled her into the conference room. "What do we know, Richard?"

Heads turned as she entered the room: Commander Jackson closed the door behind her and a captain hastily cleared a space at the table for her chair. "Inspector Alice Morgan is with the subject right now, resuming the interview. They're on the top floor. She's keeping it low-key and friendly for the time being: the subject has been cooperative so far. The only problem is, there's obviously been some sort of leak—"

"Who was the recipient?" Olga demanded.

"The General Secretary's office. Mr. Pierrepoint's deputy called the interview room on the direct line about an hour ago, demanding we hand the subject over. Whoever blabbed told them exactly what extension to call and who to ask for, so I'm treating it as a hostile security breach and will be hunting the leaker in due course. Inspector Morgan told them to come back with a warrant, but it's anybody's guess how long we've got—"

Olga cut him off: "They've got tame judges. We've got to get her out of here *right now*. You don't want to get caught up in a fight between the Party Secretariat and the DPR."

"But a transfer of jurisdiction—"

"Do you agree that this is a matter of national security?" Commander Jackson met her gaze for a second, then nodded abruptly. "The DPR is best placed to handle a debriefing and work out how to respond. If it's a matter of whatever charges you're detaining her on, I'm sure we can arrange to settle them or bring her in front of a sheriff's court in due course. But it would be a *really bad idea* to let Mr. Pierrepoint take custody of the prisoner in view of the current, uh, political situation."

"Oh hell." Jackson rubbed his eyes. "This is about the succession, isn't it?"

"I hope not, but the timing is a terrible coincidence." Olga took a deep breath, then another. She was running out of energy again. She wanted nothing more than to go back to her hotel room and sleep for the rest of the day. Her job was demanding enough at the best of times. Having a multiple sclerosis flare-up in the middle of a crisis would put her in the hospital if she didn't take care of herself. *For Lightning Child's sake, don't give him any ideas about who the spy is.* "What have you got from her so far?"

A woman in the uniform of a Transport Police lieutenant stood up. "I can fetch the latest updated transcript, sir . . . ?"

"Do that." Jackson's dismissal was abrupt. "She's from their Department of Homeland Security and we're certain she's a world-walker. They trained her as a spy and kept her in a padded cell so she doesn't know much about her operational context, but—"

"That makes her our responsibility for sure. Take me up to see her."

The lieutenant came bustling back, clutching a manila folder of printouts. Jackson took it and passed it to Olga without a word. "Right away."

In the elevator, alone with the Commander and her attendant, Olga looked at him appreciatively. "You've done well, Richard. And so has Inspector Morgan."

"We only just caught her by the skin of our teeth. We're not out of the woods yet."

"Of course not. But if you got me half an hour's lead over Pierrepoint . . ."

They rolled out into a corridor. Olga had no problem identifying the interview room. Two cops armed with short-barreled shotguns stood guard outside it. They came to attention as Commander Jackson approached. Olga glanced down at the briefing papers. NAME: RITA DOUGLAS. AGE: 26. RACE: MIXED HINDUSTANI. HEIGHT: 5'4".

Oh dear, she thought dismally. The age and ethnicity added another decimal place to the probability they'd placed on her identity. If the speculation about the Americans having worked out how to activate world-walking in recessive carriers was true, then it was hard to see who else this woman could be. She barely had time to read another line when the door opened. She closed the folder hastily as Jack lined her wheelchair up with the door frame and pushed her through.

"Good morning, Inspector, Miss Douglas. I'm sorry to interrupt your little chat, but you're both coming with me."

"And who are—oh." Alice Morgan half rose, then abruptly came to attention as she saw the Commander behind Olga's wheelchair. "Sir."

"Who—" The prisoner looked confused. "What's going on?"

Olga looked at the prisoner. There *was* a family resemblance, if you were looking for it. She steeled herself. "I'm from the Department of Para-historical Research, Security Directorate. Commander?"

Jackson knew his role. "National security," he said stiffly, nodding apologetically at Inspector Morgan. "Miss Thorold here is taking over the investigation. You will accompany her and the prisoner."

The prisoner flinched visibly: Inspector Morgan was also clearly startled. "What, right now? But we've got another six days—"

"You've got until the Party Secretariat gets a judge to rubber-stamp an Emergency Decree that will doubtless be a massive case of bureaucratic overreach, then rushes it round here with a goon squad for backup." The commander gestured at Olga. "Miss Thorold is from the DPR. She'll keep the Secretariat off our back. That's right, isn't it?"

Olga stared at the prisoner. She was pretty, in the gamine mode that was popular in the United States. Skin that could pass for a deep tan, shoulder-length black hair, eyes like a frightened rabbit's. "You showed up at a *very* bad time," Olga told the woman. She flinched as Olga continued: "I'm here to get you to a place of safety. Then I will have a message for you to take to your handlers. Are you going to cooperate?" The prisoner nodded, visibly subdued. "Okay, hood her and cuff her, then bring her along. To the car, Jack, there's no time to lose . . ."

IRONGATE, TIME LINE THREE, AUGUST 2020

Rita felt trapped in a bad dream. *This can't be happening* felt like it should be a cliché, not a queasy churning in her stomach as men in unfamiliar uniforms pinioned her hands behind her back and dropped a sack over her head, then frog-marched her out of the room. She was hungry, tired, and frightened by this turn of events. All she could do was cling to what the woman called Thorold had said: *a message for you to take to your handlers*. She shuffled, trying to keep her feet under her as they hauled her into an elevator. *As long as the message isn't my dead body,* she thought.

The cop, Inspector Morgan, had been reasonable, but that's what you'd expect of an interrogator. The art of successful interrogation was all about getting the suspect's trust. She'd been spared violence and torture only because they weren't effective means of extracting useful information; they were tools for intimidation, for making someone (often not the victim) do what you wanted. *They aren't going to torture me because it would serve no purpose,* Rita told herself uncertainly as the elevator descended. *These people are professionals.* But repeating it didn't help. For all she knew, this was another little motivational scenario: an attempt to convince her to cooperate by handing her a believable lie.

The elevator juddered to a stop. She felt fresh air on her face, heard voices: "Whatever you do, don't take the cuffs or hood off until I tell you to. We don't know if she's got a tattoo somewhere . . ." They marched her out to a vehicle, shoved her onto a padded bench seat, then someone climbed in next to her. The engine rattled, and the stink of gasoline made her nose itch. They drove for minutes that felt like hours, before coming to a halt somewhere where the air stank of burning diesel: there was a distant roaring. *An airport?* she wondered dizzily. They lifted her up a short flight of steps and onto another seat. Someone sat down next to her. "We're going for a short flight," Miss Thorold confided in her right ear, confirming her suspicions. "I hope you don't get airsick." Then someone clamped a pair of ear defenders over her hood, muffling everything.

There was more vibration, then a gathering banshee scream and a vibration that set her teeth on edge. It seemed to go on forever, until Rita felt her stomach drop away as they rose straight up. *Must be a chopper—*

Someone removed the ear defenders and hood: Rita blinked at the dazzling daylight. Without the mufflers the noise was deafening, far louder than Rita would have expected of a helicopter. She was sitting directly behind the pilots, Miss Thorold to her right. Someone in the seat behind her clamped a headset to her ears: she tried to look round, but the cuffs prevented her from turning. The chopper lurched and began to accelerate forward. As it did so the noise level dropped, as if some sort of boost motor had shut down. "What—" She cleared her throat. "Where are you taking me?" The entire front of the aircraft was a glass bubble. The view would have been mesmerizing if she hadn't felt as if she was about to throw up.

The Thorold woman adjusted her mike, then reached up and flipped a switch. "I don't think anyone can overhear us. Ms. Douglas, you are in *deep* shit, and not just because you're an illegal. Luckily for you, I'm going to throw you a life preserver. I'm even going to ask Jack to take the cuffs off, assuming you won't try to jump out the door at ten thousand feet?" Rita shook her head. Miss Thorold leaned over the chair back and said something on another channel; a few seconds later the guard in the seat behind her unlocked her handcuffs. "First, I want you to answer a couple of questions for me." Miss Thorold pulled out a bunch of printed papers. "You told the inspector that you were recruited by the DHS after world-walkers tried to abduct you. I want you to tell me *exactly* what happened."

Rita massaged her wrists and stared. "Wuh?" She swallowed. "I thought you'd know."

Thorold looked tense. "Pretend I don't. We've got nearly an hour before this flying scrapheap gets where it's going. You've got plenty of time to tell me everything."

Cold realization crystallized in her guts. "I'd flown home to Boston from Seattle," she began, then recounted her story for the second or third time this morning.

Eventually Thorold shook her head. "We didn't do it." Her tone was blunt. "Whoever they were, they used totally the wrong protocol. Amateurs! If we'd wanted you—assuming we even knew who you were—we'd have caught you. You know what I think? It was a set-piece scenario organized to motivate you to say 'yes' when they recruited you. You were probably expected to break away when they parked somewhere, or to call up those friendly DHS people who'd bugged your phone." She snorted. "Idiots."

"I suspected something like that," Rita said defensively. "But I didn't have any good alternatives."

"You could have phoned us."

"What! How?"

"Let's see." Miss Thorold put her papers away. Not for the first time Rita noticed that the woman's hands were shaking. "You're twenty-six. Born in 1994. You're a world-walker. They finally figured out how to activate the ability in by-blows, did they?" Rita nodded reluctantly. There didn't seem to be any point in denying it. "That means you're a relative. We can confirm it if you like, but at a guess . . . Indian father, right?"

Rita looked away. "I never met my birth parents," she said. "They gave me up for adoption right after I was born. Who are you and where are you taking me, ma'am? And what have my birth parents got to do with anything?"

"Those are three *very* good questions. You might also want to add, why did your Colonel send you in particular?"

Thorold sounded *approving*. As if she *wanted* Rita to ask questions. Her skin crawled. Asking questions in a classified security perimeter was a good way to get yourself a one-way trip to a jail cell. Even *thinking* the wrong questions could be dangerous. "I changed my mind. I don't want to know—"

"Tough, kid. I'm going to give you more answers than you want. Firstly"—Thorold held up a finger—"the Clan of world-walkers that the US government is so pants-wettingly scared of doesn't exist anymore. We are citizens of the New American Commonwealth—naturalized immigrants—and we mostly work for the government. In my case, I work for an agency called the Department of Para-historical Research. As you probably guessed, my specialty is para-time security. You could say I'm your Colonel Smith's opposite number. Right now we're en route to the DPR headquarters in New London—that's the Commonwealth capital, although you know it better as Manhattan.

"When we get there, you're going to meet my boss. She's a Party Commissioner, a member of the Central Committee—there is no exact equivalent in the US government, but she is responsible for an entire government ministry. And she's going to give you a message to take home to *your* bosses."

"A message?" Rita felt a stab of hope.

"Yes. Don't you think it's better if our political leaders start talking to each other?" Thorold's cheek twitched. "Talking like responsible adults, instead of shooting down drones and playing stupid cold-war spy games? They should be exchanging embassies, sending diplomats, that sort of thing. This playing footsie with spies, somebody could get hurt."

"You want me to be a messenger?"

"Yes." Thorold raised her finger again. "But let me warn you what I'm talking about. Your boss couldn't have picked a worse time to play head games with us. The Commonwealth is on a hair trigger. That's because in this world, we're one of two superpowers who are pointing lots of nuclear weapons at each other. Our enemy is a totalitarian regime that covers the whole of Europe, Asia, the Middle East, most of Africa . . . and they'd love to take advantage of any internal crisis to damage the Commonwealth. There are lots of proxy wars on the fringe, and everyone's afraid the Big One will start by accident if someone sneezes at the wrong time—just like the cold war you might have learned about in history lessons.

"I'm telling you this because it's possible the Commissioner will be too distracted to mention it, and if she *does* mention it you'll probably be too distracted to remember. But it's vitally important that your bosses get the message. The last high-altitude drone they sent over nearly triggered a nuclear war. If that happens again, the consequences will be very bad for everyone."

Rita's stomach clenched. "You're soft-soaping me. Why? What are you softening me up for?"

Thorold muttered under her breath: "*Lightning Child* . . . there's no easy way to say this. Rita. Ms. Douglas. I am not *certain* of this—I won't be until the results come back from running the DNA sample the police took from you, and that's going to take a while—but you're the right age, ethnicity, and background, and everything else about you fits." Outside the glass bubble of the helicopter, the world rolled by. Rita's sense of unreality intensified as Miss Thorold continued. "The woman you are about to meet is almost certainly your mother. She's known of your existence for about an hour. You are her only child. And I believe you were recruited, trained, and sent here to fuck with her head."

AIRBORNE, EN ROUTE TO NEW LONDON, TIME LINE THREE, AUGUST 2020

Miss Thorold clearly had some idea of the impact her words would have on Rita, for she fell silent for the next ten minutes. This suited Rita completely. She was shaking; her hands felt cold. She raised them to cover her mouth. "Mother" meant Emily, not some stranger in a foreign government ministry. Not the woman who had turned her back on her as a baby. The realization that she was going to have to meet her made Rita feel increasingly resentful. Angry, even.

Many little girls went through a phase of thinking they were different, of playing make-believe that they'd been left with foster parents but that when their real parents found them they'd discover that they were actually a princess. Rita had known better from an early age. Just by looking in the mirror she could see that she didn't resemble her parents. They hadn't bothered pretending otherwise. They wanted her regardless, and had showered her with love. Rita hadn't ever searched for Cinderella shoes to wear because she'd grown up knowing that she was a pale brown Snow White. Her make-believe queen had betrayed her, abandoning her for good. And now she found herself sitting in the middle seat of a military helicopter, thundering through the skies to answer the evil queen's summons.

When she could trust herself to speak, Rita lowered her hands. "Tell me about my—about who I'm going to, to meet."

Miss Thorold's lips thinned. "Mrs. Burgeson—Miriam Burgeson—is the Party Commissioner in charge of the Ministry of Intertemporal Technological Intelligence. If you think of it as a cross between the National Science Foundation, the CIA, and the Department of Transportation, you won't be too far off the mark. Like you, she is a world-walker. The Department of Para-historical Research, where I work, is part of MITI."

Her first name was Miriam. Another piece of circumstantial evidence to back up Thorold's assertion, Rita realized. Her birth mother had been called Miriam something or other. "She—she sounds important. Is she?"

"You have *no* idea." Thorold looked away. "Her husband runs the Ministry of Propaganda and Communications. They both report in the cabinet to the First Man—the equivalent of the President. Except he isn't—we have a different constitutional separation of powers. The point is, you are about to have fifteen minutes with one of the most important people in the government of this continent. Half of the power couple who lead one of our Party factions, if you like. She's going to give you a message to take back to *your* government, along with proof of her identity. And then we're going to get you out of there before the bad guys arrest you."

"Fifteen minutes?" Rita's voice rose.

"Yes. It's risky enough as it is. Ms. Douglas, Mrs. Burgeson has power-ful enemies. Unilaterally opening negotiations with the US government is horribly risky: if it backfires it potentially gives them grounds to charge her with treason and espionage. You they'd see as leverage—a hostage."

"But I don't even know her!"

"You know that, I know that, and she knows that. The other side do *not*. You will have fifteen minutes—then we'll take you back down to Irongate and send you home, along with instructions to contact us safely in future." Above their heads, the engine note began to change. The chopper began to slow. They were flying over buildings, three- to six-story blocks. The skyline was unfamiliar to Rita: the southern end of Manhattan in this world boasted no thicket of dense-packed skyscrapers, but an array of neoclassical domes and Gothic cathedrals and something that looked for all the world like a castle.

Well, fuck, Rita thought, staring blankly out through the chopper's bubble nose at the approaching jagged horizon of triumphal arches, pal-aces, and huge government buildings that eclipsed even the Capitol in D.C. with their bumptious pomposity. *I blew the mission, got captured, blabbed when questioned, and now they're just going to run me through an interview with the evil queen, pat me on the head, and send me home . . .* She'd thought she was at rock-bottom when the Inspector was giving her the third degree, but this was positively mortifying.

The chopper slowed, circled, and began to descend toward a lawn that separated two marble-fronted wings of a giant palace. "Don't try to world-walk from here," Miss Thorold advised her. "This whole area is built up. You'd break your neck or get run over by a yellow cab. We'll have you home by evening."

Rita swallowed. "I'll be good," she said hoarsely, unsure whether it was a promise or a threat.

Everything now seemed to happen very fast, with the inevitability of a march to a firing squad. The blades spooled down as the chopper settled on its skids and doors opened. The *snick* of a handcuff around her right wrist locked her to Inspector Morgan, who seemed mildly irritated. They walked to the building, then along endless corridors and a wide marble staircase under stained-glass windows. There were flags, flags every-where: an unfamiliar field of gold stars superimposed on a white circle on a red background. Another corridor, past windows overlooking a broad courtyard and oil paintings of men in wigs, white stockings, and polished steel cuirasses. Then a door, opening as a man's voice said, "Come in."

Now they were upstairs, the handcuff was unlocked: Rita found herself in an outer office, desk against one wall, inner office door ajar. "Come on," said Miss Thorold. "George, this is Ms. Douglas. We're expected. Please ensure we have privacy." To Rita: "Can you push my chair for me?"

"I guess so." Miss Thorold's bodyguard, Jack, gave her a warning look as he surrendered his place to her.

"We'll wait here," said Inspector Morgan.

"Yes, you will." Miss Thorold pointed: "Rita, that way." Heart in her mouth, Rita pushed the chair forward into the open doorway.

"You took your time getting here," said the middle-aged lady behind the desk as she rose to her feet. "Close the—" She stopped and stared. "Olga. Is this who I think it is?"

"Shut the door, Rita," said Miss Thorold. "Yes, I think so. What's your birthday, Rita?"

"May eleventh," she said automatically, as the door latched behind her. She couldn't look away from the evil queen. She didn't *look* particu-larly evil. She had dark hair, and a middle-aged face that had been pretty once and was now succumbing to gravity's pull. Her costume—no, that's what they wore here—was odd to Rita's eyes, something like a shalwar kameez, but tailored and draped with ruffles at collar and cuffs. "Are you my birth mother?"

"The DNA results won't be ready for another day," said Miss Thorold.

"I don't need them." The commissioner, Mrs. Burgeson, stepped out from behind her desk and slowly approached, staring at Rita. "I spent the eleventh of May 1994 in a bed in the Obstetrics Department at Mass General." Her eyes were very dark: pupils dilated, staring at some inner vista. "And you're a world-walker."

Rita stepped out from behind Olga's wheelchair. "Yeah, right," she said, crossing her arms defensively. The evil queen looked as if she'd been punched in the gut. *You're not getting to me that easily,* Rita thought silently, even though she felt shivery, gripped by a nameless emotion that she wished she could banish. "Miss Thorold here says you've got a message for me."

"Yes, I do." Mrs. Burgeson swallowed. For a few seconds she looked as if she was choking, but the moment passed. She turned and walked slowly back behind her desk, as if ten years had landed on her shoulders in an instant. "Come here and sit down. Both of you."

Rita wheeled Olga up to the front of the desk, then perched on the edge of a spindly visitor's chair that looked like it belonged in a museum. Mrs. Burgeson, she couldn't help noticing, had a very modern laptop occupying pride of place on her tooled leather desktop, leaving the hulking CRT terminal and its oddly unrecognizable keyboard to sulk in a corner.

"Rita—" Mrs. Burgeson stopped, then shook her head as some internal censor brought her tongue up short. "I'm sorry, there's so much to say and so little time. I wish we had longer—"

"Why? So you could explain why you dumped me?" Rita asked, keeping her tone light, even though her words filled her with nausea. "Don't worry, there's nothing to talk about. I get that you didn't want me: I'm chill; I've got a real family back home who love me anyway."

Miss Thorold glared at her: if looks could kill, Rita would have been incinerated on the spot. "Why don't we stick to business?" Olga suggested grimly.

Mrs. Burgeson, for her part, looked uncertain. She spoke, haltingly: "Listen, Rita, I know you've little reason to trust me, but it was more complicated than that. And I was younger than you are now. If you ever want, want to—" She stopped and dabbed ineffectually at her eyes. "I'm sorry." She took a deep breath. "Stick to business." Another deep breath. "I want you to take a sealed letter to your boss." She picked up a plain white envelope, utterly prosaic, that had been sitting on top of an out-tray. She pushed it across the desk toward Rita. "Also, this." A plastic screw-top sample tube, with a swab in it. "Please witness."

Rita watched as the evil queen uncapped the tube, removed the swab, took the end of it into her mouth, then placed it back in the tube and sealed it. "This will serve to confirm my identity," she said, placing it on top of the letter. She took a deep breath. "Olga, the contact protocol . . . ?"

"I don't have it with me. I'll see she has it before she leaves," said Miss Thorold. She added, for Rita's benefit: "It's a set of times and GPS coordinates you can use to visit this world safely. The locations will be secured at this end and I'll be available to meet you—no risk of getting run over by streetcars, and no handcuffs."

The evil queen leaned back in her chair, eyes closed, and for a moment Rita felt a stab of apprehension. "Last time I spoke to them, they tried to murder me," she remarked to nobody in particular. She opened her eyes and looked at Rita, her face composed and clear of emotion. "I want you to understand this very clearly, Rita. The history of dealings between the Clan and the US government is toxic. You must be clear with your superiors: we are *not* the Clan. The Clan tore itself apart after the Family Trade people stuck their oar into Gruinmarkt politics by nuking the Hjalmar Palace—which they did *before* 7/16. I'm not going to get into tit for tat or recriminations here. What happened, happened. The world-walkers here in the Commonwealth are refugees. We earn our keep as far as the Commonwealth government is concerned, but we don't set policy."

Olga cleared her throat.

"We *mostly* don't set policy," Mrs. Burgeson amended. "But here's the thing. The *very first time* the United States made contact with another time line, it ended in a nuclear holocaust. I want you to tell your superiors that it had better not happen again. *My* superior—the First Man, the head of state—is of the opinion that the least bad strategy to pursue is one called Mutually Assured Destruction. It's an old cold-war trade-off: both sides know that if they launch a preemptive attack they will destroy their enemy, but only at the cost of being destroyed themselves. The New American Commonwealth has an arsenal containing more than nine thousand hydrogen bombs, because we are locked in a cold-war standoff with the French Empire. More than a thousand of those weapons"—her voice wavered—"are targeted on US cities right now. God knows we don't want to use them—but if we are attacked, retaliation is certain to follow."

"You're—" Rita boggled at her. "That's insane!"

"Tell me about it." Mrs. Burgeson smiled weakly. "Which is why that letter is so important. It's an invitation to discuss the ground rules for diplomatic engagement, so we can find a way to step back from the brink. Before some idiot on either side starts World War Four by accident."

Olga cleared her throat.

"Oh yes." Mrs. Burgeson was weaving the shreds of her dignity into a cloak of confidence, collecting herself visibly from second to second. "Of course this has to happen at the worst possible time. Rita, the other thing your bosses need to know is that the First Man, Adam Burroughs, has terminal cancer."

"So there's going to be an election soon?" Rita asked. "Or does he have a vice president?"

The evil queen shook her head. "It doesn't work that way; the Commonwealth is only seventeen years old. They had a revolution, and before that, it was an absolute monarchy—think North Korea, not Disney. The Commonwealth's constitution is only fifteen years old and it has never been tested by a peaceful transfer of leadership. Adam has been the First Man since the very beginning. In *theory*, we know what's supposed to happen and how to do it. In *practice* . . ."

"Nobody knows," Olga said darkly. "Most likely there will be a peaceful transfer of power to the new First Man, or perhaps even a First Woman. But that's far from certain."

Mrs. Burgeson picked up the narrative: "The point is, we have weeks—not months—to sort out an agreement that cools everything down. If we don't get there while the First Man is well enough to sign off on it, everything goes back to square one—only in the middle of a succession crisis. Which is *really risky*, because war planners love to take advantage of succession crises, never mind the fact that one possible outcome is that our own hard-liners could end up running the show."

She met Rita's eyes, and Rita froze. She felt as if the evil queen could see right through her: and for a sickening moment she wondered if she'd fallen into the wrong fairy tale by mistake. "But we're out of time now— you'd better be going before the Specials arrive with an arrest warrant. If you change your mind, if you want answers—I'll be here for you.

"Goodbye, Rita."

PHOENIX, TIME LINE TWO, AUGUST 2020

Another morning.

Kurt Douglas yawned as he shuffled around the kitchen. His feet, back, knees, and hips ached. The kettle on the stovetop was beginning to steam as he added coffee grounds to a filter cone, measuring them carefully. Two and a half precisely heaped spoonfuls was his habit. He had a rigid idea of how best to greet a new day: he would brew his coffee, then he would retreat to the downstairs bathroom to take his morning medication, shave, and read the news on his tablet while he threw off the early morning lassitude.

He'd had a disturbed night's sleep, as was increasingly normal for him these years. And he rattled around this huge, two-thirds-empty house like a dried pea in a toothless mouth. The sheer distance from bed to bathroom was a nuisance, forcing him to fully awaken when he had to rise in the small hours to deal with his old man's bladder. If Greta had been around she could have helped him fill the house. But as things stood, he almost resented its size. Franz expected him to keep the place proudly, like a janitor in a palace that his grandchildren would inherit in due course.

Collecting his coffee, he retreated into the comfort of his morning routine. Everything was much the same as any other day, until he came to his e-mail. A letter from Rita! He read it with increasing engagement, looking for the little signs between the written words. So: she had run into a special friend? Or a friend, anyway? One of the girls from back when they'd lived on the East Coast. His brow wrinkled unconsciously. *Interesting.* Of course Rita knew better than to use e-mail for anything important . . . What was the girl trying to tell him—oh. *Of course.*

Kurt did not hurry his routine. But when, half an hour later, he dressed in sweatpants and shirt and sport sandals and walked slowly across to his son's mailbox, he was unsurprised to find a letter within, addressed by hand to "K. Douglas," laboriously and in unpracticed capitals. Someone unused to writing longhand; someone young. (Or at least young by Kurt's standards.)

His pulse quickened, but he refrained from deviating from his routine in any way. He carried the post into Franz and Emily's house, sorting the other items into two neat piles and placing them on the breakfast bar. Only after the normal delay did he go home, with the envelope concealed under his shirt.

Once inside, Kurt locked the door and shuffled upstairs to the spare bedroom he sometimes used as a study. He drew the curtains, then turned on a portable camping lantern for illumination. He placed it on the small desk beside the letter and a battered paperback and some writing materials. He pulled on a pair of disposable latex gloves, careful not to touch their exterior. Then he sat down and pulled a blanket over his head, forming a tent above desk, lamp, and letter. It was no guarantee that he was free from observation, but unless the observers in question had glued a webcam to his forehead while he slept (one small enough that he had missed it in the bathroom mirror while shaving), it was fairly certain that they had no direct knowledge of the letter's contents. (Unless it had been opened and scanned and resealed in transit, even though it had been addressed to another—but *that* way lay madness.)

It was a letter, an old-fashioned handwritten missive directed to him by name. "Dear Mr. Douglas, your granddaughter Rita said I should write to you. I've been reading the book you gave her, and I have some questions you might help me with for my comprehension class . . ."

Kurt suppressed the impulse to nod approvingly. The code words were in place, falling in their assigned word order like pins between a key's serrated teeth, ready to unlock hidden wisdom. One of the youngsters, a little cub nosing up to the pack leader for advice. He turned to his copy of the book and began to draw the grid for the one-time pad. The questions were a neat block, written painstakingly in a crabbed hand that bespoke focus and paranoia:

RITA IN DHS STOP URGENTLY NEED SUPPORT STOP CAN ORCHESTRA CONTACT BIRTH MOTHER ENDS

Kurt grunted painfully. For a moment he felt despair. He'd been afraid of this, or something like this, for many years. It was not just the very specific fear that something might reach out from the dark heart of the security state and snatch away his granddaughter (who, for all that she bore none of his genes, thought more like him than his own son). It was the broader, agoraphobic fear that the unquiet dead were stirring in their graves, a third of a century after the fall of the Berlin Wall. It was impossible to outrun memory, or to outlive one's sins. As long as the Wolf Orchestra remained hidden, abandoned in place by the state it served when the cold war ended and the German Democratic Republic ceased to exist, the temptation to awaken the musicians was there. He could summon them to their instruments and play a last devilish ditty—tempting and taunting those who knew.

Kurt had remembered, and silently practiced the necessary rituals for all the years of their exile. For more than three decades he'd let them lie, trusting that save for the annual ritual of the greeting cards—to keep track of his players—he could allow his conductor's baton to gather dust. But now *another* hand had reached out: this Angie, Rita's friend. Angie Hagen. Alex Hagen's granddaughter, another of the third-generation children, born and raised on American soil. Children trained by their parents and grandparents to serve the fatherland, whether they knew it or not.

I could try to do this on my own, he thought dubiously. Why disturb his musicians' beauty sleep? Many of the first generation were dead of old age. Some of them were senile, disturbing their fellow nursing home inmates with the black comedy of their memories, dismissed as demented

confabulators by children and carers alike as they randomly blabbed
state secrets over the dinner table. Most of the active ones today were
children or grandchildren, born and educated here like the descendants
of *conversos*, Jews living under suspicion as Catholic converts after the
reconquest of Spain. They kept to the rituals of their parents out of habit,
living in constant fear of the Inquisition's knock on the door.

Few of them were truly aware of what they had once been expected
to do, and fewer still were ideologically committed. The inner citadel of
belief in the workers' duty to build a paradise on Earth had been betrayed
by history. They'd been misled by their own leaders and teachers, then
abandoned in the dark abyss of late-stage capitalism. Nobody really
believed anymore. But it was still too dangerous to contemplate recon-
ciliation with the nation in which they were embedded like a fragment
of shrapnel from an unremembered cold-war explosion.

The bastards have Rita, Kurt reminded himself. They had stolen her
and they would use her until she broke, for they knew her to be of enemy
breeding—even if she herself did not. His resolve hardened. *I will visit
this Angel*, he decided. She cared enough for Rita that she'd written a
coded plea to the orchestra conductor. *Philadelphia? It's been a long time.*
He'd visited the City of Brotherly Love once before: it would be interesting to see how it had changed. He would talk to Rita's Angel, and then
he would commence the search for Rita's birth mother.

But he would not do so unaided. First there were notes to be written
and sent. Anonymous letters to the neighbors of his sleeping agents, letters containing signs and code words to remind them of the faith they
once held, before the great betrayal and the *Wiedervereinigung* of 1990.
Words to awaken them and call them to the flag. Words of action, saying:
stand by.

They—or their parents, or grandparents—had been loyal members of
the *Hauptverwaltung Aufklärung*, the foreign intelligence service of the
Stasi, once upon a time. They'd been sent to these alien American shores
to await an unspecified future mission. They were the members of the
Wolf Orchestra, the last and greatest Communist sleeper ring, injected
into the United States between the 1960s and the 1980s by order of the
chief spymaster of the GDR, Markus Wolf himself. Comrade Wolf was

long dead of old age, and the nation he had served was itself liquidated almost a third of a century ago, its ideology bankrupt and its walls smashed. The Stasi's foreign files had burned before the capitalists, flush from their triumph over the Democratic Republic, could retrieve them. The members of the orchestra were stranded on foreign soil as aimless illegals, unable to return home despite (or because of) the end of their mission. But if they and their descendants held the faith—faith in *each other*, never mind the failed dream of a workers' state—they would surely come to his aid when he called.

And so Kurt Douglas allowed himself to be goaded into action by Rita's guardian Angel—unreasonably angered at the bumbling conscription of his granddaughter by the amateurs and clowns who passed for spies in today's America—and raised his baton to summon the Wolf Orchestra back to life, to play the cold war blues one last time.

AFTERWORD

Extract from "Beyond the Labyrinth: The Department of Homeland Security's Secret War on the Multiverse, 2004–2020," by Bruce Schneier— the Definitive Unauthorized History of the DHS

The Office of Special Programs (OSP) was not, strictly speaking, part of the Department of Homeland Security's (DHS's) chain of command. For the first two years of its existence it was an independent agency; where it relied on DHS assets, it maintained an arm's-reach relationship just as it did with the FBI, NSA, and the other agencies from which it drew its personnel. It was only in the wake of the panicked dash to regroup after the attacks on the White House that the OSP was actually integrated into its parent agency. While everyone knew what the DHS was, what it stood for, and what it did, the Office of Special Programs stayed resolutely in the shadows.

From its initial formation as the Family Trade Organization (FTO) during the first world-walker panic in mid-2002, the agency operated on a small scale. Operationally it was divided into three departments. Forward Intelligence controlled the deployment of agents and special forces in the Gruinmarkt; Interdiction provided the Drug Enforcement Administration and FBI with intelligence leads pointing to Clan smuggling operations on US soil; and Technology drew on the resources of the national laboratories to develop and manufacture world-walking machines (under the rubric ARMBAND). Prior to the nuclear attacks of 7/16, the FTO was one of the smallest organizations in the intel community. With fewer than four hundred staff it was even smaller than the State Department's Bureau of Intelligence and Research (INR).

The events of 7/16, the retalliatory bombing of the small nation of Gruinmarkt in the Clan's home time line and the subsequent congressional hearings, changed everything. The FTO brief became the policy football of warring rival bureaucracies. And the Department of Energy, DHS, and Immigration all made bids to become the parent stakeholder in the embryonic agency—in the case of DOE, because of the access to oil in other time lines that it promised. DHS "won," much as a caterpillar that wins the race to eat the spores of a particularly grotesque parasitic fungus might be said to win. It engulfed the FTO and in the process renamed it the Office of Special Programs.

But, in short order, the business of transportation security—the DHS's prior focus, via the Transportation Safety Administration—took a backseat to the business of building and managing world-walking machinery. The new machines provided access to all the oil under all the uninhabited parallel-universe versions of Pennsylvania and California, and a similarly vast number of biospheres into which carbon waste emissions could be exported. Transportation security is not merely about terrorists and train crashes; energy security is a huge part of the picture.

Protecting airliners, trains, and Greyhound coaches is only a hundred-billion-dollar-a- year industry. Oil is everything, and the para-time frontier is potentially infinite. The iron law of bureaucracy dictates that most of the people in any large organization will, after a time, be more preoccupied with preserving their own jobs than with fulfilling the mission statement of the agency. And the best way to ensure continuing employment is to build out the organizational empire. Who could possibly argue with that?

After a decade and a half of integrating the OSP's core mission into the DHS policy apparat, there were precious few people left over from the wild ride of the early years. Fewer still understood the fraught legacy of potential disaster left behind—the legacy created by the government's initial reaction to the world-walkers' attack on D.C. These remaining individuals were the few, the proud, and the cowboys: in this respect they were much like "Wild" Bill Donovan's OSS operatives, who after 1945 went on to form the backbone of the Central Intelligence Agency but who were rapidly swamped by a rising tide of bureaucrats.

Building on this foundation, the FTO sucked in staff from the FBI, NSA, DIA, NCS, Air Force Intelligence, and other more obscure provinces of the sprawling national security empire. The embryonic OSP was largely sidelined and left to its own devices. It should be no surprise that this branch of the organization is now known (dismissively) within the DHS as "our para-time CIA"—the subagency responsible for identifying and addressing threats to the United States originating from other time lines.

OSP is small in comparison to the DHS as a whole (its budget in FY 2019 barely topped four billion dollars, making it responsible for less than 2 percent of the total Homeland Security budget), but its responsibilities are vast. In the decade and a half following the development of the ARM-BAND technology—devices that used stem cells originally harvested from the brains of captured world-walkers to enable aircraft and vehicles to move between parallel universes—OSP drones mapped out paths to hundreds of new time lines.

Three quarters of the newly discovered were uninhabited, and of the remainder, all but two held only scattered tribes of Paleolithic hunter-gatherers. However, the two exceptions were cause for serious soul-searching within (and without) the OSP.

The first inhabited nonpaleo time line to be identified was, of course, time line one, location of the Kingdom of the Gruinmarkt: the version of North America where the Clan originated. (Following the US retaliation on that time line, the East Coast is still unsafe to visit without protective gear and radiation detectors.) The other time line is Nova America four, an ice age version of our world that is dotted with the ruins of a long-extinct high-technology civilization. (This will be discussed at length in chapter 26, "A Bridge to Nowhere.")

Finally, there are the unknown unknowns, as President Rumsfeld so memorably characterized them. We know today that the world-walkers' ability isn't natural, or even evolved. It relies on self-replicating intracellular quantum-dot enabled nanotechnology, controlled by engineered genes and activated by what one researcher described as an "epigenetic hack."

Somewhere out there in the infinity of branching universes we call para-time, there is (or was) an advanced technological civilization—and almost certainly more than one of them. At least one of these civilizations understood the structure of the multiverse better than the best physicists in America today and built subtle machines to manipulate reality and bend it to their will. The world-walkers of the Gruinmarkt come from a primitive, preindustrial world. Exhaustive sequencing of the genome and epigenome of the few surviving prisoners has long since revealed interesting facts about their world-walking ability, which had been subtly damaged by a point mutation a couple of hundred years ago. Interrogated, they revealed a family history pointing back to a founder who had appeared in the 1760s. From where? Nobody knows. The obvious inference was that he was a fugitive, a runaway, a deserter. He kept a low profile, bedding in deep in the Gruinmarkt, willing to live a life of relative poverty in a quasi-medieval backwater in order to avoid the attention of . . . what?

Nobody knows; and that fact, taken at face value, is deeply disturbing.

PRINCIPAL CAST LIST

UNITED STATES OF AMERICA

RITA DOUGLAS, struggling thespian
FRANZ DOUGLAS, Rita's father
EMILY DOUGLAS, Rita's mother
RIVER DOUGLAS, Rita's sister
KURT DOUGLAS, Franz's father, retiree
GRETA DOUGLAS, Kurt's wife (deceased)
SONIA GOMEZ, DHS agent
ANGIE HAGEN, electrical contractor, childhood friend
JACK MERCER, DHS agent
PAULETTE MILAN, a spy
PATRICK O'NEILL, Rita's supervisor
DR. EILEEN SCRANTON, deputy assistant to Secretary of State for Homeland Security, Smith's boss
COLONEL ERIC SMITH, DHS, head of the Unit
DR. JULIE STRAKER, colleague of Rita's

NEW AMERICAN COMMONWEALTH (AND FRENCH EMPIRE)

MARGARET BISHOP, Party Commissioner
MIRIAM BURGESON (previously Miriam Beckstein), Minister for economic

development and inter–time line industrial espionage, Commonwealth Government

ERASMUS BURGESON (Miriam's husband), Minister for Propaganda, Commonwealth Government

SIR ADAM BURROUGHS, First Man (head of state)

THE DAUPHIN, heir to the throne of the French Empire

PRINCESS ELIZABETH HANOVER, heir to John Frederick

JOHN FREDERICK HANOVER, the Pretender, King in Exile of the New British Empire

MAJOR HULIUS HJORTH (Yul), Brilliana's brother-in-law, world-walker spy

ELENA HJORTH, Huw Hjorth's wife

HUW HJORTH, Explorer-General

BRILLIANA HJORTH (Huw's wife), DPR (espionage agency) director

ADRIAN HOLMES, Party Secretary

ALICE MORGAN, Commonwealth Transport Police officer

OLGA THOROLD, Miriam's director of counter-espionage

GLOSSARY OF TERMS

Accretion disk
A "whirlpool-like" disk of extremely hot gas that gathers around a black hole. As matter is sucked into a black hole it heats up until the radiation pressure from the inside of the accretion disk balances out the attractive force of the hole. It thus limits the rate at which a black hole can absorb matter. As most black holes rotate, the accretion disk is dragged round at very high speed: temperatures range from several millions of degrees up.

ARMBAND
Device used by US military and DHS to transport aircraft between parallel universes. Mechanism is secret; believed to include neural tissue harvested from world-walker "donors."

BLACK RAIN
Code name assigned to time line three (home of the New American Commonwealth) by the US government.

Bogies
The chassis or framework carrying wheels, upon which a railway carriage rests.

Clan

An umbrella organization consisting of five (previously six) families of world-walkers, formerly resident in the Gruinmarkt in time line one. Coordinated the world-walkers' inter-temporal trade and smuggling activities, provided security and a framework for the arranged marriages required to keep the world-walking bloodlines alive. The Clan was effectively disbanded in 2003, and the survivors sought asylum in time line three (with the New American Commonwealth).

Corvee for the Clan postal service

An obligation on world-walkers from time line one (who were members of the Clan). They had to make themselves available to transport goods between time lines a certain number of times every month. The organization is now defunct.

CVS

A big, well-known American pharmacy chain.

DHS

US Department of Homeland Security: in time line two, the agency responsible for transportation security, counter-terrorism, and para-time security (interception of world-walkers). Also responsible for organizing security of government and corporate sites in other time lines, and countering threats from all other time lines.

DPR

Department of Para-historical Research: a para-time industrial espionage agency established within MITI in the New American Commonwealth.

ELINT

Electronic Intelligence: covert intelligence gathering by electronic means (as opposed to HUMINT).

Engram

Among world-walkers, a knotwork design that can trigger the world-walking ability to transport them to another parallel universe.

Family Trade Organization

Precursor to the Office of Special Projects. It was a cross-agency organization established within the US government in 2002 in response to the discovery of world-walkers and the Clan.

FISA Court

United States Foreign Intelligence Surveillance Court: a US Federal court established to oversee requests for surveillance warrants and other espionage-related secret legislation.

Gruinmarkt

A small kingdom on the eastern seaboard of North America in time line one, founded by Viking colonists in the 12th–14th centuries. Home of the Clan. It had reached a late mediaeval level of political and economic development before it was destroyed in a nuclear holocaust instigated by the United States.

Hochsprache

A Germanic family language spoken in the Gruinmarkt; now effectively extinct, remembered only by former members of the Clan.

HUMINT

Human Intelligence: intelligence gathered by means of human agents and informers (see also SIGINT, ELINT).

ICBM

Inter-Continental Ballistic Missile.

MITI

Ministry of Intertemporal Technological Intelligence: a government agency within the New American Commonwealth. This body is tasked with accelerating technological development by disseminating new developments discovered in other time lines.

New American Commonwealth
Successor nation to the New British Empire, which ruled North and South America and Australasia in time line three from 1761 to 2003. The New American Commonwealth is a revolutionary republic created by the former Radical Party to pursue the goal of spreading democracy throughout time line three.

Niejwein
Capital of the Gruinmarkt. Destroyed in 2003.

NRO
National Reconnaissance Office: US government secret agency in time line two responsible for launching spy satellites and developing photographic/radar intelligence from satellites.

NSA
National Security Agency: the US government agency in time line two tasked with SIGINT and ELINT, the interception and decryption of enemy communications. Noted for monitoring all phone, Internet, and data communications worldwide.

Outer family
Among the Clan world-walkers, the world-walking trait is recessive: only the children of two active world-walkers inherit the ability. However, the children of a world-walker and a non-world-walker may be carriers. The offspring of two such carriers may have the world-walking ability. Such carriers were monitored by the Clan and known as "outer family" members (the Clan had a strong interest in maximizing the pool of possible world-walkers available to them).

Para-time
Umbrella term for parallel universes diverging from a point in time.

The cause of divergence may be some quantum event which may have multiple outcomes with macroscopic (observable) effects.

POTUS
President of the United States.

RFID
Radio Frequency ID: "smart" inventory control tags found on many items of packaging or clothing. RFID tags can be interrogated remotely and used to identify the item they are attached to, unlike bar codes (which need to be scanned at close range). Same underlying technology as contactless payment cards.

SCEP
Special Counter-Espionage Police: a government agency within the New American Commonwealth of time line three. The organization is tasked with tracking down subversives, spies, and agents of both the British Crown in Exile and the French Empire.

SIGINT
Signals intelligence: intelligence obtained by analysing metadata derived from enemy radio, telegraph, Internet, and other signals.

TL:DR
"Too Long; Didn't Read" (sarcastic dismissal of a long explanation or glossary).

USAF
United States Air Force.

World-walker
A person equipped with the ability to controllably teleport between parallel universes. It's an inherited ability, the hereditable mechanism presumed to have been invented by a high technology civilization elsewhere in para-time.